Rare Earth

Harry Marku

Rare Earth

ISBN (978-0-9843646-2-6)

Chapter 1

September Shiver

The shrieking Arctic breathed, buffeting Yakov's frame and holding him at a standstill. He shivered, the latent chill unfurling through to the skin beneath his balaclava, seeping around his face onto his neck and shoulders.

Having forewarned with the gale, Yakov ducked as he was sandblasted by a barrage of snow pellets. Finding gaps in the conformal headgear, flurried bits struck home, stinging his eyelids. Instinctively, he'd clenched them shut, surrendering his sight and promptly tripping over the gaping burrow of a ground rodent. Wrenching a knee, he cursed loudly. He tested the aching limb. It was tender, but had sustained no permanent damage.

Shouldering forward, he tucked his head sideways into the barrier of his hood. The parka's hollow fiber lining was far better at blocking the shotgunning snow than his soft body tissue. Through squinted slits, he alternated his focus between the terrain ahead and the precarious footing below. The clumsy tactic preserved his vision and limbs, but deprived him of steady balance. Worse, the awkward position strained his neck and eyes, causing the first to cramp and the other to create the onset of a nasty headache.

Every few minutes, he compensated by altering shoulders, first leading with the left and then the right. An observer might have chuckled while watching him shuffle a two-step across the freezing wilderness.

Not that anyone could see him. At times, the blowing snow afforded mere yards of unsettled visibility. For the thousandth time, Yakov cursed himself for neglecting to bring snow goggles. However, his oversight wasn't gross negligence; this blizzard was a full month out of season.

The geologist narrowed his focus onto a greater concern—maintaining his course. Every few minutes he held a compass to his eyes, registering its bearing and adjusting his course. Fearing he might lose his magnetic beacon, it was snugly secured with a lanyard hitched around his wrist.

Here, he could access it quickly and with minimal hindrance. Although his high tech gloves were specially designed to withstand the Arctic, they were not work gloves. Yakov could not safely hold onto a metal housing for more than a few seconds at a time. In this wind, a conductive surface would drain too much precious heat from his hands.

After each reading, he balled his hand into a fist inside the glove, slowly re-warming the chilled fingers. Fortunately, his two-piece winter suit was holding heat. It's weaved fibers cloned Nature's black-body design. The high-tech insulation was superb at retaining energy, but the fit was sub-optimal. His hood was leaky, a chink of armor the wind ruthlessly exploited.

Turning his back to the blasting gusts, Yakov dared to expose his hands to tighten the drawstring. One lace snapped, and he frantically repaired the dangling cord before numbness ravaged his dexterity. It was a poor fix, leaving his hood unevenly drawn and protecting his head less than before the botched repair.

Instantly attacking, wind gusts knifed through the skewed opening, swirled over his shoulders and cooled the gathering sweat on his back. Goosebumps raised and faded. Inexorably, he lost more heat than his exertion could fuel. As the chill penetrated and consumed his warmth, he began to fear the cold.

Redoubling his pace, he desired to both increase his metabolism and reduce the transit time to shelter. He would not succumb out here in the cold. But without good vision, progress was painstakingly slow. Another stumble, the latest nearly spraining an ankle, and he wisely moderated his pace. Slow trekking was better than zero displacement.

Unabated by the flat terrain, a gale-force gust slammed his chest, pushing him backward. He stumbled briefly before regaining his balance. Thus daunted, he leaned hard into the forcing air, willing himself to hold ground. The cold pressed its advantage, marching unchecked through his parka. Only the ice pellets were kept at bay. He shivered, a disruptive response that rattled his frame.

The wind reared and lagged, a brutish slab wall stymieing his efforts. Making insignificant progress, Yakov halted, but there was no shelter. Turning his backpack to the wind, he huddled over his knees, refusing to contact the freezing ground, beseeching the heavens to quit.

Abruptly, the wind gasped and abated. Silence ensued. Within moments the launched ice pellets settled, and the heavens gave back a mile of clear sight, unveiling a startling change in landscape.

Only an hour earlier, the prairie had been richly hued with autumnal shades. In the intervening minutes, the golden brown grasses had been violently spray-soaked with a crusting of shimmering ice pellets.

The storm was not spent, a short lull to prepare its next salvo while sizing up the foolish figure defying its assault. From the steel gray sky, large snowflakes descended gently, entombing the man in a crypt-like void, a silence punctuated eerily by the discordant compression of his footsteps on ice.

In moments, the heavens released and a tonnage sailed earthward, softly hissing, encompassing him within a downy shroud. This time, at least, he could keep his eyes open.

The heavy snow descended but a half hour, depositing a thick, six-inch layer over the encrusted grass. Insulated by the windless cloud blanket, Yakov re-warmed, and made good progress. Nevertheless, the respite would be brief. Gently stirring, the breeze returned. Within moments, wintry fingers hurled the mass-less flakes parallel over the ground. Instantly, the air embittered, cryogenic claws pilfering the last of the land's miserly summer heat. The mercury plummeted, seeking refuge within a crystal bulb den. Yakov laughed heartily.

The storm offered a peril a minute.

Exhaling sharply into the cold, Yakov's breath plumed, condensing instantly. Hovering briefly, the ice cloud whisked into the recharging wind, which now scoured the freshly fallen snow furiously, lifting and flinging the frozen grit against any entity in its path. This round, the storm's fury doubled, assailing with cold and crystal, although the wind had lost strength. Now his gear championed—as it was more readily designed for a temperature excursion than a wet snowfall.

A new menace was a slower, insidious threat—self-inflicted. Each vapid pulse of spent breath dusted his headgear with minute ice particles, whiskered strands gradually integrating into a matted frost cover. Within a half hour, ice wisps stiffened the hood's fibers, reducing its capability to insulate and his capacity to see. Neither was his face immune from his own exhaling. Through slits in the balaclava, fractal ice glued exposed facial hairs, rubbing coarsely against the fabric of his headgear.

More disconcerting than frosted eyebrows, gathered bits were glomming his eyelashes. Each time he blinked, viscous beads solidified, half melted by his body's heat, briefly bonding his eyelids shut. Re-opening them took effort, a claustrophobic frustration. Brushing his glove-tips through the mask's slits, he extricated ice blobs and tethered lashes invoking stinging tears which promptly froze into pearls at the corners of his eyes. When he blinked, they dislodged, miniaturized gems disappeared into the white vista below.

Pursing his lips together, he expelled his breath farther away, intending to prevent additional build-up. Under no circumstance would he risk frostbite now by exposing his fingertips to melt the ice away. He assessed the nuisance. The frosted deposits would stay, unmitigated. The fur bordering his parka's hood was solidified, but functional. Clearly, the fibers were synthetic, not the Arctic fur that he'd paid extra to acquire. His outfitter in Moscow would be replaced. The rest he could live with.

Yakov did not know whether his existence on Canadian soil was known. He'd not landed through the documenting portals and he had dutifully avoided contact with inhabitants, not that he'd seen any. Even if his presence was suspected, the blowing snow was excellent cover from the authorities.

Besides, RCMP patrols were random, there was no local detachment and there were immense quantities of land to survey. Budget cuts to federally-funded programs within the province, imposed by Ottawa politicians, had severed staffing to a minimum. In recent years, the world-renowned police force had become dangerously ineffective at patrolling its internal frontier.

Neither is it a simple matter to stop unlawful entry. With thousands of miles of coastline to choose from, an increasing number of intruders easily penetrated the northern coastal boundaries. Recognizing the logistical difficulties of policing so much space, some foreign interests operated with a free-for-all mentality exploiting the Arctic wilderness with little concern of being apprehended.

Unknown to Yakov, the storm was peaking, its untimely drama ending prematurely precisely because it was too early in the season to have amassed sufficient staying power. Reluctantly, winter retreated, unable to deter the slogging trekker from advancing toward his rendezvous.

Behind him, drifting snow filled his tracks, erasing his footprints. Within an hour, no trace of his presence would remain.

Yakov pictured his business partner, Sergei, a few miles ahead, keeping watch in the warm cabin of a late model Bombardier, and waiting for his return. He hoped Sergei was saving him a cold bottle of vodka. He chuckled at the thought, expecting the impossible from his friend.

Sergei was a trusted, loyal and resourceful partner—and a hard drinker. Any alcohol not secured under lock and key would be subject to consumption. Having had hours to search for Yakov's secret stash, the geologist would be lucky to have lukewarm coffee available to bolster his spirits.

By next day's end, they would be diving to depth aboard a submarine, currently concealed in a deepwater cove along the northwestern Hudson Bay coastline. After a fortnight undersea, they'd be frequenting the *new* Moscow, reveling in nightclubs, sampling expensive vintages and drinking with beautiful women. For a while, they would be well funded and popular.

Then, they would have to work again.

Beneath the Russian's balaclava, a giddy smile stretched his lips. Not for the anticipated hedonism, but rather an expression of accomplishment and pride. The prospecting venture was an unequivocal success. A month ahead of schedule, in an offbeat location, he'd located a rich ore body. His contract guaranteed a fat bonus. Certainly, his find wasn't an unknown cache, more likely it was an overlooked geological singularity. It would be ludicrous to suggest that over thousands of years of human occupation, no inhabitant had perceived the presence of its surface-borne minerals.

By necessity, native cultures are zealous in observation, embracing the synergy of natural phenomena with everyday life or deciphering the complex behaviors of predators and prey. Over time, nothing unusual would escape their collective purview.

In song, dance and legend, aboriginal traditions codify the connections between the earth and its people, a blueprint for survival. Without the capability to map, or calendar, the humans would have starved and vanished.

In mastering the land's nuances, geological abnormalities were not overlooked, frequently forming navigational landmarks. In contrast to issues of life and death, chromatic rocks were of little use, except as oddities, trinkets or tints.

In the Bronze Age cultures, the peoples needed iron and copper metals to chisel their survival, not curiously colored stones. The objects were not fashionable into weaponry, jewelry, implements or precious trade items. Neither had the medicine men divined spiritual or medicinal purposes from their pigmented properties.

Without immediate value, there was no impetus to guard its location or speak openly of its presence.

As a consequence, the ore's existence was most likely overlooked, easily lost as the cultures disappeared behind new influences.

In the early 20th century, oral legends of surviving tribes suggested that human populations once thrived along the 60th parallel, a hinterland demarcated as suspect place names on vague maps.

By the 1950s, aerial surveyors reported finding only a few isolated outposts. The original inhabitants, nomadic in nature, left little permanent evidence. The fading tales of vanquished peoples are often disregarded as sympathetic *soul-salving*.

Too easily discounting native folklore, the supplanting culture is still crawling through an infancy of rediscovery. Yakov, as an independent contractor, could not afford to bias his inspirations with arrogance. He had been wise to maintain an open mind.

The odd properties of the disregarded stones are now a gateway to immense acquisitions of wealth and power. To find new mineral sources, large sums of capital are being sunk into re-exploring the globe. Inevitably, others would learn of the same rock formations. Even time and chance would lead someone to his location. Long term, the stakes were high. Possession of mineral rights is in vogue, recycled strategic maneuvering in the economic combat zone. Rare Earths are a new gold, to be bartered for instant capital or hoarded for future leverage.

But for now, with the premature onset of winter, Yakov felt fortunate to be vacating. Once the serious snowfalls arrived, it would be impossible to continue prospecting alone. If this first storm was any indicator, the oncoming winter would be savage.

Normally hired by corporations, Yakov's sleuthing contract reeked of governmental influence. Which entity he did not know and he could not ask, the terms expressly forbid communication with parties other than an agency contact. It was an uncommon stipulation, but not the first time he'd worked through an intermediary.

There was serious funding backing the request, a commitment amply forged with upfront remuneration for purchasing supplies and meeting logistics. In return, the employer demanded frequent progress updates, digested them thoroughly, and proffered numerous suggestions—almost micromanaging his plans.

In compensation for meddling, support ratcheted to unlimited funding, even at a moment's notice.

This might even be anti-government funded, he thought.

The thought might have disturbed Yakov had he chose to dwell on it, considering the adrenaline of the adventure as more valuable lucre than background vetting. Not knowing too much was safer. Throughout his career, by not subscribing to a single sovereignty, ideology, business or governing philosophy, he maintained a larger base of contracts.

The incognito source had hired him to locate one or several rare earth minerals. Preferring a surface deposit, as did all outfits, they strongly coveted a clandestine venue. This requirement of total secrecy ruled somewhat against corporate employment. Usually, a big company needs to mine continuously and hence, openly, to be cost competitive, unless it can control the value chain from the cradle of extraction to the grave of the end product.

Smaller labs and venture capital enterprises, while desiring confidentiality, typically possess a fraction of the necessary financial reserves, unable to *carte blanche* his brand of offbeat expedition.

This employer had demanded prolonged anonymity, from exploration to extraction and some vaguely defined beyond, a premise suggesting a large firm with a deep research budget, a significant market player needing to avoid international competitive repercussions. When developing a replacement or disruptive product, reliable acquisition of highly sought, limited resources across borders on the world market can suddenly become difficult.

Purchase transactions are denied outright or, more benignly, impeded, replete with glitches such as customs procedures or shipping roadblocks. While snookering timely development, competitors catch up. More than once, a promising concept had been scuttled using an artificially created shortage of resources.

Not surprisingly, many new business products simply cross the ocean to finish development and initiate manufacturing. Several offshore, high tech industries thrive with local governments helping control the distribution of key raw materials or manufacturing components. If this scenario were true, his employer might be North American even though the hiring agency operated solely in his native Russia.

More likely, he was exploring for Chinese or Japanese interests, well known for staging industrial strategies that achieve long-term dominance. Access to high value minerals has been a key goal on their recent political-economic agenda. Conversely, new participants in this global game, the Gulf States, are only partly engaged in material stockpiling, suitably endowed for a couple of centuries with oil reserves.

It was unlikely his employer was a disruptive geopolitical entity. Few terrorist or revolutionary groups possessed the resources being supplied to him. With a submarine and crew at his call, he could travel virtually incognito around the northern hemisphere.

The crew's origin was another mystery. Speaking a variety of languages—Spanish, English and others he couldn't place; the *others* conversed amongst themselves only when necessary and rarely with him. It was an extraordinary display of professionalism, bordering on fanaticism, although their discipline lacked the precision of a military bearing. Acting like cogs turning a big, secretive corporate machine, he found determining their motivations or allegiance elusive and unnerving.

No matter who or what interests were tendering the contract, his in-pocket sample bore proof of easy extraction. His reputation for getting results was well earned, justifying his pricey expectations.

Yakov's genius for prospecting ignited from a surprisingly simple spark—downloading satellite images from popular websites. Uncharacteristically lacking in adrenaline, he started each venture searching geographical features from the comforts of his one bedroom flat in downtown Moscow.

To a practiced eye, the aerial images detailed an astonishing array of colors, forms and textures that, when properly massaged and interpreted, pinpointed potential geological anomalies.

For this rare earth expedition, he'd sought exposed formations from a younger earth, upheavals of ancient metamorphic rock. Matriculated within, forged by primordial heat and pressure, purified minerals are frequently found. Most deposits are locked deep beneath the Earth's surface, challenging to find or too expensive to extract.

Even in the rare locale where tectonic forces have exhumed the bounty, wind and rain quickly paste over a thin veneer of mud or water. If surveying from ground level alone, finding enriched strata could take one person a lifetime of pedestrian effort. But satellite images provide a disruptive advantage, macroscopic vantages suggesting where the Earth is being turned inside out.

The Precambrian Shield in Canada is truly vast, comprising nearly a million square miles in area. Sparsely inhabited, remote, subjected annually to fierce winter freezing, a large fraction remains poorly traveled and less known. It is not a stagnant landscape.

Over the past one hundred thousand years, continental glacial coverings have advanced and retreated, paring away escarpments and redistributing rubble to lower altitude lowlands. As ice packs retreat further north each summer, and melt-water erodes surface topsoil, hidden features are being exposed for the first time in thousands of years.

Yakov, or his electronic minions, churned around the clock. When the adventurer was out socializing at night, a sophisticated computer script he'd personally written was surveying, capturing and analyzing pixels. Once he set the coordinate boundaries, it took over, sequentially retrieving satellite images, examining their albedo and deciphering potential ore sites. The software was superior to the human eye at quantifying data such as light frequency, intensity, rate of change or estimating the coverage area. Using advanced optical resolution, sometimes an erupted ore vein could even be discerned. Replicating the effort manually would be impossibly time consuming no matter how compulsive one workaholic might be.

Yakov was a hard worker, but for a reason. He enjoyed life. Without leaving his chair, Yakov investigated geological features thousands of miles away, tilting his chances for success before he set foot on soil. Over time, he'd refined the program to be efficient and accurate. It was his own algorithm; a lifeblood trade secret he did not discuss.

The proliferation of his analysis software would end his career.

Following up his automated research, he would peruse the declassified annuls that many governments are publishing on the internet. Over the

previous century, most countries have hired mineral exploration teams
to scour their hinterlands. Some of the geologists' reports are publicly
available on government websites. Yakov made a point to seek these out
early.

During the initial decades of surveying in North America, rare earths
were not economically strategic; there was little risk in disclosing potential sites. But this historical omission is under reconsideration, access to
significant information is drying up.

In reading through the online briefs, Yakov was convinced that most
were either replete with errors or had been doctored to obscure important
details, such as extraction potential or exact location of findings. However, the information wasn't entirely dubious. When geological reports
aligned with satellite surveying features, Yakov elevated the probability
of performing onsite exploration.

As a final, anecdotal source of evidence, he would investigate cultural
fable—both recorded tales and published images of artifact. The existence of folklore, while never quite precise, was often referential and most
confirming.

On this venture, while searching from his flat, he had found one series
of images particularly intriguing. Near an exposed riverbed by an alluvial
gravel field, a river had broken through an oxbow exhuming the bedrock
below. Along the river's new edge, curious tints jagged over the exposed
ground suggesting the presence of a mineral vein encased in quartzite.
This signature had interested him, but he could not immediately guess
what it might be.

Neither could he immediately corroborate his computer analysis with
historical observations. Either there was none or it had been pulled from
public view.

Yakov pondered the possibilities.

The oldest rocks frequently house the heaviest elements, including uranium, lead and gold. It made sense. In recent years, diamonds have been
found in the Shield, tantalizing prospectors with the promise of an abundance of minerals yet to be found.

Yakov's breakthrough came from a most unlikely source, an anti-
fur website. Like stationery, a two hundred-year-old map underpinned
a homepage headlining a campaign assailing the barbarism of the wild
caught fur trade. The map, replete with hand drawn caricatures of navigational landmarks, caught his attention, especially a sketched cartoon of
a funeral pyre of striated stones. Captioned beneath was an unusual two-
line descriptor, *Kapuskasing wâpikwaniwinâkwan*, Cree words for *winding
river* and *pink*. From this unexpected corroboration and the language
of usage, Yakov finally unearthed folklore describing a mysterious oasis

of oversized game and a place where the ground would glow after lightning struck. The location was suitably similar to his electronic reckoning, convincing Yakov that he had a primary location for searching.

With that promising site pinpointed, and several contingencies in queue, he and his partner, Sergei, had boarded a submarine from the Baltic for Canada. Like himself, Sergei was both an adventurer and a self-professed adrenaline junkie. More importantly, Sergei was his closest friend, a brother since childhood and someone he trusted implicitly.

After disembarking along the Canadian coast, they did not rush headlong to the prime location. Testing his own patience, Yakov clumsily investigated several poorly chosen locales. The diversion had multiple purposes, mainly ensuring that his benefactors weren't tabbing his movements too closely. Experience taught him to expect a short leash. Spending a few days familiarizing the terrain provided some insight on the frequency of human traffic and, more specifically, RCMP patrols. They saw no one.

While exploring, they were stashing supplies of fuel, water, and food—caching them for the longer venture to the location he did not divulge. Placing the foodstuffs in small depressions, they covered them over with filled fuel buckets relying on the venting fumes to thwart scavengers. For the humans that might find the goods, the containers were unmarked, preventing easy identification of their country of origin. Yakov counted on a local inhabitant needing the fuel, considering it a fortunate find, avoiding contact with the authorities.

Yakov didn't trust the sub's crew. After all, they were suckling from the employer's payroll. Frequently backtracking, he ascertained that the sub's inhabitants were not trailing his daylong rock hounding. That was sensible; underneath clear skies satellites could track ground movement in real time. The fewer people above ground the better.

Choosing September to prospect was a ploy aimed at befuddling the overhead tracking eyes. At his present latitude, September was the beginning of the rutting season for big game. Large mammals like elk, caribou and moose were departing from yearlong habits of nocturnal foraging, wandering the lighted day, restless with procreative urge. Their moving forms, continuously captured by the omniscient watchers, would reduce the efficiency of software from electronically detecting his small prospecting party.

On the sixth day, Yakov and Sergei had set off, retrieving the stored fuel buckets and food on their way out, staged for a journey much farther than they admitted. Driving over land for a half day toward the river, they then turned upstream following the drainage for several hours until reaching a telltale escarpment he'd recognized from his computer images. Here, in the waning daylight, they conducted a fanning search. They began connecting dots between bedrock outcroppings, the river valley and glacial till mounds.

After dusk, they settled down for the short summer night, ate dried foods and shared a fifth of spirits. The next morning, continuing to the selected point, Yakov jumped out to survey the river valley beneath while Sergei dutifully turned the craft away.

Looking down the steep slopes through high-powered binoculars, Yakov gleefully noted that the mineral was abundant. His methodology had proven completely reliable. Overhead, the gray skies threatened and the barometer was falling. He was unconcerned, not needing much time to confirm the deposit.

Leaving Yakov behind, Sergei returned to the previous day's search pattern, eventually concentrating at the land drop some ten miles away.

There he performed another mock foray, setting off depth charges, pausing for analysis and repeating. While purporting to be prospecting, he was doing nothing of the sort. He was killing time hoping to hunt deer, coyotes, waterfowl or whatever appeared, but explosives and game were a poor mix—oil and water—so he fretted while setting the ruse, generating a preponderance of data to smokescreen their eavesdropping employer.

With a small window of time, Yakov descended the steep valley to survey the surface, mapping forty acres of exposed mineral. It was a magnificent find that would certainly attract other suitors should his employer redact payment. From the surface, he collected an indicative specimen and prepared to return to the Bombardier.

As he imbibed in his success, one disturbing thought would not subside. With this venture involving the *intrusion upon* a foreign country, Yakov had reluctantly accepted the employer's offer for assistance and had been surprised when the fully-manned submarine was placed at his disposal. Now, he was chagrined, fearing the concept of anonymous dispositioning. It would be wise to play it straight, deliver the goods and never accept a similar contract again.

That is, he would gain wisdom once he was safe in Moscow. Experience had taught him to always prepare back-up plans.

Waypointing the GPS coordinates in his mind, Yakov scattered the longitude and latitude discreetly across several pages in his logbook. Pointedly, he did not set markers, unwilling to leave evidence of his inquisition.

Chance favored the clandestine, leaving unnatural telltale markers begged others to snoop closely and a legally authorized prospector would understandably file for rights.

Besides, homing in using GPS is far more accurate than navigating by hand drawn field guides. In a previous expedition, Yakov had hired a cartographer and instantly regretted the decision, fretting throughout the entire field trip about the added security risk. Using GPS was easy, accurate and relatively private. But it also raised a security issue, whether its signals would be consistently tracked or lost within the noise of global telecommunications traffic.

Overhead, the fomenting sky threatened. A severe storm was imminent. It was time to go.

Chapter 2

Racing The Blizzard

Nimbly scrambling up two hundred vertical feet of craggy bank, Yakov left the riverbed and took note of its changing strata.

Deciphering clues to its past, he approximated the mineral layer at one billion years of age; an informational tidbit that might assist in finding deposits elsewhere. Surmounting the topmost shelf, he emerged onto taiga—a mossy and treeless landscape. No longer protected by valley walls, a blast of cold air jolted his face, rudely welcoming him to the summit.

The weather was worsening.

Overhead, ribbons of silver clouds raced at high speed, tattering and dissipating beneath a ponderous charcoal ceiling. Yakov could not mistake the warning; these were definitely snow clouds. Alongside, killed by early frost, the summer's golden grasses textured the plains, briskly bending beneath gusting wind. Pockets of heather rippled in unison, churning waves of a bladed sea.

Across the river, scrubby evergreens eked a troubled existence from cold ground and thin sunshine. Peppering the gently rising slope, the singular stands fused at the horizon, miles away and a thousand feet overhead. A half mile upstream, a deep ravine split the earth, funneling a seasonal tributary into the main river. The river's constant flow had dwindled to the autumn meander, an easy ford for a man on foot.

A short stretch of the river bed was relatively new; the annual convergence of ice and water had overwhelmed an oxbow bank, scoured a gravelly divide and exposed the shallowly buried treasure.

Within the ravine's folds, the fir trees towered, protected from the fierce winds and fortuitously capturing additional heat. Dwelling in a moderate micro-climate, the woody giants stretched to heights uncommon for another thousand miles south. Between their dark green monotony, splashes of red and golden suggested thickets of poplar and maple. Beneath their secluded canopy, there would be big game wintering.

Farther downstream, towards the Bombardier, the plateau ended, descending steeply to the water's elevation. At the nadir, the topography sputtered with chains of glacial ponds, separated by small hillocks and overlaid in scraggy muskeg. During the short summer, breeding waterfowl had visited the waterholes, rapidly rearing nestlings on the hordes of stinging insects inhabiting the wetland patches. A few incompletely fledged birds remained.

Completing his circumferential scan, Yakov reached into his jacket pocket for a two-way radio, sending a message to Sergei. It was simple...a series of three clicks...long-short-long, repeated twice. No words. A double burst returned immediately.

All was quiet at the Bombardier.

Marking his bearing by GPS compass, he crosschecked against a traditional magnet-in-fluid instrument. The two aligned. It was practical to have a low-tech backup in lieu of unforeseen difficulties. While the GPS was a superior navigational device, its batteries could fail. Compasses didn't need electricity. If the oil didn't thicken, it would provide a constant, reliable aid.

With ten miles to traverse, Yakov started briskly. The plateau plain was a fairly easy hike, unencumbered by uneven terrain, tall grasses or fallen logs. Making good progress, he figured completion in under four hours.

At first, the approaching wind prodded his back toward the rendezvous. One hour and three miles later, the river changed course, slowly turning eastward. Following the valley shoulder, Yakov felt the fierceness of the gathering gale. From the northern horizon, ominous zephyrs assembled and raced.

Fifteen minutes later, freezing rain pelted his face and Yakov stopped to slip into winter thermals. He radioed his comrade. Sergei's response was positive.

The rain ceased, but the wind intensified. Behind him, dark rain streaks feathered the horizon, a warning of limited reprieve. Vainly, Yakov hoped to outrun the storm, but fifteen miles of mercy were not enough. With a blunted blast, the storm pummeled furiously—loosing a deluge that instantly obliterated his visibility.

Again, the wet fall did not last. Within moments, rain turned to sleet, a temporary reprieve before the sleet became hail that lashed and stung his exposed cheeks. Donning a balaclava, Yakov protected his face. It brought instant improvement.

Mentally, he was stunned by the instant changes in weather. He could not have fathomed the full onslaught of an Arctic front.

Driving ice bounced over the ground, melting on contact. The prairie softened, becoming spongy, muddy and slick. Of necessity, Yakov stopped again to reassemble his defenses and briefly consider calling Sergei to retrieve him. But a sixth sense forbade him, cautioning that a second jaunt by the Bombardier would be traceable.

Reluctantly, he elected to continue on foot, relying on his high tech gear to guide, insulate and protect him.

As conditions approached white-out severity, Yakov feared that his electronic tracker would fail in the cold. While he could, he studied the route, redrawing the distances and directions in his mind. If the hardware ceased working, he needed the memorized map to direct the compass in his hand. Each ten minutes, he contacted Sergei using the clicks only, demanding himself to preserve the secrecy. It was a monster find and worth keeping discreet.

Another mile passed. This pedestrian journey would be the hardest part. On the first thoughts, he was correct, but the latter surmising was infinitely wrong.

Backtracking the morning's GPS thread line, Yakov revisited the geographical junction, a rapid descent from taiga highland into muskeg bogs. Below lay a wetland of scrub conifers, moss, lichens and glacial ponds.

But the slope between was now enameled with a wintry glazing, slick and treacherous. Seizing the advantage, the wind pummeled him, mercilessly pressing him toward the perilous slope. However, Yakov was prepared, possessing a pair of telescopic walking sticks currently attached to the bottom of his pack.

Yakov descended precariously, each step puncturing through the crisped glaze, dislodging the loose gravel till beneath. The wind howled, threatening to launch him into an unrestricted tumble. The pointed sticks offered less traction than he desired. Halfway down, he lost his footing. Twisting rapidly, he shot out an arm, bracing his fall and regaining his balance, but not before sliding several feet, nearly impaling himself with the sharp end of his dangling brace. Dusting himself off, he checked for damage.

His parka had a small tear, courtesy of a jagged rock but otherwise he was unharmed.

At the bottom, deeper snow and a flatter texture offered better traction, but numerous small sloughs blocked his way. Meandering between the watery gray ink blots of viscous chop, his forward progress did not improve. The snow layer thickened, from ankle deep to mid-shin, hindering his speed further. The carbon fiber sticks, no longer needed for towage, now helped him avoid falling into a hidden pond.

Fortunately the tempest had weakened, its flurries softly subsiding. The weather would offer no further challenges.

Yakov did not perceive that he was being followed. An expert tracker was steadily homing in, having picked up his trail on the topside plateau. This flatfoot relied not on satellites or radios for pursuit. Rather, it possessed superior senses, precision honed by its kind over tens of thousands of years. Not needing to rest or re-orient, it could track on the fly for hours at a time, conserving energy beneath a thick layer of insulating fur. It did not fear becoming lost. A fierce storm was familiar ground, as the coastal Arctic was its ancestral home.

But this hunter was miles from a typical comfort zone, perhaps having pushed inland along the freshwater conduits in search of summer sustenance when the ice pack no longer provided access to stranded seals.

Displaced didn't mean disarmed.

Once having picked up the scent, the polar bear would not relent. Time, stealth, and strength were on its side. Its only fear was another, larger great white bear. While Yakov had a two mile head start, with perhaps as much to go, under cover of the elements, the bear would steadily gain.

A mile from the Bombardier, the wind waned. Long range visibility resumed, revealing a trail of footprints visible for a quarter mile behind, progressively filled with blown snow the longer they lay.

Yakov verified his coordinates. During the white-out, he'd strayed an inconsequential half degree off course. It might cost another minute or two, but his accuracy was encouraging. In less than a half hour, he'd be warming in the heated cockpit of the ATV. The want of a strong drink graced his lips. In response, he ingested a few frigid ounces of water.

Drinking too much icy fluid was as perilous as dehydrating if the body could not economically warm it to body temperature. Too much or too little could lead to hypothermia.

Three quarters of a mile away, a trembling movement caught his eye.

An animal, he guessed, although it had quickly disappeared, perhaps descending beneath a snowy rise or else blending into the pasted white landscape. Calmly, Yakov set field glasses to his face. Thoughtlessly exhaling, he fogged the eyepiece.

"Shit!" he muttered.

It would take a few minutes to dissipate the fogged eyepiece. Scanning with his naked eyes, he sought a trace of the animal. The wind stirred snow fragments in the distance, dusted pellets which obscured his view. Seeping cold chilled the perspiration on his back. Stomping his feet in place, he struggled to keep warm. He could not afford to tarry much longer.

Resetting the binoculars over his eyes, he found the lenses cleared. The monochromatic landscape, once enhanced, was immensely detailed. Yakov was startled by the clear view. Surmounting a ridge a half mile in the distance, a polar bear was following his footsteps. Intense eyes locked on his, magnified orbs gripping Yakov's soul. In cold terror, he shivered.

Coarse goosebumps arose upon his skin. Primeval instincts ordered him to flee.

Stifling the urge, Yakov turned and trotted, afraid of provoking an immediate attack, bluffing the confidence he did not feel. Anxiously gripping his radio, he repeatedly depressed the send button, a message of urgency to his partner.

A triple click returned instantly. Message received. Sergei was firing up the Bombardier. One minor fear was allayed.

Almost immediately, the metal box on tracks rose above a steep esker a half mile away. His partner was very close. But there was no easy path to his perch. Worse, the craft turned away, winding down a muddy bank encircling a glacial pond. Frantically waving his arms, Yakov vainly sought Sergei's attention.

"This way! This way!" he yelled. "Go through the water, not around it! Come get me! Now!"

Moving as though deaf and slow-witted, the Bombardier circumnavigated methodically, a maneuver Yakov could not bear to watch.

He can't hear me!

Shouting desperately into the radio, he broke his rule of silence. A stunned Sergei tersely affirmed the transmission, bee-lining the machine at his friend. But its speed was limited.

Over his shoulder, Yakov saw the bear galloping nearer, each loping stride literally consuming the space separating them. Desperately, Yakov unzipped a side pouch housing his weapon. The gloves encumbered his movement, and he could not dig it out cleanly. He ripped one off, no longer debating the consequence of frostbite. Hanging by its lanyard on his wrist, it flopped against the pack, hindering his scrambling fingers from reaching inside. Focusing his mind, he willed his panic subservient, and felt the firm butt of an ivory handle. Retrieving the semi-automatic 9-millimeter Glock, he cocked the handle and removed its safety.

The ice cold metal edges sapped the heat from his hand, a sensation he did not acknowledge.

He stole another glance at the bear, sizing the gap. Less than a quarter mile remained. Yakov turned and ran like hell, knowing he couldn't make it.

The bear closed quickly, covering ground at thrice the speed of his prey. On rubbery legs, the hapless geologist could not will himself to sprint faster. Fumbling at his radio, he continuously squelched his distress. If only Sergei could make the Bombardier move faster. If only he could survive a few short minutes.

His lungs bursting, he accepted the inevitable conflict, vowing to hold the bear at bay until Sergei arrived. Bloody was better than dead.

And then the bear was upon him. Desperately, Yakov spun around, gun at ready. He squeezed the trigger, but his cold hand shuddered and the slug sailed over the monstrous white head, missing badly. A second bullet was closer but still off the mark. In the cold, the gun's springs were stiff and slow and his numbed hand functioned at the same viscous pace. Stepping backward to fire again, Yakov tripped, losing the gun as his hand struck an exposed rock. Rolling over, he screamed, pointing a walking stick upward, a puerile gesture.

Lunging at the bear's eyes, he grazed an ear. Amused, the bear stood, towering above his terrified quarry. It growled, a mirthless rumble wounding Yakov's will.

The bear paused, summing his victory.

Yakov crawled to his knees, holding the pointed stick outward, bluffing the bruin while trying to edge to his handgun. A simple swat knocked the insignificant rod from his hands. He was out of ammunition before the fight had even begun.

Pulling a precious rock out of his pocket, he hurled it at the bear's face. Glancing off the neck, it didn't even shrug. Awash in terror, Yakov forgot the blade at his belt and covered his face with his hand and glove. The great bear's head plunged toward Yakov's face, teeth bared in a wicked snarl. Yakov scarcely resisted, pushing weakly against the oncoming maw. Steely jaws closed over his outstretched hand, crushing his bones.

A cacophony of white noise overwhelmed Yakov, dismembering his mind from his body. The blackness of unconsciousness beckoned.

Now shedding his inhibitions, he accepted his fate, curiously liberated toward a bottom that never came.

* * *

Twenty minutes later, Sergei sped into the aftermath, the Bombardier wrenching recklessly over unseen bumps, throttled to the edge of control. Cutting power, the relentless corrugated tracks squealed in protest, blurring to a shuddering stop.

The diesel engine choked into quietude, hot steam hissing from the searing metal flanks. Sickened with dread, Sergei jumped out of the suspended cabin, anxiously approaching the grotesque scene. To his surprise, two bodies lay on the snow. A spray of crimson spots merged into a pool of thickened blood that had already congealed in the frigid air. The blood had to be Yakov's, for the bear was unharmed.

So why was the bear still? It made no sense, Sergei thought.

Pointing his own Glock, Sergei advanced nervously, not comprehending the incongruity. Imprisoned beneath the unmoving bruin, his colleague's legs hidden, pressed into the freezing ground. Alongside massive shoulders, Yakov's torso resembled a rag doll, tiny and featureless. In grim repose above, the bear was statuesque, guarding its chance meal.

Surely this stillness was a momentary illusion before breathing again, but it did not stir.

Could Yakov have killed it? A ludicrous idea he instantly rejected. Approaching tremulously, a finger firm over the curved trigger, he began to fear the surreal scene. Fighting the compelling urge to take refuge inside the iron sanctuary of his vehicle, the bonds of his lifelong friendship drew him nearer.

Close up, the macabre confusion resolved. An exposed hand, lacerated and crushed, clutched closed over Yakov's chest. The other, blood-streaked but whole, lay uselessly outstretched above his head. Radiating furrows marking desperate swaths in the snow, terminating at arm's length, failed attempts to extricate himself from beneath the burdensome bear. Above the prostrate man, enameled with congealed blood, the beast's jaws remained locked open, framing a bewildered snarl. The bear was not visibly wounded, but it was dead.

Neither had it feasted before expiring.

Instead, malignant pupils stared upward, peering vacantly into the skull. Burst blood vessels spider-webbed over white eyeballs, a clue to the bear's final moments. The venal epitaph read solemnly. A consumption of panic, a preponderance of impotence and the same uninteresting horror it had aroused in its many victims. But it wasn't death by fear alone.

At last, he comprehended the mystery.

Deep within the throat, Yakov's corrugated glove revealed its location, plugging the predator's airway. Unable to breathe, the great maw convulsed when unable to acquire its most precious resource, oxygen. The polar bear had suffocated. Spasming in death throes, it fell onto the unsuspecting, unconscious body of its own succumbed prey.

Or had the man been vanquished? On his knees, Sergei pressed his ear against his friend's chest, hearing the undeniable murmur of a fragile heart beat.

Yakov was alive.

Beside this Arctic king, Sergei was a pitiful dwarf. The contrast assailed his sensibilities. Turning his back on the bear, he attended to his friend, desperately squelching the primeval anxiety the dead animal still engendered.

Yakov might survive.

Short of blood, he was both deeply chilled and critically wounded. Within the Bombardier, Sergei could warm him and render simple first aid. But only Yakov's slumbering will could overcome the shock paralyzing him. It was doubtful whether he would ever be whole again, but Sergei surmised that Yakov would accept his handicaps readily in light of the alternative fate that he had inadvertently escaped.

Probing Yakov's neck and back, Sergei's hands quickly perused the spinal cord, reading neither dislocations nor fractures along its length. He could safely release Yakov without concern of causing paralysis. Sergei tried pushing, pulling and rolling the bear to no avail—a man would not budge its liquid bulk.

As Sergei struggled, he could not quell a restless anxiety that the lifeless beast would awaken and attack.

Beneath Yakov too little snow remained to dig him out. Moving the bear would require more power. Sergei hooked a chain around the menacing head and connected it to the Bombardier's front bumper. Gingerly backing the snow craft, he dragged the bruin off Yakov's pinned legs. As he jumped to the ground, the bear convulsed, but did not quicken. Suppressing the hackles of terror, Sergei understood the movement was borne of gravity—not of life.

Once Yakov was released, Sergei closely examined the damages. Surprisingly, there was less than expected; a snapped arm, both radius and ulna alongside a gashed and crushed hand. But other cuts were worse. Crisscrossing lacerations covered his arms and chest, gouges from which Yakov's blood had poured. A trickle of blood dribbled through, rapidly gelling in the frigid air, but Sergei could not determine whether the flow was stopped by clotting or because Yakov's supply was drained. These wounds needed rapid disinfection and closure. He was well prepared, possessing pints of blood plasma and yards of suturing thread in the first aid kit.

The fractures were troubling; he would have to set them promptly. Debating the obvious, Sergei acted judiciously. A short distance away a walking stick protruded from the snow. Sawing the carbon fiber rod into several foot-long lengths, along with tape and cable ties, he prepared to set and secure the bones. It was opportune to accomplish this painful endeavor while his unsuspecting friend harbored within the ether of unconsciousness.

Grasping the broken arm firmly above the wrist, he wedged his feet beneath Yakov's shoulder and with a steady strength pulled hard.

Involuntarily convulsing as his skeletal supports yielded, Yakov groaned, but he did not awaken. Working quickly, lest the bones slip apart, he placed the cut carbon along Yakov's arm, temporarily restraining it with tape.

Securing the splints with cable ties, he snugged them into alignment over the fractures, forming a makeshift structure resembling a solid cast. There was little he could do for the crushed metacarpals. The remaining narrow pieces of the walking sticks could be used to straighten and support Yakov's broken fingers, but it would require a doctor to properly treat the pulverized digits. Inside the Bombardier, where it was warmer and protected, he would take another look.

Using the Fireman's lift, Sergei hauled Yakov into the Bombardier. As he carried his friend, he felt the rigid, bulky form of the rock sample digging into his shoulder. The understanding that their mission was a success was only partial relief. Inside the craft, he gently placed Yakov onto a soft bunk, covering his torso with an electric blanket and leaving his arms, legs and head exposed. Adjusting the thermostat to a warm 37 degrees Celsius, he initiated the process of re-warming his fallen partner.

Next, Sergei dressed Yakov's wounds by methodically pouring hydrogen peroxide into the gaping gashes, flushing away the thickened blood and exposing multiple lacerations. Most were shallow, but several were bone deep. A pair of serious gouges on his chest exposed shredded pectoral muscles. Yet Yakov was fortunate the raking claws had not penetrated his ribs to an organ or pierced a lung. Either would have been fatal.

Sewing the chest closed, Sergei then smeared his stitching with ointment and covered it with gauze. Inserting an IV drip into an arm, he injected replacement plasma into Yakov's veins. Then he secured Yakov on the bunk using rope and his belt. The return trip would be jarring, treacherous for an unconscious victim. Last, he attended to the damaged hand, taping the good fingers against the bad. Finally, Sergei climbed into the cockpit, directing the machine towards the awaiting submarine. He forsook the vodka, valuing his faculty, although he yearned for a nip to relieve his tension.

Periodically, Sergei halted the craft, syringing replenishment into Yakov's bloodstream. With fresh fluid circulating and the heat blanket slowly warming, Yakov's shock subsided. His chances for recovery were improving.

Chapter 3

Parity Forbidden

"Sir, I have news from the geologist's survey."

Behind a stately mahogany executive desk draped in a tailored suit, a middle-aged face with a furrowed brow buffering ambitious brown eyes from impeccably cropped, short dark hair glanced up. He was a man of influence. An ornate, hand-sculpted *bas relief* of a soaring bald eagle adorned the desk front, a proclamation of allegiance, status and power.

"What is it?" he spat from pursed lips.

The orderly blinked, unable to see clearly through the backlit vantage as sunshine dazzled through double-paned windows beneath open wood-slatted Venetian blinds. It was the typical, classless theater designed for leveraging intimidation.

"Apparently he's made a find, surface lode, composition under analysis."

"Apparently?" He mimicked with sarcasm. "That's all you have? A lousy maybe?"

Backpedaling, the orderly continued. "It's reported he suffered a severe accident. He was carrying a mineral sample in his pocket, but can't tell us where he got it."

"What about his partner?"

"Claims ignorance, says they were searching in different locations."

"Well, that tells us something."

"Maybe not as much as we'd like, they were apart for several hours," he informed with assurance.

"Did the dumb bastard run into the RCMP? We don't need that complication."

"No," the orderly informed, "he crossed paths with a polar bear. It's quite unbelievable that he survived."

The executive dismissed the sensationalism. "Why weren't the two working together?"

"They were separated for several hours by a sudden snowstorm. The partner says he was lucky to have found him at all. Perhaps the partner isn't fully trusted."

"When can the geologist talk?"

"He's damn near dead, sir."

"Oh," the man said, without concern, looking up at the orderly. "Analyze the sample, copy his journals...map his movements. If you're quite certain of his whereabouts, let him go."

"Yes, sir."

"One less loose end."

"Of course, sir. I'll keep you posted."

Turning smartly, the orderly exited the room, his face hiding disgust, but beneath his passive face his thoughts stewed. His boss was a cold-hearted bastard.

Prior to the age of electronics, rare earth elements were thought to be uncommon, hence earning the self-describing moniker.

Over time, improvements in surveying revised estimates upwardly, but the adjective remained. In actuality, the minerals are ubiquitous, albeit dispersed in fractional compositions. The *rare* misnomer is more synonymous with concentration than abundance.

Unlike the noble metals of jewelry, artisan or currency, pure rare earths are not ductile, malleable or lustrous. Rare Earths are wanting; lacking the strength of iron, the hardness of tungsten and titanium, the chemical stability and conductivity of copper and lightness of aluminum. Neither were they formed into revolutionary blends like bronze or steel. They've historically had few applications in warfare, commerce or structural building.

Rare earths were mineral oddities with limited application. Traditionally employed as pigments for coloring glasses, this usage did not require exorbitant quantities or ultra-purification. Their value reflected their commodity and there was little need to locate or tap new supplies.

More recently, discovering the physics of color alteration has greatly magnified their value, directly spawning the lucrative opto-electronic industry. For example, trace amounts of erbium in solid silicon are currently used for making EDFAs (Erbium Doped Fiber Amplifiers), error-free signal boosters enabling the worldwide information *super highway*. Networking the globe, these *high bandwidth* communication lines are far superior to last century's metal conduits.

Another rare earth, Yttrium, is a true 'light fantastic.' Yttrium Aluminum Garnet, YAG, is the backbone of LEDs—a revolutionary, efficient source of radiance projected to supplant both the incandescent bulb and the fluorescent lamp. Yttrium's properties, however, are not limited to the household. When doped with a sister rare earth element, Niobium, the pair create powerful solid state lasers, essential semiconductor manufacturing tools. Phosphor powders of yttria and ytterbia are finding uses as light emitting *taggants*, unique signatures utilized in anti-counterfeiting strategies, allowing customs agents to test the authenticity of transshipped goods, easily isolating 'knock-off' distributions of CDs, DVDs and cigarettes. Not surprisingly, taggants are integral to identifying genuine, modern banknotes.

Until recently, and with less celebrity, the inclusion of the rare earth Lanthanum in nickel-cobalt blends is the game-breaking ingredient asserting the success of the Nickel Metal Hydride (NiMH) battery. Today, the rechargeable has widespread usage, found in products from low-tech flashlights to sophisticated hybrid-electric (HEV) vehicles.

When Toyota cornered the remaining world supply of Lanthanum for their HEV line, it was rumored that GM and Ford were forced to develop the immature and somewhat explosive Lithium ion technology, retarding electric and hybrid vehicle production in the US for over a decade.

More than simply a corporate game changer, rare earths are part and parcel of sovereign economic competition. The governments of China and Japan, motivated by the long-term importance, move rapidly to secure access to newly-discovered exotic deposits, maintaining a tight fist on the supply chain. This sequestering response has already affected Western companies. ENEL, the North American company that perfected the NiMH battery, was reported to have sold its technology in exchange for a guaranteed stream of the NiMH elixir rather than face the possibility of a diminished or irregularly doled supply.

Unfortunately for the West, enriched sources of the rare earth elements exist in places geographically or politically inaccessible, the richest mines found within the communist countries of China and the former USSR.

As some experts suggest, the next generation of super-economies will be built on the backbone of these minerals, their value is skyrocketing.

Suddenly, the supply is vanishingly small.

Across an open courtyard, Robb Davis ambled toward a high-tech machine shop oddly housed in the sub-basement of a theoretical physics research department.

The Hawking Building workshop was a busy lair, cluttered from floor to false ceiling with CNC metalworking mills and lathes, grinders, cutters and laser perforators, possessing few of the older, humbler trade tools such as band saws, drill presses, punches or metal sheet benders.

The pungent odor of machining oil permeated the workshop, assaulting the senses and coating exposed objects with a greasy film difficult to remove without strong solvents. However, within its cramped confines, skilled machinists sculpted dull, bar stock ingots into a myriad of shining precision components, the critical made-to-order assemblies necessary for leading-edge research projects. Custom-made parts weren't cheap, but ground-breaking research rarely is.

An outstanding student showing great promise, Robb's experimental work was published in the prestigious journals of both *Nature* and *Science*. He was among a handful of extremely talented young scientists in that he synergized a knack of scientific understanding with the more industrial applications of mechanics and software programming. Robb designed his own prototypes and programmed their operation, uniquely exploring ideas that others could only theoretically visualize.

Today, he was status checking the progress made on his self-designed sampling stage. The temperature-controlled, three-axis movement and rotation stage would allow him to characterize the rare earth compounds he'd fabricated in any number of environments, through a wide band of morphologies, temperature, field effects, chemistry and time intervals.

It was tricky to treat samples and capture behaviors simultaneously, but these new studies would complete his contribution to his doctoral dissertation. Finishing two decades of a long education that began in grade school was an intoxicating prospect.

At present, he was studying energy *capture and release* mechanisms in coupled systems of rare earths and nanoparticles. The complexes of materials were showing promise as enhanced efficiency emitters, accessing energy transfer pathways normally forbidden by quantum physics in their single components. To date, he'd been immensely successful.

His challenge was explaining why things worked so well.

Stepping through a metal framed door, Robb entered a stairway landing to the subterranean floors. Startling him, the flying form of a woman sidestepped him neatly to dodge a collision. Before Robb regained his balance, the agile form had darted down the basement stairwell. She had dark hair tightly wrapped against her head. Lithe of build, possibly Chinese, she was not anyone he recognized from the small campus.

As the woman disappeared from sight, Robb descended, considering whether he should inform campus security. It seemed a useless formality as the furtive figure would be well away before anyone would respond. But halfway down, he reconsidered. The situation was too bizarre to ignore. Recently, an Atomic Force Microscope had been pilfered from an unlocked lab, prompting a series of security briefings and restrictive regulatory changes, wasting a lot of valuable time.

Unlocking his cell phone, he tapped the campus emergency number. The phone chirped belligerently, refusing to connect. From the building's bowels there was no signal.

Quickly ascending the stairs, he stepped outside. To his surprise, a pair of uniformed security personnel were hurriedly approaching in his direction.

"Have you seen anyone suspicious nearby?" One demanded curtly, but out of breath.

"I was just going to call you," Robb answered. "A woman nearly ran over me. She headed downstairs here in Hawking."

"Is she in the building now?"

"Possibly," Robb affirmed, "I didn't see her leave."

Adjacent to the building, a narrow alley led to a second concrete pad and door landing. Either portal provided access to the building. One officer immediately made his way to its entrance. Before he'd moved the few, short steps, the young woman burst outside. Glancing over in surprise, she immediately recovered, turning her face from view and effortlessly sprinting out of sight around the brick corner.

Neither security officer took pursuit, the pair weren't fit enough to follow. As one officer radioed the sighting, the other blandly questioned Robb. His answers sketched a short chronology, but he had more questions than facts.

"What do you suppose she was up to?"

"Probably thieving small office equipment," the officer vaguely replied. "We've had several incidences lately."

"Like the missing AFM?" Robb questioned, wondering what equipment could be considered small in his line of work.

"No, nothing like that one," came the reply. "Portable stuff like computer tablets, laptops, software, sled drives and home-made research parts. *Snatch and dash* items."

Robb looked unsure.

The officer continued. "We'll check the online auctions and the classifieds, but I doubt we'll find anything." He frowned, then lectured. "It's best to keep your doors locked at all times."

"Sure," Robb agreed, excusing himself, completely dissatisfied by the evaporative explanation. His analytical mind rebelled at evasiveness. The woman was decisive, efficient and economical in flight. Without falter, her posture had been closed, robbing him of a recognizable vantage of her face. Two-bit thieves weren't that adroit.

Something wasn't adding up.

Halfway down the stairs again a recollection rifled his brain, arresting him in his tracks. Standing stock still, he relived the event, a puzzled look falling over his visage. Fellow students passed by, chuckling at his absent-minded reverie, but the observation was undeniable. Her responses were trained, not instinctive.

She was no *ordinary* thief. She ran like an Olympic sprinter.

Chapter 4

Arctic Dinosaur

Beneath polymer-thonged, carbon frame snowshoes, Evan sloughed over a crisp snow surface, making his seasonal trap circuit. He, and a short score of others, represented the last of a four-century caste of North American fur traders. As his predecessors, he harvested and peddled the pelts of mink, muskrat, fox and beaver to a market gratefully out of touch with the reality of his existence.

The licit worldwide wild-caught fur trade had collapsed a decade earlier, falling into a casket of political correctness that instantly deep-sixed his lifestyle. Extraordinarily lean years followed, with Evan weaseling to raise cash to buy staples like sugar, flour, gas and oil. Most of his associates forsook their shanties and rejoined society, usually laboring in mines or in the emerging oil industry. The stores they'd abandoned had been the difference between famine and subsistence.

Evan refused to leave, preferring to battle the fearsome north wind than perish amongst human habitation.

It took several seasons for a black market trade to germinate and mature. Once it did, his trade recovered and he could move every fur he caught. Ironically, with reduced trapping competition, animal populations were rebounding, and filling demand required less effort than before. Unfortunately, prices did not rebound, constricted within the grip of middlemen in an organized crime syndicate uninterested in profit sharing.

Once a year, Evan sold his pelts wholesale to a greasy bush pilot whose one skill was squeezing the razor thin margin of profit in his own favor.

In early summer, the wholesaler landed his plane on a nearby glacial lake where Evan met him and exchanged goods, haggling for integral supplies inflated by an obscene margin. Evan yearned to settle the dispute with his fists, but preserving his remote measure of freedom required excessive yielding. There were no other buyers for his pelts, although a nearby native village had tried to establish one. The syndicate eliminated its competition, brutally scalping the entrepreneur while lavishly levying gruesome threats, thus silencing the villagers from assisting an RCMP investigation.

Savvy that the *über*-rich were paying extravagantly for the clothing made from his material, Evan did not, however, fathom how mainstream animal pelts were again becoming. In some respects, the restructured market surpassed the old, having guillotined the low-end producers in favor of only the high margin trade. Donned by those who cared little for environmental opinion, the patrons ranged from the wives and mistresses of corrupted officials in tyrannical dictatorships to their counterparts in legitimate global conglomerates and sovereignties—most everyone that bought into conscienceless, limitless wealth acquisition.

South of the 49th parallel, furs adorned the upper echelon of an economic aristocracy and, ironically, also dressed the shoulders of fundamentalist, neo-conservative power-mongers. The politicians who claimed a superior moral code subscribed to a religious viewpoint that encouraged all forms of exploitation, both human and ecological. Such hypocrisy profited in part by questioning the tenets of basic science and confusing social conscience with a legacy of profitability. After all, God had told man to govern the world as he saw fit...to be fruitful and multiply.

Evan held no religious illusions, nor political ambitions. A generation earlier, he had abandoned society, damaged and disillusioned. Back then, he had embraced materialism with all the fervor and enthusiasm of a well-bred, teen-aged party animal.

Until that world had failed him.

One raucous night, his mind altered by a soup of alcohol and hallucinogens, he attended a friend's party on an abandoned farmyard. In a steaming, pot-soaked barn wall-to-wall with fellow revelers, he drunkenly danced his way onto the top of a rickety chair. Howling in mirth, his friend egged him on, daring him to balance his over-sized, adolescent frame on the chair back. The chair collapsed, upholstered cushions dismembered from their metal supports. Falling onto the rusted, exposed tubing, he impaled his thigh.

Insensibly drugged, he couldn't even feel the painful sensations wracking his muscles, but neither could he move. Immobilized on the linoleum floor beneath his friends' feet, he slowly bled several pints of blood until he passed out. All the while, his peers carried on their merrymaking.

The following morning he awoke in a hospital bed, bandaged and restrained, having received a blood transfusion. At death's door, one somewhat sober partier had comprehended his plight and called for emergency services.

The emergency operator had alerted the police, who accompanied the ambulance, forcibly dispelling the party. A small town scandal was in the making, but Evan could have cared less.

After a fortnight on his back, mending as only the youthful are capable, he attended drug addiction seminars, preparatory penance before reentering normal life. The balance of his rehabilitation was learning to walk without a limp, having severed several strands of fibrous tissue in his wounded thigh.

He was never the same.

The brush with death, the lack of concern from his *friends* and the damage from the drugs took a physical and psychological toll. He'd dropped out of high school, left home and made his way northward. Working at seasonal jobs that were back breaking, he eventually disappeared into the muskeg. Here he lived for a year, stealing supplies from hunting lodges and learning to poach game, honing his outdoor skills, until he was extracting a type of survival through all the seasonal extremes.

It wasn't idyllic and it didn't last.

One robbery ended abruptly as the owners unexpectedly returned. As with most northerners, they carried a loaded rifle in their pickup, firing multiple shots as Evan made his escape. Certain he'd been recognized he packed his pirated clothes, bedding, some shot and a few rifles and migrated farther northward toward the Arctic tundra.

The human population was sparse, and its rarest European inhabitants harbored secrets much more damning than illicit drug usage and petty larceny.

Standing six and half feet tall, with a lean, chiseled frame, Evan was a fearsome competitor in a barroom brawl. His strength, sculpted by hard work and outdoor survival, was not limited to Saturday night fights. Once, he'd been set upon by a foolish timber wolf and suffered a few superficial ankle bites before he gained the upper hand.

When the lone attacker had lunged for his throat he'd grabbed it by the nose and clenched its jaws shut, holding it an arm's length away. Hindered from breathing, the whimpering predator pawed the air uselessly, unable to maul his soft flesh with its shorter legs and free itself.

The wolf's complaints summoned a mate. She approached cautiously, teeth savagely bared, but her tail was tucked between her legs. Evan used the suffocating male as a shield, thwarting her advance and keeping her dangerous canines separated from his neck and legs.

She was too late. Before she could wear out the over-leveraged man, the sniveling male expired.

Feeling his strength waning, Evan pressed his advantage, tossing the anoxic carcass at its snarling, now quivering companion while aiming his large hands at her jaws. Cleaved from her companion she fled.

As the sun set that evening, Evan squatted on a hunter's porch, hearing her wail with grief, a piteous dirge so palpable that he'd broken a cold sweat.

More disturbingly, her haunting cries were answered nearby—by other wolves. Over the next half hour, Evan listened intently as the bereaved female pleaded her case and moved closer toward her pack.

It had frightened him. He fully expected the larger group to take up her quarrel against him and he prepared his camp for a night assault. But there was no attack. After the reunion, their collective calls soon faded into the distance as they pursued other, more immediate, intents.

It seemed that she had communicated the word. The pack did not bother him as long as he stayed.

The farther north he fled, the fewer inhabitants he encountered and the fewer supplies he could pilfer. One evening, he chanced upon the trap line of a grizzled veteran who had long eked his living out from the land.

For nearly half a century, the old sourdough had escaped the shame of being homosexual by hiding away from society. Far too old to make an advance on Evan, he still invited the strapping young man into his cabin for a night of roasted moose, whiskey and the telling of tall tales.

Evan spent a week with the old man before packing to continue his wanderings. As he prepared to leave, the old man revealed that he was cancer-ridden and offered to turn over his territory to the disenchanted vagrant. Evan acquiesced and spent the balance of the summer learning a trade.

By the time the old man became confined to his bed, Evan had barely learned the locations of all his traps and possessed few skills. The basics of pelt harvesting, skinning, mounting and drying were marginally executed, but time ran out for the sourdough to divulge a greater mastery. The essential secrets of enticing prey into the steel trap jaws died with the old trapper.

In late summer, Evan first met the greasy bush pilot with the ailing fur trader. They'd peddled the bulk of the old man's harvest for liquor to dull his terminal pain.

After the first snow, his mentor died. Evan buried him near the cabin. Unable to dig into the permafrost, he covered the shallow, three-foot deep grave with rocks. Unfortunately, not familiar with the tenacity of a wolverine, he failed to secure the barrow with suitably heavy stones. The old man's grave was plundered. The association of the wolverine with the human began a winter's life and death skirmish that the *little bear* easily dominated.

Having been lured to Evan's new home, the animal conveniently and repeatedly raided his lean-to food pantry, especially emboldened during fierce blizzards that the young trapper never dared to venture into. Along the trap line, the wolverine scavenged the caught carcasses, disdainfully shredding their valued fur to tatters. Many hard won pelts were ruined, and Evan retained little of value to trade for stores.

By spring, possessing only a small fraction of what he needed for bartering, Evan realized that he had to kill the marauder or move his trap lines beyond its territory. He decided on the former, but after spring's thaw, never caught sight of the animal again. Without an active trap line to raid, the animal returned to its regular food sources.

In midsummer, when the pilot first returned for his seasonal collection, Evan described his misfortunes and his need to resolve the issue. Not wishing to lose any income, the trading pilot suggested a new site, farther north, on a long abandoned territory.

Years earlier it had been harvested by an Ukrainian immigrant. Saddled with schizophrenia, he evidently lost his mind in a drinking binge before venturing half-clothed into a blizzard. The RCMP found the body the following spring, seizing the example as a poster child to pressure Ottawa to limit the alcohol trade to the region.

As Evan seemed interested in relocating, the fur trading pilot attempted to charge an exorbitant moving fee. Evan held his ground, correctly arguing that their income was intertwined. If the pilot wouldn't help, he would simply move on his own path and all the revenue would be lost. There weren't many people in tow to take his place.

The pilot gave in.

It was Evan's first victory with the fur transporter...it was also his last.

The new territory was richer in pelts than even the bush pilot realized. Because Evan's survival and livelihood depended on knowing the terrain, he scouted his new territory thoroughly, weaving a mental map of its features until he could safely navigate it during any season.

Physically separated from drugs, his memory improved and his intellect rebounded. Over several years, he unlocked the secrets of animal capture and the number of pelts he garnered annually increased. Just like his predecessors, each lesson was earned only at great expense and Evan's psychology slowly synchronized with that of a secretive, troubled hermit. If he ever chose to return to society, he would not be welcomed.

Occasionally, he would cross paths with an RCMP patrol officer. The officers treated him with deference, mainly leaving him alone. As time passed, the intervals between patrols became increasingly longer, a function of budgetary concerns debated a thousand miles away.

More frequently, and at his own choosing, he mingled at a nearby native village. Although their ancestors had long colonized the frozen Arctic, the surviving remnants no longer trapped for trade, preferring to commercially develop their land. It was an ironic cultural role reversal, a European descendant embracing a kinship with the land while the First Peoples' sought monetary gain.

Evan's visits with other humans offered more than conversation.

Evan was nearing the age of forty and welcomed contact with others. Fortunately, there were several eligible women living in the village.

Late one spring, while gathering his traps, Evan found an unusually shaped object protruding from a receding snow bank. It was a carbon fiber pole. The finding did not please him. The evidence of high tech human involvement in his domain was unwelcome.

His senses on full alert, he searched the surrounding landscape for follow up clues. However, there was nothing incongruous, no tracks, no campsite debris, no further indication of intruders. Unnerved, he cast troubled glances in all directions, slowly reassuring himself that he was alone.

Wresting the pole from its wintry embrace, he marveled at its features. Light, flexible and strong, it easily supported his weight without being its own burden. Satisfied with its usefulness, he claimed it for himself. For the next hour, he dug through the encrusted ice patches, searching for other implements. Although late in the season, the northern snowpack was unusually thick, courtesy of a prolonged winter. Determining to return after the last snow melted, he carried on his way, completing his collection circuit and returning to his cabin a dozen miles away.

As Evan moved, unseen electronics silently came to life. Embedded within the pole, the awakening circuits were intended to corroborate the veracity of the carrier's positioning and movements. Yakov's employer had reasons to be suspicious. A recent contractor, cutthroat and cagey, withheld key information during his debriefing, collected a partial payment and disappeared behind the Great Wall. It was rumored that he lived very well.

Yakov's employer had planned a step further, inserting a GPS transmitter to trace Yakov's movements in *real time*. Registered to a decade old dummy corporation, properly licensed for speculative geological exploration, it would arouse little suspicion when used. Or so they hoped. While mineral prospecting is a matter of national security, regularly monitoring companies that employ satellite surveillance in the Arctic is prohibitively expensive.

Prospectors, adventurers, scientists and other modern explorers, however, would be considered remiss had they not used the expensive lifesaving technology. Infrequent signals were easily lost in the noise.

"Update from the geologist's find," the orderly nervously proffered, feeling more like an intruder than a messenger.

"Do you have the location?"

"None sir, but we have confirmation of the mineral. It's a high grade concentration of Erbium with trace quantities of several more."

"What good is that if we don't know exactly where it is?"

"Not much," he agreed. "It appears that the geologist was either suspicious or wary. We have tracking confirmation of his partner's activities, but his movements seem to have been lost."

"Lost? How?"

"We're not sure. There is no data of his precise whereabouts."

"He couldn't have been that far away. Didn't you say there was a snowstorm?"

"Yes, sir, and that may be why we didn't get a signal. The device may have failed in the cold. It's battery activated, you know."

"You're fixing that for next time?"

"Yes we are."

"Can he talk yet?"

"Sir, we'll find where he was. Right now, he's recovering in a Moscow hospital. We're sending someone to talk to him as soon as the doctors permit it."

"Yes, of course. Who?"

"The recruiter."

"We don't have much time to waste."

The orderly stood his ground, "Sir, it's winter, even if we have the exact coordinates of the strike, we could not penetrate the target for another three months. We'll find out if he's telling the truth long before then."

"Good work."

"Thank you, sir." The orderly stepped out, surprised. *Now what the hell does that mean?* The unexpected accolade was more sinister than complimentary.

Chapter 5

Government Interference

At 15 Wing, Moose Jaw, home of Canada's NATO air force training, a white-shirted analyst collected his daily download of data, a summation of the previous night's satellite-to-ground signals, both military and commercial. The facility, strategically located within the continental prairie, monitors the vast expanse of the northern Canadian distant early warning (DEW) line.

Over his first cup of coffee, the analyst ported the files into an SQL database. Sieving the bits using automated routines, his codes isolated deviations suggesting parameters of interest; transmission origin and destination, frequency, duration, encryption, nonlinearity—signatures that suggested someone might have something to hide.

Added to his watch list was a recently isolated signal pattern originating from a trio of geosynchronous, US-owned telecommunications satellites. It was not of late origin, having beamed undetected for several months until its sporadic outbursts became statistically relevant. Before 2001, it might have remained just another series of incomprehensible packets. After the twin tower collapse, the Canadian government, like the American, enacted sweeping domestic surveillance legislation against its citizenry. Brokering intel with allies, the defense ministry plied access to the *skybirds* orbiting its soil, including encryption keys, clientéle lists, etc.

"Sir, I'm noting some unusual traffic on some GPS birds," he announced.

"Such as?"

"One-way signals, short bursts, no replies."

"No response?"

"None whatsoever, or nothing I can detect."

"Where's the target?"

"Northern Saskatchewan."

"Uranium City or tar sands?"

"Neither...eastern side, near the Manitoba border."

"That's unusual. What's there?"

"Nothing I know of. In fact, that's probably why the pattern wasn't isolated by the extraction routines until now."

"How long?"

"Three months at least."

"I thought our data mining was more sensitive than this."

"It is. We caught it in a timely fashion. In the past few weeks, transponder frequency has been increasing. Until now, it was random, never on the same day or hour." He read his printout. "Hmm, let me see. The first month, twice. The second month has the same frequency but not equally spaced. In the past four weeks, a dozen pings. Yesterday alone there were two. It's almost like someone knows our system and is working through it."

"If so, they'll know we're aware now." the boss deduced. "What do you think is going on?"

"They're looking for someone or something, I'd say."

"Yeah, why now?"

"Spring's on its way. People will be able to travel after it thaws."

"Indeed. You think they're looking for a person or an object?"

"Probably the latter, an object someone left behind."

"Perhaps a downed plane?"

"I checked the records for lost flights. There are none in this area from the past three years."

"All right, contact the local RCMP."

"Will do, sir."

Lieutenant Trakalo sat on the porch of the trapper's home, patiently awaiting his return. In addition to a Smith & Wesson 5946 pistol, he was armed with a half dozen civil complaints, a collection granting him full investigative power of search and seizure. In point of fact, the papers were several years old, the accuser having failed to spur action before a discrediting rumor surfaced that he was a blue-balled loser seeking retribution on the trapper following a gambling loss and a woman.

Even so, the documents were never filed in Bin 13. At intervals, innuendo simmered about a shady past, often enough that the detachment kept his file open in contingency. Or as leverage that could prove useful in eliciting information, although it was unlikely that Trakalo would employ the threat.

In recent years, Evan's public behavior was mostly harmless. The Force dismissed him as being a bit soft in the melon, a solitary outcast never venturing too far from his lonely hermitage. A subtle inference to restraint behind bars would likely wilt any suspicious reserve.

From his outdoor venue, Trakalo surveyed the trapper's yard. A hundred yards away, willows grew in thick abundance, edging a serpentine creek locked beneath a twisting ribbon of ice. Nearest to the cabin, a small section of bank had been cleared of bush. Atop the ice was an inverted metal tub, held in place with a heavy stone, covering a small, chopped hole in the ice. Reopened daily, it provided a constant source of fresh water.

A trampled footpath of hardened snow connected the cabin and stream, spurring once to a dilapidated shed where a long-handled axe reclined against a faded plywood door. A short length of cut planking latched the structure shut, attached by a nail half sunk into the door frame. Behind the home, a steep hill lifted the land to a large prairie meadow stretching for miles in every direction. In the early evening, it was remarkably idyllic, but in winter, Trakalo shuddered, it must have been hell.

It was not the life for him. With two seasons to complete on his assignment, he'd be happy to accept a post just about anywhere else, even Quebec, although, he couldn't speak French. His fiancé, barely attached, was drifting away with trivial waves of emotion in Winnipeg. In his opinion, they'd be lucky to remain a couple much longer. It took a full day of aerial acrobatics provided by a kamikaze bush pilot to fly the nine hundred miles just to see her twice a year.

She refused to return the favor.

Evan returned near sunset, just as Trakalo was preparing to leave, startled to find the RCMP at his cabin. Warily, he called out.

"Can I help you?"

"No, thank you," Trakalo responded. "I've made something to eat if you want."

"Sure," Evan responded dubiously. The bastard had already been through his belongings.

"Everything's on the porch," Trakalo beckoned. He had glanced superficially at Evan's goods, but his real interest was motivated by a satellite surveillance report. Anything else he might have learned about the hermit was probably better left hidden away and secret.

Evan was surprised to see that the offered food had not come from his larder. Consisting of roast beef sandwiches, some cut vegetables, and a bottle of ten-year-old blended rye, the fare was light, but nutritious.

Perhaps the blue shirt hadn't been so intrusive after all. He grabbed a sandwich wedge and poured himself a generous drink.

"Pop?" asked Trakalo, offering a cola mixer for the rye.

"For sure," Evan responded, unable to stomach drinking rye whiskey straight up. Trakalo poured the mix into Evan's cup, stopping when the trapper's eyes indicated a sufficient dilution. It didn't take much. Trakalo sat back, raised his glass and they toasted each other's health.

"How was the winter trapping?" Trakalo asked, making small talk.

"Good enough," Evan responded, giving away little. He pulled a slug of rye and cola. It went down smoothly, warming his throat with a magnificent glow.

"What was good?" Trakalo also drank, but deliberately sipped a smaller portion. He needed Evan to loosen his tongue, while he needed a clear head.

"This year, beaver and mink."

"You see many wolves?" Trakalo referred to the large timber wolves, three and a half feet tall at the shoulder, a hundred and fifty pounds when fully grown. They were fearsome predators, unchallenged when gathered in familial packs.

"No, but I hear them—and the coyotes are disappearing. I see a few more foxes, though."

"Where there are foxes, there are polar bears," Trakalo chimed.

Evan's eyes narrowed, recalling the image of a carcass he'd seen at the exact site of the carbon fiber pole. As winter had lingered exceptionally long, he'd already returned, hoping to find anything else of technological note. Curiously, he'd observed a dried, salt-encrusted glove lodged within the skull, probably in what would have been the bear's windpipe, but there were no human remains to be found.

"Aye, the two go together," he responded, downing his glass.

"Another drink?" Lieutenant Trakalo suggested. The question had hit the mark. Evan had found the expired bruin.

"Sure, another two fingers," Evan responded, reaching for the cola bottle and pouring his own mix. He didn't dilute the whiskey more than a few drops. Trakalo asked about his food supply.

"How's the caribou holding up?"

"Getting low," Evan answered truthfully, "but once the ice is gone, I'll be catching some *jacks* and grayling. I'll get by."

"If not?" Trakalo asked.

"I'll head on down to the Chippewa village. I hear they traded pelts for a bow whale pulled up onto the ice last fall."

Indeed, thought Lieutenant Trakalo. In recent years, traditional whaling by the northern coastal natives had restarted, instantly igniting a political hot potato, in part due to the worldwide whaling ban, but also because the modern hunter preferred rifles and snowmobiles to harpoons, arrows and dog teams. Once again, the biped preferred a technological advantage. The hunt seemed hardly traditional, except in name.

"Never tasted whale meat," Trakalo offered, slowly sipping from his cup.

"Neither have I, but I've had me some rabbit fried in blubber oil when I visited last winter. Tasted good, but it didn't sit well with my stomach. I had a hard time getting home." He sat back in his chair, savoring the whiskey.

Too much information, Trakalo thought. *But he's certainly not as reticent as he was a few minutes ago.*

"Ever think of getting a snowmobile? Or some dogs?"

"Nah, I'll save that until I'm older," Evan replied, laughing heartily.

Lieutenant Trakalo played a card.

"Look Evan, I'm here about a missing person. We think someone, perhaps a prospector, came through this area late last fall. Have you seen anyone?"

"Seen, no," Evan answered, "but I have found something mighty strange." He relayed the story of finding the carbon pole in the melting snow, and later seeing an abandoned glove lodged precariously in a polar bear skull.

"Damned strange," he summarized, and then it made sense. "Do you suppose some poor sucker stuck his mitt into the bear's throat and killed it?"

"Is that possible?"

"Couldn't tell you. It's an old legend. An Inuit woman is attacked by a polar bear, covers her face in fright, passes out, and wakes up with a suffocated bear lying next to her."

"I've heard the tale. Strange that it might have happened a second time."

"Yeah. If so, then there was more than one person there," he continued. "Yet I never heard of it. It couldn't have been a Chippewa. It must have been somebody from outside these parts. What was he looking for?"

He's smarter than I'm giving him credit for, Trakalo considered before asking. "Did you notice anything else?"

Talking easily now, Evan relented. "Yeah, I found a lightweight pole."

Trakalo caught himself from leaning forward too excitedly. "A tent pole?"

"Oh no," Evan corrected him. "More like a walking stick. Do you want to see it?"

"You know, that's not a bad idea. More whiskey?"

"Sure," Evan stumbled across his porch, sliding a wooden box and fumbling behind. Slowly metering another beverage, Trakalo watched from the corner of his eye. *He keeps it hidden. Why?*

Returning, Evan handed the object to the officer before sitting down to his drink.

Trakalo examined the rod thoroughly. Reflecting the evening dusk, its glossy finish glowed blue-black. Six feet in length, the lower end possessed a pointed claw opposite a knurled knob at the upper. Just below the handle, five parallel silver bands decorated the top most section.

"What's it made of?" Evan asked.

"Carbon fiber composite, just like a hockey stick," answered Trakalo. "Strong for its weight and expensive. Up here, they're used by hunters and explorers, like scientists or prospectors. They're usually hollow." Grasping the handle firmly, he twisted. It gave way easily, spinning under his applied torque.

"What the hell...?" Evan breathed.

Removing the handle, Trakalo looked inside the hollow tube. A golden glint caught his eye. Flipping it over, he gently shook and loosened its contents. A miniaturized chip fell out. The electronic button was soldered onto a tiny, round printed circuit board.

"Would you look at this?" Trakalo spoke to himself. Glancing at Evan, he noticed the puzzled look.

"This is a GPS tracking chip," he explained. "Somebody was here last year and needed to know exactly where he'd been. I wonder why."

"He wouldn't be after my furs, would he?" Evan asked. "Or a pain in the ass animal protection do-gooder?"

"Not likely, you're too remote. Neither have I heard of any recent scientific expeditions. It might have been big game hunters, but more likely, someone was prospecting."

Lieutenant Trakalo looked Evan in the eye. "Have you noticed any unusual rock formations around here?"

"When the river gets low, I've seen some bright pink rocks."

"Your creek?" he pointed nearby.

"No, at the main river a few miles away."

"Pink rocks," mused Trakalo.

"What's so special about them?" asked Evan.

"I don't know," answered Trakalo honestly. More concerned with their location than composition, he continued.

"Did you find this pole near the river where you've seen the rocks?"

"Not exactly, I found it in the muskeg, near the north end of my trap line."

"You have a *topo* map?"

"No, never needed one."

"I got one out on the snow machine. Just a minute and I'll get it."

Trakalo left, excited, returning a few minutes later. After turning on a porch light, Evan finished pouring the last of the whiskey, mostly into his own tumbler. Trakalo preferred it that way. His mind remained clear.

Spreading the folded map over the table, Trakalo placed a finger over a small 'x' mark, the location of Evan's cabin.

"From here, where did you find the pole?" he asked.

Evan looked puzzled, so the RCMP officer explained how to read the map's contours, pointing out the hilltops, ravines, rivers and glacial beds. Once Evan grasped the fundamentals, he outlined his trapping territory, tracing his trap lines along the curved printed lines. Once oriented, he delineated the walker's approximate location.

"About here," he decided.

Trakalo marked the position.

"And the stones?" he continued.

Running his finger along a dense collection of sinuous, parallel isobars, Evan traced the schematic along an adjacent river valley. In his mind's eye, he pictured each twist, recalling the surroundings, until he stopped, tapping the map.

"Likely around here," he declared, tracing a circle. "Although I can't be too sure in this light."

"No problem," said Trakalo, "I can come back during daylight if need be. Chances are it'll be nearby."

Trakalo connected the two locations, clearly bound by the serpentine river. Evan had marked the carbon pole's position above the ridge. Following the high ground might provide some clues about the owner's arrival and departing, but the river meandered for hundreds of miles before discharging into Hudson Bay. It was not likely that he would easily find additional evidence along the route.

Forensics on the pole would provide better information. Not wishing to irritate the trapper, Trakalo chose his words cautiously.

"Evan, is there any chance I could send this to Ottawa for further examination?"

The jackass gets me drunk and then... Evan thought suspiciously, staring at the cop.

"Look, it's more than valuable," Trakalo explained, "and you know I could impound it. But I don't want to, especially since I'm asking for your help. It does me no good to expect your assistance if I piss you off. But, on the other hand, you should also know that this GPS dot will have someone looking for it. He, she, or they might find it...and you."

Anger abating, Evan queried, "What do you have in mind?"

"Whiskey, fuel, some cash, what would you like?"

"I don't need whiskey and I'm good on fuel for several months. Can you replace the pole with something similar?"

"Yeah, sure, I'll get you a pair of walkers. They won't be exact, since this one is customized, but I get top notch ones for my own use. And I'll even throw in a bottle of rye."

"Deal," Evan agreed. "If only that damn pilot would negotiate."

"I hear he's a pain in the ass."

"For sure, for sure."

"Evan, if you see anything else out there, be sure to pick it up or at least mark the location and let me know about it. I'll be back in a few weeks. What you see can save me a lot of time wandering about. I don't know this country quite like you do."

"I'll do that."

Not that Trakalo was holding out much hope. The stakes were too high for prospecting teams to give away valuable information. It never paid to advertise.

As the cop churned away over the snow, Evan noticed a ghostly image on the ground, reflecting the snow machine's tail lights. When Trakalo topped a knoll, the shimmering disappeared. Retrieving a flashlight from his cabin, Evan returned to investigate. Lying on the snow tread was a zippered plastic pouch.

Picking up the flat packet, Evan re-entered his cabin.

Deliberately closing the door, he secured his abode against intruders. Not the human kind, but the four-legged type.

At this time of year, badgers and wolverines were short on food, desperately foraging for the few remaining scraps of carrion. A few seasons past, during a moonless spring night, a beleaguered badger had barged through his unbolted front door. Famished and fearless, the fanged weasel had held him hostage, snarling copious threats, while scavenging his indoor larder. In the gloom, Evan could only fume and fret, awaiting daylight's return. Before he could see clearly, the satiated curmudgeon prattled away to safety. Nowadays, he laughed about the incident, but he would not let it happen again.

Once safely inside, Evan unzipped the plastic pouch. Inside were several documents, unserved warrants with his name on them.

"Bullshit!" he yelled, instantly red-faced and livid. "I'll not help you, you son-of-a-bitch!"

For a moment, he imagined getting his gun and chasing down the cop. But Trakalo was already miles away, and even in his apoplexy, Evan knew he was far too tipsy to travel. There was great risk in becoming stranded this early in the spring. It was an easy way to die.

A card fell from the pouch, scribed with a handwritten note.

All charges dropped. Thanks for your help. Lt. Trakalo.

All the warrants were stamped in thick red letters, 'Expired' or 'Insufficient Evidence' and signed by the cop with the current date.

Stunned, Evan fell to his knees. He was a free man, but he would never leave his sub-arctic home.

"I'm not sure what I want to do now," Robb said, a bit too truthfully.

"Just what are you talking about?" The indecisive tone caught the professor's attention. With concern, she looked her star student in the eye.

Robb vented. "Look, Paulina, I got into the field of science because I loved it and I was good at it."

"Good reasons."

"And when I started, every career report I read described an immediate shortage of scientists and engineers here in the US."

"There is."

"I don't believe it."

"What are you talking about? The science and math scores of our high school students rank well below most industrialized nations. Universities can't even fill their programs with homegrown talent."

"Is that really an important metric?"

"Of course it is, it tells us where we're going to be in less than a decade."

"There's no incentive for kids to do better."

"What do you mean? It's a high demand occupation. Good money. Job security. What more incentive is needed?"

"Hah. Is that true anymore? Twenty years ago, jobs were plentiful and stable and paid well. The workplace was a rewarding environment. There were annual raises, bonuses, and commissions earned from writing patents."

"It's all still there now," Paulina smiled, motherly. "You'll get your share."

"It's not *my* share I'm concerned about. The dynamics have changed. I think there are too many workers for the jobs available."

"The field still pays well," his professor argued, conveniently ignoring the punch line.

"For you," Robb replied. "You're at the top, and you locked in at a cheaper time. For years now, the pay has been declining. And do you know why? Supply and demand. We import up to 150,000 professionals per year, saying we need them to meet the shortcomings in skills. If that were true, salaries would be rising across the board. Yet, they aren't.

Instead, dilution in the workforce is suppressing compensation. In the past two decades, lawyers, medical doctors, even top flight auto mechanics have had increases. That's market demand. Doesn't really sound like engineering is a high demand occupation, does it?"

"It's a strategic move for the country, keeping us innovative and creating new markets."

"Well, then it's not a shortage of labor, is it?" Robb challenged. "Obviously, it's not working. Most new products are shipped overseas to manufacture, taking the jobs offshore. How many of the skilled and financially connected are returning home, taking secrets and starting rival industries?"

"Espionage is rare."

"I don't just mean theft, what about legitimate businesses? The law is pretty clear: Unless a company holds patents in China or India, a competitor can manufacture and sell copies without recourse. For shallowly funded companies, especially start ups, patenting in every market in the world is prohibitively expensive."

"Well, by law, we still maintain the cutting edge here. The rest is for patent infringement lawyers to sort through," Paulina relented.

Lying on his small cot, dressed in a paper-thin hospital gown, Yakov half gazed at the only broadcast entertainment he could stomach, a KHL hockey game. Early in the second period, the contest was a farce, a major blowout hardly worth watching. It was better than staring at the wall waiting for scars to form. Although Sergei had brought him his laptop, there was little he could do with it. The hospital did not provide internet access.

He was more isolated in convalescence than being stranded in the frozen tundra of Canada.

The lacerations on his arms and shoulders were fully closed, but the broken wrist had been stubbornly unresponsive, a complication requiring a pair of surgeries to re-break, realign and secure the bones. Now, with permanently inserted titanium plates and screws, crossing airport checkpoints would be annoying. His career might be in jeopardy.

More serious were the deep gouges rancorously mending in his chest. Although Sergei had washed and sterilized the wounds, the sub's crew had been negligent. The oily, sooty, recycled air of the submarine settled onto the fabric of his cloth coverings and worked its way through to his seeping wounds. Several times Sergei had argued for better treatment, but their benefactors' stony animosity was underscored with a commensurate lax in medical care.

Out of discretion and fear, Sergei did not inform Yakov that his employer was neglecting him toward death. Immediately after arriving in Moscow, Sergei rushed him to the hospital. Fevering and incoherent, his body ravaged with a life-threatening infection. It was just in time, Yakov's heart was nigh on failure.

This Yakov knew about. Twice now, he owed Sergei. Sergei felt otherwise. Without Yakov's brilliance, he'd have to get a real job. A real low-paying job. Sergei relied on Yakov for a good living. With his friend in the hospital, clubbing in Moscow was an empty exercise, a tradition hollowed by going solo. The girls were uninteresting, the attentions he once found intoxicating he now discarded as obsequious fawning. Trite greed disgusted him, but in his heart, he understood that his pious loathing was merely manifested by his frustrations and jealousies.

With Yakov laid up, he couldn't feed his wanderlust. Most evenings he languished at home, bored senseless, drinking until he was comatose. He knew he was being pitiful, but he didn't care. And he harbored a growing guilt, having not relayed his onboard suspicions to Yakov. He was haunted by the visions of the crew's callous indifference and passive hostility.

Sergei made up his mind. Tonight, he would drink, catch a cab and visit his old friend. With Yakov's health clearly out of the woods, it was time to put cards on the table.

Chapter 6

Strategic Acquisitions

It was two o'clock in the morning and Robb was at his desk, hours after finishing a battery of experiments. He was suffering from renewed motivation. Having received his custom-made phosphor-characterizing stage a few days earlier, finishing his thesis, getting a job and earning some real money was in sight.

Outside, the air was cool and damp, but not cold. Southern California was never cold. The winter marine layer had descended to ground level, a pea soup mist filling the void between buildings, obscuring rooftops, quickening the nocturnal eucalyptus trees. Overhead, street lamps diffused amorphous orbs burnishing a medieval maze of concrete walkways between ghostly brick edifices. Some found the cloaking haze unnerving, while others were comforted.

As Robb analyzed his research, he could care less.

Parsing vats of electron wells, Robb distilled the results from an experiment probing a combinatorial size-composition matrix of rare earths and nanocrystals. With growing excitement, he noted intense photoluminescence signals expressed from several new formulations. This was good stuff. Porting the raw data into an SQL database, he charted and pared away the stellar traces into a separate table. As later scrutiny, he would repeat and perform conclusive forensics on these samples.

His computer churned, sieving the trillion points of data. Impatiently, Robb got up for coffee. It was better to keep active than remain sitting at this hour.

Five minutes later he was back.

To his dismay, the computer was still chugging. Rather than get frustrated, he would catch up on other work. He tried opening another file, a manuscript he was authoring for peer review. The cursor plowed across the screen, shuddered to a halt, and froze.

"Damn computer can't multitask," Robb muttered. Impatiently channeling the virtual move, he clicked several times over an icon and waited.

Nothing changed.

"At least I can multitask," he grumbled, grabbing a final sip of coffee from the stained porcelain. He might as well dissemble his experiment before another grad student came in and dismantled it for him. Too many critical pieces went missing that way.

Entering the lab, his awareness suddenly awakened, sensing the presence of something else. He'd not heard anyone around for hours, but when he focused his concentration, he became oblivious to his surroundings. Another student could have easily entered the lab without him being aware.

He surveyed the cluttered room, bisected overhead by an industrial rail from which hung a heavy, black stage cloth. At present, the curtain was gathered loosely and secured against the back wall. There was no bulge of human size in its billows. Every few seconds, a cryo-pump cricketed, a monotonous chirping madly grating on his nerves.

To his left, clear sight lines over a massive optical bench indicated that that side was uninhabited. On the right, a slug shaped, homemade vacuum deposition chamber owned the space from floor to drop ceiling. Its mass of kludged ducts, flanges, and stainless steel chambers thoroughly blocked his view of an office door in the opposite wall. Getting around it safely was a logistical hazard. Protruding in all directions were coiled wires, toxic gas carrier lines, coolant tubes and hot wall furnaces.

He shuffled around the machine, careful not to impale himself on multiple sharp protrusions, as he made his way behind.

The back office was vacant. The whole lab was empty. His mind was playing tricks on him.

Jesus, it's late, he thought, heading to his apparatus. *Maybe the fog is getting to me.*

At the snooker-sized table, Robb methodically disconnected, unmounted and stored his equipment. Twenty minutes later, the tedium and late hour convinced him to call it a night. Returning to the office, he noted that the computer had not finished its routine.

"Shit," he grumbled. Before adjourning, he would need to reboot the computer and verify that his data wasn't corrupted. That might take another hour, but with the experiment disassembled, he couldn't afford to lose his results. He soft-booted the keyboard, but to no avail. Absentmindedly, he sipped his coffee cup, instantly spitting out the cooled, bitter liquid. A taste of mold singed his tongue.

Hard-booting the recalcitrant machine, Robb fretted, the operating system languidly toiling through reload. Fearing the worst, he grabbed a network cable and strode back to the lab. The original data might have been left on the acquisition computer, a stand-alone unit housed beneath the optical bench. Normally, it was not connected to the internet, as firewalls and anti-virus software slowed data acquisition cards to rates below useless. Hence, it had neither.

He found the original files. Inserting an ethernet cable into an onboard jack, he connected the acquisition computer to the network. He would retrieve them, if necessary, from the comfort of his desk. Returning to his office, his desktop was up, ready and waiting.

Robb navigated the network tree to the lab computer, but couldn't make it connect. Each task took an inordinate amount of time to perform. Wondering if his desktop had been infected with a virus, Robb initiated a file search, *.exe*, looking for any recently created or modified executable.

With the telltale rat-a-tat of the spinning hard disk, the computer crawled through directories. Robb paced the room, recalling the day, trying to determine exactly when his computer had begun malfunctioning. A day earlier, it had responded normally, so a twenty-four hour search was an appropriate time frame.

He waited impatiently.

The results window was unpopulated. Expanding the parameters, Robb included every malicious program type, *.sys, *.reg, *.pif...*, that he could think of. After a few moments, one appeared, *kylg.bat*.

It was fourteen hours old.

"Shit, shit, shit," he grumbled. He did have a problem.

Noting the directory of the villainous file, Robb expanded the inquiry with a wide-ranging *.*,*, retrieving every file that had been created or modified in the last day. A list of hundreds overran the search window. Rapidly scrolling through them, he noted that most were benign, operating system files or the ones he'd been working on.

Nothing more than he expected.

Sorting the results by directory, he isolated the *kylg.bat* file. Anticlimactically, the same directory housed a second, similarly named file, *kylg.txt*.

Angrily, and with a nagging concern that he was screwed and screwing up even worse, Robb opened the second file. It contained nothing more than text. He began reading its contents.

The skin on his neck started crawling. Every action he'd performed on the computer, every file opened and edited, and each modification had been recorded, keystroke by keystroke. Bewildered, Robb sat back a moment.

"Who is doing this?" Then his curiosity ignited, supplanting his anxiety. Tapping the keyboard, he watched each symbol appear in the file.

Closing the file without saving it, he immediately re-opened it. All the new symbols were still there...along with all of his recent actions.

Closing the key-logger file again, he opened another document editor, typed a few random symbols, saved, named and closed the file. Re-opening *kylg.txt*, he found every glyph recorded. The key-logging program was robust and efficient.

Switching windows to the file search results, he scrutinized the list in greater detail, now noticing that a document in a *Security* folder had also been altered. Oddly, there was no file name listed, just a blank space, a time, and the size of the phantom file.

Changing tactics, he manually navigated the directory to the ghost's file folder. It was completely empty—except for a tag line at the window bottom betraying the skittish apparition's existence.

"Jesus..." he muttered, "there's something there and I can't see it."

For a moment, he considered deleting the directory. But as it was situated in the operating system's root folder, he didn't dare. Spending the rest of the night recovering files and rebuilding the platform simply didn't appeal to him. There had to be a more efficient way.

Running over to his lab computer, now connected to the network, he searched for and found his desktop computer. Opening the *Security* folder, he found a single file inside, *Ipsec.sys*.

"Huh," he grunted. "Internet Protocol Security System file."

Picking up the phone, he dialed the Information Technology department. At this wee hour, he'd get a student employee, but this was a world class institution, even the students were very skilled at their job.

"IT, this is Pascal."

"Pascal, this is Robb, over in Applied Physics," he began, "I've found a key-logging program on my computer."

"What's it doing?"

"As far as I can tell, it records everything I type and records everywhere I navigate."

"Everything?"

"Yeah."

"...is that so, just a minute."

While waiting, Robb felt antsy. *Should I be backing up my data?*

Pascal came back on the line, "Thanks for waiting. Are you connected to the network?"

"Yes, I am."

"Okay, before I get you off the network, I want you to do something for me, please..."

Get me off the network? Robb wondered. "Just a minute then," he interrupted.

"Yes."

"There's another issue."

"Okay, go ahead."

"A system file has been made invisible, but I can see it from another computer."

"Which one?"

"*Ipsec.sys.*"

"That's even worse," Pascal remarked under his breath.

"Okay, before you unplug from the network, go to the DOS prompt and check your ports."

"How do I do that?"

Pascal relayed the commands. Robb typed them in.

Popping onto his screen, a window began printing IP addresses and messages.

> 255.255.155.0   Port 01   *closed*
> 255.255.155.0   Port 02   *open*

The lines continued scrolling for a moment before stopping, leaving the cursor blinking at the DOS prompt.

"Done," Robb informed Pascal.

"Is there a port 55 listed?" Pascal queried.

"Yes, there is."

"Is it open or closed?"

Robb read the applicable line.

> 255.255.155.0   Port 55   *listening*

"Neither," he said, surprised. "It's *listening*."

"Thought so," Pascal said. "Disconnect from the network now."

"Okay, why?"

"Just disconnect."

"Why?!?"

"Your computer's been hacked."

"Can you fix it?"

"No, and neither can you. Remove it from all networks, save your data, and kill it."

"Kill it? You mean re-install the operating system."

"More than that. Low-level format the hard drive. Use a Linux boot disc or go into your BIOS. Wipe it clean. It'll take hours to finish. When you're done, re-install the operating system, but you must call us up and clear this computer before you will be allowed to reconnect to the network."

"Who can do this?"

"You will do this."

"No, I meant, who can hack a system this way?" Robb demanded.

Silence.

"Who did this?" Robb insisted.

"Just kill it."

"Are you up for a visitor?" the nurse queried.

"It's got to be better than this," Yakov brusquely replied.

"Then I'll send him in," she said sweetly.

Momentarily, a slender man in his early fifties entered, wearing a tailored parka. The first hints of gray flecked his short sideburns, highlighting impeccably groomed black hair. His face was soft, untouched by the elements, someone who had been indoors most of his life. Yakov immediately recognized him. It was the recruiter for the recent job.

"Yakov, my boy," he bellowed boisterously, "it is good to see you alive. What a fright you've given me."

"For my life or the contract?" Yakov grinned in return.

"You've read my mind, young man. But, of course, I am also concerned for your health."

"So you know we found the mineral?"

"Yes, indeed, and the samples scored high grades in the lab."

"As they should. Those I picked off the ground, you know."

"So I've been told, but there's much I haven't been told, I gather."

Masking his growing wariness, Yakov parried. "My notes are precise. Have you not seen them?"

"To you, perhaps, but I find them quite confusing."

"In what way?"

"Location and timing of the find."

"The coordinates are logged."

"So we hope, but not as indicated when you and Sergei went out."

The Bombardier was tracked!

The gloves were coming off.

"Of course not," Yakov argued. "You expect me to be that stupid?"

"The employer finds it insulting."

"Employers don't want details, they want results. They got what they wanted, that should soothe any irritation. Anyways, I doubt they're that thin-skinned."

"Business is about trust."

"Business is about money and protecting one's trade-craft. I should expect to be treated the same way if the roles were reversed."

"Yes, indeed."

"So why the drama?"

"He's concerned about your discretion."

"Why?"

"It's very important that you maintain silence."

"I have, I always have. And I will," Yakov vowed, thinking—*who the hell does he represent?*

"And Sergei? He's become quite the drinker, you know."

"Sergei is not a liability."

"Are you sure?"

"Yes, I am. We've been friends since childhood. He saved my life, remember?"

"Ah, yes. But business is about money, I remember."

"The log is correct," Yakov lied. "We'll go back in spring. You can come with me."

"We shall see." Abruptly, the recruiter turned on his heel and left.

Puzzling over the abrupt departure, Yakov absorbed the warning. *Watch your back*, he concluded, *and Sergei's.*

Standing in the doorway of an executive's office, an orderly announced, "Update from the geologist, sir."

"Carry on."

"He states his log is accurate, but..."

"I wouldn't believe him either. Have you checked his apartment?"

"Yes, sir, but we didn't learn much."

"Why not?"

"His computer files are well-encrypted, sir."

"He's a paranoid sort, isn't he?"

"He's a Russian, sir."

"What the hell does that mean?"

"He's seen a lot of political and economic upheaval..."

"Don't lecture me."

"Yes, sir."

"Did you copy his files?"

"Sorry, sir, the orders were to not leave a trail. We can send the team in again..."

"No, not necessary. When does he leave the hospital?"

"Within the week."

"All right. We have time..."

"Just give the word, sir."

"Or, we can wait until he gets home."

"Yes, sir."

"Can you store live merchandise?"

"Already arranged, sir."

"No leaks then."

"Yes, sir." The orderly took leave.

Dialing his phone, the executive spoke into the receiver, "Initiate phase two."

After thanking the trapper for his hospitality, Trakalo rode the bone-jarring miles to his vehicle on the agile snowmobile—summarizing his impressions along the way.

The area was recently prospected—possibly for these pink stones. The prospectors were well-equipped, used high tech equipment, and hence, were funded by deep pockets. They were also professional, having intruded and withdrawn without leaving behind an obvious electronic trace.

Hmm, maybe not, he thought, *maybe they had cleverly avoided attention by appearing normal.*

He would investigate the airwaves, air traffic history, coastal sightings and more. In the meantime, he'd follow up on the GPS dot and hiking pole.

As he drove to his barracks in Churchill, he pondered the mysteries. Someone had suffered an accident the previous autumn. Had he survived? What had been found? Would he, she or others return following the spring thaw? He would not expect them any earlier. Few dared to face any part of an Arctic winter.

The next day he submitted his report, recommending a survey of the potential site as soon as his duties took him through the trapper's territory again.

The phone rang belligerently, demanding his attention.

"Trakalo here," he growled. The damn thing always interrupted when he was making progress on paperwork.

"Kurt here, from electronics in Ottawa."

"Yes, Kurt, good to hear from you," Trakalo responded, snapping to attention. This was much better than administrative duties.

"We've been looking at that the stuff you sent us," Kurt rambled, "and there are a few things of interest."

"Did you locate the GPS satellite company?" Trakalo broke in.

"Yes, yes, of course we have," Kurt replied, a mild hint of aggravation showing. "But that's not why I'm calling. The walker is a very unusual piece."

"Looked pretty pricey," Trakalo agreed. "Maybe custom-made, certainly better than the ones I have."

"I don't mean the quality," Kurt hinted.

And Trakalo quieted down, "I'm listening."

"I'll tell you about the GPS electronics in a minute," Kurt began, "but the chip itself was just a standard, passive receiver. Made in China, assembled on a PCB in Malaysia, nothing there. Underneath it, however, there was something a bit more interesting."

Get on with it, Trakalo nearly complained aloud.

"The top half of the pole is a fully-integrated electronic device."

"What?"

"Beneath the receiver we found an embedded controller supercharged with a 256 GB flash memory module. We think it filed coordinate data every two seconds, that's the capability of the electronics and the way the circuitry is wired, but the files are encoded with 256-bit encryption. We haven't broken the code, and it's not likely that we will soon. However, we can draw a few inferences. For starters, every movement made by the pole's owner was being tracked and recorded."

"Maybe the guy wanted an exhaustive record of everywhere he'd been," Trakalo suggested, "you know, a back-up to his notes?"

"I think it's more than that, for several reasons. First, the encryption is too sophisticated for a small group to design and program. That means a whole team of people are involved. Second, the two second sampling frequency means it also recorded how long he stayed in each location. That alone makes me think the carrier didn't know it was on him, since his memory and a few GPS coordinate waypoints would be enough to remind him of where he'd been, but if a third party needed to interpret his movements based on data alone, the time element gives some pretty good clues."

"All right, so an employer didn't trust his people. Neither would I if the stakes were high," Trakalo countered.

"It gets better," Kurt crowed, enjoying the buildup.

"Okay, then what?" Trakalo answered slowly, hinting his impatience.

"Third, remember I said it was stuffed with electronics? It wasn't just unbreakable recorders. It has a battery-powered satellite communication sender."

"Whoa, you're saying it has a sat phone?"

"Yeah, someone wanted real time information on the whereabouts of his guy. You think he was a prospector, right?"

"Right now, that's my best guess."

"Well, so do we. But he was being tracked as he moved and check-pointed when he didn't. If he was lost in the field, whether he lived or died, it didn't matter. The employer was recording his movements—where he'd been, how long, where he was heading next. They didn't need to talk to him again."

"Whew. I wonder if he's alive."

"Yeah, unlikely."

"So we're looking at a very wealthy source, here."

"Absolutely, but there's more."

"Hasn't this already limited the scope of players?"

"To some degree, yes, but the next device helps even more."

"Another piece of hardware? Where did it all fit?"

"This one was external."

"What? There was nothing on the outside. I examined the piece."

"Remember the silver bands?"

"Yeah, some flashy decorating, looked like Mylar strips."

"Wrong. They're a flexible, thin-film multi-crystalline solar panel. They powered the recorder and sender and charged the batteries. But, frankly, we don't think the last message was ever sent."

"Why?"

"You say this trapper had the pole stored away, right."

Geez, this guy read the whole friggin' report word for word, Trakalo thought. "Yeah, I saw him take it out of a box."

"Away from the sunlight."

"Oh-h-h-h," Trakalo breathed, "you're saying that..."

"When we got it, the batteries were dead."

"How dead?"

"They didn't have enough juice to power the sat com. We used that to fit the data."

"What data? I thought you couldn't break the encryption."

"No, we can't. Based on the battery charge level, and being without sunlight for six months, we date-stamped the most recent file at mid-September last year."

"You believe that?"

"The flash memory module is off-the-shelf, we know its decay characteristics."

"Wait, wait, wait, you're losing me."

"Over time, flash devices lose charge. The programming age can be inferred from the charge level and its decay rate. If data has been written to the transistors only once, like with this module, the method is very accurate."

"You're kidding me."

"Not at all. The capacitance remaining in the gate stacks correspond to the date stamp. That's pretty corroborative."

"All right, I'll buy that," Trakalo answered. "But, if the batteries can't power transmission now, how about earlier, like last fall or mid-summer?"

"Not likely. We don't think it saw much sunshine, there isn't much aging on the carbon. Those glossy UV coatings tend to break down in sunlight. This one is pristine. The carrier was in for only a couple of days. Otherwise, there would be more data stored and a deeper charge cycle."

"So, he wasn't out there last summer?"

"No, it doesn't look like it, unless he was underground."

"The trapper said he pulled it out of a melting snow bank."

"Then it was dropped at the end of fall. And not much earlier."

"We had a helluva an early snowstorm last year," Trakalo remembered. "Very unusual."

"Then you might have a time interval for this intrusion."

"Anything else?"

"The PV device is very recent, a developmental type. We can't determine its origin, but a host of small companies are trying to make them. We believe this one came from a lab, or a start-up."

"Why's that?"

"Very high quality, large crystal grains..."

Trakalo rolled his eyes, he was not a scientist.

"...normally requires an Exciter laser to fabricate in quantity. We think it's an experimental prototype. Very good, but probably not profitable on the open market. Not yet, at least."

"Who makes these things?" Trakalo asked again.

"That may not matter, it could be a dead end. It might have been made in-house or been jobbed out to a small fabricator. We are investigating, and if it's a start-up, we have a chance. If it's a lab, we're out of luck."

"Let me know if you find anything else, please."

"Will do. You've got a real mess brewing there. You may want to get some help."

"I think you're right, I'll see what I can dig up," Trakalo agreed.

Chapter 7

Troika

"How about Tretiak's?" Sergei suggested as he drove Yakov home from the hospital.

"Ah, yes," Yakov agreed, "I could use a good night out."

"Can you handle it in your condition?"

"Piss off, you jerk!"

"Of course," Sergei laughed. "You still taking painkillers?"

"What's it to you, Mom?"

"I want to know if I have to carry you out tonight when you get stupid."

"Sure, makes it easier for me," Yakov chortled.

"I've set up a card game for later," Sergei parried. "After dinner, maybe?"

"Sure, sure."

Looking around, imbibing the Moscow nightlight, Yakov sighed.

"I didn't think I'd see any of this again," he admitted.

"Hey, don't get sentimental," Sergei teased, though he'd been the one wallowing in self-pity.

Outside Tretiak's, a stretch of humanity stacked like dominoes inhabited the snow-packed sidewalk, well-dressed young adults braving sub-zero temperature, wearing less than common sense dictated, pitting exposure against entrance.

"Shit, look at this line," Yakov grunted.

"Ach, not to worry," Sergei replied. "I dropped by earlier to let them know you were being released from the hospital...and that I was bringing you straight over. We'll get right in."

"Ha! How much did that cost you?"

"Nothing much," Sergei lied.

"Bull shit!" Yakov exclaimed. "This club isn't humanitarian, you know."

"Yeah, yeah. So it cost a bit," Sergei relented. "But, I've saved a shitload not going out the past two months."

"What, you've been sitting at home pining for me?" Yakov snickered. "I'm touched."

"I was losing money at cards," Sergei blustered. "I think I was being set up."

"By who?"

"Same bastards we'd been fleecing all year," Sergei chuckled. "Same guys we're playing tonight. I think my luck will suddenly change."

"Well then, we're even," Yakov laughed.

"Not even close," Sergei retorted, studying the queue outside Tretiak's entrance. "Hey, check out those two!"

Near the queue's end, two striking, blonde beauties were huddled together, impatiently fidgeting and icily stamping their high-heeled feet against the frozen walkway. Based on the thinness of their garments, they weren't planning to wait out the line. As yet, a suitable benefactor had not appeared.

"Need some drinking company, Yakov?"

"Damn straight," he replied. "What do you think, I'm on injured reserve?"

"You look the part," Sergei laughed, referring to the whitish scar lines crisscrossing Yakov's cheeks.

"Then, let's score."

Handing the keys to a valet, Sergei and Yakov exited the car. Pausing for a moment, they ensured the kid was transporting their car to the club's parking lot. Valet thefts were common at nightclubs this year. Feigning the part of North American tourists, Yakov and Sergei approached the two women.

"C-C-Can we get a picture with you?" Sergei stuttered in broken Russian.

"Sure," one of the girls beamed, a dazzling smile of perfect teeth.

"My friend's from Canada," Sergei continued. "He's a hockey player."

"I'll say," the second girl gushed. "Oh, what happened to your pretty face?" she cooed, tracing a scar along his cheek. Yakov grinned.

"I'm sorry," Sergei stammered, "but he only speaks English. He got carved up by a hockey stick."

"That's okay, handsome," she said, moving to Yakov's side.

Sergei pointed his camera at the pair, quickly snapping a photograph.

Not to be outdone, the other girl tucked against Yakov's opposite side. Lasciviously holding the ladies against his hips, Yakov beamed while Sergei took several more images.

"What are your names?" he asked.

"Marusia," the first blonde twittered, "and this is my friend, Natasha."

"Dobre Viachar," Yakov blustered.

"Good evening to you, too," Natasha replied.

"Hey," Sergei continued, "we have friends at the club. Hockey fans. No lines for us. Would you like to join us for a drink?"

Looking at Natasha for confirmation, Marusia replied, "Sure, let's go warm up. It's too cold out here."

Once inside, the quartet selected a booth along the club's back wall.

"Beer?" Sergei asked, and all heads nodded affirmation.

For the next hour, Sergei *translated* tales of Yakov's hockey prowess, regaling exploits of bone-jarring hits and tempo-setting fights. The twins fawned over him, tittering over his injuries. But three beers and sixty minutes later, their vaudeville proved boring.

"Let's order sushi," Natasha wheedled, flirting.

"I'd like another beer, first," Sergei parried.

"Oh, I can't have another," Marusia complained righteously, giving Natasha a glance.

Natasha jumped, but it was her cell ringing in her purse. "Excuse me."

"Sure, sure, go ahead." Sergei, too, had tired of the game.

A moment later, Natasha hung up, giving Marusia an insider look.

"Sorry boys, but we have to run," she announced. Leaning over the table, she gave Yakov a peck on the cheek.

"Good-bye, handsome hockey player," she whispered throatily.

The pair walked away quickly toward the front door, nearly bumping into a pair of well-dressed men confidently bypassing the bouncers. Their clothes were fitted woolen sweaters over cotton pants, fitting the club's genre, but their forty-something age did not.

"Moscow isn't what it used to be," Yakov opined.

"No, that was too easy," Sergei agreed.

Yakov looked at Sergei, grinning from ear to ear.

"You know, my friend, I think those two were working girls."

"Of course—a few weeks in the hospital has made you stupid," Sergei bellowed. "Now let's eat."

"Carp?" Yakov questioned.

"Hell no. I'm having prime rib."

"And I'll have *filet mignon*."

"Go ahead, you softie."

"I've earned it," Yakov grunted.

* * *

During the half hour wait for their food, they quietly inhaled the club scene. As it was early in the evening, the live band was sober, hitting most notes, and still louder than the patrons. It was not a marquee billing, but to Yakov, it was vintage U2.

I *am* getting soft, he chided internally.

Decorating the brick warehouse were accoutrements from an ice rink. Goal nets hung from rafters, firmly secured to wooden beams that framed the even pitched roof. On the grained walls, team jerseys from popular northern hemisphere clubs hung as centerpieces, interspersed with signed hockey memorabilia—sticks, pucks, gloves and black and white photos. Adorning the cold concrete were large, high definition images of the Soviet's Red Army conquests, including team pictures from eight Olympic gold medals, the NHL-Dynamo series of 1971, and of course, multiple snapshots of their greatest goaltender, Vladislav Tretiak.

A dozen televisions carried non-stop games through the early morning hours, progressing leagues with the time zones from the newly formed KHL to the western European contests to the east coast American NHL. It was a hockey paradise.

Of the two, Sergei was the hockey player, having skated competitively throughout his youth. An unfortunate injury, a shattered femur suffered when his blade caught a rut in the ice just as an opponent delivered a punishing body check. It all led to six months of recuperation. At the end of his rehabilitation, he was unceremoniously cut from the junior national team only a month before the international championships. His fractured leg never fully recovered its strength and power, perhaps a result of losing a centimeter of length. But he remained passionate about the sport, playing non-competitively and always ready to watch.

Immersing himself in the club's atmosphere, with his friend back from the dead, was healing, a pilgrimage to normalcy.

"You know, Yakov," Sergei began, "it's rumored that Tretiak had ligament surgery to make his knees more flexible when he played."

"Ach, only you would know that," Yakov replied. "You know, if you spent half as much time learning a profession as you do watching hockey, you'd be gainfully employed as more than an adventurer."

Eying him suspiciously, Sergei guessed, "Are you retiring, old friend?"

"I can see this gig coming to an end soon," Yakov affirmed.

"How soon?"

"No more than five years."

"Then let's make them worth our while."

Toasting his friend's health, Sergei thought, *he is sentimental tonight...*

"Sergei," Yakov began, a cautious tone in his voice, "this contract we were working worries me."

Holding back his own unspoken reservations, Sergei looked Yakov square in the eyes and nodded, "In what way?"

"Twice in the hospital, the recruiter dropped by. The last time was less than friendly."

"Why? Don't they have what they wanted?"

"Yes, but he knew we were prospecting off course the last days."

"So they were tracking us. That explains a few things."

"What?" It was Yakov's turn to be surprised.

"Yakov, on the sub, I watched you deteriorate. A doctor looked you over once or twice a day, jotted notes on a clipboard and left. He never noticed anything—or ordered anything. My requests for aid were ignored. Your wounds were not being properly treated. So I washed them with hand soap and water and I changed your bedding. They were letting you die."

A plain-faced, but shapely, waitress brought their food. The two dug ravenously into their meals, each sober in thought, but there was little time to cogitate. Five minutes into their gourmet dining the chief steward interrupted, apprehensively approaching the table, his hands wringing nervously.

"I apologize, Sergei, but I have unfortunate news."

"Yes?" Sergei answered with annoyance.

"Your card table has opened earlier than scheduled, but your opponent is not prepared. I've penciled in a party from the waiting list. Would you be interested in an early game?"

"Perhaps," Sergei replied as Yakov nodded. "Who would be joining us?"

"A Dmitriy Borisinskoff and Tomas Kapustin. Do you know them?"

Yakov frowned, shaking his head. There was something familiar about Dmitriy's name, but he could not place it.

"Can't say I know either of them," Sergei answered. "Do they play here often?"

"They've been regulars the last three months."

"About as long as we've been absent," Yakov calculated.

"Yes, I should say so," the chief steward agreed. "Welcome back, Yakov. I trust you are recovering well."

"I've had better days," Yakov grunted, "but I've certainly had worse. I could use a charity match."

His pricey food losing heat and taste, an agitated Sergei broke in. "We'll play as soon as we're done."

"I'll pass the word on," the chief steward retreated. Spinning away, his hands wrung anew as if annihilating germs from a bad infection.

Thirty minutes later, Yakov finished his dessert—a chocolate- and butter-laced creation imported from Canada and called a Nanaimo bar. Besides a hockey theme, the club portrayed Canadian influences alongside Russian hockey paraphernalia, including serving a Canadian cuisine of sorts—to get that full hockey experience.

Why not? he thought while crunching on the sweet square, *we've been good competitors for over a generation, only the targets have changed.*

"We'll have to come back again, soon," he said, with satisfaction.

"Then we better win big tonight, or I won't be able to afford you."

"I'm not a cheap date," Yakov guffawed with a broad smile, "and neither were those two earlier."

Signaling the chief steward, Yakov indicated they were ready for cards.

The *restaurateur* hurried over and escorted them through a locked door, down a staircase, and into a brightly lit, furnished underground club where several other parties were engaged in contests. Not that card playing was illegal, only illicit gambling was strictly forbidden by city and club rules. And tacitly encouraged by anyone who needed some coin—especially nightclub owners. The new Moscow, frequently listed as one of the most expensive cities in which to reside, had an insatiable list of money-seekers spanning the social classes, each striving to keep pace with the oil and gas capitalists.

"Are we still playing...?" Yakov purposely struggled at recalling the names.

"Dmitriy and Tomas," the chief steward filled in.

"Yes, those two."

"They're already at the table."

"Do you know why they come to this club now?"

"A little paranoid, Yakov?" the chief steward chuckled.

"Facing death makes one appreciate living longer," Yakov grandstanded.

"I believe they have recently relocated from Kiev. Their business is computer software, and they've moved their headquarters to Moscow. There's a bigger market here for security-based software."

"Okay, so why here and not another club?" Sergei persisted.

"That I don't know, but their money is good, and they haven't caused any problems. In fact, they took your seat while you were laid off, Yakov."

"Then we shall have to take it back," Yakov boasted.

"Go easy on them, there's room to add tables," the club servant cautioned without conviction.

Performing introductions, the chief steward initiated the evening's first match, fussing over the details of cards, score sheets and writing implements. "As you know, gentlemen, side wagering is strictly forbidden." Finishing the legislative admonition, he lingered a moment to ensure pleasantries were exchanging. Summoning a cocktail waitress, he busied away.

Yakov and Sergei took seats opposite each another, between their competitors. "I understand you are in security software," Yakov began, establishing a friendly, professional tone.

"Yes, we specialize in sizing security systems for all—big or small," Dmitriy replied, catching Yakov's eye a fraction longer than necessary.

The direct stare caught Yakov off guard. *Now what does he mean by that?* he wondered. *Does he know my business?*

He overlooked the unsettling comment as habitual sales pitching, before continuing, "It is said you moved in from the Ukraine."

"And other places," Tomas interjected. "Recently, we've contracted to companies in the Americas, in Brazil, the US, and, most recently, farther north." Again, the eye contact seemed prolonged. Shifting uncomfortably, Yakov ignored the stare down.

Software geeks were notorious for lacking social niceties, so Yakov shrugged off the strange dialogue.

"Shall we cut for deal?" he prodded.

With nods of acquiescence, the foursome moved on to the ritual of determining home court.

Bad luck followed poor taste, and Sergei and Yakov promptly lost the first position. Handing the deck to Dmitriy, Sergei fixed his focus on the dealer's movements, urging his integrity. Through a flurry of shuffling, splitting and marrying—it appeared to Sergei that Dmitriy was an honest dealer.

The game commenced.

A half hour later, Yakov gathered cards from the felt cloth, he and Sergei possessing the short side of the final score. He shrugged off the loss. Out of nowhere, the chief steward appeared across the table, lightly brushing Sergei's elbow.

"Pardon my intrusion," he monotoned, unapologetic, "but your party has canceled its appointment."

Raising his eyebrow, Yakov probed for an explanation.

Instead, Dmitriy spoke, "we'd be glad to continue playing."

Seeking Yakov's and Sergei's acceptance, the chief steward paused.

"Of course," Sergei answered, "we have some distance to make up."

"Then it's settled," the host retreated.

"Our deal," Sergei announced, gathering the playing deck. As he shuffled, Yakov again attempted small talk.

"The chief steward tells me you've been in town only a short while. How did you come across this club?"

"We were members in a similar club in Kiev, this one was recommended by our Moscow friends there," Tomas responded. "We're both hockey fans, we liked the atmosphere. A good club like this is rare ground."

A warning bell tolled in Yakov's head. Three times the odd phrasing had skirted topics from his professional life. It was not a coincidence. Yakov determined to learn who his opponents really were and what they represented.

Six hours later, and a thousand US dollars ahead, Yakov had fewer answers than winnings. The baited barbing had diminished as their take increased, making him doubt his anxiety. Perhaps the offhanded comments were meaningless quips from unsociable jokers.

He was exhausted. His euphoria at rejoining society had long been overwhelmed by a desire to go home and sleep. It was time to break the match open.

"Eight," Dmitriy announced aggressively.

Yakov grunted, his voice rang hollow through the acrid, cigarette smoke haze. Checking his watch, he rolled his eyes and sighed. His nerves were frazzled, equal measures of fatigue, excessive alcohol and odd fellows for company.

"Let's end this, Sergei," he declared, informing his partner that it was time to bend a few rules.

In concert with his bravado, a guitar twanged a concluding riff and cymbals clanged calamitously, the western-styled pop band was taking a break. The surfeiting throng breathed a collective hush of relief. The live music was simply underwhelming.

Outside, the mercury was bottoming at minus thirty-five degrees Celsius. The line on the icy sidewalk had dwindled to a few diehards, unfortunate stragglers with wallets too thin to gain entrance. As the clock ticked past four, these too, dispersed stiffly, fogged by cold and vodka.

Sergei cocked an eyebrow. He was holding the five of hearts, probably the one card Dmitriy lacked to make a confident bid. He had no need to communicate a pair of kings, as the five was all important. Barely glancing

Sergei's way, Yakov sat in repose, looking at the ceiling. Exhaling a long draught of smoke, he acknowledged the message.

Without hesitating, Sergei outbid him, "eight, no," doubling the points, gained or lost.

"Hey, no table talk," snarled Dmitriy.

"Afraid of losing?" Yakov postured.

"Can't stand card cheats," Dmitriy growled.

"Who's cheating?"

"You, sooner or later, it catches up to you. Maybe sooner, eh?"

"What do you care, it's not a lot of money," Yakov ignored the threat.

"No, not to me," he scoffed.

"Then play." Turning to Tomas, he prodded, "You bidding or passing?"

Tomas paused a moment, convinced that the bastards had been cheating all night. Now, if Dmitriy was right, they'd be weak in his strong suit of clubs. He had little chance of pulling off a large bid, but even if he lost, it would prevent their opponents from scoring.

"Nine," he bid optimistically, knowing they had better stop this hand in lieu of surrendering.

"Nine, no, going high," Yakov announced, absconding the bid round. Checking the two-card Massey, he selected the ace of spades, discarding the unneeded nine of diamonds and a useless seven of clubs from his hand.

It was good to have an extra high card, even in spades.

Efficiently, Yakov opened with the ace of hearts. Tomas tossed a low heart, Sergei delivered the five, and Dmitriy unloaded the three of spades, but the indolent gesture was inconsequential. Yakov ran the table, ending the contest.

Their winnings totaled $1500.

"Time for another?" Yakov gloated.

Red-faced and sullen, Dmitriy glowered, "No, we're done."

"Then I thank you for the game," Yakov taunted, not sure why he was rubbing their faces in his victory. The accusation of cheating had certainly rankled him, but even more—the unknown pair had interacted with an element of familiarity that made him uncomfortable.

"You mean the money," Tomas barked. "You going to spend it somewhere, perhaps Canada?"

"Now what do you mean by that?" Sergei broke in.

"Perhaps you can rebuild your hockey career there."

Doubt vanished from Yakov's mind. They were not random comments, they were being baited.

"What do you want from us?"

"We're keeping an eye on both of you. We want to protect our investment."

"Not from what Sergei tells me."

"Not true, we saved your life. Your value is required when we send a team in this spring."

"My value," Yakov scoffed, fully convinced that, to these men, his life's worth ranked well beneath his knowledge, "It's not so easy to go prospecting, now is it?"

"Hardly that," Dmitriy rebuffed, "we know the location. You left us a clear trail."

That's where you're wrong, Yakov saw through the bluff. Clearly, they were missing information and couldn't backtrack his trail. They needed him alive—for now. "You know where to find us," he leveled, a direct glance backing his words.

"Yes, we do," Tomas replied. "We'll be seeing you again."

With the warning delivered, Dmitriy and Tomas dropped a check to cover their losses and exited. Seeing the game breaking up, the chief steward hurried over, puzzled and anxious.

"Were you too rough with them?" he asked.

"No, it was just business," Yakov replied.

"I thought you didn't know them."

"We didn't—but we do now."

Tipping the chief steward well for services rendered, and for continued discreteness, the prospectors also made haste to leave. The steward bustled again, ordering a valet to retrieve their car. In silence, Yakov and Sergei waited.

Thirty minutes later, Sergei deposited Yakov on a snow-packed sidewalk outside a granite-block apartment complex.

"Great time, my old friend," Yakov grinned.

"Shall I see you tonight?"

Frowning, Yakov deferred, "not until tomorrow. I am still in recovery."

"Of course, you wimp."

"Kiss my ass."

"Not a chance," Sergei laughed, accelerating quickly and spinning his tires. The ejecting snow dusted Yakov mercilessly.

"Better a weakling than dead," Yakov whispered.

Facing the complex, he dug into his parka pocket, fumbling through pocket lint to retrieve a ring of keys. It had been months since he'd last used them. Fortunately, he'd paid for the flat by automatic withdrawal, ensuring that it was always available to him. With a pang of nostalgia, he opened the door, entering a small foyer. A myriad of scents greeted him; stale cigarette smoke, pungent cat urine, and the metallic tinge of vegetables on a hot frying pan.

Holopchi, he decided, the sour smell overwhelming his senses. *Always hated cooked cabbage.*

He stopped to collect his mail. Inserting a thin key, he twisted the locking mechanism, and wrenched open the metal mailbox door. Within was a wadded mass of envelopes and circulars. Wriggling them free, a palm-sized box slipped out.

"What is this?" Yakov questioned. It looked expensive, not something he recalled ordering. The handwriting looked familiar. It was Sergei's cursive. Inside the cardboard covering, he found his cell phone. After his long absence, he'd considered it permanently lost. Dialing his voice-mail, Yakov gathered his untouched mail and started up a cold, dark and familiar stairwell. It had been a long time since he'd been home.

There were only a few messages, any others had been deleted by his service provider. Impatiently, he skipped the requests from telemarketers, worried or irate ex-girlfriends (who didn't know they were exes, yet) and drinking buddies. Their banter was inconsequential, banal utterances from a previous life. Stepping into a hallway, he strode towards his flat's door. The final message, only minutes old, began playing. Waiting at the door, he listened intently.

"Yakov, this is Sergei," it began, "welcome home. I forgot to tell you...SHIT!!!" A loud blast that sounded like a gunshot went off, hurting his ear. The next several seconds were laced with horror, chaotic scraping and squealing over a hollow background. The hair on his back rose. Slowly, mindlessly, Yakov inserted his key, turning the lock open.

What the hell just happened?

An unfamiliar voice began speaking, "Sergei is dead. I suggest you tell the truth."

Yakov's heart plummeted into his stomach. Fear and grief permeated his soul. Numbly opening the door, he slumped inside, feeling for the light switch. Finding the lever he flipped it open. The first rays illuminated a ransacked room, but thieves were not responsible—Yakov knew. Littering the floor were open books from emptied shelves, scattered utensils and broken pottery. Crudely patching over the mess, strewn papers quilted his disheveled belongings. His paper files had been thoroughly searched.

"Shit!"

For the moment, the death of his best friend was lost in the surreal scene. "What the hell is happening?"

"Welcome home, asshole," a familiar voice rumbled.

Turning on his heel, Yakov faced his adversary from the card game.

"Tomas," he spat, "what the hell are you doing here? Get out...get out NOW!"

"Not until you've answered a few questions."

Howling in rage, Yakov attacked headlong, stretching for Tomas's throat. Answering his charge, a metallic cracking punctured the air—a muted lancet exploded into Yakov's shoulder with a burst of fiery pain. Following the impact, white hot heat remained. Spinning away from the agony, Yakov crumpled to the floor. His left arm flailed uselessly from its socket, a dark stain seeping through the charcoal hole. He struggled to stand, but Tomas felled him to the floor once more with the power of an unfettered kneecap and shin smashing into his cheek and chest. The assault was incapacitating. Twisting in torment on the floor, Yakov heard a second voice.

"Nice shot."

Wild with fear, Yakov eyed his second nemesis. Dmitriy was sitting at his computer, casually powering up the system.

"You're going to help us, Yakov," he suggested, "or you will die like your friend." He looked at Yakov with a benefactor's calm gaze. "Give us what we want, and you can get yourself fixed up again."

Yakov desperately tried to move, but the fountain of pain cascading from his shoulder made it impossible to concentrate. He sat still as a pool of crimson blood began creeping across the wooden floor. He could ill afford to lose too much blood—but he would not cooperate with these killers while they still needed him.

They wanted the files from his computer, but they needed him to unlock the encryption. What would he gain by helping them? Probably nothing. He was a dead man, now or later, whether he helped or not. Yet, they were vulnerable. In killing his partner and sparing his life, it meant they needed him alive. So their threat to kill him was a bluff. And, if he divulged his secrets, he might void the posturing. He would not aid his enemy. Resigning to the inevitable pain, he prepared his mind for the beating to come.

"Yakov, it's your turn," Dmitriy beckoned. The monitor showed a login screen, requiring both a password and a numeric key to gain entry.

"What do you want?"

"Don't be a moron," Tomas snarled.

"I'm not the one who can't type," Yakov sneered.

"Neither can you, now," Dmitriy taunted.

"Figure it out yourself," challenged Yakov. "You're the security expert."

"And you're the paranoid geologist with the all the answers," Tomas replied. "Hacking is much easier when one has the code writer."

"I didn't think you knew shit," Yakov blustered, willing to goad their ire to buy additional time. Someone must have heard the ruckus. Being rudely awakened at this hour would be alarming. How soon would the police arrive, Yakov thought, realizing quickly that they probably owned the police.

Answering his belligerence, Dmitriy cuffed Yakov's ear with his pistol. The blow was blinding, and Yakov slumped, knocked into senselessness. A few seconds later, he came to, hearing Tomas chiding his partner.

"Keep him awake, Dmitriy, we don't have much time."

"It was a bloody mistake," Tomas complained, "he's too weak."

They don't have a fix with the police, Yakov deduced in his groggy state. Hope rising, he feigned unconsciousness. Fresh blood oozed from a sliced earlobe, curling along his neck, cooling and congealing on his throat. He could not move his left arm—the shoulder was shattered.

He had two avenues for survival, the cell phone and his computer. Calling for help would alert the pair that he was conscious. Perhaps he could crank call an emergency number while moving over to unlock the computer.

"Should we kill him now, Dmitriy?" Tomas was asking, a strange tone creeping into his speech. His accent had changed. Yakov could not place the origin, but it wasn't Russian.

"Not now, not here," Dmitriy cautioned. His voice sounded peculiarly, a metallic clanging in a hollow room.

Yakov's mind raced—what could he do? In his mind, he rattled off his computer's encryption key. He was not losing his faculties, yet. But the loss of blood was taking a toll; coldness seeped through his body. He shivered.

"We need to get him out before people start waking," Tomas suggested.

Yakov groaned, pretending to rouse.

"Shit," Dmitriy grunted. A comatose body couldn't resist, but Yakov's awakening presented a better opportunity.

"Five minutes, Yakov," Dmitriy insisted. "Tell us the code and we'll let you live."

"Yeah," Yakov gasped, "help me up." His good hand, tucked in his jacket pocket, gripped his cell phone. He felt for the key pad.

Warily, Dmitriy dragged Yakov to his feet, roughly pulling his damaged arm for leverage. Pain annihilated his shoulder, incapacitating him. He could not dial for help. Tomas grabbed an elbow, un-pocketing his hand, propelling the hapless geologist into the swivel seat. Losing his grip on his phone, it clattered harmlessly over the floor. Tomas crushed it beneath his foot.

Yakov collapsed on the cushion, a relentless fountain of fluid surging from his wound. A sordid sweat flushed his skin. Nausea pitted his stomach. The room wound in lazy circles. Choking down bile, he held himself motionless to stop the careening. It didn't help. Putting his head on the keyboard, the swaying finally ceased.

"Quit stalling," Tomas barked.

Lifting an ashen face, Yakov set trembling fingers on the keyboard. Stroke by stroke, he entered the code. It was his only chance. Confusion overwhelmed him; he could not execute the task. Losing control, he slumped to the floor. *Sergei is dead,* he thought through the painful fog billowing in his head. The fog thickened—Yakov passed into unconsciousness.

"Shit!" Dmitriy exclaimed, shoving Yakov's limp body aside. Mindlessly, Yakov's finger depressed the enter key. The processor began logging on.

"Quick, get the flash drive," Dmitriy commanded.

Handing him a memory stick, Tomas glared disgustedly at the prostrate geologist sprawled beneath his feet.

"Where do you keep your files, dead man?" he whispered. Across town, a factory siren awoke as the industrial quarter stirred. Spurred by the distant wailing, Dmitriy feverishly pared through the file trees. Tomas paced the floor, picturing where the elusive geologist was storing his data. Beneath their radar, a klaxon grew louder.

"Run a time-based search for the most recently altered files," Tomas suggested.

"Doing that already," Dmitriy muttered.

From the street below, the sirens turned up the block. Suddenly they stopped. The silence was disturbing.

"Dmitriy, do you suppose..." he began.

"Suppose what?" Came an exasperated response.

"...this prick called the police?"

The dearth of noise suddenly registered.

"Shit, let's go!"

Scrambling to his feet, Dmitriy grabbed the flash drive and his gun, bolting for the door. Following behind, Tomas swept a glance around the room. Too much evidence was being abandoned, but they had no time to clean up. Covering up this invasion would be expensive, requiring the payment of several lucrative bribes, but they would avoid detection. Dmitriy had executed the impossible more than once in the past.

Descending the back stairs, the intruders quietly and calmly exited the complex's rear doors. Two blocks away, their parked car awaited out of sight and suspicion. Within moments they were speeding away as a security patrolman knocked on Yakov's door. Getting no answer, he checked his pager. A line of text authorized his entry. Readying the appropriate key from his library, he drew his weapon, unlocked and opened the door. Warily, he stepped across the threshold.

In a huddled heap on the bloodied floor was the unconscious adventurer. Above him, a monitor luminesced—a warning message emblazoned on the screen insisting that a device had been improperly removed and that its data might be corrupted.

The banquet hall was elegant. Round tables spread in regal purple linen; set with polished silver cutlery and white bone china, pleasantly aglow with candles in Steuben crystal bases. In black bow ties, the wait staff served and bussed, a practiced choreography of efficiency and invisibility, a hallmark service of the multi-plate *fete*.

The head table was uncharacteristically situated—a large, oval plateau occupying the room center. It was located at midpoint not because of a lack of hierarchy, rather, its position served as a deferential statement of thanks by the departing executive to the legions that had personally protected him or defended his policies, both domestic and abroad.

Halbert "Hal" Shaparell's presidency was in its twilight, his party embarrassed at the polling booth, his personal popularity tattered. Although it was somewhat awkward to hold his head high, shying away from a fight or quitting was not in his persona. Even so, at the end of his second term, he was fatigued and looking forward to a short respite of relative obscurity and anonymity.

Tonight he sought sanctity, peace amongst those sworn to protect him—or so he hoped. The cocktail banter was lively, as expected, but the bickering obtuse. Jobs were at stake. Party loyalists jockeyed to appear non-partisan, brush-stroking their less savvy colleagues as polemic misfits, an effort of comparative slander in hope of avoiding the impending purge. Incoming presidents were known to clean house and the more moderate might be retained.

An equal number of ideologues were unconcerned, their placement assured by power brokers who did not rise and fall every election cycle, and who were thus immune to the contagion of politics. These wandered the floor, taking note of those who held faith, those who did not, and those with exceptional skills of navigating the tightrope of uncertainty.

One such autocrat sauntered toward the head table to speak to the departing executive. As if staged, the pathway cleared as he neared his destination. Once at the president's side, he was an audience of one.

"Any upcoming plans, Mr. President?" he asked.

Shaparell turned to see who addressed him. A smartly dressed, intense man of fifty stood at his elbow, but not someone he immediately recognized. Yet the man had the bearing of someone in intelligence, a person of power and secrecy.

Shaparell wondered who the interloper could be and turned to slightly nudge his admin for an introduction, but his aide had disappeared, no doubt wooing a skirt he'd been seen chatting up earlier. *Damn kid's a walking hormone,* he thought, but in truth, being left alone was Shaparell's own doing. He'd explicitly requested his support staff to back off. His days of being handled were, thankfully, drawing to a close. After two decades of being groomed, prodded and prompted, he'd soon be able to speak his own mind. He would be allowed to compose and express his own thoughts. He could become a humanitarian and statesman, rather than a loathed politician.

In the meantime, he'd learned enough to comport himself amongst *friendlies.*

"I'm looking forward to a little fishing," he replied. A small measure of meaningless honesty never hurt when establishing trust.

"Really? I would never have guessed," the man lied. The polar opposite was true, dutifully recorded on a comprehensive dossier in his files.

"Mrs. Shaparell is not like-minded," he chuckled, "and the children were never exposed to it."

"Sorry, that's too bad," came the insincere apology. "Perils of the public life?"

"Something like that," Shaparell raised his guard...the man's bearing was too familiar. "I suppose I have much to thank you for."

"Nothing at all," the suit responded with false humility, "it's all in the service of my country."

"If these walls could talk?" Shaparell probed.

"They would not talk," the man assured.

"I must apologize," Shaparell began, but the man cut him off.

"I represent the Secure Homeland Research Group," he introduced his association.

The who? Shaparell paused, momentarily unable to make a connection.

"We're a think tank specializing in answering questions of strategy, usually on contract to the armed services. We research cause and effect models and suggest response and mitigation to scenarios concerning national security."

"And..."

The man cut him off, "I represent the policy action side of the business."

"Is that the euphemism for a political action committee," Shaparell stalled, instantly locking onto the speaker's affiliation, if not his identity. The suit represented a bastion of old money conservatives who had helped fund his original nomination and campaign.

"The PAC is the voice of an independent, civilian group of researchers who recommend policy, unencumbered by government influence or allegiance," the man purred, completing the sales pitch.

"To whom do you owe your allegiance?" Shaparell tested.

"I'm sure you're well aware, otherwise, I wouldn't be here."

"I trust you're enjoying yourself these days," Shaparell alluded to the change of administration.

"All roads require repair," the man assured, "occasionally, public opinion turns. But, the public is fickle."

"What's in the works, now?" Shaparell asked.

"We'll take a few hits, orchestrate some friendly fire, so to speak, but it won't last long. Fabrications are easily exposed and disproved, rendering the truth as questionable."

"Why wait?" Shaparell asked. The nearer he got to the end of his presidency, the more he felt like a figurehead in policy-making decisions. It was annoying, watching the economy spin out of control, experiencing the loss of public support. He was being shackled—halted from vocalizing a sound defense. He could, he wanted to do and say more, but his advisers had all virtually mutinied, shutting the door on a brawling approach. He'd suspected they were no longer following his orders.

If he wanted to be honest with himself, he'd have to admit that little had changed during his tenure of power. All he was losing was the prime place at the podium. Presidential policy setting was a mythical facade.

"We don't want a band-aid. Quash the public opinion now and it might not die. Instead, the resistance must be demoralized. Address the economy in simple terms. Speak the bare minimum. Don't provide momentum."

"This will take a lot of faith."

His defiance did not sit well. "Lay low, Mr. President," the suit ordered, "the party has big plans for you."

"I'm looking forward to the fray," Shaparell retorted.

Chapter 8

Errors

Mending a second time in a hospital bed, a battered Yakov convalesced slowly. In addition to the shattered shoulder, he had suffered broken ribs and a collapsed lung during his beating. The latter was slow to respond to treatment. Filled with fluids, pneumonia was a risk, but a regular regimen of draining and antibiotics were keeping that concern at bay.

It required two operations and an ingot of titanium to reassemble his scapula. For now, his arm was immobilized against his torso, a practical securing since his cracked ribs needed to avoid the extra stresses of torsional movement.

Although the bruises would heal and the bones would fuse, what could not fade was Sergei's terrified shout an instant before his murder.

Yakov brooded.

A pencil thin doctor, with a kind, wrinkled face entered his room. Holding a clipboard, marked with Yakov's vitals, tucked under his arm, he smiled at his patient. He was one of several doctors who had treated his first battery of infirmities.

"Yakov," he chided, "you just cannot stay out of trouble lately, can you?"

Yakov stared at the doctor, anger blazing through his eyes. "I think there will be more," he announced flatly.

"Shall I mend you, first?" asked the doctor, sarcasm lacing his query, "or shall I release you now to pursue your fate?"

"I wish to be healthy," Yakov replied.

"But you wish for more, too," the doctor sagely surmised.

Yakov stared into space.

"I'm sorry about your friend," the doctor continued, "we brought him back, but he was too weak to stay."

Continuing to glare fixedly at the void, Yakov's eyes narrowed further.

"He asked to see you, but you were unconscious. Before he slipped away, he wanted you to know something. Do you wish to hear it?"

"Da," came the dull response.

"He said he was sorry."

A cold silence ensued. The blazing orbs of Yakov's eyes penetrated the wall and beyond, an infinite gaze peering through the vacuum of hatred.

"Yakov, the antibiotics are working. The fluids are discharging from your lung and you will likely be released this week."

"That is well."

"The bruising is superficial, soon it will heal. None of your previous injuries are affected, but your shoulder will take some time to repair. Perhaps you should not seek more pain?"

Now this is odd, Yakov thought. *Sergei is dead and I'm only scratched. Why?* The warning bell chimed. There was much more game to be played.

"But, no matter," the doctor continued. "My job is to heal you. It is not for me to dispense wisdom as medication. Still, I am concerned and I must ask, do you wish to see a psychologist?"

"Later," Yakov answered. *Much later—only after I have sinned.*

"Come on in, Robb," his advisor beckoned, sitting behind a disheveled desk piled with academic periodicals, its only uncovered real estate holding a desktop computer and monitor. The keyboard was itself hidden beneath an open journal. Similarly, the office walls were cramped to capacity. Two were bookshelves, the third an open window overlooking a grassy courtyard.

The balance of the entrance wall was a giant, dry whiteboard. Splayed piecemeal upon every square inch of its white space were multicolored scribblings, design details for out of scale equipment, crude scientific models and mathematical hieroglyphs.

The bookshelves, although neat and orderly, were bursting with reference materials, a litany of textbooks, conference proceedings and bound copies of annualized academic publications. Relegated to a lonely top corner, photographs of the professor, her husband and children gathered dust.

"Probably taken the last time she saw them," Robb quipped sardonically under his breath.

In the courtyard outside, two graduate students sat at a picnic bench eating bagged lunches—lost in an animated discussion. The intense debate looked ready to erupt into a full-scale argument.

A pair of chairs faced the professor's desk. Oddly, there was no clock on any wall. In this profession, the hours labored weren't counted...only results. And breakthroughs take time, even by the brilliant. She was among the elite.

Entering the room, Robb took one of the two seats, sitting in silence for a moment while his furrowed boss completed a final academic task.

"I'm working on a DARPA proposal," she apologized. "It's due by the end of this week. You have anything you want to include?"

Thinking before answering, Robb wisely organized and weighed his notions. Loaded questions like this required careful answers. Although he had several ideas, he never knew what his advisor wished to pursue next and Robb didn't want to get into a pointless discussion about the merits of his priorities. He and his boss didn't always agree.

"I've been thinking of experimenting in a new direction with these up-converters..."

The phone rang. His advisor looked at it, frowning.

"Just a minute, Robb."

Picking up the phone, she began a short, one-sided conversation.

"Paulina here." A pause. "Good to hear from you. How can I help you?" Another pause. "Sure, drop on by. How about in an hour?" A third pause. "You're downstairs right now? Come on up, then. Sure, he's sitting right here with me. I'll make sure he stays. See you shortly."

She hung up, a quizzical look on her face. "That's a DARPA representative, Jerry Graham. He wants to meet with both of us."

Robb nodded and continued, "about the up-converters..."

"Not now," she cut him off. "We'll talk later."

Robb got the message. Although most funding institutions only doled out research money, some had affiliates that competed for ideas. A research proposal needed to first be documented in a grant application to prevent academic piracy. Once an idea was in the government's hands, it could award or deny funds, or assume the idea as its own and work on it internally. In the latter event, the principal investigator might earn merit towards the next submission or be given a token award to pursue an obscure topic.

Ha, he thought, *so much for academic integrity.*

A knock on the door jamb announced the visitor. Welcoming him in, Robb moved a chair sitting next to a musty bookshelf and the visitor took his seat. After expeditiously exchanging introductions and pleasantries, the visitor launched into his business *spiel*.

"Paulina, I'm here to talk to Robb about an internship with DARPA."

"He's my best student, perhaps the best in a decade," Paulina bragged.

"Yes, we've read his papers. His work on phosphors, up-converters and their composites has caught our attention."

"It's good progress," Paulina understated, now wishing she hadn't been so forthright.

"Yes, but you see, we think there's more to Robb than just science. Did you know that during his undergraduate education he'd been recruited by the CIA, but turned them down to work for you?"

"It's not surprising," Paulina answered, although the revelation was exactly that. "He has a broad range of talents."

"And we'd like to have use of his abilities for a short time. Having been vetted by the CIA makes it easier for us, you see."

"Yes, what for?"

"We'd like his analysis on some intelligence trends."

"Is it dangerous?"

"Hell, no, it's a desk job," Jerry lied.

Robb's head was swimming. He'd turned down the CIA because he didn't want to work on tasks that might be morally ambiguous. His skills were best employed churning out useful scientific innovations and training new apprentices. That would aid the country without compromising his integrity.

Paulina was alarmed. "Why are you asking me and not Robb?" she challenged, inviting her ace pupil into the conversation.

"We're talking to you because we know it is unusual for students to intern during graduate studies."

"That doesn't sound level to me," Robb finally spoke.

"Indeed," Jerry answered, a twinkle in his eye. "This is exactly why we want your help."

"What do you want?"

"Look, Paulina," Jerry ignored Robb again, "you're writing a big grant proposal, asking for what, $10 million? You've got every reason to believe your research has sufficient merit to win the money, right. And it probably does...having Robb work for us can significantly facilitate the allocation."

Holy shit! Robb thought. *He's turning the screws on Paulina.*

"Is there anything of scientific value in this internship?" Robb asked, trying to cool the heat.

"Nothing that will ever be declassified," Jerry answered, truthfully.

"We have an open-thesis policy in our department," Paulina debated.

"Exactly," Jerry answered. "Exactly why we need your support. There will be no official credit for Robb."

Turning to face Robb, Paulina looked him squarely in the eye. Guaranteed funding or not, she was not about to abandon her young talent to a predatory agency.

"Robb, the decision is entirely yours. I'm willing to take my chances on this or other grant proposals I'm writing. However, you have my permission to take the time off. It may be of value to your career to develop new and diverse contacts. Your field has applications in national defense and this internship can go a long way to successfully acquiring your own research money."

"This is happening pretty fast," Robb replied adroitly.

"I can give you a week," Jerry answered, "but no more."

"I won't need a week to decide," Robb announced. "I'll take the internship. It's going to take a couple of months for my new design to be fabricated anyways. And, Paulina, you're right, the relationships are needed. Not just with DARPA, but also with you."

Jerry smiled, "Told you he's a clever son of a bitch."

"Congratulations," Paulina felt her heart sinking.

The hospital ward was motionless at two o'clock in the morning, most patients quiet or sleeping. A few televisions flickered, discordantly strobing the darkened corridors, but the sleepless watchers were engrossed in reading subtitles. Late shift nurses answered requests for medication, water or help with more primitive functions, but rarely did they pace the deserted halls. A chill lingered in the night air, not surprisingly, as the boiler room had long ago reduced its activity.

On separate floors, two men garbed in surgical scrubs emerged from their respective restrooms. During the late afternoon, before visiting hours had ended, each of the two had hidden in isolation until the day's activities ceased. From their respective stalls, each headed briskly for a prearranged rendezvous point, alertly watching, listening and wishing to avoid contact with the legitimate hospital staff.

It had been a simple matter to prevent detection of their presence. As each exited his perch, he removed a taped sign that read, *Out of Order— Maintenance Alerted—Repair Scheduled for the Morning* from a flimsy commode stall door. Few questioned the inconvenience of an unavailable stall, there were alternate facilities accessible in the same room and curiosity is not normally aroused by bathroom filth. This late in the evening, the sign's wording was of better effect. Nobody expected a night shift to retain a licensed plumber on the payroll.

Slowly stretching as they moved, each worked out the kinks of a half day's worth of crouching within a cramped space. The spurious warning placards were discarded into the bottom of the restroom trash receptacles. Boarding separate elevators, one went down, the other up, meeting at an elevator foyer on Yakov's floor.

One carried a small black satchel, the other a clipboard. The items were of no great significance, except as hospital camouflage. Giving each other a nod of affirmation, they separated, one heading to an unoccupied nurses' station, the other to a fire alarm panel. It was the night shift's lunch hour, and the administrative nurse had stepped away for a cup of coffee, just like she had done on many previous nights.

Her leaving the desk was a security breach, but the graveyard staff commonly exhibited gray area rebellion against the rules. Nobody came to harm the nondescript and infirmed in the middle of the night. Justifying her absence, the desk nurse relied on the security crews stationed at the hospital entrances to prevent unauthorized entry during these hours. Nine hundred and ninety-nine times out of a thousand, this was a correct assumption.

Not tonight.

Entering Yakov's room, the intruder noted that the convalescing geologist was sleeping soundly. Whether he was under the influence of pain killers or sleeping aids was of no concern. Retrieving a preloaded syringe—taped inside his sleeve—he removed a protective plastic sheath from the tip and softly depressed the plunger, forming a bead of liquid at its tip.

Expertly jabbing the needle into Yakov's unprotected neck, he delivered its incapacitating brew. Yakov moaned at the discomfort. Pressing the needle firmly, the man finished delivering the transparent payload into his carotid artery. Flowing unimpeded into his nerve control center, the anesthetic immediately began having an effect. Yakov did not fully awaken before slipping deeply into unconsciousness.

A few meters away along the corridor, the other intruder had reached his destination. Here he halted, watching and waiting, staring through plate-glass windows into Yakov's wing. There was no activity. For the moment, they were alone and undetected.

As Dmitriy wheeled the unconscious patient, Tomas remained on alert. If luck should hold, they might not need to employ a smokescreen getaway, but luck was rarely on their side.

Holding a steaming cup of coffee, the desk nurse appeared in the hallway. Seeing a patient being wheeled along the hallway, she was startled. It was most unusual as she could not recall a move order. A look of confusion criss-crossed her face.

"Where are you taking him?" she demanded.

"Back into surgery, X-rays showed chronic damage to his clavicle that needs immediate repair. It might be causing his infection."

"I haven't been informed," she replied staunchly, "he cannot leave without the proper paperwork."

"Of course," Dmitriy answered, "I have it right here."

"Why wasn't I notified?" she pressed suspiciously, feeling a shiver up her spine.

"I don't know. The doctor ordered the procedure only hours ago. Perhaps it was an oversight. Anyways, here's what you'll need."

"Which doctor...?" she began, but she did not finish. Reaching into his bag, Dmitriy pulled out a pressurized cylinder, pointed the nozzle toward her and squeezed its trigger. A fine mist of mace nebulized toward her startled face. She gasped, instinctively covering her eyes, but wisely letting go of the coffee cup. In slow motion, the tepid contents descended.

Her stunned responses weren't quick enough. Fine droplets seared her eyelids and burned into soft nasal tissues. The first torrent of pain paralyzed her voice. Her eyes watered profusely and she could not open them.

Her sinuses gushed, releasing a flood of mucus onto her smock.

The filled cup hit the floor, instantly shattering into sharp ceramic shards. Hot, black droplets scalded her bare shins, but she could feel none of these discomforts over the fire in her head.

Watching Dmitriy's chance encounter unfold into Plan B action, Tomas sprang, finding and fingering the fire alarm switch—he didn't want to pull it. He readied its trigger, gaging the escalating situation, but no corresponding cries arose. Cautiously, he deferred setting off the alarm. It was a prudent restraint. Sounding the klaxon was a last ditch effort. It would immediately draw unwanted attention from the remaining hospital occupants and awaken a gallery of eyewitnesses. If the ruse was discovered too quickly, security would implement a lock-down. It might take a fight to make their way out. And that would add considerable complications to completing their mission.

Fully debilitated, the nurse lost her balance, collapsing to the floor, choking and vomiting. Landing in a pile of her own bile and coffee, razor sharp cup fragments embedded into her stained frock and sliced her bare skin. While she faltered, Dmitriy closed in, bare-knuckling the back of her head and clubbing her into unconsciousness. To his satisfaction, she sprawled over the cold, tile floor—her body flinched once—then lay still. In the ensuing hush, Tomas called the elevator. They waited tensely, hoping no one else was stirring, coldly calculating a lethal response.

The elevator door chimed open. Tomas pushed Yakov aboard, while Dmitriy held watch. Momentarily, the door slid shut with its normal hydraulic whisper. Quiet returned to the ward. An electronic motion sensor deactivated, plunging the foyer into darkness.

As the trio descended, a security camera transmitted a benign scene; a prostrate patient properly secured on a white gurney, attended by a pair of dispassionate medical orderlies. Descending a single floor, the three exited, disappearing from digital view.

Pushing Yakov into a public restroom, the abductors dressed him in street clothes while discarding their scrubs. Yakov's clothing fit uncharacteristically well, having been pilfered weeks earlier from his own apartment.

Inserting his fingers into his own throat, Tomas gagged, forcing himself to vomit into a metal sink. Grabbing a paper towel, he collected and smeared the noisome liquid onto Yakov's clothes. As an afterthought, he wiped the residue away, creating a tell-tale stain on Yakov's garments which underscored the rancorous odor permeating from his body. For further dressing, Dmitriy doused the hapless geologist with rotgut vodka. If the olfactory feint was crude, it was consistently portrayed.

Lifting Yakov from the frame, they supported his limp, fuming body between their shoulders. Exiting the restroom, they crept along the wall to avoid tripping the electronic light switches. Drunken patients weren't sent to this ward. Re-entering the elevator, the trio descended to the ground floor, emerging in a corridor near an emergency room entrance. Here, they would be the lesser drama. Laughing boisterously, the pair shuffled Yakov through its well-populated waiting room.

An elderly man sat on a metal bench, coughing profusely, attended by an uncaring grandson. Although his pallid face was parched with age, his eyes defied the inevitable and mocked the impatient scourging he was bearing from his youthful kin.

Facing them, a young mother tenderly held an ill infant, cheeks ruddy with fever beneath dilated eyes. Panic and fatigue cruelly aged her countenance. Her foot tapped the floor, nervously beating time as she fretted at the delay, scarcely subduing her rage at the lack of medical concern for her precious child.

Assisting their apparently inebriated companion, the two abductors strode toward the front door, ignoring the guffaws and pained glares of disgust from others in medical want. Brazenly crossing the pneumatic double door, Tomas and Dmitriy fabricated a banal banter, keeping up the pretense. Alerted by the commotion, a security guard looked up suspiciously, but smelling vodka and vomit, simply averted his eyes. Drunken young men were an all too common malady.

Moments later, Tomas, Dmitriy and the sedated geologist sped northward through the city. They had a ten minute head start before the hospital staff would notice the downed nurse and empty bed. Hundreds of kilometers ahead lay a small port in which a submarine sat at dock, but that was more than enough time to get away. Hospital bureaucracy was notorious—the police wouldn't be notified until they were half way to their destination.

At the edge of the city, the getaway car would be disposed of and pre-arranged transportation was waiting. Yakov was vanishing with little trace.

Chapter 9

The Bowhunter

Kneeling on soft ground inside a tangle of fallen moss-enameled pines, Moe kept a vigilant watch for game. Splayed roots cast patterned shadows of craggy fingers, surrounding him in a dark, woody cocoon. Cap to boot in pine foliage camouflage, his garments blended neatly with the needles, fungus and brown bark. When still, he was nearly invisible.

Thirty yards away and similarly garbed his hunting partner, Ken, had also settled within thick underbrush, silent and motionless. Only when he moved, usually to avoid cramping, could his presence be discerned.

An avid bow hunter, Moe had honed his skills hunting the deciduous groves of his native Michigan. In the parklands, he was expert at ambushing whitetails from a ground-level blind or a suspended tree stand. But his current venue was unfamiliar, no artificial tree stands and no advance time for scouting. The dual challenges tested his expertise. Yet, he welcomed the testing heartily as it was a hunt he'd dreamed of for years.

Harnessing his knowledge of deer habits, he presumed that Taiga whitetail would behave similarly to their southerly cousins. Hence, the most promising hiding places were scrubby poplar hollows harbored within rolling, short grass hillsides, but the bluffs were small and the deer within, if any, proved most elusive.

The pair kept moving, eventually progressing to the most remote corner of their hunting range—a wooded ravine which spurred into a river swollen by the spring runoff. The valley was far deeper than it had appeared in satellite views and the evidence of game, spoors, rubs and antler sheds was abundant.

Hard work created its own luck.

By pure chance he'd learned of this draw, a rarely offered springtime big game harvest. Moe had applied for the permit after seeing it advertised on his local fish and game website. The exceptional cull had been deemed necessary by several converging factors; an overpopulation of deer, recent poor hunting seasons and too few natural predators. The populations of the vast herds were not in check.

He'd jumped at the opportunity, as it was easier securing a fortnight's vacation in spring, when traditional holidays slowed the workplace, than taking time off in the fall. When Christmas production peaked, his corporate bosses were inclined to deny his PTO requests, claiming his on-site presence was essential. As a result, he'd missed two of the last five seasons of hunts.

Accessing the Northern Saskatchewan wilderness had been an adventure of patriarchal folklore, with or without regaling the accompanying hunt. The enterprise had commenced humbly, a mundane flight on a commercial jet to Winnipeg, Manitoba. At the provincial capital, he and his hunting partner, Ken, chartered a twin engine propeller Cessna, whose discerning features were chipped paint and an alarming assortment of concave dents along the stubby fuselage. Captained by an unkempt, and eccentric, bush pilot who did little to inspire confidence in his passengers, they sought to secure alternate means of transportation.

Finding none, they reluctantly continued journeying on the disheveled craft. Before committing, Moe had paused, dubiously examining the damaged aluminum. His reticence was noticed.

"Just like a golf ball," the pilot bellowed, "helps me fly faster and straighter."

"Uh huh," Moe replied, noncommittally. "You cultivate this wild man image just to keep us tourists off guard, do ya?"

As if the pilot's gruff appearance and brusque mannerisms weren't backwoods enough, the flight had been choppy. Severe turbulence, heavy cloud cover and the unceasing, mind-numbing drone from the engines nearly consumed his giddiness for the hunt. The craft, in spite of its rickety mirage, proved reliable through seven hundred miles of corrugated skies between Winnipeg and Churchill.

On their evening approach, they first glimpsed ground below the cloud cover, a land similar to their hunting range. It was replete with scattered glacial lakes, crooked rivers, rocky outcroppings and short, stubby tree cover set onto a stochastic landscape, a remote wilderness stretching another thousand miles northward toward the Arctic Ocean.

Even though spring had run its course in Michigan, here the season of rebirth was tardy. Sailing the wide mouth of the Churchill River, a flotsam of ice floes drifted into the charcoal waters of a briny Hudson Bay. Moe shivered at the obvious chill, but with *terra firma* promised beneath his feet, shrugged his reservations away.

There were yet miles to traverse before his hunt.

* * *

Littering the sleepy springtime harbor, countless ice fortresses slowly rocked in the choppy brine. This early in the year, only the sturdiest of ocean vessels could safely navigate the heaving hazards. On shore, adjacent to concrete docks and high-rise metal cranes, the dockyard was dotted with heavy mining equipment.

The metal carcasses lying in rest were being serviced and repaired; readied for the next mad dash of hair-raising expeditions hell bent on harvesting a bounty of valuable minerals. Some interior mines were accessible for only weeks each year. Impatient company executives were already calling daily for updates on the status of transport craft and the thawing wilderness. It was a nervous time.

As usual, numerous spring rains were ensuring that the inland soils remained sufficiently drenched to only let the lightest vehicles pass over. The massively built diggers, crushers and haulers would be stranded at least another month. If the drizzly conditions persisted through summer, some might not work again until the following winter's freeze.

Suitably impressed by the scale of the equipment as they drove past the industrial dockyard, Moe pondered, "I wonder if Intel ever stored any mining equipment here."

"Huh?" Ken asked, incredulous, "Intel in mining?"

"It's quite a famous engineering story," Moe baited.

"Not that famous." Ken countered, "I haven't heard of it."

"Not many people have heard of low-alpha lead."

In the mid-90's, Intel was making a substantial profit selling high-end CPUs to a meteoric need in the computer gaming market. The new cult of electronic consumers was hard-core competitive, young adult warriors with disposable income to burn and willing to parlay serious cash to wield any minuscule advantage over virtual rivals. Each release of a faster chip fueled a wave of buying, a predictable, incremental cash insurgence for the semiconductor manufacturer where it mattered most, at the apex gross margin.

But replacing CPUs had risks, requiring partial disassembling of the testy computer innards. While dismantling components into a mess of ribbon wires, fans and peripheral cards, static discharge from merely dragging a sweater across a rug could *fry* the whole system. In addition, the *flip-chip* CPUs were fragile, a pin-studded square biscuit which bent as easily as it short-circuited. Gamers didn't mind dropping serious coin to replace a chip, but they didn't want to blow a few thousand dollars of other equipment in the process.

Determined to facilitate continued windfall sales, Intel's engineers contrived a simpler CPU replacement method, the SECC, or single edge cartridge CPU, module. The drop-in replacement was a clumsy achievement, but it reduced the risks. To downplay its shortcomings, it was marketed as making upgrades faster, easier and safer. For a while, the strategy worked, even forcing Intel's competitors to adopt similar designs, but its disadvantages would soon outweigh the improvement.

The SECC adaptation was bigger, requiring additional interconnect material between the chip and the motherboard. At the time, lead was the conductive metal of choice, but nearly all lead, an end product of uranium decomposition, contains measurable fractions of radioactive isotopes. Occasionally, lead emits an alpha particle, a dense packet of energy normally passing harmlessly through thin materials. However, faster CPUs have more transistors, increasing the probability of alpha particle interaction. And, as smaller transistors provide more computing power, the energy density of alpha particle interaction could short circuit and self-destruct that portion of the chip.

In partial mitigation, Intel's CPUs were built with redundant circuitry, capable of bypassing a limited number of bad connections, but it was a costly strategy. The dilemma amply demonstrated the trade-off between pure power and robustness in chip design, between cost, reliability and market demand.

Factoring into their strategic thinking, Intel had recently learned a costly lesson. A small fraction of the immensely successful Pentium CPUs demonstrated a *floating-point decimal* error. Knowing the error had manifested during a contrived sequence of calculations, the corporate leaders chose to ignore the flaw. Even as word spread, and a few *helpful* techno-savvy folks showed it was repeatable, Intel still denied it was a gaff of any consequence.

Only after a media firestorm ignited did the company brass take note. Their downplaying strategy, albeit logical, embarrassingly catapulted the flap into leading news headlines. Intel smarted, accused of old-school corporate arrogance and greed, a culture that the paranoid start-up had been proud to avoid.

Although the best solution was not having the alpha-emitting lead in the product, it lacked feasibility. Removing all the leftover isotopes made the lead smelting process too costly. Using replacement metals was either too costly or poisoned the transistors. But there was another solution, albeit rare and out of the ordinary, using geologically old ore-bodies of lead, long spent of alpha particle emission.

Few such deposits exist, and where they do, they're in the oldest rocks on earth, like within the Precambrian formations in Northern Canada.

Buying an established mine outright created several dilemmas for the semiconductor giant.

First, logistics of climate ensured raw ore extraction was possible only a couple of months per year.

Next, the mineral needed to be kept separated from all other ores during both transit and smelting to avoid unwanted mixing that could lead to contamination. Lastly, the equipment used to purify the metal to interconnect quality had to be dedicated to processing non-alpha emitting ores only to avoid picking up alpha-particle emitters that would be left behind in the equipment following processing of other suppliers' batches.

Limited access, compartmentalized transport and normally-idled equipment created a *trifecta* of added cost.

With no better alternative, the company moved ahead with the mine's purchase, a strategic endeavor to corner the supply of the necessary conductive interconnect material, thereby locking out their competition from cost-effective competition in this high-end SECC market.

For a while, it looked like the strategy might work, but politics within the semiconductor manufacturing community made strange bedfellows. In short order, a new, disruptive invention intervened. Desiring a method of using copper for interconnects, normally a silicon poisoning material, IBM developed a method of *passivating* the chip surface, preventing copper from migrating into the transistors.

Then IBM publicly disclosed the breakthrough, allowing the entire industry to quickly adapt and phase out lead interconnects.

The mine Intel had bought was superfluous.

Within another year, Intel returned to the flip-chip design. The decision-makers who led the low alpha lead mine acquisition fell into disfavor. Finger pointing, head rolling and some internal chaos were inevitable.

The first night was frigid as the mercury receded well below freezing, raising a few doubts about the sanity of springtime hunting, but the subsequent morning began with warm sunshine and promise. Renting a four-wheel drive GMC pickup and an ancient eight-wheeled Argonaut ATV, they loaded their hunting gear, a hundred gallons of fuel and two weeks' worth of sustenance onto the bed of the pickup.

Commencing the final leg at dawn, the balance of the journey lasted an entire day. Driving along mostly unpaved roads, their progress was frequently hindered by tracts of greasy gumbo. On the slick stretches, the pickup slid treacherously down shallow inclines, anxious moments for those accustomed to asphalt. With a little luck and caution, they avoided stranding themselves in the soggy roadside.

At the end of the navigable trails, they unloaded the Argonaut and transferred their supplies to the ATV. The final four hours were fatiguing, an endless succession of bone-jarring jolts as the stiff-framed craft navigated uneven terrain, a vacant wilderness varying between muskeg and taiga.

Once inside their hunting terrain, they set camp, forgoing a fire as they had been unable to pack wood. A small butane-powered campfire stove heated a meal of canned soup and stew and the pair settled down for a cold, wind-swept night beneath a cloudless, jeweled sky.

They slept well.

On the first day, they explored their hunting terrain, now well north of Reindeer Lake, following an ice-free turbulent river. Considering the season's availability of fodder and the cold nights, they targeted small ravines feeding the flooded river, refuges separated by flattened meadows now sprouting with fresh, green grass.

Here the big mammals would find sweet sustenance, irresistible after winter's woody twigs and bitter tree bark. At twilight, the deer emerged to feed on the fresh fodder, cautiously grabbing mouthfuls of grass, but not straying far from the trees.

When Moe and Ken approached, they instantly fled into the sheltered thickets. Forbidden by law to hunt at night, they camped nearby, fresh wood in tow for a campfire. Eagerly awaking before dawn, they secured a position along a game trail, intent on ambushing the returning foragers, but the deer did not materialize, cleverly foraging on the opposite side of the watershed.

They moved on.

After two days of slowly scouting and halfheartedly hunting, Moe and Ken tracked a herd of whitetail into a massive ravine spurring away from the swollen river. This location held sufficient promise for them to stay and they repeated their strategy of lurking near the best food supplies and trails, but by the end of the first week, they hadn't recorded a kill.

The wily deer were managing to remain concealed from sight, even though the gorge seemed to be inhabited by a sizable herd.

After the first week's failed attempts, Moe resorted to insertion tactics. They prepped in full-dress camouflage, including face-paint, hoods, gloves and chemical concealment, even spraying themselves with what was billed as *doe-estrus* scents—whether it was harvested from a female whitetail or chemically contrived Moe didn't know. Neither was he certain it would work in a season other than the rut. By now, he was sure that their sweat was a klaxon of their presence.

They covered up and hid where trails converged within the natural cover of deadfall. The dividends were immediate, the small forest awakened with life.

A scant twenty yards to his left, a speckled ptarmigan male led his covey through the undergrowth, searching for tidbits to raise a brood. The careless prancing of the proud male pleased Moe, proving that their presence was undetected.

The ptarmigan sported a transitional coat, a speckling of brown and white that blended with the deep tree cover mosses, lichens and patches of snow. In behavior, they were similar to the grouses of his home state. He wondered how they would roast, but would not follow up on his desire to harvest one. He was licensed for deer, not game birds, and although it was unlikely he would be caught poaching, he had no desire to even try.

He did not have an appetite for anything illegal, he realized. Rather, he appreciated that, within his lifetime, hunts like this had become exceedingly rare—and he was proud that he could legally enjoy this kind of a sublime outing. It was this singularity that had led Moe to put down his gun and take up bow hunting. While the rifle was easier, the weapon unfairly brought down game at distances approaching a quarter mile.

He thought about his boyhood, he had hunted exclusively with a rifle, his success and failure essentially a bragging rite of passage to adulthood. As he forged a career, harvesting trophies was no longer a source of building self-esteem. Rather, he hunted to rekindle a connection to his youth, his deceased father and to reacquaint with the outdoors.

In time, he would pass this legacy down to his unborn son.

Bow hunting expressed a simple, primeval theme: without technology, humans are a weak species, wholly dependent on mental faculties.

Although Moe favored the compound bow, a device of precision engineering, its kill range was limited to fifty yards. It required sufficient skill or luck to approach that closely to any game and it had taken years for him develop the essential skills of stalking quarry, staying downwind and tuning his senses to discern the honed wiles of the deer.

He took a deep, silent breath—he was proud of his skill, he realized.

In contrast to his seasonal forays, a mature buck knew his terrain, understood self-preservation, and possessed superior senses. With a silent step, it could neatly blend into the background where it might be surprised from hiding only if the predator got a good fix on its last location.

Stumbling over a roosted animal rarely led to a shot. A compound bow is not rapidly loaded and fired. The advantages clearly tilt to the prey, he knew.

Perhaps more appealing than the thrill of matching wits was the time spent unwinding in a quiet, isolated outdoor refuge. Occasionally, Moe remembered sitting for hours, absorbing each forest's effervescence. It elicited an unfettered peace in his soul, an ephemeral escape from the urban rat race. In the city, work colleagues were pitted *friends* and foes, *frenemies*, ceaselessly competing to keep a job, a house, a spouse and the meager possessions that defined their livelihood—their civility.

There were too many mouths in the world to feed, a clear fact that materialized as the integrated global economy outstripped resources. Corporate trusts fully exploited the reality, opportunistic parasites disproportionately gorging on cash flow, without regard to human profit or loss, legally undermining employees into a class of indentured servants.

Debt, hunger and the threat of homelessness are great motivators.

Get off your soap box! Moe thought as he refocused on his hunt.

Within minutes of settling down in hiding, the squirrels were squawking, tattling his presence. Neither would they stop exposing him, abrasively broadcasting his daily defeat. A half hour later, they finally tired of their childish rite, re-engaging in the age old passions, feeding, squabbling and reproduction.

Once his sounders were distracted, the forest enlivened.

Rustling through the treetops, a light breeze nodded the head limbs of the tall pines, which crackled and creaked a fractional compliance. Inspired by the staccato bursts, a redheaded woodpecker answered, tapping out the same rhythm and cadence—his repertoire was not in mimicry.

A moment later, a driven rival took up the challenge, re-sounding and one-upping the percussive taunt. The two sparred back and forth, moving closer together each round until they inevitably clashed. Attended by their ladies, each tatting her own epithets, the dispute persisted without blows until one pair abruptly conceded, surrendered their claim and flew away. Within an hour, another skirmish would renew.

On his pine log, hidden behind the radial root tangle of a windfall, Moe had a comfortable perch for observing. Smiling at the woodpeckers' antics, he relaxed, envisioning the movements of the deer, trying to predict their movements and motivations. Were they searching for food or water, or were they returning for a midday siesta? He chuckled at the thought, applying a *south-of-the-border* term in a frozen land—two expansive countries to the north.

A quarter mile downhill the fluid ravine discharged into the main river.

In the afternoon, when the deer were down, Moe and Ken intended to fish for grayling, a trout-like species with an over-sized dorsal fin reminiscent of an ancient mariner. If they were lucky, they'd reel in enough for a meal, a welcome relief from the cans of stale dried food in his cool locker.

A wolf mourned the close of his day, his eulogy echoed across the cavernous divide.

Instantly, Moe doubled his alertness, quietly shifting to protect his back against the exposed root pack. Not that he was under-armed, in addition to his *Bowtech* Allegiance, he holstered a 9-mm Glock. The pistol protected him from the wolves he could see, but it wasn't a perfect defense. It had questionable stopping power against the monster grizzlies roaming the area in spring and summer. Had it been winter, he would not have trusted the hand-held weapon against the greater menace, a polar bear. For that, he would desire a large bore rifle or a metal-walled sanctuary.

In the realm of animal danger, the polar bear was king.

Alarmed by the howl, the ptarmigan bevy cocked their heads, took a few jerking steps and simply...disappeared. Astonished, Moe stared, unable to distinguish plumage from foliage—impressed by the cleverness of the flock's retreat.

In contrast, he was an intruder, not a player.

Some distance from his dirt-plastered root shelter, a droning arose. Moe stilled, scanning his pupils left and right. The humming intensified to a ponderous pitch, heralding a swarm of inch long horseflies. Perpetually whirling, they spun in random motion briefly punctuated by inexplicably short respites on hanging foliage before skittishly alighting. Insects of this size and number meant a large, warm-blooded mammal was nearby.

Gingerly, Moe unstrapped the Glock's holster. Ensuring their safety was more important than arming for a kill. Reassuringly, his hand brushed against the pistol's smooth, custom-contoured palm grip. It was free to retrieve. Having mollified his instincts, Moe silently removed a carbon-fiber arrow from his bow-mounted quiver. It was lethally tipped with a spring-loaded arrowhead that would release on impact. Guaranteed to fly like a target point, it had cost double to acquire, although expanding blades have a terrible reputation for failure. Now, he questioned the logic of replacing his high-drag, but reliable, *broadheads.*

The flies, and presumably the deer, were moving closer, but Moe could still detect no movement in the surrounding thickets. Lifting his field glasses to his eyes, Moe smiled. Evolution was a generation behind image magnification.

Only seventy-five yards away above the mossy floor was the form of a large buck sporting magnificent antlers, the trophy rack was coated in velvet. He was sniffing the air, tasting its myriad scents, a precautionary habit of self-preservation.

Moe waited patiently. Unless the stag moved closer, it was a difficult, low-return draw.

Gently letting the glasses return to his chest, Moe readied his bow, extrapolating his aim between fluorescent sight pins. Without the visual aid, the buck was difficult to distinguish from tree bark and branches. He put a reed to his lips, crooning the gentle grunt of a doe in *estrus.*

Immediately, the low growth stirred, thin twigs whipping recklessly. Harried antlers scraped the tree bark up and down, but without the passion and agitation of full rut. Staring hard at the noise, Moe waited patiently, noiselessly notching the arrow into the d-loop, and setting the trigger's mechanical jaws. Once readied, he started drawing.

Hooves approached.

At half draw, the bowstring tautened against an iron wall of resistance. It didn't feel right. Maintaining a steady rhythm, Moe pulled harder, his index finger mistakenly gracing the mechanical hair-trigger.

It let loose. Instantly, the bowstring twanged, impotently nudging the arrow a few feet forward. Short on propulsion, the carbon shaft fell lazily, clattering against a tree stump.

In the language of the forest, the unnatural sounds reverberated as foreign.

The buck froze. For a surreal moment, it looked straight at Moe, no longer unaware—neither would it tarry. Leaping sideways, the stag bolted nimbly into the thick cover, galloping hooves drumbeating the ground. Within seconds, he was gone, his hooves muting as he slowed, suitably distanced from his disabled reaper.

The bush rustled softly as Ken emerged from cover.

"What happened?" Ken asked.

"I'm not sure," Moe answered, inspecting the bow. He was immediately dismayed. Pinched between the aluminum bow frame and the lower cam bearing, a small length of the green and black striped bowstring sagged limply. During draw, it had escaped the cam's groove and snapped fast into the frame mounts, relieving only a fraction of its draw tension. The arrow had barely launched.

"Dry fire?" Ken queried.

"Can't be," Moe replied dubiously. "All my arrows are properly weighted."

Irritated beyond words, he glared at his weapon. It was now useless, unless he could restring it by hand. He had not brought a back-up bow, although Ken had prudently packed his own, but Ken's bow was not a drop-in replacement. It had a different manufacturer, and a shorter and lighter draw. More pragmatically, Moe was unfamiliar with its capabilities or sighting adjustments, so he couldn't confidently aim it. For success, he needed to repair his own bow.

Taking the instrument to Churchill and back would consume a minimum of two hunting days. Determining to attempt to remount the string, Moe began his field repair.

First, he tried drawing, hoping to roll the string into the groove by brute force, but that proved impossible, the limbs were as stiff as slate.

Worse, the imparted action caused the bowstring to slip further.

Leaning atop its upper limb as if he were a vise, he tried compressing the device against the ground. This proved puerile. His arms were obviously too weak, but perhaps his legs might be strong enough, he thought.

Mindful of the energy stored in the half-coiled cams, Moe expressed his reservations.

"What if the string snaps, Ken, or a cam breaks away from its mount?"

"The cams could be braked by inserting hunting knife handles into their spindles," Ken countered. "They'll prevent recoil if I lose my grip."

Moe agreed with a nod, accepting the implied risk. If the braces damaged the bow, the hunt would be over. To repair, he'd need an archery shop. Similarly, if their field attempt failed, restringing required the services of a qualified bowsmith.

Setting the aluminum frame atop a fallen log, a twig protruding through a hole preventing pivoting, Moe put one foot on the bow, two hands on the string, and pulled.

Slowly, the cams began turning. It was working. As Moe made gains, Ken inserted, withdrew and re-inserted the *shivs* into the cam, finally locking its position at three-quarter draw.

Gently, Moe released the tension on the string. The supports held, but the bowstring was not freed from the cam-mount. Worse, the inserted knife-stops prevented him from coaxing it away from the frame. The bow needed to be taken to full draw.

Moe steeled himself for the effort. Readying the removal of the shivs, Ken watched as Moe pulled, synchronizing removal as he saw slack in the cams. Quivering from the effort, Moe took the bow to full draw. Scrambling, Ken re-inserted the knives, locking its position. This time, the string fully cleared its paralyzing mount.

Reaching down, Moe realigned the string into the cam grooves. Checking the string and its two supporting cables, he was relieved to find them unmarked—with no resultant fraying either.

"Let's get those knives out, Ken," he said, not willing to linger longer with the cams pressing against metal stops. Agreeing, Ken cautiously pulled out the knives as Moe held full draw. Once the locks were removed, Moe slowly let the string down to avoid another dry fire, all the while watching the movements of the cams.

They retracted uniformly and in unison, reloading the bow. Inspecting their efforts, Moe was elated. Their improvisation had not damaged the thin cams. More importantly, the string was nestled properly in its grooves.

Having solved his problem, Moe puzzled to find a root cause, his memory obscured when he'd concentrated on his prey. Recasting the events in frames, the simplest explanation sequencing was that his fingertip had tapped the trigger. It hadn't been a classic dry fire; his arrows were properly weighted, having loaded the bowstring with the correct resistance. While excess momentum can unleash a string from a cam and deform the limbs, this mishap lacked the essential kinetic energy.

It was clear the only plausible explanation was that he'd accidentally depressed the mechanical trigger. But why? Had his excitement got the better of him? If so, it was the first time he'd lost his head since he was a teenager. Worse, he'd lost his best opportunity for a successful kill.

Needing to ensure the bow's integrity, Moe prepared a test: a full draw, no release. If it failed, the hunt was over until repaired professionally. Hunting with an out of tune bow was a waste of time.

Thoughtfully notching an arrow, he set the trigger, this time firmly positioning his fingers behind the release.

There would be no accidental discharge. Smoothly he drew back. The cams obeyed dutifully, rotating freely on their pivots, channeling the energy of the flexing limbs. At half draw, Moe slowed, glancing at the top cam. The alignment was true. Relieved, he continued.

And his luck ran out. Without warning, the string flung loose again, snapping his right arm backward, accelerated under its own tension, before being roughly jerked forward by the whirling cam.

There was no pain, only surprise.

"Shit!" he cursed softly, stunned. The bow had mechanical issues, needing professional repair. The next two days were lost.

The string had lost its loop, hanging outside the twin bars of the lower cam mount, a sleight-of-hand restructuring that defied logic. To remount it without removing the bearing or its rotating pin was humanly impossible. He needed a magician.

"It's not worth trying," Moe grumbled once he understood the root cause. While walking through the low branches and whipping bushes, he'd snagged a wanton spline within the cam's groove. As he'd drawn the bow, the lodged twig displaced the bowstring, forcing it to roll off. Had he removed the stem the first time, his bow would have been properly restrung and restored.

Rotating the free-spinning cam, Moe gathered its freed string, a little housekeeping to reduce the probability of snagging it on a wayward bough. Without warning the cam reversed, instantly under tension. Brushing his hand, the spinning sprocket snagged a fingertip, dragging it through its center plane until the aluminum frame suddenly presented an unforgiving barrier. With a sickening snap, the last carpal on Moe's ring finger crackled, splintered and disjointed.

The cam's thin edges bit through flesh.

He shouted, convulsively pulling to extricate his damaged finger. It wouldn't move. The pain seared a lightning bolt surging from his pulverized finger directly to his head. The agony would not relent. Compressed between the frame and dialing cam, his finger tip slowly severed. Finally, the stub caught fast, a thick fleshy digit pinched between dull scissors. From the hanging fingertip, the craggy carpal angled upwards through crushed flesh.

Writhing against the metal pincer, Moe spun in a half circle, desperate to free his hand. Ken rushed in, his stomach sickened, an imprinted visage of shredded sinews at the forefront of his bewildered gaze, but Moe was flailing frantically and Ken held fast, not risking to rip away the last fragment of his friend's fingertip.

"Cut the string," Moe begged. He held still.

In an instant, Ken reached into his pocket, withdrawing a sharp jack-knife. With precision, he caught the taut bowstring and, in a single motion, sliced through its fibers. The limbs splayed open violently, rupturing both cables. The compression relieved, but Moe's finger remained trapped.

With his free hand, Moe gripped the dappled green aluminum frame. With brute force, he pulled, panting in short gasps, painstakingly extricating his mangled finger from its grasp. Profusely bleeding, the crushed fingertip flopped against his knuckle, an elliptical, purplish mass attached by a mere flap of skin. From its bloody center, the ghastly white bone tip protruded, no longer resembling the human digit it had only recently been.

"Thanks for cutting the string," Moe muttered. The paralysis was gone, but each heartbeat still enlivened his nerves, a pulsing hammer wracking his tattered finger through his arm and into his forehead. He wanted to scream, but refused to even moan. He was sick, nauseated to the verge of vomiting. As a chill wormed through his back, he felt his legs buckling. He sensed he was passing out but fought the urge.

"No problem," Ken replied, surprised at the gratitude and incapable of fathoming the agony before him. In his mind, there was no question of priority—Moe's finger or a bow—but clearly, his friend held the integrity of the weapon with higher regard. Ken shuddered at the thought that his friend was going into shock and his comment was a harbinger of an impending state of delirium.

He would monitor his friend's behavior closely.

The pressing concern was sterilizing and wrapping the finger. The bleeding needed to stop, and a tourniquet was the most expedient solution. Searching through his backpack, he found only friction tape. His first aid pack was at camp, a two-mile jaunt over rough terrain.

"Moe, do you have a first aid kit," he asked as nonchalantly as possible.

"No," Moe wheezed, "but there is some toilet paper in my pack."

Quickly, Ken retrieved the roll and began wrapping the wound. The first windings blushed crimson. With some dismay, Ken realized that the damaged digit was Moe's ring finger, and that the stump was sporting his wedding band. He wondered if the ring would perform the duties of a tourniquet or do the opposite and kill the whole finger, but there was too much swelling to remove the thick band.

He looked for some ice. Beneath the low-lying underbrush, small patches of crusted snow remained. The snow was unusable, visibly dusted with a thick layer of debris and invisibly inoculated with the voracious micro-organisms of spring.

Instead, Ken secured the soft ply with two parallel strips of friction tape, wound twice over so that the blood couldn't wet and loosen the binding glue. A third loop bound his ring finger to his unbroken middle finger, a rudimentary splint more convenient than small, knobby sticks.

As Moe fiddled over the dressing, Ken inspected the ground, picking up the fallen arrow, the distended bow and the scrapped toilet paper. He would not leave a blood trail, as he was not carrying a sidearm.

"Can you walk, Moe?" Ken asked.

"I think so," Moe responded. His ashen face spoke volumes, etched creases beneath each eyebrow, despondent fear glazing his bloodshot eyes. Moe stood up and slowly stepped forward, testing himself.

He was steady. He wondered if he could climb the five hundred feet necessary, unsure of obtaining medical assistance without aggravation or further mishap.

Ken felt useless, ill-equipped to field dress wounds more serious than scrapes or sprains. A partially severed digit was beyond the scope of his experience in field surgery. Without proper care, Moe could deteriorate into shock. If that happened, his only recourse was abandoning his friend to retrieve medical supplies, a journey of at least two days. It wasn't a viable option. The map indicated a nearby reservation village, but it was out of the way, didn't advertise its services and wasn't worth the diversion in time and energy.

He swore under his breath, cursing their oversights, no satellite communicators, underestimating the logistics presented by the lack of human settlement in their hunting locale.

The fragility of life was unnerving.

Moe pushed the pain to the fringes of his consciousness. The initial explosions had subsided, replaced now by a betraying numbness frequently punctuated with sudden, throbbing pain. Fixating on the stream bed, he watched the liquid tumble over a cascade of scoured rocks. Adjacent to the flow, in an exposed, dry bank were polished stones of abnormal geometry and color. In spite of his injury, he moved closer, intrigued, disbelieving his eyes. Was he really seeing blocks of crystalline ore?

With his undamaged hand, he selected a choice specimen and stared at the truth. Encased within quartz was a thick, metallic vein, separated from the milky matrix by transitioning tones of vibrant colors. The striations, shaded from brown to off-pink, were distinctly similar in hue to the mineral precursors he used during his daytime job.

Through his mental haze, an excitement fomented. Scraping his thumbnail over the rock's scaly surface, he flaked a brittle coating away. Freshly exposed, the hues intensified. Smashing the rock against a granite boulder, the quartz cleaved, revealing a jagged, bright pink layer within.

It was real. He was sitting on a deposit of rare earth minerals. He selected another promising sample. Without evidence, no one would believe it. A flood of nausea swept his strength away. With his hurt hand, he palmed a sturdy branch from a felled poplar, jarring his injury. Shards of light detonated inside his eyes, nearly driving him to pass out. Closing them tightly, he held his balance and pocketed the strange stone.

Noticing Moe half bent over in discomfort, Ken looked him in the eye. He'd been finishing his own preparations, but was instantly perplexed by his friend's discordant behavior, striking rocks before losing his balance.

"Ready to go?" he queried.

"Yeah," Moe replied.

Carefully ascending the stream bank, they walked the ravine bed, picking through the tangled forest. The route was not easy as barriers arose at every turn—fallen trees, stony obstacles and eroded potholes. Along short stretches, they traveled game trails, temporarily easing their progress. Ken kept up a rambling conversation, a banal chatter gauging Moe's condition, keeping his friend talking. He could not afford to let Moe slip into shock.

"You feeling okay," Ken interjected frequently, waiting for Moe to either falter or lose his temper. Either response would be telling.

"Yeah," Moe responded firmly.

"Good, just checking," Ken conceded.

Moe wanted to give Ken a piece of his mind, but he knew why Ken was pestering him. Instead, he puzzled over the unusual mineral find.

As far as he knew, rare earth stones were mined from the earth's oldest rocks. His taggant precursors originated in Australia or from the Rift Valley region in Africa. These were pricier alternatives to Chinese sources, but fear of changing geopolitical conditions had cemented his purchasing decision. It had been a hard sell to management, more concerned with quarterly earnings and cashing in stock options than establishing a friendly pipeline to raw materials. Ironically, his powders were used to make anti-counterfeiting labels, a coincidence that met stony silence when he dared connect the sovereignty of sourcing to the flood of knock-off products it intended to expose.

A mineral strike in Canada could ease the latter concern, and by avoiding intercontinental intrigue and shipping charges, give him a competitive advantage in pricing. It was no secret that competitors were trying to duplicate his products, wooing the suppliers and his technical staff, but to date all their poaching had been unable to match his consistent record of improvement.

He'd experimented with several materials, including yttrium, ytterbium, and dysprosium. The actual blend he used was an unpatented, undisclosed trademark secret, a viscous mixture he vaguely referred to as *psychedelic opals*, one that proved impossible to duplicate, and instantly exposed counterfeiters, but to remain competitive, he was thinking ahead, considering several new alternative product lines. This find might enable the next generation of development on another special sauce he'd been cogitating about for over eighteen months.

Still at the ravine bottom, Moe looked up the steep incline with trepidation. He was weakening, partly from fatigue, and partly from dealing with the incessant pain. The hard walking kept his heart beating strongly, each pulse painfully coursing through a fingertip that still felt fully attached.

"I have to rest," he announced.

Ken looked around for an object to sit on. Only large rocks were present.

"Have a seat over here," he suggested.

Moe lumbered over, sitting heavily on a craggy boulder.

"Let me look at your hand," Ken requested. Moe acquiesced, holding up his hand. Stained deep crimson, the wrapping stopped any fluid from seeping through. The ring was an effective tourniquet.

"Can you feel your fingertip?" Ken questioned.

"Yeah," Moe responded.

"Good," Ken replied. The ring tourniquet was not killing the tissue.

Next to the path lay a washed out stream bed. Large chunks of quartz rocks sat exposed, a rock hound's dream, but not today. Scattering through the wash, Moe saw dozens of pink-rippled stones, enough to suggest the obvious. He was sitting on a mother lode.

"Can you gather me a few more of those stones?" he asked Ken.

The question concerned Ken and he wondered if Moe had lost it—it was challenging enough to get him out safely—now was he supposed to lug rocks, too? Electing an intuitive approach, Ken agreed, selecting several colorful pieces meeting Moe's approval.

"What's so special about these rocks, Moe?"

"It's an unusual mineral, normally found on the other side of the world," Moe responded, with lucidity.

The answer surprised Ken. Moe was alert and cogent.

"Okay, are you ready to continue?"

"Yeah, let's get up this slope," Moe challenged himself.

Halfway up, they rested again until Moe caught his breath. Topping a ridgeline, his heart fell as the ground before them also descended. He'd forgotten they were crossing a forked watershed. Steeling his resolve, he found his stride improving on the descent, but near the bottom, the fauna thickened due to growth after a fire from a decade ago, and the undergrowth became difficult to navigate.

It took a toll.

Winding between charred deadfall, thickly growing saplings and stair step drops over exposed root mounds, Moe was taxed. Tottering, he asked to stop again. Fortunately, they were nearing the truck.

Ken eyed Moe carefully. "I could go get the first aid kit."

"No, I'll just be a minute," Moe mumbled, wavering in place. Ken took note. Moe was at his limit. It was a damn good thing they were close to camp.

Moe thought about his new discovery, the pink-veined stones. They could make him rich and he wondered if anyone else knew about them. The thought was assuring, but a dozen other questions surfaced—from investing help to filing claims to establishing mining schemes. The implications were overwhelming. It could quickly become expensive, avoiding a lawsuit from his employer. The business he was in was similar enough to make it lucrative for a well-funded corporate legal team to wrestle his prize away.

Modern employment contracts are notorious for claiming the rights to all employee finds, even without offering compensation, and protecting them against future development strategies—even by the employee's heirs. It seemed ludicrous, abdicating due process of the unborn to garner employment, but it was necessary to sign such documents if one wanted a job. Otherwise, the employer would outsource the job, or, equally farcical, offer it to a foreign national claiming that a *qualified* American could not be found.

The assignation contracts were immunized with blanket protection clauses. Challenged portions could be struck down without undermining the rest, no matter how egregious the offensive text had been. Realistically, it meant that only the rich, or well-funded, could oppose them. People like Moe couldn't even begin, didn't even dare try. The lawsuit procedure would ruin them, consuming their funds, homes, marriages, families, and ultimately, their health. The right of the employee was approaching new lows, a nether untested since the labor movement won reforms a century earlier.

"Qualified, my ass," Moe rambled, "I need more money to live on. I gotta pay back my student loans and day care. I don't have my parents living with me to help. I didn't get my education for free at a state-sponsored school."

"Gotta rest," he murmured, immediately sitting down. He thudded onto a grounded tree trunk, eyes dulled, his breathing was coming in short, panting gasps.

Ken wondered if his friend had finally gone into shock. Sitting next to Moe, he inquired.

"Is it hurting badly, or is it numbed?"

"Hurts like hell," Moe responded.

Good, Ken thought. Acute sensations indicated alertness of mind.

"What did you pick up back there?" Ken queried, changing the subject.

"Maybe nothing, some cool stones, could be a mineral," Moe answered, cautiously.

"Valuable?"

"They're not gems."

"You didn't answer my question," Ken challenged.

"Huh? Oh, maybe for a pet rock collector. I'm not sure what it is, but I've never seen anything like it."

"Ready to walk again?"

"Yeah."

Over the final kilometer, Moe felt his strength waning quickly. The nausea was building while numbness consumed his severed digit. His head ached from an intense pressure behind his eyes, his forehead cleaving from within, floating above his brow. His coordination failed and he stumbled over fallen logs, lumbering through tangles of disjointed deadfall.

Several times Ken helped him maintain his balance. A desire to quit gnawed his will. It would be much simpler to just lie down and sleep. A sweet escape. Ken would do what was best. The money from the rocks would take care of him.

"C'mon, Moe, just a little further," Ken encouraged.

No reply.

"Do you want to rest?"

"No," Moe grunted.

Turning a corner, a meadow opened in front of them. In its center stood base camp and the four wheel drive truck that would get him to safety and care.

Propping Moe beneath his undamaged arm, Ken half dragged, half carried him to the truck. Opening the tailgate, he lifted his friend onto the exposed platform and leaned him against the hard metal side.

"Wait. Rest a minute," he commanded. In the cabin was the first aid kit, with antiseptic wash, antibiotic ointment, bandages, tape and gauze, but there were no sanitary cloths. Fearing infection, Ken grabbed a fresh roll of toilet paper. Although it would wad up when wet, it would also wash away when soaked. A piece of sterile paper stuck in the wound was better than a bacteria-laden towel.

"Moe, I'm going to redress the wound," he warned. "Are you ready?"

"Yeah," Moe answered firmly, a smidgen of strength in his reply.

"Tell me when it hurts too much."

"Yeah."

Gingerly unwrapping the blood-soaked coating, Ken's trembling fingers peeled away the topmost layer. Wincing and gasping, Moe absorbed the assault, skirting the threshold of shock. Ken worked quickly, afraid Moe might react impulsively, pull hard away and restart the bleeding. He needed a diversion. Removing a composite arrow from the bow's quiver, he unscrewed the razor-sharp broadhead and handed the thin shaft to Moe.

"Bite on this," he suggested. "Look, it won't take away the pain, but it'll give you something else to concentrate on while I'm cleaning the wound."

Moe obliged, inserting the shaft into his mouth and clamping his teeth. The distraction was minimal, but it was something.

Pouring drinking water liberally from a plastic bottle, Ken worked at accessing the wound, slowly peeling away wadded toilet paper with his fingertips, balancing efficiency with gentleness. Moe poured the torment into the arrow shaft. Grinding beneath gripped teeth, Ken wondered if the stiff shaft would soon be crushed.

Rinsing away the final bits of tissue, the wound was finally fully revealed. The truth was repulsive. Apart from the compressed flesh and broken bone, the swollen fingertip, deeply purple and misshapen, was now barely attached, hanging by a quarter-inch flap of skin. The fingernail was gone. Ken found it on the ground, glued in the wad of blood-soaked toilet tissue. Whether it could be salvaged was questionable.

How can a body heal something like that? Ken wondered. He couldn't find a single matching feature—tissue, skin or blood vessels. Ken mused over the surgeon who would be able to align these mashed parts.

Considering whether he should splint the finger, Ken examined the swollen stub further, but was unable to ascertain if the fracture continued below the top joint. Most likely it did, but the injury was superfluous compared to the severing. To set this injury, the pain would be excruciating. Calculating the length of their return journey, he elected to stop thinking about setting the finger. He could not effectively treat this part of Moe's injury.

"I need to wash it again, Moe," Ken ordered. "I can use antiseptic or water, which do you prefer?"

"Water," Moe gasped, unable to bear the grueling burn from a peroxide dousing.

"No problem," Ken answered, cementing the decision to coat the new dressing with an antibiotic ointment. No need to push for more disinfection than was needed.

Moe tensed, teeth gouging the carbon fiber shaft and preparing for the agonizing sensation. With his free hand, he dug into his pocket and grabbed his precious ore sample, tightly squeezing it into his palm. In his mind, he chanted a mantra...*upon this rock, I will build*...a biblical passage not heard since boyhood, as he hadn't been inside a church for three decades.

The repetitive phrase sapped his sanity. After a time, he could no longer clear his mind of its ponderous message. Drowning in delirium, he let go, and found peace, suddenly immersed in a comforting certitude that he'd be all right.

Roughly jarred by the trail's potholes, Moe came to, slamming his shoulder against the cold metal of the passenger door. He groaned.

Looking over while driving, Ken saw Moe squirming in discomfort.

"Sorry, Moe," he said. "How are you making out?"

"Okay," came a stoic response.

"I've got some Tylenol if you want."

"Can't," Moe answered. "I'm allergic. You have any Ibuprofen?"

"I don't think so," Ken denied. "I have some whiskey, though."

Moe wanted a drink, but the reserve of his judgment warned against imbibing alcohol.

"Won't be given painkillers if I have whiskey on my breath."

"Shit," Ken muttered, incapable of softening the ride. Bumping and jostling over the unimproved trail, he tested the limits of the truck's suspension. He could not afford too great a risk, he was not equipped to repair a broken axle.

Two hours later, he vacated the dirt track for a grid and sped up. The dust billowed as Ken now pushed the vehicle's traction limit, but at least they were edging closer to medical care.

Periodically, Moe writhed and groaned, an involuntary plea for relief. Lacking any painkillers, he stroked the stone in his pocket. The tactile sensation seemed to dull the throbbing of his damaged finger.

From grid they transitioned to super grid, an oiled road... and finally... hardtop.

After a full twelve hours, Ken neared Churchill. Moe no longer sat upright. Rather, he slumped against the door, apparently dozing, his face frozen in a taut grimace. Creases of fatigue lined his cheeks. In the past few hours, he had aged a decade.

"Almost there, Moe."

At the outskirts of town, a large blue sign emblazoned with a white "H" and an arrow pointed him toward the hospital. The building was alarmingly small, serving a community of only a few thousand people during peak season.

Yet, it existed.

"Benefits of a government-run medical program," Ken rued aloud, knowing this profitless medical enterprise would never be operating in Michigan.

The emergency entrance was easy to find. Pulling alongside into a drop-off zone, Ken parked adjacent to its double sliding doors. Moe labored, putting himself together, fumbling with his good hand to zip his jacket. He couldn't get it more than halfway up his torso.

Rushing around the truck, Ken opened the passenger door and helped Moe out of the truck supporting his rubbery legs so he could walk. In the waiting room were three people, an elderly man coughing coarsely and a young mother holding her infant. The former looked doomed while the latter was consumed with worry.

"Excuse me," Ken said to the receptionist nurse, "my friend here has a nearly severed finger."

"Oh," she gasped, surprised, "let me get someone."

Fifteen minutes later, admitted to triage, Moe was at long last receiving professional care. With no small amount of agony, the makeshift bandages were stripped away revealing the crushed black and purple fingertip with the ghastly yellow carpal poking through.

Sedation was administered as a portable x-ray cart imaged the skeletal damage. Curiosity spread through the small hospital and every nurse on duty wandered by to view the damage, but it did not bother Moe, the drugs were having their blessed effect. A half hour later, he was fully prepped for surgical reattachment.

The surgery required six hours of cleaning, slicing away shredded tissue, setting bones and inserting titanium pins before reattaching the finger and reshaping the compressed digit into its former semblance. Finishing the procedures, the tired surgeon analyzed his handiwork. Having done his best, he still frowned. The chances for complete success were less than half, but he'd seen much worse. He managed mangled limbs sustained in the shipyard and compound fractures from airlifted miners.

Over time, he'd honed the expertise to put them back together.

The bow hunter had an excellent chance of having a fully functioning hand again.

Chapter 10

Intelligence

Six dilated hours after arriving at his new job, Robb had painstakingly read, digested, sorted and scribed through all the starting day paperwork, perfunctorily returning them to the HR representative. The documents ranged from the simple, such as contact information, to the more complex, his benefits declarations, but the bulk were hard core legal treatises, his proof of legal right to work, non-disclosure agreements and, most troubling, assignation of rights of liability and invention.

It was somewhat shocking to realize that, other than a paycheck, there would be no revenue sharing for his creative contributions.

Human resourcing, my ass, it's exploiting my mind, Robb thought darkly. Yet, in spite of the limited remunerative context, he was glad for a change of pace. This work might be intellectually stimulating in a down-to-earth way, not restricted to a strict scientific rationale and rigor.

The HR representative, expressing an overtly bubbling veneer of charm and manners, showed him to his office. It was little more than a box-sized cubicle in a maze of half-walled metal partitions, each cluster separated by well trod, all-weather carpeting. Voices babbled over the arrayed austerity, constant and unintelligible.

Occasionally, discrete bursts broke through the din, snippets of conversation resolving clearly in his ears. Heard out of context, they captured inane snapshots of the daily mundane.

"...yeah, sure lunch at 11:45, meet you in the foyer..."

"...not one, but *two* flat tires..."

"...my mother-in-law is in town, we're putting her up in the spare bedroom. I had to get out, I needed a drink..."

Settling into his new weekday digs, Robb closely examined his six-by-six cube. On the desktop, a name brand laptop nestled into a docking station that cabled, wonderfully, to a flat screen LCD monitor and not a squealing Cathode Ray tube that eventually made your temples throb. Arranged neatly in front of the display sat a keyboard and mouse pad, primed and positioned for movement.

Above the computer were a pair of gray metal shelves and below on each side, similarly manufactured file cabinets. Opening the top drawer, he found an assortment of pens, pencils, permanent markers, paper clips, sticky notes, highlighters and file labels.

No mistaking what his daily tasks would require.

Those essentials portrayed the positive aspects. On the flip side, there was no window, no outdoor view, no hint of sunshine. Instead, an air conditioner vented overhead, positioned exactly at his chair, a continuous blasting of frigid, humid air. Although the DC summer was hot and muggy, once inside his office, he would need a sweater.

Frankly summarized, it was ponderously boring. The stale air made him hungry, the fluorescent lighting fatigued his eyes, and his co-workers appeared off beat or aloof. Underscoring his impressions, his churning stomach, a product of jangled first day nerves, simmered into a growling assailant. He would eat as soon as he could escape unnoticed.

The clock ticked slowly.

Every few minutes someone would walk by, cast a sideways glance, and scurry away. Weirdly, a few smiled to themselves, smugly enjoying a private joke that revolved around him but didn't include his assent.

Robb liked to think they were missing an important nutritional supplement or an essential social vitamin.

Infrequently, gregarious passersby stopped and introduced themselves, swapping a few lighthearted tidbits of advice before taking their leave. After ninety minutes of meeting colleagues, Robb's head was swimming, floundering in the distillation of first impressions and pairing names with new faces.

It was like treading water. Indexing the more congenial, the few that seemed normal, he resolved to quickly make contact again, but the anti-social garnered no sympathy. A bunch of oddballs and nutcases he didn't need to know he decided, not sure if he was being an intellectual snob or if the think-tank environment inherently fabricated its own dysfunctional culture.

If so, he would rebel, refusing to return to grad school having assimilated a plethora of anti-social quirks.

Before long, he felt exhausted, a mental aggravation of the self-imposed confinement borne of his indecision. He desired to leave and go home, but felt compelled to wait and meet his new boss.

Another thirty minutes dragged by.

By now Robb had mapped each coffee stain on the carpet and was mischievously planning to make a few stains of his own. He would have already succeeded except that he didn't know where the break room was located.

This is ridiculous, he thought. *I'm getting out of here.*

Pushing back on his chair, Robb stood to leave.

"Welcome to the CIA," a voice boomed, volume and sensationalism overshadowed the tardy appearance.

"Huh?" Robb answered, surprised, "I thought this was DARPA."

"A simple misdirection," came a smiling response.

"Misdirection?" Robb laughed, "it sounds like a play action fake."

"Well said," the man chuckled, "sometimes we don't wish to advertise when we're recruiting."

Robb smiled, but he was still wary.

"Rolfe Ottley," his boss extended his hand.

"Pleased to meet you, sir," Robb shook it firmly, masking the welling concern that his advisor wouldn't approve of his employment, but without this sleight of hand, neither would his mentor be receiving her funding.

His brow creased with concern. Looking his new boss directly in the eye, Robb began, "Paulina's application...?"

"...was approved. She gets her grant. A big one. Welcome aboard."

Leaning her head into his room, a nurse, clad in the traditional white frock of her profession, intoned blandly.

"There is a phone call for you." Her face was blank, unreadable.

"Is it my wife?" Moe groaned, reticent to explain why he was a patient in a foreign hospital. Neither was he motivated to be forthcoming and admit that his injury resulted from a cascading series of human errors.

His own errors.

"When the phone rings, just pick up the handle and press the blinking light," the nurse suggested with false cheerfulness, dutifully disappearing outside the door. Desiring to ignore the call, Moe watched the contraption's synchronized lighting and ringing routine. Each burst chided that he couldn't ignore the caller forever. Whoever had tracked him down to this hospital would call back repeatedly until they spoke.

He might as well be done with it.

Besides, he was bored out of his mind, languishing in a stark room a thousand miles from familiarity. He'd grown tired of the monotonous view outside his window, a featureless expanse of bleak winter giving way to spring. Deciding he would welcome a call from his family, he reached for the cradle. He would fend off their *blustrations* and he would finish the hunt before returning home.

Deliberately grasping the handle with his injured hand, testing his coordination, Moe answered the call.

Obtusely, his bandaged finger pointed into the air, a proclamation of his attitude.

"Moe here," he spoke into the receiver.

"Moe O'Connor?" An unfamiliar, masculine voice queried. "This is Lieutenant Trakalo, RCMP. I understand you've recently had a hunting accident."

"Yes," Moe responded carefully. *Now what the hell does a cop want with me? I wasn't poaching.*

"I was wondering if I might ask you a few questions?"

"What are you wanting to talk about?" Moe hesitated, wondering if he needed a lawyer, immediately cognizant of his ignorance of Canadian law. He was afraid to speak freely and more afraid to hide anything.

Reading his mind, Trakalo responded. "You can retain a lawyer if you wish, but this isn't a criminal investigation. It's a routine fact-finding conversation. Since you were injured in my jurisdiction, I need to file a report with Ottawa."

"I think I understand," Moe answered. "But, frankly, I'm a little confused here. I don't know Canadian customs and laws."

"No," Trakalo agreed. "I wouldn't expect you would. If you prefer, I can call back later."

"No, no, this is a good time."

With Moe's acquiescence on record, the cop continued, friendly in tone, but professional.

"I've checked up on a few details of your visit. I know you are holding a legal game permit and that you were injured in an accident by a bow, which incidentally, you are licensed for carrying, and that you were hunting with a companion named Ken, also from your home state, Michigan."

Holy shit, Moe thought. *How the hell could he know all that?* During his morning visit, Ken hadn't mentioned having any official conversations.

"The border crossing records give me all the details I need to know," Trakalo clairvoyantly answered.

"The worldwide *Big Brother* network," Moe sighed.

"Yes, indeed."

"The injury was pretty much my own doing," Moe admitted without provocation. "I had a misfire, and rather than take two days to get my bow properly repaired, I tried to restring it in the field on my own. I should have known better, but once I saw the loose string hanging there, I figured the all the tension had been relieved..."

"Slow down, please," Trakalo politely interjected. "I haven't got the gist, yet. In fact, I haven't got much of a picture at all."

"Sorry," Moe responded, equally polite.

Canadians could be infuriatingly formal. Not combating against a pushy, in-your-face investigator was unnerving him, rapidly loosening his tongue. Maybe there was some skill in the interrogator's style, after all.

"You're saying a string came off your bow?" Trakalo prodded.

"I drew the bow..." Moe began the story, coherently and chronologically organizing his thoughts. On the other end of the line, Trakalo recorded and took notes. The recorder was necessary as he couldn't transcribe quickly enough. Subtleties in spoken conversation were impossible to scribe in real time.

Finishing his monologue, Moe concluded by favorably mentioning his current stay in the hospital. This formality was going much easier than expected. He'd been able to control the conversation, not having been interrupted over a single detail, carefully avoiding the mention of *his* precious mineral find. After all, it had nothing to do with his accident, the hunting trip or his convalescence.

He was pleased with his off-the-cuff rendition.

Trakalo, however, had a different objective. He was grasping for evidence relating to his find at Evan's cabin. His sole reason for calling was knowing that Moe might have been hunting near the fur trapper's territory.

Not knowing Moe's occupation, he wasn't considering asking questions about mineralogy.

"A few last questions," he began, and Moe began relaxing. Perhaps there was no guile in the cop's approach.

"We've had a series of criminal activities in the area you are hunting," Trakalo explained vaguely. "I'm wondering if you found any unusual objects or artifacts, perhaps evidence of recent human traffic. The area is not normally well-traveled."

"Can't say I saw anything," Moe answered, truthfully. "No camps, no fire pits, hell, we didn't even see a cabin until we left the ravine."

"Which ravine?"

Moe gave a description, but Trakalo couldn't seem to place it.

"You have GPS coordinates?" he asked.

In typical pocket-pencil fashion, Moe rattled them off the top of his head.

Writing them down, Trakalo questioned, "How can you be so sure?"

"I read them at least a hundred times setting up a buck ambush," Moe answered. "I wasn't moving around very much."

"Uh-huh," Trakalo doubted.

"Look, I'm an engineer," Moe quipped. "I can remember numbers, not people's names."

"Just a minute while I look these up," Trakalo spoke tersely.

Shit! Regretting his brevity, Moe nonetheless remained polite, translating the epithet as a simple, "Sure," to the cop. It was another useful engineering skill he'd picked up during endless *blame-storming* meetings with executive managers.

The phone clicked, connecting him with elevator music, but leaving him *live* on the voice recorder.

Staring disgustedly out the window at the springtime lowlands, Moe chided himself for having provided too much information. Now he really wanted to get off the phone, get out of the hospital, finish his hunt and get back to the good, old *US of A*.

Not that he didn't like Canada, he was starting to feel like he was floundering in foreign customs and protocol that were just unusual enough to confuse him. The subtle differences grated on his already ragged nerves.

"You were in a ravine?" Trakalo's voice returned, a measure of urgency and tension in his question. "Where? Describe it."

Picturing the location, Moe gave a thorough description, failing only to mention the mineral stones.

"Did you get down to a fork?"

"Yes."

"Was there a large, exposed gravel bed next to a major river?" Trakalo persisted.

"Yes, yes," Moe responded, trying to speed up this conversation, "it went on for at least a mile, maybe more. It looked like an exposed riverbed, like it had been underwater until some recent time. But there was no game there, so I didn't get much of a chance to walk over it."

"You're an engineer, right?" Trakalo questioned.

"Yeah," Moe replied guardedly.

"What did the gravel bed look like to you?"

"I don't understand your question," Moe bluffed.

"Was there anything unusual in the gravel?"

"Look, I'm not a civil engineer or a geologist..." Moe blustered.

"I know that," Trakalo curtly cut him off, "what's your field?"

"Chemical engineer."

"Oil and gas?"

"No, materials."

"Such as?"

"Taggant powders," Moe replied, feeling the floor falling from beneath his feet.

"They're made from uncommon minerals, right?"

"Yeah, a group of elements known as Rare Earth's and Lanthanides," Moe sighed.

"And they're used as coloring agents," Trakalo continued.

"Historically, yes," Moe monotoned, "but we use them for their light-emitting qualities."

"Why?"

"We make powders for anti-counterfeiting devices, used in cigarettes, DVDs, software and more," Moe explained.

"Is that all?"

"That's all we do."

"Let me rephrase," Trakalo pushed, "What else can be done with these minerals?"

"Some people are trying to make optically-manipulated electronic devices, too."

"Such as?"

"IR amplifiers."

"Which are what?"

"Signal boosters for infrared communication frequencies, the one used in fiber optics. The signal travels well through glass fiber, but are too weak to send through the air over any long distances. Your computer probably has one, and few people know it or use it. It's a bit of a dud."

"Can these rare earths change that?"

"It's possible."

"And you work with these substances every day?"

"Of course," Moe answered.

"Then you wouldn't have to be a geologist to know when you've found them, Moe."

"No you wouldn't, I see your point," Moe conceded. "Look, I've not told anyone, not even my hunting partner, about them. I've been debating what to do next."

Trakalo ignored his introspection, "Describe what you saw."

Pulling the cherished rock from his pocket, Moe detailed the pink-veined stone. Finishing the description, he emphasized again his quandary between assisting his company or himself, and the uncertainty of knowing how to proceed in his neighboring country.

This time, the cop followed up on his dilemma.

"I imagine you wouldn't know," Trakalo agreed. "But I could recommend a few places to start. When do you get out of the hospital?"

"Probably later today," Moe answered. "I'll either be released or I'm walking out."

"Getting cabin fever, eh?" Trakalo chuckled.

"Yeah, pretty bad. This hunt was a special one. I'd wanted to try something like this since I was a kid. To lose it by my own stupidity is grinding my nerves."

"You going back?"

"As soon as I can leave."

"Good luck, Moe," Trakalo answered.

"Thanks."

"Your information has been very helpful." Trakalo paused a moment. "Since the minerals you saw may be critical in this investigation, I'm wondering if I can keep you on my list as an expert reference."

"You mean, possibly go to court...?" Moe inquired, dubiously.

"No, not at all," the RCMP officer assured, "I might need some help interpreting information I pull off the web or get from our usual science experts."

"I'll do my best," Moe agreed.

"Thanks, again. I'm sure you will."

"What are we working for, Adam?" Robb ranted, on the phone with his close friend from his lab. "Today, I signed contracts that assign all my inventions to the company. Back at school, everything we create, the institution owns. Even what you and I publish becomes the printed intellectual property of the publisher."

"Next thing you know," Adam laughed, "some corporate strategist will bury what we innovate because some company someplace else will reverse engineer it and beat us on labor and material cost."

"I am being serious," Robb informed.

"So was I," Adam returned. "Why do you think I came back so soon from my internship last semester?"

"No kidding."

"Yeah, it was kind of embarrassing, I didn't tell anyone."

"Sorry to hear about that."

"Look, be truthful," Adam queried. "Is this about money?"

"Partly," Robb answered truthfully, "but so much more. I cannot in good conscience continue to be a scientist when I have no ownership over what I discover."

"The job was an eye-opener for me," Adam replied. "Everything I worked on was poised to be ported overseas in eighteen months. I was expected to support the technology transfer, meaning I would spend two years overseas working long hours, with no appreciation and little contact with my family."

"I thought we were creating new products and jobs," Robb mused.

"Not really," Adam rejoined, "we're the frontline in *trickle-out* economics. You know, when I joined the company, they hired a foreign national, using my citizenship as proof to the government that they were not discriminating against hiring Americans."

"Are you sure?" Robb doubted.

"I know," Adam assured, "he told me as he made his application. When I left, he took over my project. He's back overseas, being paid as an expatriate, living in his hometown. As long as we continue to grant so many specialty visas, we're *in-shoring* our occupations to becoming low priced, commodity careers."

"And you know what," Adam continued grousing, "This morning, I had my car repaired. I could have fixed it myself, but I didn't have the time. I paid *one twenty* per hour for labor, plus a two hundred percent mark-up on parts, plus environmental disposal fees, plus who knows what else was buried as fees and overstated surcharges."

"The shop rate alone is a quarter of a mil per year. We don't make that in our profession. Yet, it takes ten years of study to qualify for it, and another ten years to master it."

"You want to be a mechanic, then?" Robb teased.

"Probably not," Adam lamented, "but, I used to think our government's policy was strategic, keeping our technology cutting edge. Now, I see it as *good for the country* doubletalk. Employers own us, and our creativity, while monitoring our habits, our finances, even our medical commitments. Nowadays, you can be fired and sued for comments made on social networks. We've been goaded into silence and submission."

"I didn't know you felt this way," Robb commiserated.

"I can't say much about it. I can't afford to be political. I have a family to feed. When I was at the job, we worked like rats, and I was going into debt—and so were my co-workers. By laboring long hours to pay bills for essentials, they were exhausted and distracted, unable and afraid to resist."

Adam laughed, but it was a harsh, bitter sound.

"275,000 H1Bs in 2008 alone, the year the economy crashed, under the guise that they're all aces. What a crock! Most are talented, but certainly not *paradigm shifters*. Without the flood, corporate America loses its supply side control over the profession. Hah, I could pinpoint the gifted in a few minutes. It would be barely a thousand people per year. We're being played, Robb."

Two months after his abduction, plus or minus a fortnight, Yakov was on the downhill side of mending. His body had healed, his mind was recovering and his resolve had returned with fire. His only drawback was formulating an ironclad escape plan. At present, he'd barely construed a rudimentary outline, but that wasn't really a failure.

As his circumstances continued to be bound by significant hindrances, the necessity lacked urgency until he could see more clearly into the future. He could let his fire smolder as red hot coals.

Locked within a closet-sized cell, behind an imposing metal frame door, he could not escape. Not that there was any place to go, aboard a submerged naval vessel, the hurdle to freedom was insurmountable.

Assuaging his impatience and fear, he constantly reminded himself that there was no place to run, but neither would they harm him during transit.

Presumably, once moored, he'd be within a hundred miles of civilization. Certainly, their destination was Hudson Bay, their timing scheduled in concert with the spring ice breakup which was permitting a return to the Canadian interior.

His opportunity would come onshore.

He possessed one strategic advantage, firsthand knowledge of the geography. Having trod the virgin terrain twice more than his adversaries, he alone knew that the ore body was not accessible by land craft. An interval would arise when an exploration party would need to abandon the vehicles and proceed on foot.

When that happened, there would be some measure of confusion and disorientation. With luck, it would provide a portal to bolt free. If he could muster a short head start, he would simply disappear and survive on the bounty of the upcoming summer months.

Before winter settled in, he would need a more fortuitous habitat. He would deal with that reality in time. How he would get back to Russia was a separate troubling matter. Unless he could destroy his assailants, Moscow would never be a safe haven.

Remarkably, his forthright prognosis was an abrupt change from the depravity of the early hours of his incarceration. His first days aboard the submarine, an indeterminate time period, were spent in solitary within a secure, soundproof room. Without freedom, without a clock, and lacking vigor, he brooded, angrily and with too much grief. In no small part, his mental condition reflected the austerity of his surroundings.

Devoid of normal chronological telltales, such as sunrise and sunset, he tracked time by shift changes, his own biorhythms and the less reliable sustenance schedule. He soon realized he wasn't being fed at regular intervals.

It might have been oversight, but more likely a simple plan to keep him off kilter.

Compounding his confusion, he remembered little of the period between the card game and his on board incarceration. He recalled a period of violence, pain, and loss, followed by a nightmarish sequence of awakenings, each dominated by intense physical and mental discomfort.

During his first semi-lucid days, he had slept more than he was awake while his body began healing from the second round of wounds inflicted upon it. He estimated his semi-comatose state as lasting a week, maybe two, but as he recovered, the need for sleep subsided, and matters affecting his mind and pride rose to the forefront of his daily thinking pareto. These mental ailments festered mercilessly, a rancid froth of anguish fomenting from his heart.

Once his body no longer required extra rest, his imprisonment was most cruel. Yakov was not accustomed to extended periods of inactivity. He could not suppress his agitations with constructive behaviors. Yet, it was not the adventure void that was sapping his spirit, it was his personal tragedy.

Having lost his best friend, his liberty and his youthful swagger, he journeyed the depravity of mortality, his mind dominated by negative emotions and fears.

Fear of his captors. That waned quickly as he understood they wouldn't terminate him before achieving the mineral site. They needed his expertise. Reinforcing his conclusion, they frequently left him alone rather than harassing him with questions, but his anxiety could not be permanently put asunder. His life was forfeit once the job was completed.

Denial. An inability to accept that he was irrevocably captive...that Sergei was dead...and that his own reckless naiveté was at fault. When his rejection of reality waned, grains of suspicion coalesced into a cogent truth, and he overcompensated by accepting his blame and viciously self-flagellating his shortsightedness.

Flight response. Like a cornered rat, he sought to escape, at first furtively bargaining for freedom with his keepers, but his negotiations were harshly rebuffed, blunting his robust demeanor and splintering his psyche.

Worse, the emotional wounding highlighted the immutable: To his captors, he was loathsome. He could not talk, cajole, coerce or bribe his way out.

Next began a slow descent into hopelessness. An abyss had opened. Once exposed, his frustrations had been supplanted by grief, absorbing the loss of his lifelong friend. Rapidly, grief gave way to anger, rage and inviolate, venomous hatred. In part, it was self-loathing for his own mistakes, but he was fermenting a psychosis for revenge too. In his dark soul, he knew he was drifting towards insanity, but he was sliding willingly, not caring to arrest the cancerous vitriol consuming him, afraid that stemming its upwelling was giving up.

He dreamed of escaping his cell, surreptitiously moving about the craft, surprising his enemy and tearing their horrid bodies into tattered shreds. He would roast their flesh to the gods of revenge on the altar of his life, but after a time, the hatred burned a hole in his soul, leaving him wanting, unsatisfied, guilt-ridden and depressed.

He'd never been suicidal before, except, as he facetiously boasted, under his own terms as a self-confessed adrenaline junkie. Not familiar with depression, he resisted its urges, and fortunately, this emotional tide was short-lived.

A phrase he'd heard from his grandfather turned the battle for his heart. "Yakov, my boy, the best revenge is outliving one's enemy." Outliving his captors would, at a minimum, require health and strength. Needing a fitness level that his injuries had eroded, he began working out. Wisely unwilling to broadcast his efforts, he targeted the periods when he was left alone, quietly performing routines that wouldn't attract attention.

Isometrics for power and strength pitted Yakov against the rigid walls of his steel box—stasis versus sinew.

He invented prolonged isometric contortions, seeking to expand his anaerobic potential, needing the capability of exertion through prolonged muscle fatigue.

For explosive power, plyometric movements, once taught to him by Sergei. Springing against the metal floor, over and over, he stubbornly tempered his muscles with bursts of inertia, restoring quickness and agility. *Great hockey training,* he heard Sergei taunting boisterously, mocking his first feeble efforts, but the technique worked. Yakov was amazed at the rewards; muscle growth, better balance and a feeling of power.

Even in death, Sergei was his partner.

Performing countless repetitions of traditional push-ups and sit-ups, he rebuilt his shoulder and thickened the core fibers inside his torso, but he could not effectively target an aerobic regimen. Trotting in place was mindless, a loathed task more about honing his determination than his endurance. In a footrace, he might not outrun his captors, but a persevering spirit might tilt the balance when his body wished to quit.

Yet, the cards weren't all stacked against him. His adversaries were also on a submarine and not capable of preparing for a triathlon. Recalling his first voyage, Yakov knew there were treadmills on board for the runners, but artificial spin trails are a destitute substitute for the real thing. Perhaps the odds of matching physical prowess weren't leveraged so heavily against him.

As a child, Yakov had studied karate, but he remembered little except rudimentary power movements and flexibility routines. Instead, borrowing the concept of a *kata*, he improvised a system of rhythmic movements that strengthened his muscles, focused his mind, sharpened his coordination and fine tuned his balance. The graceful routines had a surprising, secondary effect; self-imposed discipline and mental relief helped to heal his mind.

Lastly, he stretched, returning his body to the supple condition that he formerly possessed, one that served him well while prospecting the harshest of terrain. Like the kata, the mere act of flexing and breathing was calming. It took weeks of sustained and determined effort to integrate the improvements, but it was better than rotting in place.

The beneficial effect of exercise on his psyche made perfect sense. The less time spent hating, the more he immersed in living, for the exercise bloomed anew his sanity and natural spirit.

Riding the crest of his healing soul was a burgeoning confidence that he would prevail. He would mete out justice, but not at the expense of his future. He could not forget the past, never would he become its victim. It was a new mental maturity.

"So what is success on this job?" Robb slipped in annoyed, desiring to curtail the meeting before the obscenely late hours advanced. Outside his boss's skyline office, the cityscape silhouetted a setting sun, crisply edged block shadows in front of a pastel horizon.

"Not missing the obvious." His superior responded, a bland reply to an obsequious question.

Since being blocked in his bolt for freedom, Robb had spent a succession of super-charged hours with his boss, establishing position and gathering details of his internship. He was, of course, being oriented to his lowly perch in the office power structure.

In spite of the surprise of *where* he was working, there were no shenanigans regarding *what* he'd be doing.

As touted in Paulina's lab, he was *the* Technology Analyst. No longer a burgeoning researcher in a lab developing new science, he was now dubbed a *subject matter* expert who examined others' work, deduced immediate applications and inferred the long-range potential of their discoveries.

Pragmatically, it meant that the next few months would be spent in his cubicle sifting terabytes of data, algorithmically sieving binary tidbits from the electronic screen. With luck, and sometimes good sense, he'd isolate indications of high tech threats against his country, alert his superiors, and, having received a *go-ahead*, delve further into the root causes and effects.

"...with your background in applied science, your practical skills, and your analytical abilities," Ottley had blathered, "we expect you to provide expert opinions, identify potential threats, and suggest, from the technical side, how to deal with them."

"What kind of threats?" he had asked.

"Specifically, we want data analysis covering several genres; chemical, biological, electronics and more."

Concern creased Robb's brow. *How the hell do I do that?*

The boss noticed his growing reticence and moved quickly in response.

"It's not blind digging on your own. We have a team of data analysts working 24/7, paring out the spurious stuff, flagging the interesting. Most of your source documents will be handed to you by librarians or be electronically available at your fingertips." He paused, giving Robb a chance to respond.

"Just how open-ended are these assignments?" Robb queried.

"Good question. Each project has written objectives, but do not become bound to answering the stated questions only. Feel free to extrapolate. Of course, there may be several investigations on your docket at any time."

"You will need to multitask without losing focus, weaving several threads together independently without overlooking unimportant details on individual tasks. I don't suppose you'll have much difficulty on that score. I've read, well, have had your work explained to me. It's uncommonly clear and thorough."

"Thank you, sir, but I'm still not clear on specifics."

"Okay, I've been purposefully vague. Here's a typical example. Suppose someone is creating advanced materials capable of significantly improving present armaments or, even more alarming, inventing novel, sophisticated weaponry. It's important we know and have time to plan contingencies."

Robb cocked an ear, an unspoken question that Ottley jumped on.

"We can respond in several ways; stopping them, getting there first, buying them out, or worst case, covering our ass and preparing for the deployment."

Robb's face steeled in seriousness.

"Another scenario might entail uncovering evidence of foreign nationals incorporating our technology into their products. As you might guess, we're constantly alerted to accusations of industrial espionage."

This will be interesting, thought Robb.

"You'll consider everything and suspect everyone," Ottley continued, "you'll map the assemblage of knowledge, skill and matériel from both friendly and unfriendly entities; whether they be sovereign nations, corporations or splinter groups. If it catches our analysts' collective attention, we dig deeper. I've brought you in to formulate expert opinions when our security or economic integrity is being undermined."

"The data I'm analyzing...where does it come from?" Robb asked, ignoring the hyperbole.

"Published dossiers and reports, some you're familiar with, like scientific journals and conference proceedings. In-house data is gathered routinely by existing US agencies, like national security or customs. This intel is helpful in detailing movements of people of interest; what they are carrying; where they say they're going. Other knowledge you can dig up yourself, like recent IP filings, mining and minerals reports, business mergers, attempted or successful acquisitions or publishing of business contracts."

"Regular reports?"

"Yes, and along that vein," Ottley continued, "don't underestimate the mass media. They report more than they know. Sometimes it's like a puzzle, fitting commonality into disconnected pieces, but once the picture is assembled the evidence is immutable, having been self-disclosed."

Robb remained dubious.

"Okay, another example," Ottley grinned, pleased to impress the neophyte. "Seems that tantalum is a desired commodity in the electronics industry, specifically, it's used in making popular gaming equipment. No big deal, but a large fraction of the world's supply of tantalum comes from a country that reputedly uses child labor in its mines."

"Sierra Leone?"

"Of course. Now, no reputable corporation would admit to purchasing resources furnished by such a disagreeable practice, but yet, the fact is one large company used more tantalum than could be accounted for when combining the output from the other mines. A couple of mineral reports and the company's own sales volumes sealed the verdict in the court of public opinion."

"Was that a security issue?" Robb wondered.

"No, a leverage one, one that we put to good use to get some intel that helped us solve another, unrelated security issue," Ottley gloated for a moment, clearly enjoying a recollection of personal triumph.

Robb waited until he spoke again.

"The most sensitive data will be eyes-only, inside governmental information, covertly gained of course."

"Spy stuff?"

"Yes, but not a joking matter."

"I wasn't..."

"No, you weren't. But it's imperative to remain aware of the sensitivity and the vulnerability of this information channel."

"I wouldn't divulge anything, sir."

"Be careful what you say, and what you don't say. Be circumspect when strangers approach you in public and begin chatting. Never wear your employee badge in public and always lock your personal effects in the trunk of your car when you leave it unattended. Do not use your personal cell phone in this building, nor may you browse the internet while using our system."

"Yes, sir."

"You'll receive more training on maintaining secrecy during orientation," he said, checking his watch and frowning, "which is scheduled to start tomorrow morning."

Robb took the cue. "When should I report for work tomorrow, then?"

"Let's meet first thing and I'll give you a dossier to review. By jumping in head first, you'll quickly get up to speed on utilizing our resources. It'll be a good experience for you."

He paused, scribbled a note on a desktop calendar, and continued, "Hmm...I'll assign a mentor for the first project."

Looking Robb in the eye, he leveled his voice, "...but after that, you're on your own. We're too short-staffed to hold each other's hands."

"Understood," Robb agreed, ignoring the snub.

"Because it's a summer project, you won't be given any nuclear projects, nor those that are software-related. You won't have time to obtain a full security clearance. Most of your opinions will be handed to senior personnel for further review. Don't have an ego."

Then he softened, becoming complimentary again. "Your expertise is applied physics and specialty materials, understanding applications and potential, hence data mining, weaponry and industrial espionage. Along that vein, your first assignment will be probing whether a domestic venture has had its thin-film solar IP breached."

"Sounds interesting."

"This is not academic, Robb. It is real. If this technology has been stolen and duplicated, the poor, invested suckers are losing a fortune. Not to prejudice your conclusions, but it's usually an inside job."

Robb's eyebrows raised.

"Many of them are. So it's really the fault of companies and its investors for not performing due diligence and completing proper background checks on all their scientists, both native and foreign born."

"Is this for a legal defense?" Robb probed, his insight into his boss' social agenda instantly improved.

"Not at all," Ottley chuckled. "We use the information to influence matters of national security and trade policy, we don't give a rat's ass about the legality, neither does the intelligence we gather factor in providing restitution."

"Sorry, sir," Robb winced, and covered up with a broad smile. Ottley had gone out of his way to express a lack of sympathy for failure.

"See you tomorrow then."

Chapter 11

Whispering Gallery

"What do you think they're doing, Robb?"

"They might be building advanced, lightweight weaponry..."

"Big deal," Ottley scoffed.

"I haven't finished, sir," Robb continued. His boss was such an asshole, fortifying the office gossip that DC connections were worth far more than competence. In fact, it was people like Robb that provided the expertise to make the division look good. Another old adage in play.

"Then please enlighten me, Oh, wise sage," mocked the asshole.

...if only you had a brain..., Robb thought, desperately stifling the insult.

"It looks like ultra-light, ultra-small robotic flying devices, perhaps less than an inch in size."

"So what? We've been making flying insects for years," came the brash response. "Great concept, but they're dumb, short-lived and have an essentially unusable short range. They can't be controlled very well and they're too small to program with a smart, adaptive response."

"That's the catch," Robb broke in, enduring a harsh stare.

"What? Small body neural net programming?" Came the sarcastic response. "We've tried that. The electronics aren't ready, the chips are too heavy to fly."

"No, radio control," Robb defended. "Actually, sir, long range IR control."

"Not possible."

"Why not?" Robb responded.

"Never been done right."

"So far, but that doesn't mean it can't be done. Look, a few years back, the *holy grail* in opto-electronics was an integrated circuit-sized IR amplifier."

"You mean the erbium-doped integrated circuit amplifier myth?"

"It's not a myth, it's achievable, and the basic idea is simple."

"So simple that good minds wasted careers on it, heh?"

Too bad you didn't, then I wouldn't be speaking with you... Swallowing his sarcasm again, Robb continued, "the EDFAs used in fiber optics are inefficient."

"I thought they're state of the art."

"They are, but the physics work best at large scales since erbium absorbs the necessary optical frequency poorly."

His boss glanced sharply.

"Without energy absorption, there is no power for signal gain. And, instead of relying on erbium alone, it's more efficient to add small amounts of a sensitizing material, such as silicon. The sensitizer is a thousand-fold more effective at capturing energy. The trick to enhancing amplification is transferring it to the erbium."

"How? Print tiny wires? That'd be cost effective and reliable wouldn't it?" Ottley scoffed.

"It doesn't need wires, *sir*," Robb began losing patience, then toyed with him. "In fact, the erbium needs to be separated from the silicon."

"That doesn't make any sense. How could they work, then?"

"There's a good working hypothesis for that, although it followed a rousing debate in the scientific community."

"No history lesson here, Robb."

"At the nano-scale, energy can cross barriers normally insurmountable through a process called *tunneling*."

"Tunneling can be predicted by probability arguments and spatial separation. But that mechanism didn't seem to apply here, the length scales were too long to obey the normal stochastic model."

"Get to the point."

"It's simpler, a more classical, description," Robb pontificated. "When a silicon nano-crystal absorbs enough light energy, an electron is ejected, leaving behind a positively charged *hole*. The hole pretty much stays put, but the electron is mobile and bounces all over the crystal. In a quantum dot, the volume is small; the electron spends so much of its time around the outer edge that it acts like a wave flowing along the surface, especially when the dot is coated with a thin layer of insulation—like an oxide shell."

"So, the wave overflows into the erbium, right?" Ottley guessed.

"It's a bit trickier. The electron surface wave is just the basis for another phenomenon called a *Whispering Gallery* effect."

"Which is?" Ottley's patience was wearing thin. It was too much detail for a bureaucrat.

Robb wouldn't let him off.

"It's the way you hear small sounds along the walls of a big room. Have you ever noticed, at a noisy cocktail party, that somebody's quiet talk suddenly materializes in your ears clearly. You don't know where it came from, and nobody else seems to notice, but a whole sentence rings clear as a bell?"

"Yes, we use it all the time to eavesdrop."

"The same idea. You stand near a wall. Sound waves traveling along the wall meet up with waves traveling through the rest of the room, sometimes adding, sometimes canceling...over and over again...creating hotspots and dead spots. You can be far away from the speaker, but you move an inch and the waves add up inside your ear. You hear the conversation almost like you're standing next to him or her."

"What's the connection?" He sounded interested.

In the nano-crystal, the electron wave behaves similarly. It spins round and round the outer surface, trying to rejoin the hole. Sometimes, it goes across. While the electron pops about quickly, the hole tries to follow, but it's very slow. Over time, the hole migrates toward the center, creating a quasi-stable electric field, called a *dipole*. This electron-hole pair is called an *exciton*, but that's not important. What is important is that their positioning stabilizes the charge balance for a moment, but a moment is a lifetime for an amplifier."

"Meaning it has time to do something unusual, like tunnel?"

"Exactly. The field's effect travels through the insulator to the erbium ion. The erbium responds by mirroring the field, setting up an *image* of the first dipole, much like a piece of iron responds when a magnetic field is placed nearby. Now, the erbium is poised to amplify. Just add the carrier signal..."

"How does the energy get across?"

"Once the dipole sets up, the energy is there," Robb repeated, realizing Ottley did not understand. "It's called a Förster process."

"You think they've made the amplifier work?"

"No, they wouldn't need to."

"Why not?"

"The integrated circuit EDFA is only needed to match the wavelength of transmitting signals through fiber optic glass. There's no reason to have to use that wavelength. They could use any other Rare Earth signal to control a miniature device."

"...and operate outside our normal signal jamming ranges?"

"Absolutely. Each Rare Earth amplifies a different frequency. I don't think we're adequately prepared with countermeasures, sir."

"Shit."

"Well, at least it tells us one thing," Robb offered.

"What's that?"

"There are only a few people that can do this stuff. It's a narrower scope to investigate."

"Yes it is," Ottley agreed, picking up his phone. Robb was dismissed.

"Moe here," the engineer spoke into the phone.

"Moe, this is Lieutenant Trakalo. Do you remember me?"

"Of course," Moe answered with impatience, "how are you doing?"

"Good, good. Glad you remember me. How did your hunt go?"

"The best and worst," Moe answered.

"Meaning?"

"Didn't get my buck, but it was still a superb hunt. Great fun."

"Glad you enjoyed your stay with us," Trakalo charmed.

"I sure did," Moe replied, "hope I can make it back some time."

"Drop in if you do, except, try not to make it an emergency."

Moe laughed, "It won't be my intention."

"I'll say. Look, do you have a few minutes?"

"Of course, what would you like to discuss?"

"I need your expertise."

"This won't take long then," Moe quipped.

"Well, depends on your opinion," Trakalo rejoined.

"That will take longer," Moe self-deprecated.

"Okay, good. What do you know about thin film photo-voltaics?"

"Huh?"

"Flexible solar panels?"

"Never worked with them."

"Moe, you're not on trial here."

"Yeah, sorry, conference room reflex reaction here. Hmm, let me think..."

"Take your time."

"I've had some friends work for a solar start-up, I could put you in touch with them, but their jobs didn't last more than a year or two."

"Why's that?" Trakalo ignored the offer of talking to Moe's friends.

"Not sure, they claimed they made great cells, but nothing came of it. I always figured the technology cost too much to mass produce."

"Could a competitor have improved on the idea and been making a cheaper version?"

"Probably not, that kind of breakthrough *tsunamis* the market."

"So, what you're saying is, the field is limited. Typically, only a start-up or a research lab are making thin-film devices."

"Yeah, I guess you could say that."

"Any idea who the players are?"

"Yeah, the big names are obvious. IBM, Kyocera, Sharp—a few others. I would look for well informed corporations who see the potential, understand the payoff, and have enough money to play the risk."

"How about start-ups?"

"Too many to know all of them, but you might want to check the patent database."

"Huh?" It was Trakalo's turn to be surprised.

"Some companies will patent their ideas immediately, especially if one is too easily copied or reverse engineered. You might look at the USPTO to see who has applied for patents recently."

"I thought there was a time lag between application and full public disclosure."

"Correct. The application is held by the patent office for a year before its published, so there's a dark period you might have to contend with," Moe thought for a minute. "Can you subpoena information before it's published?"

"Probably not," Trakalo responded. "That's a political ploy, not a legal one."

"Of course," Moe changed gears. "For an established company, the critical stuff is kept in-house."

"Why?"

"Trade secrets are hard to ferret out, usually involving and implicating the internal staff. On the other hand, a big company, with a thicker wallet, can afford to develop new technologies close to the vest as its immediate survival is not staked solely on the emergence of a single hot product. Since you don't make money long term by exposing your angle to profitability, it's better to avoid being out-innovated or reverse engineered after committing to costly development."

"Could a start-up also move this meticulously?"

"Depends on the need for money. To attract investment, start-ups frequently establish a strong intellectual property portfolio while begging suitors to sign restrictive non-disclosure agreements. There's a lot of risk in exposure. Once backed, a win can be forged in two very different ways. One is to sell the technology to a deep pocket interest, the other is to successfully take a game-breaker to market. The latter involves perfecting a manufacturing process and scaling it to high volume, not a simple task."

"The scaling expertise...?" Trakalo began asking.

"Very good ideas are developed by the R&D folks. Usually, they're concept innovators, not versed in driving their idea from lab to pilot plant to high volume manufacturing. Self-propelled companies have to hire the proper skills or farm out their early production work. Both have risks."

"If a product is made by a unique process, no one has the experience to scale it. If it can be made by commercial *tollers*, it doesn't take a rocket scientist to copy it. If patient money is behind a breakthrough, the company will be harder to find until the product is on the market. Even so, a nut doesn't fall far from a tree, right? I'd look for companies with core competencies similar to what's being developed."

"Anyone else?"

"Any good university lab," Moe thought aloud.

"Will academics make an actual device?"

"Not likely," Moe admitted. "A superb researcher makes his name demonstrating *proof of concept* research, the victory is in getting there first. Once the ball is rolling, the top echelon races on to the next projects. Those who want to convert research to applications usually bust their butts launching incubator projects. Their venture funding efforts are well documented or publicly disclosed. Do you have any VC contacts?"

"I haven't had the bandwidth to speak with venture capitalists," Trakalo admitted.

"Why do you ask?" Moe queried.

"It's part of an investigation," Trakalo cut the question short.

"I'm in no position to cause trouble," Moe reminded, "I'm not even in Canada."

"Indeed," Trakalo replied, pausing momentarily, then decided, "we found a GPS transmitter embedded in a telescopic walking stick, powered by thin-film photo-voltaics wrapped along the shaft."

"No shit," Moe breathed, "that's smart stuff."

"Indeed," Trakalo agreed.

"Then I wouldn't look to industry," Moe guessed, "I'd consider a small operation, a nondescript lab, maybe secretly-, privately- or governmentally-funded."

"You sure?"

"Absolutely. It's a one-off or a prototype. No for-profit company does this stuff, no matter how lucrative the contract is for making a single-ton. Earnings are tied to bulk processing and margin, not *Mom and Pop* piecework."

"Best guess, Moe...Government or private?"

Without hesitating, he answered. "Government involvement, one way or another, even if it's funding a private venture."

"Thanks."

"My pleasure."

"Come back anytime."

"I'm looking forward to it. It's a beautiful place."

"I think so."

"Oh," Moe remembered, "one more thing."

"Yes?"

"If you're looking for an expert on the potential of the mineral find, I think I can suggest one."

"Someone you work with?"

"No, someone I've been reading about in the science journals. His papers have been keeping the scientists in my company scrambling to rip off his ideas to make new products. This guy really has a handle on both the science and the technology."

"Trying to get out of talking to me?"

"No, just trying to help."

"Fair enough. Who is it?"

"A scientist named Davis...R. A. Davis. I think his name is Robb."

Ottley stewed at his desk. Drawbacks were looming. Snatching a defenseless citizen, twice injured in the previous months, would draw significant attention from Russian authorities. It was becoming increasingly difficult to palm their tracks clean. Implementing a kidnapping only underscored his logistical roadblock.

He picked up the phone and dialed.

"Have you secured enough material?" Ottley demanded.

"We're tendering bids," his chief project engineer responded.

"Why not? What's the delay?"

"We've bought enough to arouse Red Star suspicion."

"Change suppliers."

"We've done that. They talk to each other over there, you know. They've cornered the supply."

"So what. Work it out," Ottley's tongue cracked like a whip. "How much do you have?"

"Enough to complete a couple of prototypes, little more."

"That's all? What happened to the rest?"

"We've had complications."

"What kind of complications?"

"Contamination."

"From what?"

"Metal residue."

"How the hell did that get in there?"

"Sheared off during an equipment malfunction."

"Don't have any more," Ottley ordered.

"Then we'll need some purchase requisitions signed," the engineer negotiated. "They'll be on your desk later today." Tiring of the badgering, he fought back, "how's the alternate sourcing coming along?"

"We're two months away, best case scenario."

"Why so long?"

"It's winter."

"Keep me in the loop, sir, the critical path is stalling," the engineer warned belligerently.

"No excuses, stay on schedule."

Chapter 12

Toad Strangler

How can I escape before they kill me? Yakov pondered sullenly.

After months submerged, Yakov stood on solid, open ground. Unfortunately, it wasn't entirely dry. The icy recesses of winter were receding, trickling from shaded strongholds over the saturated earth. Unable to soak in, the plain had become a seasonal bog. Yakov, shackled to his search party, was a mere fifteen kilometers from the ore body, although only he knew the exact location.

With surprising accuracy, his captors had closed the gap from the Hudson Bay landing to the inland proximity. They were now nearing the wretched location where Yakov had survived his violent encounter with the polar bear, but that memory mattered little to the geologist.

Facing his fears was the least of his worries.

Once again, his future was hellbent toward forfeit, requiring no small endeavor of skill or chance to elude the designs stacking up against his life. Correctly, Yakov had surmised that the confirmation of his mineral strike would diminish his value toward zero.

All that would remain was the answer to the macabre, intellectual question. Would they slay him immediately and toss his body onto the tundra? Or would they maintain a modicum of discretion, waiting to re-board the submarine to eject him at sea?

It would be facile, and twice as clean, to discard a lifeless body onto the open water rather than abandon one on the open prairie. Though common sense suggested it should be the latter, either outcome foretold that he would not be alive for a return oceanic voyage. Hoping for any measure of life before boarding the submarine was foolish optimism, but today he was alive, and the silent stalking of death would not take him by surprise.

For a rash moment, he considered attempting an immediate break for freedom. In the early morning hours, the members were distracted by a myriad of activities, finishing breakfast, breaking camp, repairing gear.

It would be a fool's quest. He could not outrun a quad and he was unarmed.

This morning, the sodden ground was deteriorating progressively, already too buttery to hold the distributed weight of the versatile ATVs. A quorum was in progress, the leaders were debating whether the venerable craft should be parked in favor of exploring on foot. Their discussion was all the more vigorous as, on the previous day, there had been several strandings when their iron beasts had bogged to the axles, uselessly sinking on their flat underbellies while squeezing out a slurry of mud until they could be heaved onto firmer ground.

Rescuing the craft had been a constant source of embittered merriment. Teams of men struggled, cursing in aggravation, to extricate their mired lifelines from the suctioning mud. After a trio of arduous recoveries, the entire party of men were filthy and the individual temperaments ranged from disgruntled to foul.

With each subsequent recovery, even the most cheerful lost their good humor, weighted beneath an accumulation of grime on clothing. In a single day, the collective mood had soured. Frustrations mounted and tempers tilted. Perpetually wet and chilled, the men were snarling and surly. The more volatile temperaments were losing their professionalism and lashing out at their brothers.

With daybreak's promise of constant drizzle, the expedition members were visibly displaying their disenchantment.

Though he partook of their physical misery, Yakov did not have the luxury of sharing their emotions. The time was ripening for his escape attempt.

With mounting hope, Yakov kept a watch on the ATVs. Half the fleet was marooned, floating on their iron pans. A faint smirk creased his lips. Over the night, the craft had slowly sunk into the rich gumbo. An engine fired up, and entrenched wheels spun uselessly, flinging a geyser of soggy droplets. There was no traction.

Altering the transportation modes would work to his advantage. Having walked the ground before, he possessed a unique familiarity of the upcoming terrain, of the sheer mud bank valley and the hidden ravines.

The intruders were ignorant of the geographical changes and the difficulties only kilometers ahead.

Misting rain softly graced his cheeks, keeping the biting bugs down in the grass. Overhead, thick, gray clouds billowed, stretching toward the horizon. The albedo was hauntingly similar to that he'd experienced a half year earlier, indicating continued inclement weather. Fortunately, their color was sublime suggesting rain, not an icy, Arctic gale.

The decision was subtle, but imperative, imparting a scurry of motion. They would move on foot, investigating the local area. The data suggested the ore's location was at hand. An aura of tenseness rippled through the camp. Yakov sensed the seeds of distraction in germination.

It was a mixed blessing. Already Yakov could hear the distant roar of the turbulent water cascading over the plateau shelf. If they followed the river, the valley ahead would funnel their search to the exact location. At that juncture, even a dim-eyed geriatric could stumble upon the exposed mineral bed.

Yakov cemented his own decision. He would seize any opportunity to escape, though nothing plausible came to mind. Since landing, he'd been under constant observation. During daytime travel, he shared an ATV with the group's leader and a pair of hard-jawed sentinels.

At night, his tent was guarded by a rotation of indefatigable men not prone to the dereliction of sleeping. Even his forays to relieve himself lacked privacy.

Even if he could escape notice for a few moments, he could not hide. The open, boggy plain was devoid of cover for several kilometers in each direction. He plotted feverishly, peering into the distant mist.

Ach, yes! The drizzle was undermining visibility and the overhead skies forecast worsening conditions. In the confusion of a major rainstorm, he might be able to quickly disappear behind a wall of water.

Yakov felt the first flutter of hope.

Could he hide nearby? There was cover beneath the silvery skins of the numerous glacial potholes, but their water was too chilly to drink. No human could survive more than a few numbing minutes beneath their placid surfaces. Instead, he would have to run, an exercise of endurance. He knew his conditioning was lacking. That wasn't the only sobering aspect. Every step imprinted the ground, depositing a vector of footfalls easy to follow.

Farther ahead lay the river valley, where he recalled a shroud of small bush cover beneath a tree-carpeted ravine, but his mind revolted against that play. Leading the party toward the ore would advance his doomsday timepiece. His captors would get there eventually. For now, he would remain vigilant, taking advantage of present opportunities but not adding to his risks. Surely, one would arise today.

Perhaps the Canadian authorities will find me, he wished, valuing incarceration and deportation above an appointment on death row, but if they were located by DEW Line surveillance and subsequently intercepted, it was doubtful he would survive more than the first few seconds of armed conflict. To protect themselves, his captors would personally see through his execution.

In truth, he held little hope for an intervention by the law. In the previous autumn, he and Sergei had traveled for days without seeing another human. Of course, they had worked for their success, avoiding satellite detection by taking cover within the seasonal migration and rut.

Unfortunately this spring, overcast skies were blinding the satellites. Disgusted, Yakov realized he hadn't seen the sun for more than a few hours since disembarking. He was at the crossroads. His tensions mounted and his mind spun out of control. It was do or die, or...stay and die. He was scared, but detested his choices of action over these last few months. He couldn't forget the moments preceding Sergei's death and all the tidbit warnings he'd overlooked from the recruiter's threat through to the unsettling card game.

He should have foreseen the contract signed in blood was only a mandate of grief. At least then Sergei would be alive. It was impossible to grieve at present, he knew, anxiety commingled with grief would not help him dig out from the present circumstance.

Occasionally, he forged limited truces with himself. Other times, he went through dark moments where he blamed himself, his recklessness and an unforgivable lack of foresight. His conflicts were palpable, an obvious barometer that he'd been deeply wounded and now doubted himself.

Clear your mind, he urged. Steeling his emotions, he began formulating the practical, assessing needs, options and priorities.

First, he needed thirty minutes of freedom to have a chance to escape, a scant half hour on his own to create a margin between him and his captors. With the scarcity of tree cover on the pressed landscape, it would take that much time, flat out running, just to get out of sight, but with that interval, he might completely elude a pursuit. He would force his captors to re-commit to their key goal and choose between an inconsequential man and the coveted minerals.

Second, while the persistent rain was cutting visibility, the soft ground was deforming easily. His footprints would leave an easy trail to follow. To prevent making tracks, he would probably have to go through a stretch of water risking severe chill. Hypothermia was a better alternative to stone cold dead.

Last, he recalled the increasingly familiar features in the upcoming terrain. They were camped in a lowland flat, situated beneath a high ground prairie and above soupy muskeg sloughs. Towering into the foreground mist, a glacial esker dominated his view.

It was the same hill from which he'd first seen the polar bear. A chill shivered up his spine, a eulogy of his past life.

Yakov finished his breakfast and walked about, sharpening his mind, every step observed by the fanatical eye of his guard. The greening ground was soft and uneven, rounded islands of slick moss on which his feet easily slipped down and sunk into peat-bottomed puddles. A half meter above the permafrost, the earth was cold. The solid ice barrier stopped all moisture from percolating through and sapped what little heat the spring was offering.

In the wetlands below, overflowing glacial ponds were receiving summer residents in pairs. Colorfully garbed ducks, geese, coots, loons and mudhens landed gracefully, each staking a watery claim. New aerial splashdowns were not welcome, vigorously challenged by earlier arrivals, earnestly cackling and clamoring, chasing perceived rivals from *their* chosen nursery.

A mist descended again, dissipating his long range vision. Nearby, a chorus of birds shrieked in alarm, a prelude to a ponderous fluttering of integrated wing beats as the multitude startled into flight. Their haunting complaints gave Yakov a pause.

An idea emerged.

I will die either way, he considered, *better by my own hand than theirs.*

Moving beyond the perimeter of camp, he stopped to relieve himself, buying a few seconds of privacy. Surreptitiously, he bit himself on his forearm, drawing blood. Using his last piece of breakfast jerky, he smeared some blood on the dried sinew and discreetly dropped it out of sight on the ground behind a tuft of moss. Turning to leave, he stepped on the offal, twisting it sideways, trying to crack it open and exude its fragrance.

He would leave a scent trail. At midday, he would discard a few scraps of food. With luck, help might be lured in. Exposing himself was unavoidable, but in the mayhem of an animal attack...he might find freedom. If a trapped fox could bite a leg off to free itself, he would also be self-sacrificing. If necessary—a limb for life—he could play the fox.

Nine hours later, they ascended the land drop and descended into the valley floor. Raging with melt water, the river flowed over its shallow banks. Yakov smiled, the exposed gravel basins of his last visit were underwater, their coveted stones submerged. It would not be so obvious that his journal's false recordings had led them to this juncture, several kilometers from the convergent conduits where the true deposit lay.

By order, Yakov accompanied the leaders. Once at the bottom, he was required to stay put, idly observing their prospecting from a rocky perch. On either side, he was flanked by a pair of cold and miserable guards.

Twenty minutes into scouting, a sharp-eyed searcher found the first colored rock lying along the riverbank. The men doubled down, intensifying the search. The fist-sized finding confirmed the location as the mother lode, but during the next hour, nothing more was unearthed and restlessness arose.

No one voiced the thought that the singlet stone might have originated upstream.

Directing the effort, the group leader devised the now necessary disposition of the geologist. With the minerals at hand, the men's attention was diverting, focused on winning the reward he'd offered. The afternoon waned but the inclement weather did not desist. With each passing fruitless moment, his suspicions grew that the strike would not be easy, that what they sought would require at least another day.

Prudently, he elected to have Yakov removed from the valley. A sixth sense argued that the geologist should not be eliminated. He couldn't get rid of that unwanted baggage just yet. He alone held the responsibility for determining if Yakov was playing a cat-and-mouse game. Sitting amongst his party, Yakov might unearth more than minerals. The bookish adventurer had proven his resiliency several times already.

Although outnumbered a dozen to one, if Yakov managed to secure a weapon, he might inflict serious damage on his party. In the stifle of the river's roar, a lone gunman could move undetected, and slowly change the odds.

As a precaution, the group leader ordered Yakov's guard pair to return their captive to the tundra plateau above. Separated from the distractions, the two men could easily keep watch over him and he'd have one less worry nearby. If Yakov managed to escape, there was no place to run and hide. He'd already made sure of that.

"Keep him occupied," the leader hinted. The sentinels smirked, a little fun would combat both the weather-borne misery and the tedious guard duty. For their topside duty, they'd been promised a fraction of the finder's fee.

Walking in single file, with Yakov at center, they made their ascent. Climbing the steep, soggy hillside was far more difficult than descending. Greased by the rain, the ground frequently slid out from beneath their feet. Digging his feet into the mud, Yakov defaced the trail to make it difficult for the following man to stay upright.

With satisfaction, Yakov watched the lead guard lose his footing and fall backward onto an exposed rock, savagely impacting his tailbone. Cursing angrily, the man checked himself for serious injury. Although Yakov rued the resulting absence of blood, he welcomed the short pause.

A moment later, they were climbing again. His captor did not appear hindered, although his pace had slowed and he exhibited additional caution. Stumbling, slipping and sliding each gingerly ascended the unreliable slope without further mishap.

Three quarters of the way up, the incline increased and the footing became treacherous. Holstering their guns, the guards resorted to crawling on hands and knees a few centimeters at a time, pulling on pieces of exposed vegetation to assist their climbing.

Is this a good time to make a getaway? Yakov wondered, faring no better. It was too much to leap past, scramble over, and remain out of gun sight, but once over the top, he might be able to make a break. The guards were slowing, winded from the exertion of climbing. Their pistol holsters were caked with mud. Yakov felt his anticipation building.

He would seize his opportunity when it arose. There would be only one good chance.

"Let's rest," the trailing guard announced, as if reading the prisoner's mind. They stopped, pressing their backpacks against the bank to keep their balance. The guards refreshed, drinking water liberally and snacking, pointedly refusing to offer anything to Yakov. To his chagrin, the scales were tipping away.

Twenty minutes later, they worked the last fifteen meters of hillside. A hundred meters in either direction the summit was vertical, a shear wall three meters in height formed by sliding erosion when the saturated spring ground could no longer grasp the tundra plain.

The embankment they had descended was no longer navigable, having fallen away in the intervening hours. Freshly exposed, the permafrost boundary was evident. Water seeped from the rubble, trickling toward them.

Traversing horizontally below the cliff face, they searched for a new egress to the flat land above. Presently, they found a hidden cutaway etched into the steep bank, an ancient trail the game used to escape the river valley. Packed by the hooves of countless deer, the thirty centimeter width appeared solid, with only a small seepage of water draining down its slope. Above their heads, snaggled white roots protruded providing handholds for hoisting themselves toward the top edge.

"You'll go first," the rear guard ordered to the lead sentinel. He pointed at Yakov, "Then you."

Beginning his climb, the front man dug his knees into the adjacent hillside for traction. He was covered in mud. Wedged against the path bottom, he dug his fingers and boot tips into the soft soil, methodically gaining a few vertical centimeters at a time. It was exhausting work.

Pleased by the duration of the guard's painstaking effort, Yakov nervously plotted an escape. With the front guard thoroughly preoccupied, an opportunity was at hand. The longer it took for the men to climb, the more he could rest. Opening his mouth, he faced the rain, catching a few precious drops of moisture, but it could not slake his thirst.

"Help him up," the rear guard commanded to Yakov, realizing his vulnerability. Obstinately, Yakov complied, but not until a drawn gun convinced him that rendering aid was an act of sanity.

With Yakov's pushing, the lead ward neared the top, but the final ascent was on his own, out of Yakov's reach. Remaining in position below, Yakov readied his turn. A meter below, thwarting any escape plans, the rear guard held position. Leveling a weapon at the geologist's back, the guard warned that his prisoner should not make a break.

Positioned between the narrow cut bank and the two men, a tightly restricted space, the humidity was overpowering. Yakov felt claustrophobic, overwhelmed by his confinement and its peculiar odors, an unpleasant sensation enhanced by his proximity to those he hated. Besides the smell of human perspiration, rotting vegetation and broken roots, a nauseating odor of damp fur seemed to waft into his face. He stifled the twin urges to panic and retch.

Reaching over the top bank for a tuft of grass, the lead guard suddenly trembled. A massive spasm shook him, rippling down his back and tunneling through his legs until his shins flailed free of the mud bank. Suspended in midair, he quivered, but curiously, he did not slide downward. Instead, slumped against the slope, his body shivered once more, wriggling in horrific pain.

Perplexed by the guard's strange actions, Yakov gazed impassively. Above the curving path, the guard's head tilted awkwardly. A ragged gash was ripped across his neck. Blood spurted from the laceration, surging with each heartbeat, spurting onto the dark ground. With a peculiar grunting, the severed windpipe flapped and bleated.

As horror replaced consternation, Yakov stared, transfixed by the macabre image of the pallid tubing flexing and falling.

Against the gray sky above, he saw a broad white paw, armed with four extended razor claws, swinging toward his head. Stopping well short of his face, they instead impaled the guard's outstretched torso and pulled upward, dragging the lifeless body up the bank.

"Aaaargh! You bastard!" Hearing the primeval scream bellowing behind him, Yakov tensed. He clenched his teeth, waiting for the inevitable gunshot to take his life, but none came.

Instead, the great bear's head extended above Yakov. Two rows of serrated ivory snarled wickedly, framed in pink flesh above a gleaming black jaw. Saliva glistened between the gums. Its eyes caught his, and a torrent of hideous memories churned his mind. Turning to run, Yakov slipped, sliding toward the rear guard's feet below, whose attention was riveted on the bear.

Precariously balanced on two legs, he pointed his weapon at the bear's face, depressing the trigger as often as the mechanism allowed. His face was ensconced with rage. The pistol barked angrily, renting the air alongside Yakov's ears and paralyzing his hearing. Lead projectiles struck the bear's face repeatedly, mortally wounding it, but it was not dying quickly enough for the man.

Yakov reacted, driving his shoulders into the distracted guard's legs, propelling him off his feet. The ward bellowed in gall, but only for a moment. As the ground fell away, he could not regain his footing and began tumbling down the steep embankment. Suddenly terrified, he grasped haplessly for a handhold, a rock, a bush, even the pathetically weak blades of last season's grass, but failed to secure an anchor. With each haphazard rotation, he gathered speed, and a bloodcurdling scream burst through to Yakov.

Abruptly, the howling silenced.

Colliding severely against an exposed boulder, the captor had broken his neck.

Above Yakov, the bear was stumbling groggily, profusely bleeding and half blinded from a bullet that had perforated one eye. Another projectile had pierced its nose, fracturing the rear bones protecting its brain. It wheezed, spraying a cloud of crimson droplets into the gray heavens. Mortally angered, the bear struck after his escaping attacker, stumbling over the cliff side toward the shooter's fall.

Seeing the bear leaping down the wall, Yakov dived into the hillside beneath its trajectory. He was just in time. Clubbing his back, the bruin's body knocked him roughly into the soft ground. He tasted mud, his face driven an inch deep into the soaked soil. But it was a glancing blow, and the bruin continued past him unabated.

It would not return.

Yakov gasped in pain, knowing he'd narrowly avoided being crushed or dragged down with the bear, but he still was not fully free. Far below, he heard disarrayed shouting, quickly changing to calls of alarm. The rest of the party, alerted by the gunshots, would soon be on their way. If he could get over the ridge top quickly, they would not be able to shoot at him. Once out of sight, he might have thirty minutes to flee.

Or would he? If the bear wasn't alone, his foray above would be brief and violent.

Still blocking the path of his exit, the body of the deceased guard quivered in terminal throe. Without pity, Yakov snatched his canteen, roughly pulling it over the half-quartered neck, bloodying the leather strap. Next, he removed a food pack, a long-bladed stiletto, and a gun from the man's gear. But with his own hands encumbered, he could not move past the corpse.

Slinging the canteen over his neck, he shoved the food pack into his back pocket and inserted the knife into his belt, emptying one hand. The dead man's blood wetted his shirt collar. Yakov dared not stow the gun in his pockets, not knowing its condition. As a precaution, he tossed it over the bank, hearing it discharge upon landing.

He stepped on the limp body, gaining a first foothold. With the meager momentum in tow, he leaped upward, clawing at the scraggly roots of the topside plants.

Below him, a frenzy was building, men shouting intensely. Some were noising fear, others expressed anger or confusion. He heard gunshots, but they were distant reports, not pointed in his direction.

Except one.

Whizzing by his head, an errant bullet churned into the soft ground, biting the mud with a heavy thud. Dirt splashed outward, followed by a puff of white vapor. The randomly discharged bullet seared his mind, propelling him to frantic action. Yakov scrambled and clawed upward.

Below him, the cacophony rose to a crescendo in prelude to a massive roar. The belligerent voices instantly ceased barking, dispelled by fear and horror. A cluster of gunfire erupted. The infuriated bear whined in disapproval as several marksmen found their target. As each searing thump consumed an iota of its life, Yakov fled, painstakingly surmounting the top of the ridge.

Rolling away from the edge, the din below instantly quenched. He looked around the plateau quickly. His heart leaped in fright. He was not alone. Only meters away, two white, bulky forms were approaching. Terrified, he screamed, losing his composure. The world went white as Yakov went berserk. Jumping to his feet he ran for his life, unwittingly fleeing between the two bears. The world transformed into a vague, blurred hemisphere, blended hues on a translucent palette.

Blinded by his crazing, he tripped over a shallow hole, stumbling to his knees. Panicking, he fumbled in place, unable to regain his balance on the uneven ground. A second misstep sent him cascading, head over heels, onto the tundra, mercilessly smashing his ribs against the ground. The wind was brutally driven from his chest. Cruelly, his sense of sound was restored. He could hear and feel everything; his breathing, his heart racing, the hammering of blood pulsing in his ears. In the silent spaces between, he sensed the bears closing, grunting in excitement, their padded footfalls gently squeezing the wet grass.

Gasping for air, he spun over, feebly pushing himself upward to run again. He was powerless, exhausted, winded, damaged. His fearful, twice beaten body had nothing more to give.

He was finished. Beside himself in sheer terror, he gave in.

Slowly rolling onto his back, he faced his final adversaries. The twin beasts closed in on him, teeth bared, confidently consuming the distance remaining between themselves and their quarry.

Fearing the horror of a painful death, Yakov covered his face, cowering behind his trembling hands. This time he had no miracle gloves to save him. A heavy breath exhaled near his face. The end was near. Lingering at death's door, he whimpered, powerless, succumbing to the inevitable. A warm, wet sensation stung his cheeks.

He screamed his last breath.

The breathing evaporated. The rasping sensation did not return.

I must be dead already, Yakov thought. *I feel no pain.*

Opening his eyes, the world was cast in a featureless gray. Vaguely, he focused on a dark cloud wisp curling beneath the monotone mask. *So this is hell,* he thought.

Turning his head to his side, he saw fresh green grass on wet soil. It was not the *after* world. He was still on the tundra. A half dozen meters away, a timid shuffling captured his attention. His two adversaries were patiently waiting, sitting on their hindquarters, watching his fear-filled antics with amusement. One stood on his hind legs, pawing the air as if swatting a fly. Its long, white fur drooped gracefully even though it was drenched, but the predator's arm was short, and its claws nearly invisible.

Yakov began to laugh...he was three times lucky...but the tortured tone in his mirth stopped him short and startled the infants.

"*Spaceeba, Tietra*" he whispered in thanks.

The polar bear cubs could not have been more than a few months old. Now orphaned, they too were abandoned and exposed in a harsh and unforgiving wilderness. Although stronger and better adapted, they were more helpless than him.

The cubs were doomed.

Relief seeped through his tortured soul. Yakov ignored the twin bruins and prepared again to run from the human danger. Pulling himself onto shaky legs, he failed again to stand, this time a gripping nausea overpowering his core. Pinned to his knees, he vomited repeatedly, each purge expelling vile liquids from further inside his bowels. With a shuddering gasp, the last of his fluids dribbled down his unkempt face.

Although wrung out from inside, the heaving convulsions would not cease. Remaining perched on all fours, Yakov contorted through wracking dry heaves that collapsed his intestines. Tears welled in his eyes as he repeatedly shuddered, waiting for the spell to desist. Once it did, he blinked fiercely until he could see clearly. The instant sickness chilled his body. Worse, cold rain was dousing his back, soaking through the mud on his clothes. On the open plain, the wind blew coldly through him and he shivered. He needed to get moving to keep warm.

Half buried within the middle of his vomit, a golden glint caught his eye. Cautiously reaching out with his fingers, careful not to contact his alimentary residue, he retrieved the object. Recognizing the device, the realization was astounding and revealing. It was a miniature GPS tracking dot.

Shit! This is why their security was so relaxed, he deduced. *They would track me if I ran.*

Another, more serious, thought followed. If his body was bugged, so was his clothing. Shakily, he approached the edge of the muddy embankment, dropping onto his stomach, and pressing his head over the edge. He looked for his pursuers. Already, three men were cautiously working their way up the greasy valley wall, but their progress was severely hampered by the worsened conditions.

The balance of the party was gathered around the felled mother bear, weapons pointed, ensuring that it could not rise again.

Disappointed, Yakov observed that none seemed to have fallen prey to the Arctic warrior. From far below, a man shouted the alarm. *En masse*, they turned his way, weapons pointing upward. A burst of firing instantly commenced. The bullets rent the air at close proximity. Rolling quickly away, Yakov was astounded that he hadn't been struck during the barrage.

But the firestorm had found a target. Following him to the hillside, one of the cubs had also been peering over the edge. It now bore the brunt of their attack. Cruelly bloodied, its life pouring onto brilliant white fur, the cub lay twitching, its brown eyes dulling in death.

Taking pity, Yakov crawled on his stomach to the dying infant, pulling it back from the edge. The shell-shocked eyes caught his, and for a moment, sought answers for its beleaguered spirit. Closing his own eyes, Yakov looked away, unable to console the youth. Absentmindedly, he stroked the cub behind its head, vignettes of Sergei's last fearful shout flashing through his brain. He seethed, a florid fury flashing from his soul.

He vowed anew, "I will yet avenge."

Chapter 13

Flight Of The Geologist

Peeling off his soaked, clinging shirt, Yakov cast the suspect garment to the ground.

How will I survive without clothing?

Unbuckling his belt, his pants followed similarly.

I will not survive with this clothing.

Flailing off his boots, he paused, thinking that had to be the end of the GPS devices, but he could not risk keeping any garment.

Exposed and naked, the cold rain stung his skin, frigid needles sapping warmth from his back. Scouring the open tundra, Yakov's eyes searched for anything useful the prospecting party might have left behind, but there were scant few, man-made items on the plateau, mainly the dead man's materiél that Yakov had thrown over the edge.

Unscrewing the half-filled water canteen cap, he thirstily imbibed. Attached to a strap was a small stainless steel utility knife, fashioned in the manner of the traditional Swiss army style. The water vessel was an essential keeper and the miniaturized knife might prove useful.

Harvesting the utilities, he purposed to head toward the ravine that he'd prospected the previous autumn. More important than containing the mineral mother lode, it housed an arboreal enclave. Within the thick stands of trees, he might find shelter and sustenance. At the bare minimum, safely harbored away from the windswept open plain, he would increase his chances for survival. Yakov was shivering, his skin cast slowly changing pallor from red to blue. Exposed to the elements, his muscles would not function well for more than a few hours. Already he understood that, without warmth, he would not survive the night. Underscoring his concerns, the damp, cold wind swept mercilessly, painfully penetrating through him.

He started slowly, with the stilted gait of chilled muscles. Slogging past the dead cub, his survival instincts awoke.

The animal isn't bugged.

Spinning on his heel, he hurried to the cooling carcass, rolling the limp body onto its back. A bloodstained hole on the neck marked exactly where its youthful life had drained. Stiffly, Yakov's fingers pried open the benevolent knife blade.

Clumsily attempting a first cut, a straight line slice from belly to chest, he failed to pierce the fur. The bearskin was thick and tough, resisting laceration, and Yakov's muscles were thick with chill. As desperately as he needed the bearskin, the North would not offer it freely.

The hunting knife! he recalled. Darting back to his pile of discarded clothes, he retrieved the workhorse blade. Returning to the dead cub, he pinched the gut and sawed back and forth, quickly cutting through. Inhaling the sickening stench of sliced entrails, his knees weakened and his stomach tightened in revolt. He shrugged off the discomfort, bearing down with the blade, quelling the urge to vomit again.

Accidentally gashing through the stomach cavity a noisome odor enveloped him, but by now his saturated nostrils had ceased rebelling. Instead, Yakov found himself pitying the senseless death of the toddler.

Terminating the first cut above the front paws, he crosscut the second seam from shoulder to shoulder and around the neck. It was getting easier, his hands warming from the cooling carcass.

A third gash went circumferential around the abdomen above the hind legs. Lastly, he sliced small perimeters above the front paw wrists. His heart was burdened, it was disturbing to be flaying an infant, but as he executed the gruesome task, he assuaged his conscience with the fact that the cub's life was forfeited, and that its death was prolonging his own breath.

He would not waste his opportunity.

Working methodically for the next quarter hour, he separated hide from flesh. Using broad sweeping strokes of the knife tip, he shaved away the fur skin, careful to not pierce it through. Between his knees, the dead cub's entrails tumbled onto the ground, a rancorous writhing of gray-white tubes. Their latent heat warmed his legs.

With a final effort, he pulled the skin inside out and tugged it over the front paws. It slid cleanly, giving him a bloodied cape equipped with two sleeves. Concerned it might drip a trail for others to follow, he dragged the pelt over the soaked grass, rinsing away a fraction of its damning evidence.

Wrapping the fur over his shoulders, he pushed his arms through the front legs and pulled the edge flaps around his chest. It covered his torso and thighs, although his arms were exposed at his forearms. Once donned, he took care of other necessities. Slicing off a kilogram of flesh, he clenched the raw meat between his teeth and sucked its juices. After hanging the canteen around his neck, he searched for and quickly found the guard's pistol.

To his disgust, the short barrel was stuck in the ground. The clip lay alongside, damaged from striking the only rock in sight. Worse, the clip was empty, the loading spring having discharged the unspent bullets when the housing bent open. He pawed over the nearby grass, but couldn't locate a single round. In disgust, he discarded the useless weapon.

His hunger brought to mind the guard's food packet stowed in his pant pocket. Placing the raw meat on the discarded cloth, he broke open a wrapped energy bar. Wary that it might contain another bug, he crushed pieces between his fingers and sifted through the crumbles.

There were none. Ravenously, he consumed two bars, and sought a third, but there were no more. The balance of the sustenance was dried vegetables, offering too few calories for him to expend the effort of carrying them.

Replacing the flesh in his mouth, Yakov set out jogging, less clumsily than before. Immediately he felt the difference. The cold no longer permeated through him unchecked. Slowly, his stride relaxed and his speed increased. Rainwater beaded on the dense fur, but did not soak through. It gathered into droplets and dripped away. The polar bear's hide was superior to his discarded clothing.

Glancing behind, he saw a line of dark-toned footprints, a depressed grass trail paving his movements along the valley's edge, but to his surprise, the grass was quickly springing back to full height as the persistent rainfall re-soaked the discolored blades. Within minutes, the evidence would be obliterated.

Running alongside the ridge line, he kept out of sight of the bottom.

He expected his pursuers to guess his choice of direction, but to follow him might not be appealing, for it meant leaving their safety net of ATVs and electronics farther behind. Perhaps they would not have the fortitude to follow him very far, and would abandon him to his chances against the unforgiving season.

He ran at the edge of fatigue, but progress was slow. Yet, he could not afford to slow or rest. With an unobstructed view over a kilometer of ground, it was impossible to hide. Ten minutes into his flight, Yakov could still clearly see the darkened form of the immobile carcass.

Somewhat unnerving to him, the surviving cub was following at an uncomfortable distance.

It was impossible to run and chew raw meat, so Yakov abandoned the idea. Instead, he punctured the mass with the hunting blade, and slid the sinews down onto the handle. The extra leverage unbalanced his stride, forcing him to constantly shift the knife between arms, making his arms ache.

Frequently, Yakov looked back over his shoulder, checking his growing concern that his pursuers were about to scale the steep banks. Only two kilometers away from the starting point, he had not run far enough to lose sight of the dead cub. If his captors reached the plateau before he was out of sight, they would pursue him relentlessly.

Fortunately, the wet weather was not letting up and his original line of tracks had disappeared. Less fortuitously, evening was nigh and the heavy overcast was hastening the loss of late afternoon daylight.

Without a sudden hiss, the drizzle intensified. It worked in his favor, rendering far off objects as indistinct, opaque shapes. In spite of the cold downpour, Yakov smiled, knowing that the white pelt on his shoulders was blending into the falling sheets. Behind him, the lonely cub effortlessly kept pace, frequently bleating a raspy, high-pitched call, probably grieving over the loss of its mother and sibling.

Pelted by the hard rain, Yakov ignored its bereavement, holding its sibling's pelt closely over his shoulders while he drove himself to maintain pace. His effort was rewarded. Twenty minutes later, as the downpour thinned, he could no longer see his point of departure, but the hard running was exacting a toll.

His biceps were cramping, locked in his uncomfortable pose, and his neck was aching from holding the bulky canteen. Unexpectedly, the miserable weather amplified an arthritic pain in his repaired shoulder. The gunshot damage had left him with a lifelong internal barometer, but these weren't his only vulnerabilities. He was running out of energy. He ran sloppily, his bare feet slapping the frigid tundra, a cue that his limited endurance was spent. If he did not regain control, he risked wrenching an ankle or slicing a foot open on the few exposed rocks.

Rainwater dribbled down his dark locks onto his neck and cheeks and slipped beneath his cloak. Even with continuous exertion, he was not warming up. Yakov had few fat reserves to draw on. His hair was soaked, matted close to his skull. His head began throbbing, an unrelenting vise grip on his temples from a headache borne of chill.

His condition was deteriorating.

The rain slowed to a drip. Across the divide, he sighted the hidden woods. As he had hoped, they were already greened.

Sensing a small margin of safety, Yakov stopped trotting. He could not see or hear his pursuers. He needed to eat. He cut away and chewed a piece of *bear steak*. It was tough, greasy and flavored with a slight hint of salt. His body welcomed the nourishment. For the next several minutes, he pared away the chunk in generous slices, chewing and savoring each fresh morsel. With the last of his canteen's fluid, he washed it all down, knowing that he would soon replenish his water supply.

Fifty meters behind, the trailing cub had stopped short. It paced the ground nervously. Whether it feared the man or was alarmed by the familiar smells of its dead mother and sibling, Yakov did not know.

A distant call emanated through the muting mist, startling him. It resembled a man's voice. The cub dropped to the ground and held still. Yakov stopped fast, staring fixedly at the sound's origin, but the source did not speak again.

Is it just my imagination?

The answer eluded him, and without assurance, he could not supplant the only truth he trusted, a primeval mandate to elude the threat. Yakov ran again, robotically forcing limbs into motion, an automaton escaping one danger, ill equipped for the next.

With only a kilometer separating him from the sheltered ravine, another grain of truth crystallized. It was not a pleasant grist. The ravine lay across the valley on the opposite side. To reach its safe haven, he would have to cross the deep divide, but crossing the midpoint was a fool's quest. More treacherous than simply an excursion over slick hillsides, the swollen river blocked his passage, an imposing and impenetrable barrier.

Fast, strong and icy cold, it could not be safely forded on foot until the water drained to a normal level, a process that would take several weeks.

During his late autumn visit, the river was barely fifteen meters across. Now charged with spring melt, it was at least doubled in width, and unfathomably deeper, surging above the summer banks at a dozen kilometers per hour.

The unassuming truth arrested his flight. From the valley's rim he examined the silver ribbon, searching for a natural crossing. Where the river was narrowest, the current was strong, an unstoppable force drifting beneath a placid mirror. Its smooth glass top looked engineered, deceptively easy to cross, but atop the veneer, floating foam puddles swept peacefully, the best indication of the water's speed. At the edges, the water's power was evident, occasionally shredding away chunks of amber clay.

As the river widened, the ponderous flow loosened, cascading over sunken ledges and churning above submerged boulders.

These were not places to cross. Ironically, at its widest and most shallow places, the flow was most violent, a whitewater fury of churning murk. Yakov doubted he'd be able to stand.

Deeply sobered, Yakov searched the upstream riverbank for tree cover on his side of the valley. The gently falling drizzle reduced his vision to a few kilometers, too short a range to sight another ravine. While a similar haven probably existed farther upstream, he lacked the time to chance finding one. There were only a few hours of navigable light left. If shelter wasn't within walking distance, he would not survive the night out on the plain.

For a moment he considered turning back, locating his pursuers and robbing them of supplies. Just as quickly, he decided against that suicide. Even if he still had the pistol, he could not sneak into their camp and overpower a cadre of professional fighters.

Slowly walking the ridge debating his options, Yakov came upon a well-trod game trail leading down the hillside to a wide, seasonally shallow section of the river. At present, it was a tumultuous froth. Beaten ground reappeared on the opposite side, converging into a path and disappearing into the woods. Unfortunately, there were few fresh imprints. No doubt the animals that frequented the trail also avoided crossing until the water level fell to safe depths again.

Seeing the path surprised him. He had completely missed it during his previous visit. If this was the animals' best known highway, perhaps he should also use it. The slope looked gentle, inviting him to travel. He paused with indecision, unable to determine a place to ford the river. The young cub did not share his reservations.

It darted past the hesitant human and scrambled down the slope. Instinctively, Yakov followed, tethered to the purposeful cub.

Fifteen minutes later, they stood on the valley floor. The rain had fully let up. Now the river's roar dominated, eliminating his situational awareness of movement or sound from the topside. The bulk of the vegetation was thick blades of grass and reed with a few willows growing in spindly bunches. Across the hazardous divide, the tree cover beckoned.

Beneath his feet, marbled stones lay half-buried in the saturated mud. Picking one up, Yakov observed a two-toned, red-brown striation over its surface. He struck it against a larger rock, cracking it open. Inside was a bright pink vein.

This was the place he'd remembered. This was the lode that had initiated his nightmare.

A dozen meters upstream, the young cub paced back and forth along the river's edge. It seemed agitated. Alarmed, Yakov looked all around, but saw no apparent danger. He walked toward the cub, calling to it softly.

For an unknown reason, perhaps an inclination of loneliness, he did not wish to lose its company.

Hearing his soothing voice, the cub halted and sat down, its pink tongue drooping from its mouth. The organ looked rubbery and parched. Obviously, the young bear was thirsty, but whether it had been weaned from its mother's milk yet, Yakov could not know.

Taking his canteen to the water's edge, Yakov purposed to refill the empty vessel. Where he stood, the river was narrow and deep. Up close, it was an ominous current. The bank's edge was soft and slippery. Digging his feet into the yielding earth, Yakov squatted, balancing the hunting knife across his lap. Reaching forward, he carefully submerged the flask. The melt water was ice cold, instantly chilling his hands. Beneath his feet, the saturated incline felt ready to give way.

The young bear pushed beside him, brusquely bumping into his calves.

"Whoa there," Yakov warned, "don't knock us into the water or we'll both drown."

The youthful bruin paid no heed, fearlessly dipping his face into the frigid bath, nearly knocking Yakov off his haunches. Scurrying sideways a couple of paces, Yakov put an interval of safety between himself and the exuberant cub. The bear was better equipped to survive a glacial plunge than he, confidently raking its claws into the muddy bank for traction. The cub eagerly lapped large gulps of the revitalizing fluid. It did not seem to be having any issues staying put on the unstable bank. Yakov envied its surefootedness.

His canteen only partly filled, but fearful of being pushed into the current, Yakov wedged his heels into the earth to back up the sharp slope. The slick ground would not comply. Without warning, he lost his footing. Feet flailing forward, he landed on his backside, one leg splashing into the current. The water was so cold it burned.

Startled by the sudden movement, the cub lost its grip and fell into the water. Immediately, the toddler began drifting downstream. Righting its face toward the shore, it paddled hard, dug its claws into the moist clay, and tried hauling itself out of the raging current. The cub floundered, barking calls of distress, unable to secure a winning grip.

Yakov was preoccupied. Precariously positioned on the slippery slope, he too was sliding toward the current. Spinning onto his chest, he stabbed the knife blade into the soft ground, inching himself to safety. Regaining his feet, muddy and disheveled, he first noticed the plight of the poor cub.

Rushing over, he stood atop the bank, unsure of his ability to safely intervene. Floundering against the slurried clay, the cub could not secure a winning grip. Yakov reached forward to help, but immediately pulled back, his benevolence undone by the harsh reality.

He could not risk his life to save the hapless animal.

Then the river seemed to surge, the friable bank giving way under his weight. Howling in fear, Yakov plunged into the raging flow, dislodging the stalemated cub. The brutal force broadsided the large-bladed knife from his fingers. Instantly shocked by the icy water, his chest constricted tightly. He gasped against the vise, staccato spasms tearing through his lungs.

Reaching for shore, Yakov flailed at reed stalks growing along the bank, but he was too far away. Instinctively, he clutched at the young bear's back, grazing the soft fur and desperately seizing hold. Yakov scissor-stroked toward the bank, already several meters away, but the little bear had the opposite notion, pulling him into deeper water and the coursing current.

"This way!" he screamed. The stinging water numbed his muscles, but the young cub turned its neck and snapped its teeth, nearly impaling the geologist's arm.

He's spooked! Why?

The answer was immediately apparent. At the top of the valley, the capped heads of two men were visible. In moments, his presence would be discovered.

With a sudden clarity of mind, Yakov fathomed that he had awkwardly stumbled into his chance to escape.

Now that he was in the river, there was little reason to stop his desired crossing, but time was very short. The bone-chilling immersion would incapacitate him within minutes. If the cold didn't do him in, a short stretch downstream were life-threatening rapids.

Kicking toward the opposite bank, Yakov pushed at the young cub, but the fur cloak and canteen lanyard mired his efforts. With his free hand, Yakov tried shedding the impediments, but he could not overcome the water's force. His futile efforts slowed his legs and the added burden pulled the infant's head beneath the water.

The frightened animal paddled frantically, struggling to breathe. Thrashing to stay afloat, a hind leg slammed into Yakov's arm, dislodging the man's grasp and tearing itself free.

The cub immediately pulled away.

Horrified, Yakov chased after the bobbing bear, but the midstream current pulled him away, toward the violent whitewater doom in the rapids.

"Aim toward the shore," he whispered, overcoming his instincts to turn upstream. The quickest route, with the least expenditure of energy, was swimming at right angles to the bank. He fought against his leaden chill, but each stroke seemed to have no effect. He watched with fear as the youthful bear scrambled onto the gentle bank.

Doggedly, Yakov wormed forward, unwilling to be outdone by a toddler, willfully ignoring the approaching rapids. The cold water assailed his strength, a millstone in league with the billowing fur skin and canteen lanyard.

With each determined push he was weakening. The shore, only meters away, was unreachable.

The current quickened beneath, accelerating him into the turmoil fringing the rapids. Sensing the change, Yakov pulled hard against the cold, water slab. His meager gesture had little effect. He would be swept away and die within reach of the bank, bested by a baby bear.

In desperation, Yakov rolled onto his back, struggling again to shed the pelt. An overhanging tree branch came into view. Feebly, he reached for the proffered stem. His hand made contact. Squeezing his stiffened fingers, he caught the suspended lifeline and was immediately rewarded by an immense burden on his cloak and neck.

The water plowed into him, cutting a wave in the fast moving current, urging him toward the rock-laced froth.

Yakov knew he could not last. Feebly, he worked for a second handhold, but his strength was fading. Dangling beneath the overhanging tree, one hand tenuously gripping the slippery bark, he fought to hold on.

Above his hand, the wooden trunk suddenly splintered, jagged white shards of shattered kindling spewing onto the water where they were instantly swept away. Above the river's roaring, he had not heard the gunshot.

His pursuers had spotted him and were intent on killing him.

With a surge of fear, Yakov pulled again. He caught a second hand hold. With the double grip, he finally gained some leverage. He plunged his feet along the surface beneath the tree and then down into the frigid stream, shielding his body. To his surprise, his feet scraped against the rocky bottom. The water was barely thigh deep. He had not realized the shallow depths of the frigid current.

Wedging his feet between the bottom stones, he inched forward, using the protection of the fallen timber to shield himself from his attackers, hoping he wouldn't slice himself open on a sharp rock edge. Step by precarious step, he fought the raging current, walking his hands until the branch lifted overhead to the suspended trunk.

Shots rang repeatedly, some shattering and bouncing against the water, others thudding into the wood, but pistol accuracy at long range is poor. The shots were missing their target. Yakov expected his pursuers to quickly close to a better vantage. His legs rubbery with cold, he trudged into shin deep water, exhausted and numb. His back stooped beneath the unforgiving burden of the soaked fur. The sagging garment whisked roughly against his bare calves, threatening to trip him and plunge him back into the swift current.

But the water's force had abated—and none too soon. The tree branch was rising out of reach. Diving headlong onto the soft, slippery slope, Yakov let go of his handrail. Crawling up the bank, he inched over the mud and reeds toward a thicket of willows a few meters ahead.

"I must get behind the trees," he gritted his teeth and staggered to his feet. Lacking coordination, he swayed like a drunken man, lurching forward until he was hidden within the brush. A final pair of shots assaulted the gnarled cover, splaying unfortunate stalks beneath the ballistic impact, but none found their intended target.

Even from a few meters away, Yakov could not be seen. He had escaped his pursuers. It was unlikely the mineral seekers would attempt to cross the torrent and follow him. Now he had to survive the night.

As the dark sky slowly blackened, the temperature plummeted. Beneath the deep forest cover, Yakov was sheltered from the chilling wind. The heavy spruce boughs slowly dripped their excess rainwater. He could not dry out nor shake off the deep cold that had invaded body and bone during his plunge.

In the dim of dusk, the prospector found nothing suitable for generating heat. Everything insulating or combustible was too damp to function. His fur garment clung to his skin, exacerbating the coldness.

Shivering uncontrollably, Yakov pushed together a pile of fallen leaves, but soon abandoned the effort. The soggy mass was useless. In the waning light, he looked for food, anything edible that had eluded the foragers. A riverside thicket held a small remnant of hazelnuts, but he had no tool to crack their shells.

If the frightened young polar bear was nearby, it wasn't revealing itself. Perhaps it feared the obvious. Suddenly pragmatic, Yakov knew he might need the cub's flesh for his own benefit. But he'd lost his cutting tool, all he possessed was the fold-up knife. At least it was something.

A few meters away, another bush exhibited a welcome surprise, clusters of desiccated berries. He debated whether he dare eat them. Dark clumps of dried bear spoor on the ground indicated that the fruit was edible. Bending the tall branches, Yakov ravenously inhaled a handful of dark red tidbits, nearly breaking his teeth on bony pits inside.

Instantly wiser, he chewed the mass of flesh softly, extracting every microgram of sugar he could tease away from the mess of stones. The berries were the first calories he'd ingested since the raw bear meat. His body's engine slowly cambered to life. The second handful smelled awful, bearing an odor of sweaty socks, but the sharp taste was pleasant.

Above the contentious roar of the rushing water, Yakov heard a man shouting in anger. Dropping to the ground, he waited for the inevitable gunshot, but the vitriolic cry was not about finding him, his pursuers were having difficulty finding their way out of the valley. It reminded him that his options were limited. He could not forage the river's edge without being detected. He immediately moved deeper into the bush.

Although his canteen contained fluid, it was too cold to drink. He set it on the ground beneath a pine tree where a carpet of needles promised a soft bed and offered one more tidbit. In the last light, he found early season mushrooms growing. He wolfed them down, a sweet fungus on his famished palate, ignoring the morel's rubbery texture.

As darkness fell, the loss of light dimmed his sight and the cold consumed him. Yakov leaned against a pine, knees to chest, sitting on the soft needles beneath. He pulled the pelt tightly around his body, but it was too short to cover his feet. Huddling inside, he shivered and his limbs ached. He was too miserable to sleep.

The sun dropped below the gray horizon, but the twilight was lost, too weak to penetrate the tree canopy.

The day's inhabitants settled down. A flock of crows noisily took roost in the treetops. For a full half hour, their incessant arguing overcame the river's roar. After their squabbling quieted, an unnerving stillness remained...as if the river itself was at slumber.

A wolf's howl funneled into the ravine. Yakov listened intently, but the answering calls from its pack were faint, so the predators were moving away.

Closer by, nocturnal creatures rustled through branches, needles and leaves. In the night's void their bustling was unusually loud, alarming Yakov, but he soon realized they held no threat. If anything, they indicated safety.

An owl hooted and all movement ceased. The small critters were eager to avoid detection by the sharp-eyed aviator, but the owl's warning was not for the rodents, nor for him. A large animal was moving nearby. Shuffling through the ground-litter, the footsteps moved closer in short, deliberate bursts. Yakov froze, motionless and attentive.

In the inky blackness, he could see nothing. Periodically pausing, the animal took reconnaissance, punctuating the uneasy silence with coarse sniffing and heavy pawing. Evidently, it was homing on the scent of something interesting.

The small creatures stayed hushed.

Yakov stiffened, clenching his teeth tightly to prevent their chattering. In his mind, he tried to construe the animal's size, a weighted guess based solely on footsteps and breathing, but the exercise was counterproductive, liberally fueling a rampant run of fears as his mind conjured a creature of lethal proportions.

Cruelly, his jaws started cramping, a reward for his prolonged clamping. Yet he could not relax his grip. In his fleece cocoon, his terrified exhaling wheezed like a homing beacon. Somehow, he had to stop making noise. Holding rigidly still, he suppressed his breathing, erasing the evidence of his existence.

A minute passed.

The urge to inhale soared powerfully, but Yakov refused to comply. The beast was within earshot and getting closer.

A second minute ticked by and the compulsion weakened. The footfalls were fading, quieting into the distance. He would wait just a moment longer...Yakov passed out...awakening with no idea how long he'd remained unconscious. The pitch black entombed him and the forest remained deathly still. The animal was out of earshot, but until the small creatures began moving again, it would not be far off.

Unarmed and exposed, the terrors of the night unleashed his frailties. Refusing to sleep lest the beast return, he clutched his wrapped skin like a life vest and shivered and stared into the black gloom, mindless with fear.

Hypothermia set in and Yakov hallucinated, restrained in a dreadful twilight where he battled against an endless succession of cartoonish foes. Each confusing skirmish peaked with the bloodthirsty predator's return, ponderously closing in, teeth bared in conquest.

He hid beneath his shroud. He heard it breathing in his ear, savoring the sweet aroma of an easy feast. Yakov crumbled, shriveling into a deep, imaginary void, not daring to emerge for fear of the violent end. Entranced in anxiety, his eyelids screamed wide open, eerily reflecting the rising soft moonlight and thinning clouds. Even when his exhausted body fell to unconsciousness, he could not calm his soul. The horrors proliferated unabated in his subconscious, a cancer consuming his mind. His body twitched incessantly.

Then, suddenly and unexpectedly, it all ceased.

On a cluttered desktop, a complicated phone purred, interrupting a busy executive from his electronic tasks.

Picking up the cradle, Ottley screened the caller and made a mental note of the time. Details were forthcoming from the expedition.

He mentally noted his calendar. It was early in the timeline. A small measure of satisfaction traced his tight-lipped mouth.

"Ottley here," he grunted.

"First minerals in hand." Came a dispassionate reply.

"As *dispositioned?*" Ottley questioned.

"Slightly offset, we're closing in on the source."

"Make him pay," he snapped.

"He's been lost, sir."

"How the hell did that happen?"

"We were attacked, sir."

"By who?" Ottley suddenly had concerns.

"A polar bear. His guards were killed. He was being held in a separate location while the men searched."

"Jesus!" Ottley swore, fury displacing relief. "Find him!" He slammed the phone into its dock.

Dawn's rays tentatively kissed the mottled treetops, a pastel embrace too soft to displace the lingering chill.

Coaxing the crimson foretoken, rejoicing songbirds broke into chorus. The glowing orb smiled in answer, benevolently dispelling the petulant night's cold.

Beneath the canopy the mercury held fast, stranded a fraction above freezing, exactly where it had hovered for hours. Ironically, the flora no longer protected Yakov. Instead the overgrowth absorbed all the radiant energy for its own needs. Any creature remaining in the undergrowth would have to wait longer to partake.

The spring rain clouds had dissipated, unveiling a dazzling turquoise sky. Glimpses of blue brilliance flashed through swaying pinpricks in the leaf cover, but the geologist, imprisoned by cold on the ground, was unaware of the approaching warmth. Clenched in fetal, he lay atop his pine needle roost.

He had survived only because he wasn't alone. Moments after losing consciousness, his skittish companion had joined him, approaching only after it felt safe to move. Now the toddling cub was nestled against the geologist's head, exchanging companionship for warmth. Unwittingly, the orphan had extricated Yakov from the depths of hypothermia. As the man awoke, dazed and disoriented, it startled and fled.

Unaware of his benefactor, the geologist was surprised, even euphoric, at surviving ghosts and near freezing temperatures. His body was stiff and sore, punishments from running hard and then lying in prolonged contact with the spring ground.

Plying his muscles to bend, Yakov broke into shivering spells which shook his frame and rattled his teeth—fits which gradually subsided as he warmed. He grew acutely aware of basic cravings, hunger and thirst.

Surveying his surroundings, he found little of sustenance. The ravine's interior, bountiful in comparison to the open tundra, was barren in spring, an indigestible tableau of timber, fungus and moss. For life support, he would need to return to the river.

Treading downhill toward the watershed, Yakov paused frequently, listening for indications of the sub's crew. Only the chatter of a morning calm conversed, small mammals rustling leaves while foraging for hidden morsels, vibrant song birds in full throat, the muted notes of gurgling water trickling along the ravine.

Nearing the ravine's mouth, the roar of the rushing river rose in volume, masking his approach. Here he exercised a final caution, peering through the willow network until he was convinced there were no other humans in close proximity.

Fortuitously, his captors had taken leave from their pursuit, however, Yakov was not fooled. If the overriding reason was a want of provisions, then the return of promising weather would have them back on the hunt within a day.

And when using mechanized craft, they possessed significant advantages. He would have to make the best of his short time.

Kneeling on the greasy mud, he dipped his canteen into the frigid current, marveling at its strength and his fortune in crossing. At his leisure, he lapped the precious fluid until the liquid chill made his stomach rebel and spasm, but it was of no great consequence. For the next few hours, time was on his side. As soon as his intestines stopped aching, he would search for food.

Although it was early in the day, he began preparing for his next cold night, first tending to his ill-fitting garment. Braiding together slender willow branches, he fashioned a makeshift belt. He wrapped the flexible cord around his waist, securing it with a double hitch knot. Immediately, the improved insulation delivered a dividend by preserving precious heat.

He was still hungry and thirsty.

Although he felt exposed on the riverbank, he topped his canteen, nervously maintaining a sharp lookout. There was no human activity. The slick bank did not support his weight well, and Yakov struggled against falling into the torrent once more. As the filling water reached the canteen's cap line, he backed away. Even abundance had pitfalls.

He searched for the hazelnuts, quickly locating them. This time, however, there was something else, something he'd missed the first time. Next to the bushes, a well-worn game trail spurred into the trees. Determining to follow it, he hoped it might lead to shelter or food.

Selecting a pair of stones from the ground, one flat and the other blunt, Yakov fashioned a crude Stone Age implement for harvesting the nuts. Their casings had wintered attached to the bushes, shriveling to a brown, leathery covering. He pinched away the crumbling housing and, using his tool, easily cracked the rigid shell.

Twenty minutes later, he'd consumed enough to pass for a reasonable meal. There was enough food in this one thicket to power him for another week. How his empty stomach would handle the rich in fat fare was a different question.

Seeking a safer place to replenish his canteen, he trampled the bank's foliage, soon finding a small overflow pool. Bordered by man-sized reed skeletons, foam dollars circulated lazily on the protected surface. New bullrush shoots were rushing up the decimated sentinels to take their season standing guard. With the rain subsiding and the sun shining, clouds of insects had returned. Fine black flies fogged the misted air, hovering above the tender stems.

With a start, Yakov noticed a pair of translucent, yellow-rimmed eyes lurking beneath the surface a half meter from shore, safely removed from the surge. The eyes peered from a fist-sized body of mottled black spots on emerald green skin. Webbed feet pressed against a dead reed, holding itself in place. With hungry eyes, Yakov recognized the leopard frog and salivated.

The protein would do him good.

Needing a small stick, he tore a thin willow branch and returned to the back pool. Flies followed above his head, a few landing gently on his face. He did not brush them away, not wishing to alarm his prey. Riveting upwards, the frog's eyes rolled in their moist sockets, warily watching his approach. Yakov kept his movements slow, deliberate, without threat.

Lining the stick a half meter above the frog, he set the action. For a moment, he paused, imparting a false confidence to the amphibian. An insect landed on his pupil. He blinked it away. Several more flew into his nose, tickling his nostrils. He stifled a sneeze. Snapping his wrist, the rod whipped into flight, striking the frog mid-back and knocking it senseless. Without hesitation, Yakov plunged one leg into the muddy water to claim his stunned catch. Tearing it apart, he dined on the raw pink flesh and smiled, ignoring the apparition of flies swirling above his head. The meat was delicious.

Satisfied, he washed it down with fresh, pure ice melt. Insects flew into his mouth, each speck tickling his throat with increasing annoyance.

He needed to leave.

Filling the canteen in the back pool, he returned toward the game trail. His face itched. Reaching up to scratch his cheek he felt a curious wetness. Withdrawing his hand, he was horrified. It was dripping with blood.

He hadn't felt a thing.

Darting to the water's edge, he sunk his face into the icy bath, dislodging the flies and rinsing it clean in a trail of crimson streaks. His open flesh stung on contact. Without wasting a moment, he withdrew from the water's edge for the trees.

The minuscule black flies did not follow. Checking his face, he found the damage to be superficial, but his face felt puffy. It was beginning to swell.

Entering the timber, he climbed a steep trail leading to a course fifteen meters from the top ridge. Here he traveled, within the protection of the forest, parallel to the external plain. On occasion, alternate paths veered downhill, but nothing of interest appeared.

An uneventful hour into his journey, he stopped to peruse his surroundings. They were little changed. He was immersed in pine cover, occasionally interspersed with bluffs of birch or poplar, completely lacking the essentials he needed. Infrequently, he'd passed deadfall rows, ruins of trees that had toppled beneath fierce winds, perhaps even tornadoes. Intact horizontal trunks adjoined large, upended root mound umbrellas that might serve as overnight shelter. If he could find a flint, the birch bark would be invaluable, easily igniting damp deadfall to fuel a larger blaze. He regretted not thinking of it when he had been at the river's edge, but then his need for food had superseded his need for fire.

From behind, a crisp rustling of leaves arrested his attention.

Heart pounding, he stood stock still, eyes darting to locate promising cover. Something was following him. Yakov crept behind a thick pine trunk, quietly preparing his undersized utility knife. A moment later, the cub ambled into view. Yakov sighed, his knees nearly wilting beneath him. This land was no place for an unarmed human to roam.

His face itched, the skin swelling from the chorus of bites. Pressure built around his right eye and his ear felt oddly distended. It was uncomfortable, but he was not alarmed, confident that he was not suffering an allergic reaction to the insects' anesthesia.

Continuing along the gentle, sloping trail for a couple of hours, Yakov's search was fruitless. The ravine was barren, lacking suitable sustenance. If there had been any, the pickings were obviously slim and the more adapted inhabitants had already foraged through it for six ever-dwindling months.

Behind him, the young cub was keeping pace, but remaining just out of sight. Yakov debated between descending to the ravine floor and ascending to investigate the open terrain. Not having met his basic needs, food or shelter, but not requiring additional water, he decided on the latter. He walked straight up the hillside, picking through the tangled low-growth brush, vines and ferns. At the top, a thick hedge of bushes bordered the plain. Decorated with pluming blooms of pink and white, they promised a future banquet; but that bounty was for another day.

Nothing edible was available today.

He set out uphill along the ridge, remaining parallel to the ravine. The broad highland plain stretched for at least a dozen kilometers, textured with undulating hills. In sheltered recesses, scrub trees grew sparsely, while the hilltops and hillsides fluttered with a carpet of grass in the crisp, spring breeze. Peppering the open ground were numerous, foot-high conical earthen mounds, construction zones of digging rodents.

The dirt piles demarcated entrances to underground homes and an opportunity. Food was at hand.

But while a ground squirrel might make a suitable meal, Yakov was ill-equipped to catch one. The diminutive rodents easily outran him, pointedly refusing to be sacrificed on the altar of his nutritional needs. After a number of frantic attempts by the geologist, the colony grew wary and no longer tarried above ground when he neared.

Instead they darted into their subterranean lairs, screeching an alarm, inciting all other nearby creatures into vanishing. A length of thin cord would have tilted the odds, allowing him to noose their burrow holes, but the willow belt he wore was too rigid.

The sun shone brightly and, under better circumstances, Yakov thought it might have seemed peaceful. Overhead, a vortex of hawks circled, gracefully gliding midday thermals. Smaller than eagles, their patterned charcoal and brown plumage appeared somewhat drab but for a splendid black-speckled redtail.

At intervals, their voices pierced the air with haunting screams that disconcerted his nerves. From their lofted vantages, they hunted the same rodents that he could not catch. Yakov watched begrudgingly as one swooped and captured a hapless ground squirrel.

Within moments, the raptor was airborne, swallowing its prey whole even while its companions bore down on it with intent to steal. Yakov trotted after the commotion, hoping the gopher would be dropped to the ground wherein he could enter the fray, but the bird was too cunning to squander its kill.

Yakov welcomed the strong sunshine. Its heat pared away the remnants of his nocturnal chill, fueling a hopeful swagger in his steps. Assisted by a brisk wind, the pelt began drying. The swelling in his face was subsiding.

For the first time in weeks, his confidence began to soar as the fowl above him.

A cotton cloud intercepted the sun's flame, briefly darkening the land. Instantly, it chilled. Yakov shivered, his exposed legs bearing the brunt of an accompanying brisk zephyr. Rippling the grasses, the cool breezes firmly reminded him that summer was still a season away.

Another unbearably frosty night would soon arrive. He hurried his pace.

Still climbing the ridge line, Yakov felt compromised. He was maximizing warmth and safety to cover more ground, but sacrificing his search for food. Alongside the forest, the terrain was changing too slowly to offer new ground.

An hour later, he was nearing a decision break point. Soon, he would need to re-enter the ravine, scour the valley floor below, and prepare for the night. But he was reluctant to return to known dangers so early in the day. He elected to boost his search range by climbing a tree. From its height, he might pinpoint a more promising location.

Ascending a tall tamarack, he gingerly picked through fanned levels of pliable fronds, his hand was quickly coated with a sticky, pungent resin that would not rub away. The fur-skin snagged the tightly packed boughs. He dropped it to the ground, promptly abrading his chest on the coarse bark, but that minor pain was of little hindrance.

Scaling the tree until he perched nearly two dozen meters above the ground, he beheld a wide vista of open land beyond the adjacent rolling green carpet. While he saw no hint of civilization, nearly two hundred meters uphill there was something of interest; a worn dirt path that appeared uncommonly wide. The trail projected orthogonally from the ridge top, linking the ravine's bowels to the expanse beyond.

Eagerly dismounting, Yakov hurried to investigate. In short time, he stood abreast of the incongruous feature. In breadth, it was much wider than a game trail, but that wasn't the only oddity. The longer he studied the ground, the more certain he became that it held the weathered indentations of boot prints in the bare earth.

Again, Yakov felt hope stirring.

The character of the trail was suggestive for another reason. Game animals did not leave the shelter of the forest on a whim. Forays outside their comfort zone were limited to pursuing things necessary for life. There was none of that within view. The junction of tree and plain formed a dangerous ambush point for predatory carnivores to exploit. Whatever made this path did not care if it was a telltale for bears or wolves to find. The incongruities premised a basic assumption.

It must have human influences.

He set out along the path, following up on his hypothesis. Several minutes later, his intuition was rewarded. There was the unmistakable tread mark of a snowmobile belt in the dirt. He sighed, a mixture of relief and fear. The knowledge that the area was visited by humans bore blessings and curses. Most of all, he felt an enormous burden lifting.

Measuring his water supply, Yakov determined that he could sojourn for the balance of the day before needing to refill his canteen. If he didn't find an alternate source of water or shelter within three hours, he would return to the ravine, construct a grassy bed and sleep beneath the trees. The next day, he would prepare early to travel a much longer distance.

Reckoning the sun's position, it was early afternoon. This far north, he'd have about six hours to explore and backtrack. Even after sundown, there would be several twilight hours during which he could prepare to rest.

Plenty of time, but the more he recalled the previous night, the less certain he was that he wanted to return.

Following the spur onto the grassy plain, Yakov abandoned the secluded comforts of the ravine. To his chagrin, he left alone, his youthful companion refused to forsake the trees. Before venturing out, Yakov peered into the thickets, coaxing the cub along with soft calls, but it remained hidden within the shadows.

Endlessly rounding hillsides, the path hugged the slopes below the invisible boundary of the shearing wind, diminishing long range visibility, but he wouldn't leave the path to surmount a hilltop, unwilling to expend precious time striking out where others refused to tread.

Time passed and fatigue set in. He found nothing to support him. No shelter, no food he could easily gather and no water beside the dissipated morning dew. It was a greening grass desert sculpted by wind and winter ice, its productive season too brief to enrich with a yearlong supply of plenty.

His spirits flagged, but before he would return to the ravine. He would expend some energy climbing a hillside. Here he garnered the first glimmer of hope. At an indeterminate distance, rising above a small knoll, he thought he saw a wisp of smoke.

Is someone living out here? He hoped. His heart and mind sparred, conflicts of need and fear, but the decision was inevitable, he could not survive another night without shelter. He would now chance being caught.

If arrested, he would broker the mineral find and information about his invading kidnappers to purchase reprieve. With luck, he might face only deportation.

From the hilltop, he traced the twisting trail ahead, marking the point at which it disappeared from sight and predicting its reappearance farther away. In general, it led toward the rising gray vapor. Confident in his assessment, Yakov set out, rejoining the path at a brisk trot.

Twenty minutes later, he climbed another rise. This time, the signature was clear. He was looking at the exhaust from a woodstove blaze. The plume rose briefly before the breeze stretched it thin over the horizon. Elated, Yakov doubled his pace.

Within an hour, he neared its source.

So close to shelter, his trepidation grew. The site was obviously inhabited. Who lived here—how would he make contact, he wondered.

He sensed subtle changes in the rain-washed air, evoking images of habitation, but he could not fully discern the smells. Borne by the gathering wind, hints of smoke, machine oil and damp fur drove his preoccupations. He looked back sharply. The cub was not following him. Whoever lived here might have large dogs, Yakov realized glumly, although he hadn't heard any barking.

A grayish form floated like a ghost on the perimeter of his vision. The hair on his neck stiffened. *Be calm,* he commanded, but naked fear is difficult to control. Deliberately, he looked over his shoulder. A meter behind were a pair of great timber wolves, one silver, one black, trotting on the packed earthen trail.

Noiselessly, three more followed in single file, effortlessly matching pace with the lead pair. Their coats were woolly and ragged, still discarding thick winter fur. He could barely hear their soft panting.

Show no fear, Yakov willed.

Having made eye contact, the lead pair bounded alongside, flanking him left and right. Yakov was stunned by their size. Over a meter tall at the shoulder, the alpha male's canines could easily reach his throat. The wolf could easily serrate his jugular with a casual snap of his neck. The female, while smaller, probably weighed sixty kilograms and was capable of taking him down just as easily.

They did not attack. Instead, they pranced alongside with an easy gait, a hunting pack simply returning with its master.

With each hundred meters, the lead pair inched discernibly closer, tightening a vise from which he could not escape. These were not the mere men he'd eluded a day earlier, who relied on engineered teeth and technological claws. These wolves were capable hunters. Their casual manner mocked his apprehension and taunted his frailty, amused faces set in wicked grins.

What are they waiting for? His mind screamed in agitation. The long stroll with death was an unnecessary courtesy. Terrified, throat knotted, Yakov fixed his eyes, straight and level, refusing to acknowledge the three trailing wolves. He steeled his arms toward the pair beside him, a superficial stance to hold them at bay. He was convinced that the wolves were sizing him up and that dropping his pitiful guard would provoke the lethal attack.

Silently, the six marched, oddly stalemated.

Topping a small knoll, the trail slanted slightly, vectoring toward the cabin's porch. There he could see a small, unpainted log shanty, fashioned in rough timber and plastered mud. It was at present—occupied. Above a slanted slat roof, a chimney belched vibrantly, charcoal puffs whimsically curling skyward. The urge to sprint to shelter was powerful, but he refused to break stride. If he stumbled, if he flinched, the wolves would attack.

He would die within sight of safety.

With four hundred meters to go, the alpha pair closed in. The male's shoulder towered above his breastbone, the female's to his elbow. He sensed their body heat. Desperately, he mustered a confidence he did not possess, ignoring an insane instinct to pet them.

Whispering across the vacant hollow, a hinge creaked.

Silently, the lead wolves turned aside, drifting beneath Yakov's periphery. The geologist did not alter his pace. His heart leaped in his chest, the attack was imminent—surely they would tarry no longer. He could see their curved canines puncturing his neck and crushing his skull, a vindictive slaughter within meters of sanctuary.

Unable to see his stalkers, his senses sharpened acutely. Time dilated like an elastic band. The short grasses flexed painfully beneath a pressing breeze, the cabin's plume of cloudy molasses slowly billowed toward a languid blue sky. His heartbeat resonated hollowly in superimposed discord atop his ringing, tinsel ears. Over the white noise, he listened for a tell; the rustling of bent grass, a thudding paw, any presaging signal heralding the lethal lunge.

He planned his defense. Above all, he would protect his neck and not let the wolves take him down. The wolves might bite his extremities, but he would endure their superficial wounding. With luck, he might avoid deadly damage until he neared the homestead. There he might find a weapon—a piece of metal or stick to wield as a club.

Nothing materialized, no aberrant claw scraping against gravel, no heaving breath from an airborne canine. Not a whisper arose behind him. Five seconds passed, then ten...

Stoically, mindful of provoking the predators' killing instinct, he pivoted his neck, stealing a glance behind him. He was alone. There was
nothing but vacant space as far as he could see. At one instant they
had been trotting next to him...and the next...they were gone, vanishing
without so much as an irregular footfall.

The stretched band of time snapped shut.

Yakov would not wait for them to return. He ran, screaming for help
with every breath.

Sitting at his kitchen table, a flat butcher block covered with a faded,
frayed linen cloth laid out before him, Evan busied himself with summer
maintenance. Arrayed along the table's edge, within instant reach, were a
squeeze bottle of oil, dirty rags and a cluster of tools. He worked methodically, dutifully oiling, servicing and repairing his work line of *Conibear*
traps.

Once advertised as a more *humane* method of trapping, the Conibear
model didn't just vise-clamp on to the animal's leg. Rather, a spring
loaded top bar snapped over the back, breaking the spine, intended to kill
the hapless animal outright. In that vein, instant death was considered a
lesser evil in comparison to the enduring pain, terror or vulnerability of
further predation when gripped within steel jaws.

Many animals other than the fox—mink, other weasels and coyote
included—refuse to accept the inevitable when caught in a standard trap.
Given enough time, they embrace the only alternative, tolerating the un-
fathomable pain of self-mutilation by chewing off the captured limb.

Whatever the degree of humaneness Evan felt toward his quarried
bread and butter, it was tempered by the reality that a dead animal in a
Conibear clamp needed to be harvested promptly or the valued pelt would
be lost to scavengers. An un-serviced tool was useless, wasting a prized
resource and endangering his wellbeing.

Placing an oiled steel frame onto the cloth, Evan inspected the springs
for wear. In the distance, he thought he heard a man's voice calling.
The sound was faint and vague and very unusual given his isolated locale.
Looking up at his radio, Evan confirmed that it was off.

The howling noise was getting louder. *What the hell,* he thought,
heading for his front door.

A kilometer away, the strangest sight accosted his eyes. A half-naked
man was running towards his cabin, wild with fear. A white pelt draped
over his shoulders, covering his torso clear down to his knees and slitting
open with each halting stride.

Shouting hysterically, the man spewed a barrage of unintelligible gibberish that did not resemble language. As if blinded, the man ran clumsily, frequently stumbling, although his head was steady, staring at Evan's front door. The singular gaze was unnerving.

He's mad! Evan thought, reaching for his rifle. A WWI sniper's .308 rifle was hanging above his head, resting on a pair of steel nail pegs embedded in the wall atop the doorjamb. Loading a cartridge into the chamber, he cocked the firing pin, unlocked the safety and reduced the long-range sight to close quarters.

Already regretting his precautionary measure, he strode out the door onto his small patio. Firing the weapon would be a final resort. The last thing he needed was to initiate a new police record. Holding the rifle across his chest, ready to raise and fire, Evan nervously watched the *off-kilter* stranger approaching.

Now less than two hundred meters away, the runner was close enough that Evan could resolve smaller details. The man's face was unshaven, a tangle of unwashed, greasy dark hair covering his head. His ashen face appeared young, but its expression held age. The body build was Slavic. Beyond that, he was clearly naked beneath a draped polar bear fleece. His bare feet wore a thick coat of dried dirt and moist mud streaked his legs from his hips to his ankles, but it was the eyes that were most revealing. Held at full bore, beaded pupils steeled through him, set inside unblinking white circles. They revealed a man on the edge of sanity.

How the hell did he get out here? Across the short field separating them, Evan heard a familiar word.

"Help!"

Whether it was spoken in English, or in Russian, the language of Evan's Doukhobor grandparents, he did not discern, but the plea connected a switch in his mind, instant comprehension that the man was a foreigner from the Old Country and that he did not belong.

Few others dared intrude on this godforsaken hinterland. In an instant, Evan wondered if it was the mineral prospector that his RCMP visitor was looking for and had said would return, a suggestion he'd originally received as a threat.

How could he have survived the winter? It was too early in the season to travel over the thawing ground with anything but the lightest ATV. *Why is he coming here? Is he after me, or the walking stick? Are there more?*

The vulnerability of the trapper's isolation billowed front and center in his plume of thoughts. With measured alarm, he gripped the rifle firmly, double-checking its readiness, and raised it to his shoulder. The frantic man was a hundred meters away and not letting up his torrid pace. As the spacing dwindled, he could hear the man gasping for breath between terrified outbursts.

It was the terror in the rasping shrieks that arrested Evan's finger from releasing the firing pin. The approaching madman was neurotic, not a harbinger of murder or theft. In an instant, Evan made up his mind and his resolve was firm. He would get the man to Trakalo, but first, he would have to make sure he survived the encounter.

Evan's fear was completely unfounded. Pell-mell on his maddened dash, Yakov never made it. Blinded by fear, he'd focused on the building's form, unable to discern anything but the proffered haven. Nearing the cabin, he at last sighted the burly bushman guarding the front door. By then, it was too late to turn around.

As Yakov comprehended that the gargantuan settler was holding a weapon ready, the last hurdle of anxiety tripped him. He collapsed into an unconscious heap on the cold ground, his tortured body giving way a mere thirty meters from the porch.

Awakening later, he found himself immobilized, wrists and ankles secured within tight rope windings. The bristly cords dug into his flesh, enough to restrict blood flow, but not endanger his limbs. His extremities alternated sensations, between pins and needles and burning as his blood dammed and coursed. His arms were pulled behind his back, but his captor was not merciless, having stoked a strong fire in a cast iron pot belly stove at the room's center.

Already warming from the heat, Yakov's temples throbbed with a headache borne of dehydration, fear and defeat. And his stomach was again feeling the pangs of hunger. For now, covered in a thick woolen blanket, protected from the elements and wildlife, Yakov was thankful for his safety.

The frontiersman was not in sight. Outside the one-room cabin, Yakov could hear noises vibrating through the wall, probably arising from the porch. It was general rustling, the bumping and thumping of life, such as spindly table legs dragging over a wooden floor. After a few seconds of quiet, there was a burst of static, followed by a high pitched squeal that lingered. Suddenly, the electronic shrilling stopped, as the burly bushman locked in a ham radio signal.

Then a brief conversation commenced, unintelligible to Yakov, ran its course and ended. A few moments later, the man reappeared, holding his lifeline in his massive hands. Beneath his hat, long auburn hair flowed over his ears and down the nape of his neck. A classic mullet.

The man's face was weathered and grizzled, a coarse reddish-black stubble sandpapering his cheeks and neck. The facial hair was thick, as the man was young. He wore a green and black plaid felt jacket, both for warmth in the springtime chill and, more practically, to prevent insect bites. Below his torso, he wore old blue jeans, a creased leather belt and a pair of brown leather stub-toe boots. The clothes were sturdy, matching the frame of the outdoorsman.

It was no wonder Yakov had been bound so securely. The man was a beast.

But, uncharacteristic of a wild animal, his eyes twinkled with merriment, as if enjoying a private joke. Opening his mouth to speak, Yakov could not have prepared himself for the surprise.

"*Dobre dehn,*" greeted the trapper. "*Kak vi pozyvaesh?*"

Replying in Russian, Yakov answered, "Hungry and thirsty."

"Then I will fix you something to eat and drink."

Hours later, a warmed and sated Yakov was transferred into the custody of the RCMP and Lieutenant Trakalo.

The political game had begun.

Lying on a lumpy, coiled spring cot—a rusted, camp-style contraption— inside a cramped three meter by two meter cell, Yakov contemplated his next move. At a minimum, he was facing deportation, but whether a lengthy incarceration would precede expulsion, he could not begin to fathom.

He might request asylum, but first he would have to prove that his life was in danger. And, for starters, he didn't know who his captors were, but he could talk about the mineral, the submarine and the cut-throat machine of efficiency behind his contract. Those were the first items to bargain.

In a few days, an interpreter would arrive and he could begin bidding for his freedom. Maintaining discretion about his recent client was irrelevant, only his continued safety mattered. But he would bluff hard and sell high.

Although he desired to return to Moscow, he could not go unless the Canadian authorities protected him. That was something he did not feel confident about. Until he knew the identity of his employer, he would never feel safe again. They were a professional group, backed with wealth and lethal in their plan executions. In his heart, he was positive that he would never again see his homeland.

Chapter 14

Omissions

An hour's drive south of the Puerto Vallarta airport, the ex-president navigated a winding, two lane coastal highway. Driving a nondescript, late model Volkswagen Passat, Shaparell and his wife, Iness, passed through the city without being recognized, barely glancing at the modern Marina, the rebuilt Old Town *Malecon* and bypassing the upscale communities of the southern resorts.

Trailing a short distance behind, his secret service detail-for-life struggled to prevent two cardinal *faux pas*, losing him or tailgating into an accident. The two seasoned security men were nervous, having been unable to stop him from driving. Shaparell had argued that it was an unscheduled foray for some rest and relaxation; rules could be relaxed.

Since no one knew where they were at present, the risk was minimal. Reluctantly, they had acquiesced.

The asphalt snaked a dozen rocky meters above the water. On the seaside, luxurious multi-storey villas stretched vertically from roadside to sand. Being high season, the superlative houses were fully leased and quartering the well-to-do. Although Shaparell could have displaced a lesser lessee, he had deferred, preferring to remain incognito.

Besides, the private villas posed exorbitant security risks for his small crew. Their lodging destination was both public and remote. If news of his presence leaked, within two days, they'd be departing. This was a private vacation, a quick escape from the claustrophobia of constant illumination in the public spotlight.

Passing the submerged arches of Los Arcos, Vallarta's world famous diving mecca, Shaparell finally inhaled the scenery. He slowed to a sightseeing pace. The first domes, with underlying arches and tunnels, were a mere hundred meters off shore. Between the rocky structures, the warm, azure waters were filled with small boats, snorkelers and scuba divers.

Beyond the arches, however, the sea plunged over two hundred meters toward the edge of the continental shelf. A constant upwelling of cool, nutrient rich water surged toward the surface, feeding an abundance of intensely colored tropical marine life. Sighing as he drove past, Shaparell resumed driving speed.

Regrettably, he was not visiting to dive.

Bypassing the provincial dwellings, they entered a coastal, mountain-side jungle. Here, through his open window, monkeys shrieked from the dense foliage. Closer to the beach, he'd heard that native crocodiles were present. Those he would like to see.

Turning westward with the outgoing bay, Shaparell drove over a short rise in the road.

"LOOK OUT!"

Slamming on his brakes, he brought the Passat to a skidding halt. Blue smoke billowed from the pavement, roiling past his window. Behind him, anti-lock brakes engaged, the secret service car raised up and shuddered to a halt, narrowly avoiding his back bumper.

Shuffling across the road, a gargantuan Brahma bull obstinately thwarted transit. Of menacing size, it would have seriously damaged any vehicle upon contact. Protruding sideways nearly a meter from its bony skull, two curved horns resolutely proclaimed strength and power.

Shaparell shuddered. A sideways swat and the goring tip could pierce a window.

"Where did that beast come from?" Shaparell muttered, breathing a sigh of relief.

"Up there," his wife pointed ahead. Alongside the hardtop, a rusty old pickup truck was marooned on the dirt shoulder, its underbelly resting on the road's edge. Having blown a tire and partially sliding off the two-lane, the truck was now immovable. Its damaged rim spun lazily in free space.

A flimsy, wooden ox-cart, built onto the truck bed, had ruptured under the weight of the sliding bull. Bursting free from his disjointed slats, the unharmed bovine shook off a few harmless splinters and ambled away. Free to roam the seaside, it chose to stay nearby, foraging on roadside shoots.

"We're damn lucky," Shaparell muttered.

"Do you think they need help?" he heard his wife asking.

"Uh, sure," he answered, preferring not to get involved. Reluctantly exiting the car, he was immediately apprehended by his guards who, show-ing good sense and sufficient presence of mind, were performing their job again. In their opinion, the American ex-president did not need to play the part of a good Samaritan.

"Sir, let us handle this," one suggested, and Shaparell could not have agreed more. With relief he re-entered his car.

The first agent, pulling out a cell phone, made a quick emergency call. After securing the promise of help, the two men strode forward to reconnoiter the victims.

"Necessite ayudar?" one proffered in rudimentary Spanish. The offer was quickly accepted.

Obscured by tinted glass and hat brims, the Shaparells hid from the accumulating motorists. The helpful gathering vociferously presided over each aspect of carriage repair, tire replacement and vehicle re-seating. A vigorous debate over the integrity of the axle broke out, inciting a fretful delay during which the two agents discreetly positioned themselves in front of the Shaparells' vehicle to block the line of sight.

Finally the crowd cleared, continuing on their respective ways, and the farmer concentrated on recovering his prized specimen.

It was vaudeville. The bull, a lumbering, cantankerous beast, bore little respect for his bipedal handlers. Fortunately, he wasn't holding a grudge for the earlier rough handling that had landed him in the ditch. Attempting to shepherd the ox toward the truck, the remaining men prodded it with sticks, pokes and shouts, all the while keeping a respectful distance from the huge animal.

Carefully marshaling their quarry, they enticed it to the truck side and no further. Each attempt to persuade it onto the truck bed resulted in either of two extremes, indifference or an irritated sideways swat from the sharp horns. With each outburst the men darted out of the range of the perforating daggers, sometimes landing within the prickly brambles of the roadside foliage. Then they cursed their luck and plotted the next attempt.

Shaparell smiled in amusement.

Twenty minutes later, as a new queue of vehicles grew behind the scene, little progress had been achieved.

Then, with obstinate timing, the bull plodded next to the rear tailgate, drawn more by a sense of familiarity than coercion. At the pull out ramp the bull stopped short and stood in place—a last act of defiance—perhaps motivated purely for its own merriment.

At this juncture, Shaparell could not resist smirking broadly as his two streetwise, but gentrified, security agents attempted to corral the recalcitrant specimen up the incline.

At last they succeeded. As the gate slammed shut behind, the two agents retreated. A whipped dog could not have skulked away more obviously.

"Gracias!" called out the farmer.

"De nada," responded the bilingual agent, although he had more personal phrases to vent at the ox. Wisely, he held his tongue. This was not his country. Without so much as a glance toward their boss sitting within the Passat, the security detail re-entered their vehicle. The skilled driver pulled out into the road and slowly drove forward, blocking the frustrated drivers from overtaking the ex-president.

Shaparell understood the routine, rolling by the grateful, waving farmer while staring fixedly on the road.

There were no further events of significance, apart from the mesmerizing beauty of the Mexican Pacific coastline. Majestic in its vistas, it riveted their attention and, on more than one occasion, Shaparell drifted dangerously across the road median while enjoying the view.

The trailing security agents, less inclined to attention lapses, kept mental notes. After all, it was their ass if something serious occurred. With palpable relief, they finally approached a small, hand-painted sign, half hidden in the roadside foliage. In simple block text, it read—Hotel Mismaloya 100 metros. Their annoying journey would soon be over. Letting their half-baked retiree boss have his own way was all too often an exercise in recklessness. Preventing it was nigh to impossible.

As the road rounded a last a rocky spur, the roadside shoulder fell precipitously away—a sheer cliff. A hundred meters below, dazzling azure water rolled into a diminutive horseshoe bay. On three sides, noble basaltic bluffs presided over the water's edge, towering sharply upward before fanning into a deep mountain bowl nearly two thousand meters in height. Where the slope eased, tropical plants took hold and dense foliage grew luxuriantly.

If the jungle was merely interesting, what lay below was simply remarkable. Bordering the water's edge, a narrow strip of gleaming white sand contrasted starkly against turquoise water. It was a perfectly sheltered private hideaway.

Along the open ocean, the powerful Pacific gyred southward, restricted from entering the protected cove *en masse*. Atypically weak wavelets lapped the shimmering shore, akin to an island surge, rather than the usual pounding surf of the California coastline. Above sea level, the constant onshore breeze also met resistance by the hemispherical mountain bowl, rising to plateaus high overhead.

The result was a paradise, strong sunshine, warm air and cool, calm water for the swim set.

Along the back rim of the bay, an immense four-star luxury hotel had been built into the sandy strip. In girth, the hotel occupied a significant fraction of available beach. Paralleling the cliff face, the multi-storey edifice's penthouse lofted to roadside height.

An opulent privacy, invisible from any urban life.

But geography is not so completely magnanimous. The resort had a tragic past, and an equally uncertain future. A decade earlier, Mismaloya had nearly vanished, a victim of tectonic pressures and grinding surf. Beneath the sand, the subterranean rock bed weakened into a degenerated, fragile foundation of scoured rock.

On a single night, without a prelude of fore shocks, a shelf collapsed. While not damaging the hotel, the loss of real estate reduced the beach-front by half. Whether by oversight or by politics, the catastrophic failure seemed to have been a surprise to all involved. For a period, the hotel had closed. Concerned parties vigorously debated different fates, divided between permanent demolition and optimistic recertification of the resort.

Skewing the tilt, a consortium of well-compensated, influential civil engineers convinced the authorities that the next major oceanic event would be generations in the future, well beyond the lifetime of any who presently cared.

The hundred year risk was statistically small. Within short order, the hotel had re-opened.

The secret of the structural collapse was then vigorously put under wraps. Few of the public who patronized its extraordinary charms were ever aware of the possibility of disaster.

Reserving the penthouse for seventy-two hours, Shaparell quickly settled in. The booking did not require special consideration. A fragile economy had bankrupted the scheduled tenant, leaving it vacant for a fortnight. The opulent quarters had nearly remained empty, but a discreet word of mouth promotion through exclusive travel agencies had alerted him of its availability a few days earlier and Shaparell instantly accepted.

The hotel's roof, visible from the highway, was a security risk to pent-house deck loungers. Leveraging his influence and his bodyguards' expertise, Shaparell obtained a round the clock detail to patrol the roadside perimeter.

A localized guard could deal firmly with trespassers and loiterers. It was common protocol at the resort and wouldn't raise any eyebrows.

Well before his wife awoke Shaparell organized his trade craft; a collapsible, graphite fishing rod and an open face reel spooled with four-pound line. For tackle, he packed an assortment of ultra-light spinners and a dozen flies, mainly midges, mosquitoes and insect larvae. His outfit was not designed for fly-casting, but if the current were strong, he could still coax a floating, hooked tidbit into position.

Without announcing his intentions, he spent a few minutes on the computer, studying satellite images of the nearby mountains. Locating a deeply cut ravine on the nearby mountainside, he'd marked the telltale silvery thread of a fast flowing stream. The surrounding jungle appeared uninhabited, except near the coastal highway.

There, nestled by the creek's mouth lay a tiny, unstructured village. From the sky-borne images, he saw a single, earthen street randomly flanked by a sprawl of flattop buildings and huts. It looked promising.

Deciding to park at the village and ascend by foot alongside the stream bed, Shaparell hoped to find pools stocked with trout. Not that he really needed to angle, this venture was more about solitude and peace. Going fishing was a convenient excuse.

Leaving a cursory note, but omitting the destination, he departed his suite shortly before sunrise. Avoiding the elevator cameras, he took the stairs to a topside parking lot, tipped the valet extra, and drove past a hired sentry who failed to recognize him in the dim of dawn. A quarter of an hour later, he located the village and parked along a dusty roadside. Gathering his equipment, he locked the car doors and began hiking uphill.

Even in the early hours, the first half kilometer was the most interesting, though he paid little attention.

His mind was enamored by the freedom.

Had he stopped to notice, he would have observed that the square brick buildings barely resembled modern design or architecture, having been erected almost a century earlier. Adjoined into a single block row, the edifices soon gave way to tiny adobe houses, time-stepping further into the previous century.

Here, the inhabitants' relatively large yards showcased meager possessions. Devoid of pricey ornaments or manicured gardens, they instead housed a plethora of automobile hardware, mostly early-model Fords, VW's and Tsurus. In some, there were junkets originating from long deceased manufacturers. Nothing was newer than a decade.

Strewn over bared earth, many junks were devoid of essential parts, such as doors, windows, seats or wheels. Some were completely gutless, hoodless fronts and gaping engine compartments now supporting cobwebs and cats. Ostensibly, these dismantled carcasses had been harvested for parts, but even the drivable craft seemed only a backfire removed from retirement. The usable workhorses held a place of honor, parked closest to the habitations.

At the edge of the forest, the junkyards ended, as did the dirt road. Beneath the tree canopy the village continued: individual abodes spread out along a dirt path following the meandering river. The farther he penetrated the hidden village, the fewer the trappings of industrial civilization. Brick gave way to adobe and adobe to unpainted shanties of varying shades of gray obviously pieced together with surplus timber.

In small backyards, thin rail fences penned burros and pigs. On earthen front door stoops, lackadaisical dogs stretched. A few mutts lazily lifted their heads at his passing. None barked in warning. The thickening humidity of the advancing day sapped their energy, pinning the curs to cool ground.

Alongside the dilapidated frames, the shallow stream rippled over a bed of boulders. Within the churning water, Shaparell saw no signs of his coveted fish. Likely none could live in the village area, where raw sewage from humans and all manner of animals seeped through the soft loam into the rushing water.

A kilometer upstream, the human population waned, but the transparent streambed remained disappointing.

Sweating profusely, Shaparell peered into the shallows, seeing only water spiders skittering beneath a cloud of insects at a stagnant side pool. He proceeded uphill.

Another half kilometer upstream, the forest silently closed in, becoming a den of isolation. Tiring from his ascent, he decided to fish anyways. The water was clean and bubbling—thereby injecting oxygen and suitable for trout.

Wading into the gravelly shallows, he sought a target for casting. Twenty yards upstream, a slanted tree bough hovered over the water's edge.

If it's anything like Montana, he reasoned, *a lunker is lurking in the shade.*

Expertly casting upstream, his fly landed past the overhang a meter from shore. Satisfied, Shaparell waited patiently for the fly to drift, gathering in the slack line. The small fly dawdled downstream, held aloft by surface tension, and floated beneath the limb. It was not attacked.

"Damn!" Shaparell grunted. His polarized glasses let him see into the rippling water and he sought the tell tale reflective flash of scales. Not a living fish was within view. Not even a minnow.

Through the water, he slogged upstream. Beneath his feet, small stones dislodged, sweeping downstream in the swift current. Stumbling over a large rock, he fell into the rapid surge and was carried a few meters downstream before he regained his footing. Returning to shore, he repacked his small tackle box. As he finished snapping the lid shut, a sharp rustling beyond the near bank caught his attention.

Staring at the origin of the noise, he was surprised to see a swarthy, shirtless, well-muscled man approaching him. The man possessed a lethal machete. It was slung over his torso, held by a thin cord around his neck. He looked serious.

"*Bueno!*" Shaparell called amicably, stifling a pang of nervousness with friendliness.

"*Chinga te, cabron,*" the man grunted, belligerently.

Alarmed, Shaparell looked around, hoping to find a quick way out. It wasn't across the rushing water where a steep bank hindered passage to the opposing jungle. Heading upstream was worse. There was no instant refuge available. From behind, sloshing water caught his attention. Snapping his head smartly, he craned his neck again.

A second man was approaching, trudging upstream, holding a square pistol in his hand, finger over the trigger housing. Realizing his presence was noted the man nonchalantly raised the gun, aimed at Shaparell and repositioned his trigger finger.

"There is no escape," he spat. "Get out of the water!"

Dutifully, but taking his time, Shaparell complied, steadily climbing the soft earthen bank toward the machete-wielding man. His mind blazed through his few remaining options, the most daring being to outrun the shorter foe. He needed to eliminate the line of sight to the gun. Angling toward the thick cover, he attempted to put a thick trunk between himself and the gunman.

"Not that way!" commanded the man in the water. Cracking sharply, the pistol discharged, backing up his demand. A few feet away, splinters of wood exploded, shattered by the impact of supersonic lead. A smell of scorched wood wafted over the stream.

Cowed, Shaparell froze. Turning to face the shooter, he benignly raised his hands, exposing their harmless contents in full view. His eyes blazed angrily, staring down the gun-toting shooter, who was approaching the cut bank below him.

"Hurting me is very unwise," he warned.

"We do not wish to kill you," came the answer.

Shaparell did not feel assured. They knew who he was.

Before he could bluster further, the handle of a machete hammered onto the back of his head. Flashing nerves crisply turned to darkness as his consciousness subdued.

* * *

Roughly jarring against a rigid surface, Shaparell's head bounced painfully onto a thin, wooden rail platform on which he found his body tightly secured. Small stems and leaves whipped his face. Slung on shoulder straps between two men, he was being carried uphill along a rarely traveled path.

If the awakening was rude, he had little time to gripe. His renewed consciousness was dominated by discomfort. Besides a blinding headache, a remnant of the machete's handle blow to his head, his hands and feet were tightly bound with sisal twine bindings, stinging from where his skin was rubbed raw. His mouth ached, stretched open and gagged.

For the moment he lay quiet, assessing his predicament.

The front man was burly, with dark hair, broad shoulders and a thick neck. He was wearing the uniform of a *Federale*, his back muscles standing in etched relief against the sweat-soaked cloth. Clearly, he was fit, a well-trained professional, skilled to kill.

Shaparell did not buy the garb. His abductors could be from anywhere in the world. Strangely, his gait looked American, muscles conditioned by sustained exercise, heavy weight lifting, and fed a rich diet. Not all militaries have the luxury of three nutritious squares a day, rendering a physique leaner than their American counterparts.

Around him, the foliage and stream were unchanged. He deduced they were only a few hundred meters above the point of his capture, a supposition confirmed by the occasional fragrance of a wafting sea breeze. However, they were moving deeper into the jungle.

Why are they carrying me uphill? he wondered. If they wanted to kill him, it would have been done already. If they wanted a public execution, he'd be going downhill.

Do they want a ransom? Possibly. And that begged deeper questions, like who they were and how did they know he was in Jalisco. Furthermore, how could they mobilize overnight to snatch him and secure a safe harbor along this very path. It didn't make sense, but Shaparell did not believe it was an intersection of blind luck and coincidence.

Timing the swaying of the platform, he slumped his head rhythmically toward the stream. Within the bubbling water, a woman was bent over washing her laundry. Her clothes were shapeless, draping loosely over her huddled form. They looked homemade and poor, but functional. Dipping a garment into the stream to wet it, she raised it onto a weathered washboard set over a rock and began scrubbing.

On the opposite bank, a small wooden hut stood, built over a small patch of level ground beneath the tall trees. Fashioned from weather-beaten, rough-hewn timber, the humble home also served as a corner post to a line of fencing, hand-cut and lashed with plastic twine. Inside the corral lazed a short-eared donkey and a pair of piglets.

What the hell? Astonished, he stared at the peasant woman. *Do people live like this in North America?*

Transfixed, he watched the woman working her daily ritual, craning his neck and rolling his eyes to keep her in sight until the trees blocked his view. Walking along this stream was like stepping back into time. No one would find him here. No one would expect him here.

A few dozen meters uphill was another timeless surprise. An actual one-room adobe hut, built from matted straw and stream mud, barely two meters tall. Behind a fence made from thin samplings, three young children played on the ground. Wearing only faded and ragged shorts, they scrambled barefoot over the soft earth, engrossed in a game of tag. Behind the fence, another burrow slurped water from a trough, tied to a post. Its lazy eyes seemed to sum up his intrusion by saying, "You, too, shall pass."

With his head positioned awkwardly, Shaparell began assessing the man behind. He squinted but could not properly assess the trailing assailant without giving alert that he was conscious. Instead, closing his eyes, he listened to the footfalls, determining the number of men, their relative size, and strength.

After a few moments, he had gathered several details.

There were just two men, each treading similarly, sporting cat-like power over the damp earth. Transporting the human load over rocks and fallen obstacles, they did not falter. In disgust, he realized that his burden was of no great exertion. They were strong, agile, and fit.

Damn, he thought. *They're well-trained light infantrymen.*

He would not be able to fight his way out.

Hours later, the three men entered a small clearing. The men were finally showing signs of fatigue. Both sweated profusely, bulging veins ribboned over heat-soaked, swollen arms. Shaparell was faring no better. In addition to chafing and aching, the increase in altitude was rendering him lightheaded and dizzy.

The odds were not tilting in his favor.

The warm coastal air had cooled as they had climbed. Here, at fifteen hundred meters above sea level, the air was temperate, although the humidity was still saturated. Rolling fog banks graced the trees and a light dew frequently misted. It was much more comfortable here than down by the seaside.

Carrying him into a small hut made from thin poles and covered with a thatched straw roof, the men deposited him on the soft earthen floor still bound to the rails. Checking his lashings, and satisfied that he was securely held, they finally spoke to each other.

"*Vaminos?*"

"*Si. El hefe esta aqui en dos ahoras.*"

They left.

In two hours, Shaparell would learn his fate, he would not wait idly.

Two hours later, however, he was still bound. His failed efforts to fray the binding against the rough wood surface had done more damage than good. During a moment of extreme agitation, he had flipped over, landing face first in the dirt. Thus turtled, he could not turn the wood bed over again to right himself.

Worse, covered in sweat and dirt, he was an insect magnet. The voracious predators crawled over his body, sipped his sweat, drank his blood and stung his arms to numbness.

Somewhere down the mountain, there would be a full-scale manhunt searching for him, but he could not take heart in that effort. No one else knew where he had been, nor where he was. As afternoon wore on, the cabin dimmed. In the shadowy interior, he could not resolve any tools that might assist him.

Shaparell was grateful for being indoors. Outside, he swore he heard a primate species chattering in the treetop. What size of troupe; how big they were or what they ate were beyond his knowledge. Being indoors kept the large beasts away, especially the snakes that, in his helpless state, could have feasted on him. Not that the mosquitoes hadn't had their way with his blood supply. He feared malaria might be an inevitable payment...provided he survived at all.

From nearby, he heard a forced rustling of trees and branches. Muted voices teased the limits of his hearing. There was no mistaking. The boss' party had arrived.

Entering the small hut, a gray-grizzled, bearded face appeared, first peering warily throughout the small space. Satisfied with Shaparell's bindings, the remainder of his extraordinarily fit, middle-aged form crossed the threshold. Pausing for a moment to let his eyes adjust, he held a pistol poised *at ready* with his left hand. On his strong face presided an authoritarian manner, a smart, disciplined military bearing.

Making eye contact with Shaparell, his eyes briefly opened wide, either in surprise—or disbelief. Clearly he recognized the captive. Closely scanning over the bindings, and seeing little to alarm him, he turned Shaparell over onto his back again.

Shaparell's eyes blazed in anger, and the dark glance further motivated his captor.

"*Descanso, pronto!*" he demanded, calling outside the rickety door frame.

Almost immediately, another slim man entered, bearing a medic's bag. Retrieving a syringe and an auburn five dram vial, he pierced a needle through the bottle's plastic end, withdrew the plunger and filled the hollow tube with a clear liquid. Having loaded the needle, he turned to face his superior.

"*Diez millitros,*" he announced.

"*Bien,*" affirmed the graybeard.

Realizing he was about to be drugged, Shaparell struggled against his tethers, writhing onto the dirt floor, straining against the gripping bonds. It was a pitiful effort. Moments later, exhausted, sweating and slathered in dirt and debris, he lost his will and let go.

Immediately, the medic stepped forward, plunging the needle into his carotid artery. Depressing the plunger, the narcotic flowed into his blood. Just as quickly, the man stepped back, fearful of a final fit of fury but the former president did not move.

Quickly following the sting, Shaparell felt the fluid swelling uncomfortably. His skin felt numb, but the punctured tissue ached as though snake bit. Seconds later, a drowsiness descended, consuming him in chemical isolation. He felt hollow.

Inside the tunnel of his mind, he heard his tormentors taunting, a mocking rant, although he could not decipher a single phrase he was not going down easy. He was fighting back, tearing their flesh from bones with sharpened fingernails.

A moment later, he blacked out, kicking and screaming inside the confines of his captured mind.

Shaparell regained consciousness, the nightmare of screeching banshees encroached above his head instantly dissipated, replaced by the voluminous calls of jungle birds arguing in the tree tops outside.

Full clarity of mind took longer, inhibited by an overwhelming malaise from his chemical hangover. His neck ached, swollen and sore where the injection had penetrated his flesh, but his shoulders, back and legs were also tight through the nape of his neck, a result of chilled immobilization on moist ground. To his surprise, he could move his limbs freely. He was no longer bound.

"What the hell?" he muttered aloud. "I've been let go?"

He tried to stand, but failed. Pulling himself onto his elbows, nausea sank through his stomach. He vomited putrid bile, prolonging the queasiness. He collapsed on cleaner ground, too dizzy to move. From his prone position, he analyzed his surroundings.

They were familiar. He'd been abandoned in the tiny hut.

The shack was dimly lit by light shafts entering slatted chinks in the wall, it was day. The beams shone from the opposite end of the shanty, it was morning. He'd been unconscious for at least one full night. Gathering his balance and bearings, Shaparell was acutely aware of thirst. His first task would be wetting his burred tongue in the mountain stream, parasites be damned.

Over the next hour, while his equilibrium recovered, he pieced together thoughts of his capture.

Had it been random, or had someone been tipped off? Being left alone and unrestrained in the cabin suggested the latter, a sinister reality. There were a handful of people, *in the know*, that he was outside the US. Apart from the chance incident of the farmer's accident, he'd not been in the public enough to be recognized. Neither had he broadcast his presence at the resort.

Someone was keeping tabs on him. Was it his agents? He doubted it. They were personal, loyal bodyguards, participating in family celebrations, birthdays and anniversaries. They were well compensated, and now that the spotlight shone infrequently, their task was simpler, even mundane, and infinitely safer.

Who were the kidnappers? They appeared to be Mexican or Latino, both in discipline and skills. Although they did not display sophisticated communication equipment, they must have been tipped off to find him so quickly.

Who had done that? And, why was a military group operating out of a tropical jungle on their homeland?

He had many questions, but his first business was trekking down the mountain, back to his worried wife. He was not concerned about political consequences. His short abduction could be pawned off to a number of excuses, few people would know the truth, but he needed to know why it happened, and once that was determined, there would be hell to pay.

He still had connections and favors owed.

As his strength returned, Shaparell awkwardly stood up and walked out the rickety door. Stumbling to the water's edge, he imbibed of its salving freshness. A thin remnant of a trail snaked downhill. He was surrounded by strange jungle calls. From high in the treetops, vocal monkeys shook branches and screeched while unseen birds hooted loudly betraying his presence. Yet, he saw no one. The path contained few distinctive footprints, an overnight downpour had washed away his captors' tracks.

Of one thing Shaparell was certain. He'd not been captured by a cartel. If he had, he would not have been left alone. His detention was a political shenanigan, a gut-wrenching tactic. Thinking within that vein strongly begged that there was an inside connection.

Four hours later, Shaparell re-entered the coastal village, taking pains to avoid contact with anyone or anything.

On the way down, he'd abandoned the dirt trail on multiple occasions to hide when hearing sounds arising from others' movements. In each instance, worry constricting his throat, he'd failed to catch a glimpse of the sojourners, suggesting they were animals, not humans. It was just as well. Although he was convinced he'd been let go, he had no desire to test his hopeful hypothesis.

There was little else alive to see. A few tree frogs hopping over leaf litter, several four-foot long snakes slithering beneath broad leaf ground cover. Ducking beneath fallen timber at one bend, he'd nearly brushed his face against a lime-green serpent curled in a forked tree branch. Whether it was poisonous or not, he did not know. Instead, his chest heaving, he'd prudently walked around, fearful he was stepping toward other venomous creatures hidden in the undergrowth. It would be a terrible irony, cheating death from the hands of organized fighters, only to lose to a few grams of evolutionary fury.

In humble honesty, he realized that he feared the multi-legged creatures far more than his bipedal adversaries.

Stepping out of the jungle, he again crossed the boundary from the natural to the engineered. Two rows of dilapidated buildings formed a town: domiciles, downtown and beachfront. Peeling paint proclaimed that profits had long ago vanished, and the quaint lifestyle was decaying into extinction, but it would be a mistake to assume that all of the town's inhabitants were cut off from the modern world.

In this part of the country, the drug trade had silent sentries posted in forgotten places such as these.

Standing on the dusty street a few doors ahead, next to the decayed frontage of his shop's porch, a proprietor spoke rapidly into an ultra-modern mouthpiece. From the corners of his eyes, the wary business-man watched the approaching fugitive closely, his agitation and animation growing.

Shaparell paced steadily, behaving in a non-threatening manner. He did not want another altercation. Unfortunately, it was too late for that.

Once seen, there was no place to hide, except to return to the jungle. Realistically, even that option was gone. Evading a couple of men had been difficult enough, he would not elude a troop of village locals.

"*Si, si,*" he heard the man repeating into the cell phone. The old man was not allowed to express a personal thought. The cartel's reach and payroll were too deep.

"*Si, es aqui, es aqui,*" and the man turned to face him, looking straight at his face, hard brown eyes bearing a warning, "*Ahora! Si! Muy bueno.*"

He pulled the phone away from his face and addressed the fugitive.

"*El Presidente?*" he queried.

"Yes," Shaparell's jaw dropped.

"*Una momente, por favor.*" He gestured for Shaparell to stay.

Five minutes later, a solid blue Tsuru fiercely drove the earthen street, spewing a small cloud of dust and debris, impatiently eliminating the gap towards the pair. Seconds later, the car careened to a stop, a bodyguard emerged, gun in hand, sprinting to his side. He looked scared.

"Sir, we must go now."

Needing no further encouragement, Shaparell followed his trusted aide toward the idling vehicle, where the other guard was holding the rear door open. Turning to thank the elderly benefactor, he found himself viewing a faded, redbrick wall. The old man had vanished.

Pain ballooned in his neck, the piercing explosion of a sharp lancet delivering a pungent dose. Immediately, Shaparell felt his muscles giving way, succumbing to an elixir of slumber.

"You son-of-bitch!!" he choked feebly.

"Sorry sir," the man answered, pushing the elder statesman into the car, but his eyes were intense, inharmonious with his apology.

As the sedan sped away, Shaparell slumped in his seat, once again held tightly in the bond of a pharmaceutical coma.

Chapter 15

Missteps

"What the hell were you thinking?" Ottley scolded.

"I'm not following you, sir," Robb answered.

"Your IR-gadget idea."

"What?"

"The one you've been arguing to your co-workers in the lunch room. The one you discussed with me. You know, *Whispering Galleries*. You've been on a campaign."

Robb ignored the sarcasm and the threat. "What's wrong with it?"

"We pitched it, we worked it, and it's turned up nothing. We look like fools."

Robb was confused, but stayed silent, shifting nervously in his chair while awaiting the next outburst from his unusually florid boss.

"We've devoted resources to ferreting out your high-tech hypothesis, and this is all we found, an obsolete transmitter." Tossing a tiny, plastic-looking, electronic ferrule across the table, he underscored his rant.

"Where did this come from?" Robb questioned.

"Shaparell's idiotic excursion."

"The media says he was kidnapped by a Xacatecas drug cartel and made a fortunate escape."

"They're writing that to cover up his stupidity and our ineptness."

"I haven't been cleared to hear this, sir," Robb countered. "Why would they do that anyway?"

"You are now, since it involves your dumb-ass idea."

"In what way?"

"The director thought your remote-controlled gadget idea warranted serious analysis. He ordered an investigation. I told him we lacked resources, he told me to reassign manpower. We diverted people from other projects to work on it. We looked under rocks, crawled through jungle caves, paid off a bunch of low life, bloodsucking informants trying to find your phantom army and its techno-gizmo product. But it's been a boondoggle, a waste of time and taxpayer money. We haven't found anything because there's nothing to find."

"I definitely haven't heard any of this," Robb puzzled, "...and how can you be so certain?"

"It was a simple kidnapping by a rogue army group," Ottley stated, noting Robb's ignorance. "Following the recent Mexican presidential election uprisings, an entire battalion disappeared. During campaigning, they'd been assigned to protect the opposition candidate. They were fiercely loyal, but when he conceded, they disenfranchised.

The group simply went AWOL. Presumably they went underground, hoping to re-emerge if a revolt started. That didn't happen. The aftermath ended more or less peaceably and popular support waned. They were forced into hiding. After several years on the run, they're probably broke and deluded, desperate to re-establish a populist following."

"Where have they been?"

"We didn't care until now, but new intel is coming through. They're hiding in the jungles of Jalisco. Apparently, they wish to avoid confrontation with the cartels or having to courier drugs for funds. It looks like dumb luck that their path and Shaparell's crossed. Don't get me wrong, the group is organized, disciplined and tough, but they're not high tech, and couldn't possibly possess advanced weaponry. In fact, they implanted this, a crudely made homer, nothing more," he handed the object to Robb. "It works on a standard frequency and was routinely uncovered during the initial body search."

"That makes no sense."

"You have a better idea? I'm listening."

"First, how do you connect them to my hypothesis? I see no obvious correlation, not even based on their military origins. They're after power in Mexico, not here. Second, what's the point of planting an obvious bug? Not much, except to follow Shaparell's whereabouts. And what good is that if they lost him? They'd know full well a simple device would be found and they couldn't follow up on his movements for long. Unless, of course, they planned to keep him in Mexico, which is impossibly naive. The only thing that makes sense is that they need money, but certainly not at the expense of harming Shaparell."

Robb reasoned further, probing the other flaw, then exclaimed, "Wait, you said they implanted the bug. Where?"

"Behind the nape of his neck."

"Fully beneath the skin?"

"Embedded flush with the surface."

"Did you check for more? How many did you find?"

Ottley stared at him malignantly, "Of course we fools stopped at one..."

Still an asshole! Robb thought. An alarm chimed, *he isn't answering my questions...*

"What army is this ignorant?" Robb argued further. "Either the device keeps him on a close leash or it's a blatant gimmick. Prejudice is not intelligence."

"Insubordination doesn't keep jobs," Ottley threatened. "Maybe they're so short of funds this is the best they have."

"They'd have to be working on fumes to be attempting something this Neanderthal and to ignore its inherent repercussions."

"Exactly our inherent conclusion, Mr. Academic."

Ottley was getting under his skin, exasperating him. The conversation was nonsensical. Robb pushed back. "Shaparell was acting impulsively, sir," he justified. "Random chance is too convenient. Any of his enemies could orchestrate an abduction. You can't fault my analysis."

Beyond this obvious flaw, his argument lost steam, "he has quite a few adversaries around the world, you know?"

"Yeah, don't I though, and I can't waste the taxpayers' funds chasing an intern's science fantasy."

"I don't see how the two are related, sir," Robb replied, subdued but adamant.

"Trust me, they are. You're not cleared for it."

Sitting alone at a cafeteria in the Space and Science Smithsonian, Robb savored his garlic-soused curly fries, cuisine neither lean nor gourmet. He found it difficult to abandon a college diet just because he had steady income.

Vibrating in his pocket, his cell phone yanked an omnipresent tether. He screened the caller. The number was unfamiliar, as was the area code...he'd never seen 306 pop up on his phone before.

The phone buzzed again while he debated rejecting the oddly-originated call, but he was bored, a solitary trespasser adrift amongst vacationing families.

The escape beckoned.

"Hello."

"Is this Robb?"

"Yes, who's calling, please?"

"Robb, this is Lieutenant Trakalo of the RCMP. I'm calling from Reindeer Lake, Saskatchewan."

"Okay...who?"

"The Royal Canadian Mounted Police. I'm based in Churchill, Manitoba, but I cover both northern Manitoba and Saskatchewan."

Robb puzzled. "Why are you calling me?"

"I got your number from a colleague of yours, a Paulina. I'm wondering if you can lend me a few minutes of your time to discuss something in the line of your work."

"It's the weekend."

"Yes, I know. I thought it best to contact you away from the office."

"Yes?"

How the hell does he know I'm at the CIA?

"I understand you're an expert on Rare Earth phosphors," Trakalo continued.

"Thanks for the compliment," Robb deferred, exhaling in relief, "but I'm not an authority, I'm a graduate student."

"Well, your work was referred to me by someone in Michigan, an engineer who thinks highly of it."

"Can't say I know who that would be," Robb puzzled.

"No, you probably wouldn't. He described himself as being 'in industry, not academia.'"

"Doesn't sound flattering."

"Not the way he said it," Trakalo explained, "he meant that he wasn't up to your par."

"Sorry."

"Don't mention it."

Slightly embarrassed, Robb changed the subject, "how can I help?"

"We have a man in custody here, a Russian national who was apprehended while illegally prospecting for minerals. Apparently, he's found a fairly sizable surface deposit of what he thinks is a, how did he call it, a Lanthanide ore."

"Did he say which one?" Robb was immediately interested.

"Erbium, I believe, but he mentioned others, too."

"No kidding," Robb breathed, "this would be the first major North American deposit found in quite some time."

"Is that important?"

"Maybe not immediately, but one day, yes, it will be," Robb conjectured.

"Why?"

"Lanthanide's are showing promise in creating emerging industries. At present, Erbium is a key ingredient in several small sectors, like pigments, taggants, and optical communications, but other than those, it's pretty much a commodity product. Most of the world supply is controlled by overseas' interests, so presumably, an artificial shortage could be made.

Actually, I quite expect one if breakthroughs are made on current research ideas, you know, the inventions that could help spawn new economies or revolutionize the technology of mature ones."

"Such as...?"

"Optical gain in an electronic chip."

"What's that?"

"Amplifying wireless communication signals."

"What good is that?"

"Imagine a device connecting your camera, PDA, or a mini-computer directly to your home computer from half way across town. You could social network, have a spoken conversation, or transmit photographs without paying large data transfer fees to the cellular company or having to sit in a fast food joint or coffee shop. I think it would be pretty popular. Inventions that connect people have a huge economic impact."

"So it's a minimal money maker now, but maybe a blockbuster for new industry down the road?"

"That's one of my hopes."

"Anything else, maybe defense related?"

"Yes, but I'm not really authorized to discuss that."

"I thought so. You're at DARPA, right? That's what Paulina told me."

Uncomfortably facing the question for the first time, Robb was finding it hard to lie outright.

"No need to tell me, Robb, I can read between the lines. Perhaps this Russian prospector may be of interest to you."

"I'm working as an analyst..."

Trakalo cut him off. "Then my gut check was correct, calling you on your personal cell phone."

"Yes," Robb agreed. "Look, what exactly are you asking for?"

"I need an interpreter."

"I don't speak Russian," Robb reflexed, then caught himself, "Oh, sorry, I know what you mean. Why me?"

"There's more than just the mineral find," Trakalo baited, "some serious money was bankrolling his expedition. The prospector's toys were top-notch."

"Is this an official request? I'm not sure..."

"No, not at all," Trakalo backpedaled, "this is a sanity check. I need someone to come up here and sniff around, tell me if I'm on the right track, or if I'm losing my mind. I think you're more up-to-date on the technology's cutting edge than my own department. If it goes further, all official channels will be dialed in."

"I've got your number," Robb said with no intention, "can I call you back later?"

"Of course," Trakalo smiled. The odds were in his favor.

I'm never flying on a bush plane again, Robb groused, a small measure in disgust, the balance white-knuckled grumbling. The twin-engined propeller plane cantered haphazardly through pockets of surprisingly hard air.

Harnessed in place by seatbelt and shoulder straps, each jolt still launched him perilously close to window and ceiling.

Sitting beside him, the eccentric pilot grinned smugly, fluidly absorbing every impact. He enjoyed his passenger's discomfort. Doubly amused, in fact, as he was both transporting a lucrative load of goods for trappers' furs and his squeamish passenger was covering the round trip fuel cost.

He would be rewarded with maximized profits and a bonus.

Fortunately for Robb's stomach, the choppiness did not persist and the Cessna's flight smoothed out, although it never quite approached the leveled, powered glide of a larger jetliner.

Robb relaxed a fraction, but the atmospheric turbulence had perturbed his mind. He tried to fathom why he'd ultimately accepted the RCMP officer's invitation for an on-site visit.

There had been several reasons, but none seemed quite so compelling anymore.

Initially, it had made sense to him to be acquainted with the minerals on a level beyond the academic pale. In his R&D genre, field trips were virtually nonexistent. Daily life operated within a lab-coat universe that he occasionally found tedious. There were times that the practical side of his mind rebelled, demanding a hands-on experience. This urging had motivated him to accept the 'DARPA' internship.

A second factor resonated less; there *might* be something big being discovered here and of benefit in his dual life as junior analyst and scientist. The scientist required timely access to research materials, whether in the university lab or in the corporate setting. Being close to a discovery could expand his network and aid his placement into the corporate world.

On the other hand, what he was about to see firsthand had not filtered across his desk via the normal channels. Getting a close up view of a possible mineral find of this magnitude was something of strategic value to his industry and the future economy.

He briefly debated whether he should have let someone in his office know, but quickly shrugged his misgiving away. Too often, discoveries like these were vastly oversold and the first heralds irreversibly lost credibility once the claims were better examined.

It was better to treat this as an adventure.

Hours later, after a rock hard landing, Robb disembarked, weak-kneed and wobbly, regretting having paid for the return flight.

What next? He worried, recalling that Trakalo's territory was hours away across an expanse of undeveloped terrain. To his relief and gratitude, the final journey was unnecessary.

"Robb, I presume?" Asked a square-jawed, clean-cut man. He was dressed in jeans and a light, navy leather jacket emblazoned with a regal coat of arms on the breast and three yellow stripes on an armband.

"Lieutenant Trakalo?"

"Last I checked. Welcome to Churchill."

"Glad to be on the ground, sir."

"No doubt. I prefer a larger plane or the train," Trakalo suggested.

"Good call," Robb answered, "I think I'm calling in sick on Monday."

"Good. You might need Tuesday then, too."

Several hours into questioning, a closed-lipped Yakov had relaxed—comfortable he was not facing physical harm. Across a rectangular table, Trakalo and Robb supplied a steady stream of queries, with the Lieutenant leading the dialogue. On his end, a Crown-appointed lawyer translated and mediated. It was slow going, ensuring the lawyer had sufficient bandwidth to support both roles.

For his part, Robb was busily taking notes, doodling logic diagrams, and identifying gaps in information.

Yakov's strategy was obvious, trade inconclusive details for assurances of safety, obviously saving the choicest information for a promise of freedom. As yet, the geologist feared he was slated for immediate deportation, so he withheld critical details while his interrogators continued upping the ante.

Strangely, he sensed he was overplaying his hand, that their requests were guileless. They were merely seeking information, not accusation, but he was unwilling to abandon his game plan until the bureaucrats were involved, people who better understood the connection between wealth, power and justice.

"Why were you held captive?"

"Ya ne znayou." Yakov proclaimed ignorance.

"You must know. Is someone still assisting you?"

"N'yet," he winced. Noticing the discomforted gesture, Trakalo realized an opening.

"You lost your help."

Yakov did not answer.

"The doctor's examination reports you've been seriously injured twice recently. Your shoulder is mending from a gunshot wound, and there is scarring consistent with deep flesh wounds. The doctor suggests a mauling. Now how could that have happened?"

Yakov's eyes slowly opened wide in amazement, re-awakening a hurtling train of memories.

"Furthermore, an ultrasound of the scar tissue indicates these wounds are less than a year old. Who did this?"

Yakov stayed silent, tongue-tied by the accuracy of forensic evidence.

"Am I to believe you are a criminal...?"

"Careful," the lawyer shot Trakalo a glance.

"...or is there another explanation?"

An uncomfortable silence followed the question. Trakalo matched suit, leveraging for a minor win. By saying nothing, the lawyer couldn't object. Finally, the geologist whispered, "I was attacked twice, once by a bear, and once in Moscow by my employer."

The choked bear the natives described, Trakalo surmised but pressed the human threat. "Last autumn, all your movements were tracked by GPS. Were you aware of this?"

"N'yet!" But on his recent escape, he'd discarded his clothing, fearing the same thing. *But those weren't my clothes...The Bombardier!* He'd been wise to extricate himself from the net of his employers' equipment.

Wasn't I carrying something else of theirs? He couldn't recall, his memory weighted beneath an avalanche of experiences.

Watching Yakov's reactions, Trakalo knew he was steamrolling into pressure points, but it was painstakingly inefficient. The need for translation inhibited momentum.

"There were hours of signal transmission only kilometers away from where you found minerals."

It was the Bombardier! His evasive ploy, in spite of the eventual mauling, was the only reason he was still alive.

"Someone got you out of there, Yakov. It had to be trusted help. Otherwise, you would have been left for dead."

Yakov's brow furrowed again. Trakalo jumped forward in time, shortening his sentences, decreasing the length of time between translations.

"The gunshot wound has barely healed. I'm guessing this is a separate incident. Perhaps after you returned to Moscow?"

Recognition in Yakov's eyes. He was nearing the threshold of talking.

"I presume this is where your helper was killed."

Anger and grief swirled from the captured Russian's eyes.

"They will find you at home again, Yakov."

Yakov steeled against the panic welling. Trakalo noticed.

"You fear you're still in danger," the cop sallied.

"*Da.*"

"Do you wish asylum?" Trakalo tendered.

"In my heart, no," Yakov replied through the translator. "But..."

"It may be necessary," Trakalo pressed.

Pausing, doubting, with pain etching deep lines on his face, Yakov relented. For a moment, he looked ill—deathly so.

"*Da.*"

"You're afraid then?"

"*Da.*"

"You really don't know who you worked for?"

"No," he admitted, as Trakalo sighed, a measure of exasperation and satisfaction, "but I have suspicions."

"Meaning?"

"They're not Russian, nor Middle Eastern..." Yakov opened up.

"Chinese?"

"I don't think so."

"Why?"

"They did not speak Chinese."

"Who could they be?"

"I can't say."

"An opinion, please."

"I think they're American."

"Why?"

"They had technology—electronics, gadgets for everything; pagers, radiation badges, heart rate monitors. And their attitude...they were weirdly fanatical, maybe religious. But it wasn't a common religion, not Muslim, Catholic or Orthodox. It was political. It was Western." He paused, struggling to assemble his last thought.

"And..."

"...and what?"

"They were well fed."

Raising his eyebrows, Trakalo glanced over at Robb. Taking the cue, he plunged into the interview.

"Can you describe some of the electronics?"

"Who are you?"

Robb paused, fumbling for the correct lie. Ironically, Trakalo answered truthfully. "He is a government scientist whose specializes in Rare Earth minerals."

"So you know what I found?"

"I believe so," Robb replied, his eyes burning intensely, "a surface deposit rich in Erbium?"

Yakov surmised that he wasn't a cop or a spook, just a smart kid. Sensing sincerity, Yakov fractionally unwound. He'd not expected to be talking to a technology expert, rather, he'd prepared mentally to being strong-armed. With asylum on the table, a safety net had been drawn.

"The stones were everywhere," he replied proudly. "With my bare hands, I could fill a train."

"How deep do you think the ore goes?"

"A few hundred meters, perhaps more," Yakov ventured, "but I did not have seismic equipment. I think the veins run deep."

"Do you know the uses of the Rare Earths?"

"No."

"Do you know why you were hired?"

"Other than finding the mineral, no."

"Can you describe who hired you?"

"It was an employment agency in Moscow."

Trakalo made a note, intending to return to this line of discussion. For an amateur, Robb was rapidly unraveling threads into Yakov's past.

"Please describe the use of any electronics that you witnessed onboard the submarine or during your capture."

Leaning back on his chair, Yakov closed his eyes and thought. After his ordeals, and because of his prolonged isolation, it wasn't easy to recall details. Living in terror has a way of suppressing curiosity. Robb waited silently, masking a growing impatience. He could not rush the man, but the next words from Yakov might crack the question of who he was connected to. Finally, the geologist began speaking.

"There was a man of importance who would talk to me, but he couldn't speak Russian. He had electronic help."

"Say again?" Robb was surprised.

"He would speak into a flip phone and seconds later it would translate into Russian."

"And you could understand it?"

"It was formal, but yes, I understood every word."

"Was there another translator?"

"No."

"Was there anyone else in the room?"

"A pair of armed guards, but they didn't speak."

"Was he wearing an earpiece?"

"*N'yet.*"

"Then how did you talk to him?"

"I just...spoke...in Russian, of course, and the machine made its translation."

"Did you know what language he spoke?"

"No, it sounded harsh and guttural, nothing I've heard before."

"Hmm," Robb paused. The tale had a farcical flavor that he could not ignore, but the odd description made it hard to phrase his next question without focusing on the ludicrous and undermining its veracity.

"Yakov, what languages can you speak?"

"Only Russian, and a little English," Yakov answered, "but I am familiar enough with hearing Punjab and Mandarin to know them."

"Any African languages?"

"Once I hired porters to climb Kilimanjaro. They spoke Swahili. This was not."

"Could it have been Farsi?"

"I don't think so."

"Can you venture a guess?"

"I'll try." He puzzled a moment, "it didn't sound real."

"What do you mean?"

"It sounded fake...contrived noises I could almost understand, but not real words. I think it was gibberish."

Robb sighed as his progress seemed to arrive at a dead end.

"Okay, were there any other electronics that caught your attention?"

For the next thirty minutes, Yakov described a few intriguing devices, but none as bizarre as the mystical cell phone that translated an unidentified language, or as eerie as a professionally disciplined, fanatical crew.

Seated in a small cafe on the wharf front, the scientist and the cop were watching the season's first freight ships offload heavy mining equipment. The norm seemed to be machined beasts outfitted with twelve foot high tires. It was impressive.

"Thanks for coming up here so quickly," Trakalo expressed his gratitude, "and on such short notice. I know it must have been quite a journey."

"I'm glad I did," Robb assured him, "and it has been an experience." Shifting in his chair, he noticed Trakalo's upraised eyebrow.

"A good experience," he repeated, returning to business. "This Yakov is an interesting character. His ore find, if confirmed, is truly remarkable."

Before Trakalo could reply, an aging waitress approached their table. Neither smiling nor frowning, she carried a small notepad and a stubby yellow pencil.

"What would you two gentlemen like tonight?"

"I haven't had much time to look at the menu," Robb smiled.

"Let me order," Trakalo suggested.

"Sure," Robb agreed, dubiously.

"You're still in college, right?"

"Yes."

"Then let's see what I can remember about the college appetite," Trakalo smiled.

Robb thought, *I can't escape the stereotype even up here.*

"A pitcher of *Labbatt's Blue* on tap," Trakalo began, and Robb's ears perked up. "An order each of chips and gravy," Trakalo continued, "and for my guest, chicken balls with fried rice."

"And for you?" the waitress did not bat an eyelash.

"For me, some *pyrohe* and *kybasa.*

"For sure," the waitress responded, "and I'll be right back with your beer." She left the table, ears pointing backward, straining to catch the subsequent conversation.

"Chicken balls?" Robb quizzed.

"Not exactly the politically correct thing to say," Trakalo laughed, "but you might know them better as sweet and sour chicken."

"And what did you get?"

"Some Ukrainian food, the stuff I grew up on," he answered, "perogies and sausage."

"Ukrainian and Chinese food in one place?" Robb chuckled.

"They serve what people like to eat. The town isn't large enough to have restaurants dedicated to one ethnicity."

"I like it," Robb deferred.

"So do we," Trakalo agreed, then continued, "what do you think of Yakov's assessment, that the perpetrators might be American?"

"I'm not sure I agree," Robb replied, "since I can't think of any group that fits the bill. The people I know have nothing to hide."

"Are you sure?" Trakalo's eyes frowned.

"Yes, I think so," Robb replied quickly, surprised by the hollowness of his answer.

"It's not so simple, is it?" Trakalo pressed.

"I...I guess not," Robb defended. "It sounds naive, but I've never thought..."

"You're picking up the fine details quickly," Trakalo praised, "but you cannot let on that you suspect anyone."

"Fortunately for me, I don't," Robb admitted. "At least, not until today."

"Keep your ears open, your eyes focused and your mouth closed," Trakalo advised.

"Yes, sir."

"Thanks," Robb replied. "Why did you ask me to come?"

"I had a suspicion Yakov would talk more freely to a scientist than to a cop."

"Because he's innocent?"

"Well, not innocent of invading a foreign country," Trakalo smiled. "I'm convinced he is a pawn, not a player."

"Do you believe his story about the translating device?"

"Do you?"

"It is feasible, an ingenious idea, and possibly too clever to be pathologically concocted."

"For sure. Can such a device be made?"

"With a powerful processor, yes. Voice recognition software demands hard-core CPU power. Language translation is a snap. They usually have to be trained by the user's voice to be effective."

"They had time on board to adjust it for Yakov's speech."

"Yes, but a handheld device cannot be made, yet," Robb concluded, then backtracked. "Not to my knowledge at least."

"How would a handheld translator be made?"

"It might require a quantum computer, and nobody makes those yet."

"Are you sure?"

"Pretty sure," Robb responded, confidently, "the top researchers are making transistors and circuits, not a whole processor."

"Too bad," Trakalo sighed.

"You were hoping for what?"

"To narrow the field."

Sitting in silence, Robb thought through his denial, pausing only to eat. Trakalo dined slowly, observing the young man churn. The kid was bright and did not give up. Through the window, the cop spotted a large cargo ship being tugged into dock. It was the Nanuk.

"Hmm," he mused to himself, somewhat distractedly, "the great white bear has appeared again."

"I have a second idea," Robb began, squelching Trakalo's reverie, "if not a quantum computer, than perhaps a traditional one built by ALD."

"ALD?"

"Atomic layer deposition—a growth process of building a material one atomic layer at a time. Theoretically, it will make a computer much faster. It is a slow process, not cost effective. But some companies are finding it a necessary technology if making a precise layer is key to an electronic device."

"This computer would be powerful enough?"

"For a device translating one or two languages, yes, I think so?"

"Could it be powered by a regular battery?"

"Not for long."

Again Trakalo felt his idea eroding.

"But it could use a disposable fuel cell," Robb suggested.

"Help me here," Trakalo began dubiously.

"Not to conclude too quickly," Robb bypassed, making a discrete shift in analysis, "but perhaps Yakov is right. Making this kind of a device strongly suggests an American connection."

"Why?"

"Money, access to technology, and cutting edge fabrication techniques."

"Government or industry?"

"Either, or both, but it could be funded by a very wealthy private person."

"Who?"

"I don't have a clue."

"Why not the Japanese, or Chinese, or Europeans, for that matter?"

"The scale and scope smacks of a defense-related project. And you know Americans strive to stay ahead on that front. We have a number of national labs engaged in projects encompassing all imaginable frontiers."

"Such as?"

"NREL, PNNL, Sandia, Oak Ridge, just to name a few," Robb half-ignored the question.

"Any one in particular?" Trakalo rephrased.

"No, each of the labs has projects that fit to some degree," he puzzled, teasing the next idea, "perhaps this work is interrelated."

"Meaning?" Trakalo queried.

"Fabrication of a one-off, an integrated piece of hardware could be spread amongst several facilities, each working on a separate, but related, component. No single designer would be able to fathom the composite goal."

"I'm not following you."

"One project could be making a circuit board, another a logic chip, a third might be programming code to operate the device. Each project could be compartmentalized, need-to-know clause and accomplished independently."

"But one central group would be contracting, assembling and testing the components, right?"

"Most likely."

"Then don't the labs have a governing authority overseeing contract work so this won't happen?"

"Yes..." Robb paused, "but not the spin-outs."

"Explain."

"Both universities and the labs spawn high tech ventures, but in different ways. Universities have incubator programs in which they underwrite high potential ideas generated by professors and students. The labs, on the other hand, are forbidden by law to compete in the marketplace, but an employee may obtain permission to develop his invention in the private sector. Some of these spin-outs are then contracted to supply unique products back."

"Then we should focus some time on investigating groups fitting that bill."

"Yes, I see your point."

"Maybe there is a possible avenue to explore."

"Who do you suggest?"

"Someone close to you."

"A relative?" Robb smirked.

"Yes, an uncle," Trakalo alluded in return. The *entendré* was not overlooked.

After departing, Robb considered Trakalo's assessment of potential perpetrators. Much like his own work, the process was marvelously simple. Pare away the extraneous until logical leads remain. Robb frowned, it was a disturbing implication that his co-workers might be involved. He was glad Trakalo hadn't asked him to delve into this hypothesis.

Chapter 16

Connections

"You feeling better today?" Ottley snarked carelessly.

"Yes, much," Robb answered.

"One day flu, eh?"

"Something like that, an angry stomach, I think it was the water."

"Uh huh."

"I went...camping," Robb fabricated, already comfortable with telling white lies.

"I don't need to know the details. It happens," Ottley acknowledged, then disappeared.

Weird, Robb thought. *He hasn't talked to me in a week, and now he's commenting on my health?*

Nothing was mentioned again during the balance of the day. At 16:45, Ottley called Robb into his office.

"Come in, Robb," he beamed. "Sit down."

"Thank you, sir," Robb answered warily, recalling the morning's dialogue.

"You've been doing excellent work," Ottley gushed. "I believe you're due a full assignment."

"I'm ready."

For the next hour, Ottley defined the objectives and milestones. Dutifully, Robb scribbled abbreviated notes while committing essentials to memory. As the meeting concluded, he aimed for his desk to flesh out the project's goals while the information was fresh.

Halfway out the door, he was called back. "Oh, Robb?" Ottley intruded.

"Yes, sir?"

"I'm hosting a Fourth of July party this weekend for the department. Can you make it Saturday night?"

"Yes I can, thanks."

"I'll send out the invite and directions. That is all," Ottley concluded.

Shit! Just what I needed, Robb groused, mentally canceling more appealing plans, *...to be part of a happy, neurotic, bureaucratic family.*

He bee-lined to his desk, eager to escape the sudden onset of claustrophobia. Entering the cubicle, he paused, sensing something had been altered. His bookshelf was too neat. A large manila envelope lay on his keyboard.

Geez, this is a bit fast, he thought. *Surely it can wait until the morning.*

But, like any compulsive workaholic, Robb relented, opening the envelope and preparing to ingest its contents.

Inside was a single photograph, black and white, taken from an overhead high definition camera. In the image was a square, metal booth on a concrete pad. Alongside was a recent model sedan. In front of the car's grill, a metal lever gate hovered, blocking immediate passage.

Two people were visible in the security photograph. A smartly dressed, uniformed official stood beside the car, a maple leaf pinned on his shoulder. The agent was leaning forward, observing someone within the car. Stomach churning, Robb recognized the driver as himself, only days earlier, sitting behind the wheel of his car, waiting to be admitted into Canada.

Glancing outside his cube down the aisles, Robb searched, but saw no one. He listened. A dull hum of forced, refrigerated air pushed through angled vents above his cubicle. Nothing else. This late into the evening, the office was deserted. Whoever had dropped off the *gift* had waited until after hours to deliver his present.

Nervously transcribing his mental notes, he delayed departing, hoping someone would appear, claim responsibility and shrug off the photo as a gag. No one came by. Tarrying further, he organized his cube, each passing moment convincing him that his *benefactor* wished to remain anonymous. An hour passed in restless solitude.

Staying later was futile. Robb packed his possessions and went home. The rest of the week passed uneventfully.

Cocktail in hand, Robb strode across the plush green grass carpeting of his boss's backyard, searching for a restroom. The party was boring, and he was carefully monitoring his beverage intake so he could soon take his leave and drive home—or any place else. Company parties and booze don't mix, he judged, as several of his coworkers felt otherwise and were obviously half-inebriated, overly loud and boisterous in banter and behavior.

Stepping through a patio door into a summer kitchen, he could not find his desired destination. Instead, wooden butcher block tables, laden with *hors d'oeuvres*, filled the room, outfitted with tidbits from shrimp to chicken to vegetables. Most of the food prep staff were serving in the yard, conveying similarly loaded trays to the guests.

"Excuse me," he asked a man wearing a white kitchen smock.

"*No habla*," came an instant response.

Me neither, Robb sarcastically thought. *Oh, well, I'm on my own.* Crossing the summer kitchen into an adjacent room, he found himself within a regular family kitchen. On the opposite side of the functional room, two closed doors portaged to unknown spaces beyond. Passing between an island kitchen and mahogany cupboards, he chose one door, opened it and stepped through.

It was pitch black beyond. To his chagrin, the spring-hinged door slammed behind him. Fumbling along the doorjamb with his open hand, he felt the plastic projection of a switch and flipped it. Fluorescent lights shuddered on, expelling the darkness.

He was in a voluminous, but busy, three-car garage. Two stalls were occupied, one filled with a recent model black Mercedes C-Class sedan, the other virtually bubbled with a vintage champagne Cadillac convertible. The third had been converted into a workshop, a row of three stainless steel benches burdened with equipment.

It wasn't typical home-handyman stuff, not table saws, drill presses, nor tool boxes. Rather, the benches housed electronics. Curiously, a billowed plastic barrier enclosed the tables, hanging in straight, clear sheets from an enameled white metal frame and terminating a few inches above the floor. Above the structure were large stainless steel boxes containing filters and fans. It was a fully functional, portable clean room.

Interesting, Robb thought, stepping in for a closer look, *I would never have mistaken Ottley for a science geek.*

At the center of the first table, a small square-shaped device captured his attention. Obscured within a plastic shroud, the hardware within vaguely resembled an optical microscope, but was more box-like than usual. He lifted the covering. The device was outfitted with a sample staging tray, binocular viewing port, and adjusting knobs for "x,y,z" stage movements, but the scope was electronic, not optical, evidenced by a thick computer cable that connected to a desktop computer.

The staging tray was atypical, not built to hold glass slides. His curiosity piqued, Robb examined it closely. In the center was a small metal disk. Above that, a thin, reedy fitting reminded Robb of a cantilever holder for an Atomic Force Microscope.

Now who has an AFM in his garage? he wondered. The equipment of choice in Ottley's workshop was puzzling. *Geez, who can afford an AFM?*

Wondering if the scope was a high-end piece, or just a run-of-the-mill, second-rate knockoff, Robb gently lifted the housing off the table and looked underneath for the manufacturer's insignia. There was a foil stamp glued beneath. Adorned with shifting holograms and a corporate logo, it indicated both authenticity and that it was a high quality, high-priced instrument, but the trademark failed to command his attention for long. Instead, he noticed a shiny stamp riveted into the bottom of the scope, inscribed with an eight-digit serial number and a printed barcode. In tiny painted letters, above parallel bars, was a simple inscription, *Property of Hawkings Physics Lab.*

Robb felt goose bumps hackling his neck. *Could this be the missing AFM?* And then the obvious, *I should get the hell out now.*

But with a pair of drinks under his belt, resisting the urge to leave was simpler than it should have been. His curiosity won over. *What connection does Ottley have with the thefts from my school?*

Equally troubling was the complementary question of why would he even need one.

In denial, and desiring the coincidence to be benign, Robb gently replaced the AFM, deciding to immediately vacate the premises. Halfway across the garage, he vacillated and returned. He would leave with a souvenir.

The simple change of heart enlivened his suspicions and a fear of being caught snooping. Feeling exposed, like a disgruntled employee scratching for dirt, he feared that the clandestine moment would end abruptly with his host barging angrily through the kitchen door. He would need to work fast.

How can I remove the secured plate?

He searched for a wedge to pry the tag free, a screwdriver, a knife blade, anything thin and rigid. But the orderly top surfaces were devoid of essential utilities. His tension mounted. Sliding open metal drawers, he perused the cabinets, quickly glancing inside before softly pushing them closed. Plastic rollers grated against the steel housings. The shrill scraping would soon attract attention. Robb gritted his teeth, slowing his pace to a crawl, unsure of which was the more dangerous adversary, the noise he was making or the time he was taking.

Fortunately, the latter worry was soon allayed. On the concrete floor next to the Cadillac was a small toolbox. Inside was a selection of screwdrivers, exactly what he needed.

Returning to the AFM, he wedged a flat-bladed screwdriver beneath a rivet edge, gradually working the blade underneath the cap ridge. The metal did not give easily. In seconds, his nervous hands were sweating, a victim of the dank, mid summer's air and his adrenaline.

Without warning, the screwdriver handle slipped, nearly slicing his palm open on the sharp tag edge. Fortunately, it peeled only the top layers of skin. The sliding blade left a half-inch gouge of exposed metal on the housing, a gaff he could not hide, but his efforts paid off. The fragile rivets crumbled under repeated stressing, springing the ID band loose. The two-toned paint signature left behind was unmistakable, even a casual observer could deduce that something had been recently removed. Disavowing his eyes from the damning evidence, Robb slipped the thin band into a pocket, hoping he could slip out unnoticed. Holding still, he strained to see into the next room with his ears. For a moment, he imagined hearing scuffling from within the house. Robb froze, deathly still, but the sound was unanswered.

Curiously, he felt pangs of guilt interspersing with his fear. What had begun as a simple navigational error could now be construed as something criminal. He needed to make some effort to cover his tracks.

Resetting the AFM upright, he covered the optics with their plastic dust shield. With relief, he saw that the evidence of his intrusion was now out of sight behind the scope. With luck, the instrument would not be moved for days or weeks, and in the interim, the missing metal stamp would escape notice.

And then he saw something even more intriguing, a metal file cabinet box beneath the final table. Cautiously, he tested the drawer. It was unlocked. Inside were reams of documents stuffed into folder files, creased and dog-eared from frequent usage. The folder tabs were mysterious, a sequence of Roman numerals proffering no promise of their contents. In the back of the drawer, a leather bound notebook had been sloppily sluffed against the back wall.

Furtively, he removed the notebook, cracking the binder open and thumbing through several pages. It was a lab journal, neatly annotated, but nonsensical as it was written in code. Terms such as *pseudo-amine* and *zippered stencil* were the only words he recognized. They were not illuminating.

After a moment, he returned the book, debating whether he should abscond with it, too, but it was too large to hide beneath his clothes. And, if he were apprehended on the way out, it was better to portray an illusion of ignorance. His presence in the garage could be chalked off as a simple mistake of unfamiliarity.

Mustering an air of nonchalance, Robb exited the mysterious garage, refusing to look back. To his luck, the kitchen was devoid of people and he rejoined the party, anxiously preparing to take his leave.

* * *

Fifteen minutes later, nerve-wracked, but thoroughly sober, the junior analyst left the party. Driving home at a thoughtful pace, he considered the significance of the mini-lab, the questionable origin of an AFM scope, and all the *whys* he could muster. The equipment was fully operational and all the more sinister because of his suspicions regarding its origin.

In the morning, he would call Adam, his close friend and colleague from the Hawkins lab, to learn more about the inscribed plate. Hopefully, it was surplus equipment, long ago discarded and replaced with newer and better technology.

But against that plausible notion, Robb's mind was already rebelling. Academic institutions did not donate equipment to individuals in the government. Usually, schools received donations, especially when companies decommissioned fabrication facilities or process lines. And, when that happened, the equipment was old, out of date and suitable only for small scale research, such as performed in a university lab.

No, Robb decided, *there is no credible explanation for what I've seen.*

Returning to his apartment, Robb retired to bed, but could not sleep. Two fitful hours later, he checked his alarm clock and gladly remembered that the time difference from east coast to west was in his favor. Anxiously, he made his call. Not surprisingly, Adam was working late at the lab on a Saturday night, finishing the final touches of starting a new experiment. In the midst of a tedious set up, he asked Robb to wait a moment.

"No problem," Robb agreed, "I'll hold until you're done." In the background, a cryogenic pump kicked on and off every few minutes, punctuating the rustling of his friend's movements. He imagined the routine of the final preparation; positioning a sample stage, aligning valves, double checking that each gauge and read-out were working and the computer was data-logging. Robb felt homesick.

A rotary pump started, gross evacuation of a process was commencing. Adam should return presently. As expected, he did, and Robb began relaying the basics of his request.

"Ah shit, just a minute, Robb," Adam interrupted, "I forgot my lab notebook."

This short delay was frustrating. Of course, in scientific research, details needed to be recorded meticulously. Robb fretted, feeling out of touch with his former life. In the few weeks since he'd taken his furlough, his daily repertoire of activities were so distinctly altered that he identified poorly with the actions and concerns of his lab mate.

Reclining against his bed's headboard, he put himself back into the lab, imagining every nuance, feeling the heavy humidity of a falling fog on a southern California night, smelling the sweet fragrance from eucalyptus trees curiously blended with the ever present remnant of smog. Nostalgia swept over him, a longing for the simplicity of his graduate student life.

Frenzied footsteps approached the earpiece, disturbing his reverie. Breathlessly, Adam spoke into the wire. The news was anticlimactic. The serial number matched the missing device. It had not been given away. There was no benign alternative to explain the high tech equipment's disposition.

Swearing his friend to secrecy, for reasons he promised to explain later, Robb ended the call. He could feel the crushing weight beneath this immense burden of indecision, damning news and sleepless fatigue.

It was not his preferred state of being.

Chapter 17

A Macabre Success

"Thank you all for coming tonight, it's good to see such a large crowd. We're gaining ground in New Mexico!"

From behind an elegant mahogany podium, Shaparell looked over the feting throng. Adorning the stand was a round, hand-carved *bas relief* sculpture of an eagle, majestic in flight. It suggested power, freedom, the American spirit.

Acutely aligned at each stage corner, secret service sentinels manned the stairs. Behind Shaparell, a curtain backdrop hid a small army of security personnel charged with guarding the venue. Deploying from their backstage command center, out of sight from the dinner guests, a regular phalanx cycled through the field. At any moment, a dozen guards were mingling throughout the makeshift banquet turf.

Encompassing the outdoor field's perimeter, the greater number held obvious positions to accost and prevent curious onlookers from approaching too closely.

Two hundred yards east, atop the Citi building, lonely figures armed with sniper rifles kept watch over the infield of Albuquerque's International Balloon Fiesta Park. A few more sentries occupied building tops within a half-mile perimeter.

To the New Mexico city, Shaparell was a stranger, its citizens regularly voted against his party. But a recently exposed pay-for-play scandal had tarnished the Democratic governor's reputation, creating disenchantment amongst the voters. It was an opportunity worth seizing.

Blatant corruption on display. An opportunity to divide and conquer.

By upending the unquestioned loyalty of a sizable fraction of the voting population and re-engaging those with ambiguous affiliations, the state's citizenry was motivating to vote out its ruling incumbents. This made the Rio Grande desert town a critical stop for wooing electoral votes in a swing state.

As usual, the most damaging dirt gathered against the governor's administration was not yet intended for publication, at least not until the right moment.

As a young politician, Shaparell had laughed at the notion that behavioral statisticians could effectively time the choice moment for news releases. Attempting to engineer mass action sentiment seemed a pipe dream of election alchemy.

Over time, he became a believer. So once again, following retirement, Shaparell was stumping, setting the stage for a political ruckus. It was a rush.

Tonight's marquee moment was his discourse covering free trade policy, although his primary agenda was fundraising. A well-heeled crowd, comprising the local rich and elite, was in attendance. The invitees were heavily weighted by executives from local defense contractors whose highly profitable companies served the nearby military and government installations at Kirtland AFB, Sandia, White Sands and Los Alamos.

For the most generous donors, the twenty thousand dollar plate fee was paltry compared to the potential *lucre* from understanding forthcoming policy efforts. At backstage meetings, they would be privy to verbal diamonds, insider information allowing them to *clairvoyantly* forecast the market and initiate product designs and services well ahead of their competition. Over time, they would be repaid a thousandfold.

For show, support, and a little obsequious backslapping, a smattering of rabid party loyalists and local government officials were present, hoping to elevate their personal agendas into nationally prominent political careers.

The interests that had supported the ex-president through two Oval Office terms were the executives' lifeblood, proven strategists capable of keeping the country an armed camp, a state that had seemed obsolete only two decades earlier following the East-Bloc meltdown of a post-Soviet world.

Addressing the open air theater at AIBF, Shaparell soaked in the throng's admiration. Rapidly quelling its post dinner din, the audience hushed in anticipation.

"Welcome friends," he reveled. "We gather here tonight, our economy in recovery, celebrating our freedom. We rejoice as free Americans, with freedom and democracy advancing throughout the world. Many around the globe are now, for the first time, tasting what we hold dear. By opening our markets freely, by spreading prosperity around the globe, democracy is triumphing..."

With a hand gesture underscoring his point, he swatted away a fly, seamlessly continuing his discourse. For the next twenty minutes, the audience strained in their chairs absorbing the nuances. Shaparell's message alluded to continued unrestricted trade, privatization of government services, renewed access to strategic offshore resources, and an unrestrained focus on business alliances, first with China, then India.

An insect pestered behind his head. Landing lightly on his neck, the bug crawled beneath his shirt collar. Hairy legs pinched his skin, nearly sidetracking his concluding remarks.

"But, of course, we have much work to do—we will succeed. We will stay the course."

A furious applause erupted. Shaparell faced the crowd, smiling with certainty and pride. Gauging the enthusiastic response, he'd allayed concerns, relaying a 'business as usual' message from his party. Its power base was secure, retrenched and fortified after the carnage of the previous election.

Turning smartly, he began walking off stage. Overtly, a pair of secret service guards met him, escorting him off stage. Pausing in the middle of his exit stride, Shaparell acknowledged the admiring, still-applauding crowd, stepping forward and waving to a well-known benefactor seated at a premier, front row table. The guards dropped back a full step, giving him full access to the theater.

The ovation reached a crescendo.

The insect under his collar stung his neck. He winced. A seasoned professional performer, he tempered the impulse, avoiding a public faux pas. Pointedly, he refused to slap the feisty bug.

The surrounding skin numbed immediately, an icy cold sensation diffusing from the wound. He hoped he wasn't having an allergic reaction.

He worried, then shrugged away his concern.

At the stage's edge, Shaparell lingered, imbibing on the audience's homage, beaming and shining. Flashing cameras captured his image, an eye-catching lead for the media. Finishing his acknowledgments, he quarter-turned feeling lightheaded and strangely thirsty. The audience disengaged, a murmur of personal conversations swelling.

Shaparell yearned for a drink, striding toward the backstage stairs. Fortunately, the evening's private meetings would be conducted from his luxury suite at the Tamaya Resort.

The insect struck again, piercing below his collar. The second lancing could not be ignored, provoking an involuntary response. He slapped at the stabbing pain, pulling away a large, bulky bug. Compressing it in between his fingers, he dropped it to the floor. It landed with a dull thud.

A few still watching noticed Shaparell's discomfort, exhaling in a collective gasp. The uncharacteristic sounding instantly pulsed through the crowd. Heads craned, but they were too late.

Only the few watching saw him fall.

Chapter 18

Revenge

Shell-shocked, Robb paged the internet headlines, each heralding a pithy one-line synopsis demanding to be read. The blogs were less informative, mostly 'copy and paste' plagiarisms from the newswire. Ironically, beneath simpler titles, he found the most useful and compacted information. The most lucid details were written by the writers in attendance. From this subset of articles, he assembled the few tidbits into an incoherent picture.

Shaparell is dead!

The essential fact was crystal clear, but additional details were not forthcoming. As a result of the information vacuum, wanton speculation pointed four dimensional fingers of castigation in all directions, indicting security, secret service, the city, and, of course, political and military shortcomings. Several hours later, another electronic consensus was singular.

Shaparell had been poisoned.

Following this shocker, the news outlets inferred terrorist involvement, although no legitimate group was stepping forward with a claim. The opinion polls thus alleged al-Qaeda's involvement, the most obvious of perpetrators. In the words of one blogger, "Who else had the motivation, moxie, and monetary wherewithal to achieve...this cowardly execution?"

Other comments were even less helpful, myopic diatribes expelling political slant, "Where is the president's response? He is a weak and inexperienced POTUS. Recall him now!"

Who writes this shit, Robb wondered. Strangely, the focus on the manner, method, or elixir of poisoning was rat-holing beneath an outpouring of vehemence.

Frustrated with the dearth of data, Robb tried the TV, hoping to view footage of the assassination. It was disappointing. The networks were competing to outshout their rivals with continuous, intellectual-sounding coverage. The ceaseless chattering of the talking heads became repetitiously irritating, so Robb muted the volume.

Soundlessly perusing, he concentrated on the rolling background footage, studying the president's strange behavior, the wince, a slap and then flinging something away before collapsing.

Was the poison delivered by air, he wondered, then discounted his thought as, *not possible...or is it?*

Ottley had admitted that multiple R&D projects had worked or were working to make button-sized, remote-controlled flying devices, but the logistics were difficult. A payload was added weight. Memory, logic chips and feedback sensors preprogrammed with *smart* flight instructions required additional electronics and more weight. Besides inventing a lightweight flying device, a 'flying bug' would probably need to be remotely controlled. And that should have been impossible, as all usable frequencies were scanned and jammed.

What about acquisition assistance? Robb wondered. *Could Shaparell have been* implanted *with a homing device...Perhaps in Mexico?*

That notion also seemed far-fetched. Unless a novel, carbon-based homer had also been invented, standard imaging equipment would have found any standard homers when examining Shaparell. Two novel inventions were too many.

Flipping past the major networks, he tuned into a public broadcasting station, finding a more comprehensive presentation.

"Show me the speech," he commanded his television. Obligingly, the presenters did just that. And one better, isolating excerpts of significance so that the footage distilled Shaparell's final hours to a vignette of agitation, frustration or discomfort. At the seminal moment, Robb saw the intriguing anomaly. Just before the president waved his arms, a small shadow moved across the screen and disappeared behind his neck. He replayed the scene several times. Although in high definition, he could not resolve the object. Most likely, it was an insect, some hideous desert creature neatly blended into the screen backdrop.

...conveniently colored like the stage, he realized. *This could not be predicted. Then again, the stage was backdropped in a desert motif...*

Robb clicked through the networks again. The facts had not changed, but the sensationalism was ratcheting up. Something was askew, but no new information broke. He debated whether the truth was being shielded, suppressed underneath rancorous arguments about motivation, financing and opportunity. The denouncements were loud and superficial, contrived implications against terror groups, left wing radicals, and anarchists. Spurious folderol.

I'm becoming a conspiracy theorist, he rued.

Another broadcasting beauty took a potshot at the living president. "Swiss cheese," he suddenly muttered. The sound of his own words shocked him. He was talking to himself.

For a fortnight, it was a non-stop political inferno, a bipartisan conflagration raging at full burn. It would only have been more explosive if the current president was the victim. Instead, fueled with prejudices and fanned by incompatible ideologies, passions were hotly divided.

The question of responsibility was still unsolved, and subject to vigorous and vacuous debate. Lacking resolution, there was no action. Without action, an incoherent, angry sentiment festered. The uncertainty volatilized a rift between the so-called left and right that threatened to ignite in the streets.

Caught between wildfires, those of moderate viewpoint counseled caution. Deliberate and retributive action would be applied, but only after the facts were known. In the ongoing rabble, their voices were snuffed out. The dissatisfied sentiment was ripe for leveraging a manufactured solution.

Not content with levity, a factious front screamed for blood. Presenting patchwork clues and disingenuous half truths, some media outlets broadcast a stream of talking points, sometimes mocking the sitting president's calm and patient rhetoric, other times advocating that the killers were 'obviously' known terrorists. The incessant innuendo chipped away at viewer rationale. Even senators and congressmen championed the transparent analysis, lambasting any that believed otherwise. Invoking claims of patriotism, violence was promised to the perpetrators and, more disturbingly, inferred toward the emerging archenemy, an American moderate.

At first, Robb discounted the deleterious groundswell, optimistic that cooler heads would prevail. But, in a troubled economy, reason took a backseat, and calls for vengeance were a conduit for expressing other, suppressed vitriol. Day by day, chants for retributive action were protested from city venues. With newscoverage amplifying the volume, it was difficult to realize that the noisy throng was not the representative majority.

For reasons he did not fully comprehend until later, Robb worked from home to prove the existence of flying, bug-sized weaponry. This public execution was not being explained by traditional applications of guns, germs or steel.

The assassin's technology might reside within his scientific wheelhouse.

Outside his door the divided masses, force-fed daily on volatile fodder, moved in concert towards dual outcomes, vendetta or mayhem. All that was needed to catalyze action was a well-timed, well-placed spark.

It wouldn't have to be truth.

Watching his country straddle a razor's edge, Robb internalized another truism. Without a resistant counter front to violence, rather, by unanimously vowing a lethal response, all were goose-stepping to conflict's beat. He worked harder, caught up by his own persuasion that he might be counteracting the threat of civil conflict.

Blankly staring at his computer monitor at four o'clock in the morning, the text blurring beyond recognition, Robb's eyelids sagged above aching, indigo eye sockets. His normal life had vanished. After working each day, he nightly burned the midnight oil to validate his suspicions surrounding Shaparell's death. His investigation had become an obsession, not unlike the long, late hours of graduate school. He was nearing exhaustion.

Fortunately, the populace had retreated from the brink of madness. On the morning of Shaparell's state funeral, a drone raid on a known al-Qaeda camp harvested a top five general. With a measure of closure, public sentiment waned minutely, saddling toward a lesser state of angst. Dissatisfied with the loss of momentum, talking heads now reflected that the actual perpetrators were still unknown and at large. It was, obviously, another failing of the current administration.

The converted poured support into funding.

As the public noise abated, Robb's resolve was eroding, realizing that his endeavor was merely motivated for personal reasons. Ottley's rebuke had both rankled his ego and whetted a suspicion that his boss was somehow complicit, if only in a cover-up. Darkly, he understood that his former reason was more galvanizing than the latter, especially since his *bug* analysis had been rejected as science fiction fantasy. In hindsight, he admitted that it was an overly complex conclusion when far simpler explanations were available and more likely. Institutions such as his employer could not afford to spend time chasing idle, academic speculations. Though no one else outside of Ottley's office indicated he or she knew of his chastising, he felt the humiliation.

And his solitary efforts had not been productive. Other than the bizarre discovery at Ottley's party, and Trakalo's suggestion that his agency could be involved in something *up north*, his personal connections were biased, suspicions from left field. Interesting, perhaps, but not murderous. He'd been fooling himself. Of course his agency was involved in clandestine operations around the globe.

In truth, he had nothing connecting Ottley to Yakov or Shaparell. Although the overbearing rejection of his prognosis stung him personally, it wasn't a link. The border-crossing photograph was a heavy-handed warning, perhaps one he deserved. His boss was an ogre, and apparently a thief, but Ottley was a contributor who aligned with Shaparell's politics. Robb's suspicions were predicated on personal inclinations, a summation of personal experiences that were oddly coincidental. Finding the stolen AFM was serious, but not indicative.

Or is it the tip of an iceberg, Robb argued, unable to easily let go of his invested effort. He grunted in disgust, his premonition was flimsy, circumstantial, entirely intuitive.

He needed reasons and facts—not feelings.

He consoled himself that he was stymied because he was relying only on publicly available information. Until now, he refused to use work resources for personal sleuthing. As tonight's media montage had added little to his analysis, he perused his notes from the visit with Trakalo for the umpteenth time, seeking a fresh interpretation.

It was fruitless. He needed better sources. Or to just give up.

Sighing, he looked at his clock. Six AM.

Shit!

He'd stayed up all night. Again.

Stepping into the shower, Robb tried to jump start his day. Hot water, cold, lukewarm, it made no difference. After several weeks of sleep-deprivation, no combination of thermal shock would dispel the fog from his mind.

He needed rest and exercise, not a hot and cold dousing. The lack of exertion was telling, an unflattering layer padded his physique. He had to get himself back in control. It didn't pay to be a fat geek. Perhaps he should abandon his personal quest and get over his disgruntled feelings. He needed thicker skin.

Ten minutes later, sipping caffeine, Robb habitually checked his cell phone. No messages. He fixed breakfast, two fried eggs over easy and a piece of toast. Nutritious and low calorie. His phone buzzed—a text message.

Plate in hand, he unlocked the keypad and retrieved the text. It was from Ottley.

Do not report to the office. Your personal effects will be delivered this afternoon. Have your badge and keys ready.

Robb read it twice, but there was no mistaking the meaning. He had just been fired.

Pacing the floor of his dingy, decrepit studio, Robb's emotions oscillated between joy and rage.

He was elated at leaving. The job had been boring, his co-workers bland or neurotic, and the atmosphere of dusty paper and overheated computers sterile. The demanding hours prevented him from making friends outside his department. On weekends, his studio was an overpriced hole in the wall, with a crappy wall-unit that was supposed to be an air conditioner, an oppressively hot shoebox on the muggy DC nights. It would have been both restful and expedient to have had a cot in his cube, but then he would never have escaped work.

Good riddance.

But being fired has its own sentimental toll: Frustration, futility, failure. With a single text message, Ottley had blindsided him with a knockout punch an hour before he entered the daily ring. There was no sport to the curmudgeon's game.

A harsh reality was materializing. He was under surveillance and it was by his own doing. The garage incident was probably a tip-off. Then, Robb had gone rogue, lying about his weekend whereabouts, becoming a security threat. The latter fabrication was sufficient justification for dismissal. Now, Ottley's jurisdiction was broad enough to invade his personal life, and would already be monitoring his phone calls, banking transactions and credit card usage.

Although Ottley had the authority to fire him, why today? Why not earlier, like when he'd identified the ID tag? He thought back, drilling into the layered past few weeks. With a start, he remembered the notebook—and its strange text.

In his tunnel vision to leave the party and identify the AFM, he had overlooked something equally unusual.

Or was it paramount?

The journal was extraordinary for two reasons, he could not read it and Ottley was no entrepreneur researcher. Why was Ottley staging covert experiments in his garage? Perhaps his ex-boss's secrets were as sinister as he sensed. Perhaps he was close to discovering something, but what?

Robb was at a crossroads. If he wanted to know the extent of Ottley's scheming, he would have to plunge back into the fray. If he lacked resolve, he could skulk back to grad school. No further damage...and no salving his injured soul.

Why hire me and fire me?

Reaching into his work backpack, he removed the photograph of his border crossing. The mere sight raised his ire.

The bastard fired me for this?

Seeking revenge was a powerful motivation, but was it a sustaining ambition? *No.* The admission was disheartening. He flipped the black and white document over onto the table—staring in disbelief. Scribbled in light pencil on the back was a message.

"That wasn't there before," he muttered. "Who wrote this, and when?" Robb lifted the sheet toward the kitchen light.

God does not play dice, was scrawled across the scrap of paper. The Einstein quote was of no personal significance. He never used it, not in his lectures, nor his presentations, nor the classes he taught. If anything, it was merely the indication that the great man of science was fallible, having first rejected quantum mechanics and its heretical notion that probability governed the universe.

And then, the idea struck a chord.

Events were not happening by chance. Being in the vicinity of a foiled theft might have put him on the radar, but more importantly, he was making breakthroughs at the cutting edge of Rare Earth R&D. His hiring as an analyst was years out of context and contrary to the promise his career was showing. Before today, it would have seemed ludicrous, but his hiring was a litmus test, a feedback generator on the transparency of something Ottley was orchestrating.

But what? Until now, Robb accepted that Ottley was merely participating in a public cover-up—cloaking the pampered politician's reckless venture. The nagging doubt resurfaced: Should he have considered that his former boss was somehow complicit in the murder?

"There's no basis for thinking this way," he argued aloud, but Ottley had been most evasive when discussing Shaparell's post-capture physical condition and had lambasted...

How the hell could someone have isolated a photo so quickly?

It was impossible for human eyes to sift and sort data that speedily. Unless, he was on a computerized watch list.

How long have I been under surveillance?

The obvious realization was unsettling...*from day one.*

Is Trakalo part of the charade? Robb couldn't fathom how. The Mountie had sought his expertise to better understand the stakes surrounding Yakov's claims, and more than once expressed his reservations about the upcoming politics to be played. Yet, if Trakalo hadn't suggested that an 'Uncle' might be involved, Robb would never have lied about taking his trip.

But why? Snaffling minerals lacked rationale. If Ottley was coordinating events in Canada, it would neither be limited to mining nor, in spite of the journal and science equipment, to feed the mythological, garage-based start-up venture. There would be political intent.

Connecting his recent boss with both Yakov and Shaparell seemed pretty far-fetched, but the coincidences were stacking up. If his actions hadn't rattled Ottley somehow, his fib should have resulted only in a perfunctory slap on the wrist. Robb did not hold a security clearance; he could travel out of the country at will. What he did on a weekend was his business. That realization spun his firing into focus. It wasn't his work performance that had earned the bitter excommunication.

It was the company he kept—and therein was the key.

"I've met Yakov."

At precisely four o'clock that afternoon, Robb's doorbell rang. Stationed outside his apartment were Ottley's admin and a mindlessly cheerful HR representative.

He handed over his office accoutrements, keys, electronics and office supplies. He kept the photographs stashed out of sight. The process was cordial, but infuriating. In exchange for two weeks of pay, he'd have to watch what he said for the rest of his life.

"What is 'disparaging' language?" he asked.

The HR lady smiled, "It's speech that disparages."

No shit! Robb looked at her, incredulously.

She continued, "it can be spoken, written, or inferred."

"What if it is true?" Robb asked.

"Doesn't matter," she smiled sweetly.

"How can it not?"

"Because it disparages," she completed the circular reasoning. Clearly, she understood her logic at a depth to which Robb could not descend.

"Why would you care?" Robb retorted.

She became uncomfortable, shifting in her chair, not used to an intelligent argument. "We wouldn't normally..."

"But you could."

"If you need more time, you have one week to return the agreement," she cooed.

"I want more time," Robb ended the talk, dismissing his unwelcome guests. They stood up to depart, leaving the unsigned documents behind. He ushered them to the door, escorted them through, and closed the wooden slab firmly behind them.

I need to get the hell out of here, he decided. After waiting a moment for the hallway to clear, he left too, speeding down the back stairs and emerging on an alleyway below. Robb double-timed to his car, parked nearly two blocks away on a congested side street. Returning home late every night ensured he could not park any closer.

In his hands he clutched the termination papers, his indecision at signing the documents extended to an inability to set them down.

He needed a lawyer, but couldn't afford one. Too embarrassed to contact Paulina, too ashamed to call home, he would work through this one alone for awhile. The gig would have ended in a couple of months anyway.

He turned the corner, pressing his remote. The car responded, a familiar double chirp and winking lights. The door opened. *What the hell?* A figure emerged, a young woman, her head tucked sideways, shielded by an open hand. Her other hand was empty.

"Hey!" yelled Robb. She took off running. Robb darted after her, but it was immediately obvious he would not catch her. He stared hard at the lithe form, creating a snapshot in his mind. She sprinted away, her jet black hair flowing behind. Her gait was smooth and effortless.

Deja vu. Robb's jaw dropped. *God does not roll dice.*

Chapter 19

Into The Fray

"Trakalo here,"

"Sir, this is Robb."

"The scientist spook?" Trakalo teased.

"Scientist *sans* spook," Robb confessed.

"Well, it was temporary work. How can I be of assistance?"

"How's our friend?"

"Could be better, I suppose. He's certainly not cut out for confinement."

"That's too bad. Will he be deported soon?"

"No, not at all, he requested asylum."

"Why?"

"I'm not sure." A long pause. "I think it's the lesser of two evils."

"I see," Robb answered, grasping the gist. "When does he get out?"

"Not my jurisdiction."

"How long will he be with you?"

"I can't tell you that."

"What can you tell me?" Robb persisted.

"Why do you want to know?"

"Sorry," Robb apologized, "I'm struggling to figure out how to say this, but I think...I think I have an idea that might help us both."

"You and me?"

"No, Yakov and me."

"Hmm, I see," Trakalo stalled, working through Robb's intentions and motivation.

"Were you fired?" he deduced.

A pregnant pause. "Yes."

"My turn to apologize."

"Don't bother. I was photographed crossing the border. Someone gifted me with the 8x12 on my desk."

"By 'someone,' you suspect an associate?"

"I have no one else in mind."

"For sure," Trakalo agreed, "but do you have any proof?"

Robb sighed, "Absolutely none."

"Hmm-m. And your interest in Yakov?"

"To ask a few questions," Robb answered blandly, wishing he could be more forthright, suppressing his desire to blurt out that he didn't think they knew Yakov was alive.

"Hmm-m-m," Trakalo considered. "It's risky. He's not a free man."

The silence was enduring. Having exhausted his short ledger of trite innuendo, Robb lacked the confidence to argue further. He wanted to voice his suspicions linking Shaparell's death to Ottley's makeshift laboratory and maybe even Yakov, but he dared not utter them over monitored, international lines. Besides, if he were correct, his discreet dealings might flush out an unspoken confession from his ex-boss.

"Yeah," he grumbled at last, buying time, trying to gauge Trakalo's acquiescence.

Another protracted pause.

"Can't do it. It's unethical."

"I don't understand."

"We're a small, short-staffed outpost."

"Thanks for your time," Robb closed politely...*that doesn't make any sense.*

"Sorry." Trakalo hung up.

Docking his own handset, a disheartened Robb stared out his naked window at the brick fortresses lining his block. It was a decaying neighborhood, half way between blue-collar occupancy and slum, a thin sediment above poverty. He was glad to be leaving.

The latest loss was hard to accept. His idea, if understood, was simple and innocuous. But after the obvious rebuff, he could not call again. The window was firmly shuttered. Trakalo was no fool.

Why did Trakalo apologize? Robb wondered. *Of course! He's not a fool!* The conversation was a charade.

After surmising that Robb had been involuntarily terminated, Trakalo also had to assume the call was being recorded. By posturing outright denial, he'd enunciated the necessary words to forestall any subsequent legal proceedings.

Although Robb didn't know it, the Mountie's investigation was stalled. Worse, the cop was running out of time. Within a few weeks, the bureaucrats would move beyond shock and outrage and take full charge. He would then be required to surrender the geologist to higher authorities. From there, politicians and lawyers would bicker over Yakov's fate while corporations jostled and tendered graft over the mineral find.

An investigation was a complication to development. The Russian would vanish from his radar. Robb's phone call was the timely jolt needed to jump start the case again. Admittedly, it was a dangerous power surge.

So Yakov is bait, Robb mused, *but I'm forcing the timeline.*

Over the next hour, he planned his trip and packed his effects. He elected to drive to Winnipeg, crossing the Canadian border through Minnesota, and board a train for Churchill.

Thirty-six hours later, day broke sullenly over the Winnipeg perimeter highway, its gray cast a belligerent salutation to the swollen-eyed scientist. In his haste, and misjudging the marathon distance, he'd driven through two nights, stopping only to catnap at Interstate rest stops.

As best as he could determine, his car was unaltered following the break-in. Nothing was outright missing. His abrupt curtailing of the exit interview might have reduced the young woman's time to rifle and plant.

Wishful thinking, he thought.

The timing of the two events indicated they were planned and staged activities. It was only prudent to consider that a tracking device was installed and operational.

Out of spite, he made a dozen phone calls, rendering a homer as superfluous by mapping his progress through the wireless network. Most calls were to colleagues and mentors. He couldn't tell anyone his exact predicament, but neither did he refrain from asking for generalized advice. To a person, a pro-active course was advised.

Whatever that means, he debated. The hardest call to make was to his advisor, Paulina.

"Hello Paulina, it's Robb."

"How's the job?" Paulina responded, not returning the greeting, reminding him that she still didn't approve of his furlough, grant or no grant.

"That's why I'm calling," Robb replied awkwardly.

"I see," Paulina responded, immediately understanding, and instantly concerned that a character flaw had surfaced in her academic ace.

Robb sensed Paulina's reservation and paused, allowing his advisor to sift through the admission. Remaining silent, he waited for Paulina to query him further. It was a trivial showdown, but necessary. Paulina had to welcome him back, or his return to grad school would be brief and clouded in suspicion.

The short quiet solidified his thinking. He was stained, in part by the loss of employment, more so by the very time he'd spent working on an incomplete project. From here on, his resume would contain a blank space, betraying a gap of activity that he could neither professionally nor confidently discuss. The only way to cleanse the tarnish was to eliminate it.

"What happened?" Paulina finally asked.

Robb breathed a sigh of relief. He wasn't back in the fold, but the door was open.

"I traveled to Canada to meet a prospector who claims he's made a Rare Earth mineral find. The location is pretty remote. I was invited by a cop to provide some technical assistance in understanding the importance of the find."

"Why you?" Paulina challenged.

"He got my name from a hunter, an engineer who makes taggants. I suppose the engineer might be familiar with our work, although the recommendation is a bit bizarre."

"That's only half of what I asked," Paulina pushed further.

"It's complicated," Robb faltered, "and I don't know the whole story."

"What do you know?" Paulina was beginning to sound annoyed and suspicious.

"The prospector is foreign, and his prospecting was illegal."

"That has nothing to do with you," Paulina remarked, thinking it very well might.

Robb sensed the unspoken query. "No, it didn't," he assured, "I was asked to provide leads on who was financing him."

"How would you know that? And why wouldn't the prospector know?"

"I really can't say," Robb answered, realizing that by revealing more, he was confirming Paulina's concerns. It was time for careful damage control. "The prospector claims to have been hired through an agency and didn't know his employer. There was a language barrier, but more importantly, there was a discussion of high tech gadgetry, the kind made by start-ups and university labs, that made a grad student's comments worthwhile."

"How did the cop know you were at DARPA?" Paulina made a connection, albeit incorrectly.

"He knew what you told him," Robb dodged.

"Huh?" Paulina recalled vaguely. "Oh yes, the Mountie."

Before Paulina could turn the advantage, Robb pressed his point. "I gave the Mountie a list of names and companies who could help him further. I don't know if he followed through. He didn't call me back."

"So why did you go?"

"I went because a mineral find like this is relevant to our research. I went for the adventure of traveling. I didn't do anything wrong."

"Of course," Paulina smiled. "So why would this affect your employment?"

"The short list of organizations I suggested included various government agencies. The manufacturing was cutting-edge piecework, something like we do. Within a couple of weeks of returning to DC, I was fired. Technically, it was an 'at will' employment contract. No reason needed, no reason given."

"Perhaps you are right. Now what are you doing?"

Robb was jolted. Paulina was not inviting him back. He thought for a moment. Paulina let him think, reestablishing a stand-off. Immediately, Robb saw things from Paulina's perspective. His advisor needed to gauge the level of his commitment.

"I'd like to finish my thesis."

"You aren't due back for another month," Paulina reminded him.

"Yes," Robb understood. "I'd rather not answer questions about being back early."

"Get some rest," Paulina advised. "Go travel."

"How do you know what I'm thinking?" Robb started.

"Keep in touch," Paulina replied, hanging up.

For a moment, Robb was confused, but then it made sense. Time needed to pass. Whether he was lying or telling the truth to Paulina, a month was long enough for rumor to percolate through the small community. And Robb required time unfettered to help his own cause. Rightly or wrongly, he needed some kind of closure, win, lose or bluff. An uncontested stalemate was the worst of outcomes.

Paulina was the last associate he had called. A baker's dozen of hours had transpired since he'd talked to anyone. Now that he was in Canada, he wouldn't be calling anyone for awhile. He couldn't afford the long distance charges.

Robb glanced at the seat at his side where a food-stained, dog-eared set of directions indicated that he was seeking a commercial train yard, not a bona fide passenger depot. Within the busy industrial yard, he would find a single terminal housing the only passenger liner, Via Rail. Exiting the perimeter byway, he headed toward the city center and its industrial yards.

The depot would be easy to overlook, submerged in the volume of commercialized freight transport. Its insignificant placement served to trivialize his mission.

"What mission?" he sarcastically chided aloud, "I'm not a cop. I'm a student who didn't hold onto a summer job."

The snarling commuter traffic wound alongside an overflowing riverbed toward downtown, choking at a promenade leading to a massive brownstone structure. Over a city block long and three stories high, the sprawling edifice was center-pieced by a magnificent, six-storey pediment rising above a colonnade patio. The architecture suggested ancient Greek and Crown influences. Between a turret and supporting columns, a triangular-framed *bas relief* of Olympic deities depicted an unfamiliar scene.

A simple sign proudly proclaimed that this was the Manitoba Legislative Building, seat of the provincial government.

Balanced atop the turret was a statue, a young man, clutching a torch over his head, at full run. Its hue was distinctly golden, and it might have promised a positive omen, but the morning sun was uncooperative, and the sculpture instead appeared embattled, dull and forlorn.

Rejecting the negative foreboding, Robb concentrated on navigating through a historical downtown, maneuvering an endless maze of narrow one-way streets. Clumsily executing a left turn, he misjudged the unusual sight line and narrowly avoided rear-ending a stationary transit bus offloading commuting passengers.

Harried, angry glances shot his way.

"Wake up," he commanded. Fortunately, the transportation yard was at hand. He pulled into a lot, parked his car, and gratefully disembarked. At the lot's edge, parallel parked Greyhound buses gruffly dieseled in unison, drowning the impatient chatter of passengers queued alongside. A solitary driver in a blue uniform worked diligently, checking tickets and stowing baggage. Grabbing his gear, Robb headed to the opposite side and into a nondescript terminal, making his way to a ticket counter.

"Port Churchill," he requested.

"Do you mean Churchill, sir?" the woman behind the kiosk politely countered.

"Is that a different city?"

"No sir, but no one calls it Port Churchill anymore."

"But my map..."

"...was probably printed for tourists," she chuckled.

"Well, that would be me," he smiled.

"Welcome to Winnipeg, then. Hope you enjoy your stay, sir."

Unable to clearly see the scuffed timetable beneath the laminated countertop, Robb inquired, "How long does this trip take?"

"Twenty-four to thirty-six hours."

"Oh." He desired to peel off his disheveled clothing, shave his itching stubble, then bathe and sleep. He looked a mess.

"Would you like a berth, sir?"

"Maybe. How much is it?"

"An extra five hundred dollars."

"No thanks."

"Okay. May I suggest something else?"

"Yes," Robb replied dubiously, not really wanting to listen.

"The berths to Churchill are never fully booked at this time of year. In the evening, the conductor will walk through, offering the available empties. Catch him early and you'll probably get one for twenty dollars."

Thanking her profusely, Robb sensed a small measure of relief lying ahead. After thirty-six hours of non-stop driving, he would get some shut-eye after all. He could almost taste the downtime.

Twenty minutes prior to boarding, Robb made a necessary phone call.

"Trakalo here."

"I'm in Winnipeg, taking Via Rail to Churchill. Can I meet you?"

"I see. I hope it's important."

"That's for you to decide."

"Don't waste my time."

"I'd wouldn't waste my own. Be prepared."

"For what?"

"For the unexpected," he stammered. *For what, indeed? Sounds more like a threat than a warning. Helluva comeback!*

"I always am."

"Good. Later, then?"

There was no answer, but it sounded like he heard Trakalo chuckling as the phone disconnected.

En route at speed, Robb settled into a comfortable, newly upholstered foam and fabric cabin seat. Much like the airline equivalent, it reclined a few degrees, providing immediate, if short-lived, comfort. Fortunately, the coach car was fairly empty and he squatted on a seat pair across which he could stretch out at will.

Although exhausted, he resisted the urge to sleep, captivated by the railroad's magic and the infectious excitement of his fellow passengers. He monitored progress with his handheld GPS, preloaded with a topographical map and a paper foldout map.

Less than an hour after departing, they rumbled with the scent of diesel through the outer suburbs of the Manitoba capital. Almost immediately, civilization lost its stronghold, irregularly reappearing as sparse villages.

Between were long, open spaces of pasture, crop, and till, frequently dotted by humble farmyards.

At rare intervals, houses assembled into burghs, fewer still displaying the classical prairie icon, a wooden grain elevator. Painted in monotone browns, whites, greens, and yellows, stenciled corporate logos and faded surnames identified the town's ancestry. For an entire century, the monoliths had localized and anchored the commercial hubs of an agrarian economy.

More common, however, were the larger, austere plant silos. These gray cylinders were juggernauts, fashioned in cold concrete, siphoning the commerce into singular, insatiable sinks. Erected along the streamlined confluence of railway and highway, these superstructures had footnoted the wooden grain elevator into triviality.

At the same time, the hamlets and burghs, lacking the landmark vaults, were economically famished, unnourished by a value stream now flowing into the industrial-sized reservoirs.

"They are ugly, but inevitable," Robb sighed, realizing that his own work was having a similar squeeze on current economies.

As the hours passed, the procession of spring fields, fallow, bush, cattle and sloughs became routine. With waning enthusiasm, he returned to the surreal comfort of his electronics, catching up on reading he'd long neglected.

In early afternoon, the iron horse galloped into the periphery of a medium-sized prairie town, reducing speed to the customary tune of wasted, screeching momentum.

Peculiarly, the town had a foreign atmosphere, a panorama dominated by exotic architectural features—two Byzantine style church buildings. The elegant white structures set within immaculately landscaped foliage contrasted crisply with the vibrant blue summer sky. Impeccably trimmed in silver and blue casings, each rectory was jeweled with images of Christian deities, molded in hand-crafted, multicolored stained glass. On their rooftops, brilliant white turrets supported shimmering silver domes, each beseeching immortality through an iron-crossed spire.

Even the ubiquitous Christian symbol was unfamiliar, possessing three crossing bars of differing lengths. The lowest did not intersect at the perpendicular, instead angling by several degrees.

What religion is this? He wondered. The churches' existence seemed out of context. He attempted an internet connection. To his surprise, one was readily accessible. He grinned, the coach car was equipped with a wireless signal, and its daily connection fee was paltry. Robb gratefully paid with plastic, electronically tattling his real time position once again.

He punched in the town's name. *Ukrainian Orthodox,* appeared as the ethnic background of the town. Intrigued by the text of the top level article, he delved further.

During the early 20th century, a surge of Slavic peasants moved westward, their enhanced mobility courtesy of the Russian czar's diminishing
power. The dispersion was short-lived. Following the Bolshevik revolu-
tion, emerging communist power dammed the flow. In the New World,
emigrants regrouped, coalescing into new communities with common her-
itage, faith and language.

A sizable number settled the Canadian prairie, freeze-framing a culture
facing homeland extinction. While their Old Country cousins were no
longer vassals to feudal landsmen, the cost of collective ownership was
atheism.

Interestingly, their traditional religion was rooted in a thousand-year-
old creed cleaved from the Catholic exegesis. Steadfast in schism, the
immigrants constructed new enclaves, cathedrals and architectural symbols even while their Homeland's were eradicated. Each basilica was an
oasis, isolated and proud, embracing two worlds: the historical faith of
their forefathers, and the present fresh start in the melting pot of North
America.

For the Ukrainians remaining behind, the new regime would prove brutally unkind. Recognizing a significant threat to his dictatorship, Stalin
dismantled their society: renting the country of its educated, wealthy, and
religious. Serrated from their traditions, including their language and al-
phabet, the septic tear through the psyche of those who survived could
not heal.

Some historians estimate the death toll at numbers approaching 20
million people. A reliable count has never been substantiated, but even if
grossly overestimated, the destruction to the country's political will and
infrastructure was undeniable. An entire generation of the rich, elite,
educated and connected simply disappeared.

As the news filtered across North America, the immigrants responded,
fiercely driven to preserve their language, literature—and a religion. They
held to cherished idiosyncrasies, uniquely celebrating Christmas and New
Year's Day on a Gregorian calendar. Not that they believed the ancient
chronology, tradition was far more valuable than solar accuracy.

Undeterred in spirit and pride, the children were invited three generations later, after the ideology of secularism passed, to seed a modern
revival in their homeland.

Watching the newcomers board, Robb noticed an elderly couple boarding with difficulty, arthritically shuffling toward him. The conductor was
not to be seen. Heading to an open seat pair a row ahead, the old man
dragged an ancient, scuffed leather satchel, bumping roughly against each
seat back, too weak to maneuver his belongings under control. Waiting

for his unsteady wife to sit, he fumbled and failed to stow their luggage beneath his seat.

"Can I help you?" Robb asked.

"Tak, proshou," the old man acquiesced, his eyes speaking English to Robb.

As Robb carefully tucked the luggage, he did not notice a solitary man, dressed in a tailored business suit, entering the car. Distinctly not Slavic, the boarder glanced intrusively along the aisle, but did not proceed farther. Not finding satisfaction, he turned around and departed, just as Robb completed the menial task.

"Dyakouyou," the old man profused.

"You're welcome," Robb replied.

The sun's height reckoned late afternoon, although his watch and stomach disagreed, proclaiming the supper hour was nigh. The endless iron trail pierced Flin Flon, a mining town proudly displaying a billboard plastered with a famous hockey son.

Mildly intrigued, Robb investigated the player's bio, finding glowing renditions of a toothless, diabetic warrior of relatively short stature who was considered a hockey legend. The diminutive skater had earned all-star status, captained his team to a pair of championships, garnered diehard respect from blue-collar fans across the continent, and enraged a political power with his feisty, sometimes mean-spirited play.

A tough town, he deduced. Decelerating through the outskirts, they drifted through yards filled with logs, sawmills and mining implements, the industries of the northern frontier, for an extended period of time before lumbering to a stop in front of a five-storey hotel. Facing the train yard, the brick edifice towered above its adjacent two-storey brethren.

Prominently displayed at a second-floor corner, a blue and gold *Labatt's* neon sign advertised the main attraction, a pub, while covering over the original signage; a plywood base humbly read 'Hotel' in faded, black letters.

Beneath a patio canopy, two broad-shouldered young men, with out-of-fashion mullets falling onto even more dated green plaid jackets, were slouched in bored repose and smoking. Looking up, they snickered as they made eye contact with the pale, slightly-built scientist peering through the train plate glass window.

I'll do well to avoid this bar.

But, rather than accelerating into a new outbound pace, the train brakes fastened tightly, grinding and screeching with a shrill complaint.

Within the coach car, the noise level was uncomfortable, but it didn't seem to dissuade the pair outside.

In between drags, they gawked at the iron horse.

The conductor strolled leisurely through Robb's car, calmly announcing that the train would be stopped for exactly two hours. Passengers could disembark and re-embark at will.

"Be prompt or it'll be four days before the next train," he warned, trying to sound concerned.

Seconds later, the brakes locked fast, and the creeping metal monolith slid slowly, vociferously protesting against losing all pace. It could not resist forever, and slowly gave up, shuddering to a complete stop. In defiance, the passenger cars swayed gently in place. Encouraged, pneumatic jets hissed, relaxing their grip on the brake shoes, and the iron snake lurched once in epithet before freezing.

The journey had reached its psychological midpoint.

Not wishing to remain aboard for the full layover, Robb elected to spend the next ninety minutes exploring the novelties of a frontier town. Quickly gathering a few effects, he left the train.

At first glance, the downtown was typical. A brick and mortar frontage, dominated by the five-storey, square-built edifice of the hotel and pub dominated the town's center. Attending on either side were a series of antiquated Mom & Pop shops, businesses on the first floor and proprietor dwellings overhead. Parallel to the rail line, similarly constructed frontages stretched in both directions.

Along the three blocks, the storefront lights were dimmed, the enterprises closed for the day. None would re-open until the following morning. Separated by concrete sidewalks, rows of parked cars gathered in their parallel spots, a collection of models spanning a half dozen decades of Fords and Chevrolets. A steady shuffling of vehicles inched the main street, carting bored occupants who, thirsting for an excitement their town could not slake, would gladly settle tonight for the limited street side parking.

Disembarking stiffly, Robb sampled the fresh, cool evening air. Invigorated, he walked away from the train yard toward the residential town, slowly loosening the kinks of seven hundred kilometers of travel.

Compacted into discrete sections, venues changed every few blocks. The business row gave way to petite, century-old, wood-framed homes where, in front yards, tottering ancients busily tended immaculate botanical gardens.

The sweet fragrance of blooming lilac filled his olfactory.

Past the old town was a small park featuring a central pond filled with cheerful people and bustling waterfowl.

Stopping to observe the idyllic scene, he smiled at the small children who were eagerly feeding breadcrumb tidbits to the birds and laughing with delight at the frenzied fowl.

The diversity of birds was impressive.

Dressed with the season in mating plumage, there were ducks, geese, coots, mudhens, swans and others he did not recognize. Frantically paddling over the surface, the famished birds squabbled and hissed for each food tendering. Robb chuckled at the fierce commotion. Smaller females, bellies bloated with developing eggs, aggressively out-muscled the stronger, but less determined, males.

The analogy was not lost on Robb.

Moving unobtrusively amongst the families, he snapped dozens of digital stills, temporarily banishing his worries. His actions elicited glances ranging from amused to suspicious. He was an outsider, but harmless.

A half hour passed by quickly. As afternoon accepted the onset of evening, the families began drifting away.

Across the main street, two men leisurely strolled the sidewalk, engaged in a boisterous conversation. One glanced his way and stopped, projecting a direct, disdainful stare, startling him. It was one of the toughs he'd seen loitering at the bar entrance.

Are they following me? He halted, surveying his options. The two men also paused, eyes boring across the gap, scrutinizing his indecision. Clearly, they had recognized him and were marking his movement.

What do they want with me?

Electing to forego further exploration of the town, he turned and walked purposefully toward the train depot.

"Hey!" It was a man's voice, shouting loudly, originating behind him.

Shit! Robb ignored the call, rapidly covering the first block, now strangely deserted. *Where did everyone go?*

"Hey!"

He heard again, much closer. Insistent footsteps sounded mere meters behind, and were closing in quickly. The business district, with its bustle of protection, was beyond reach.

Turning around slowly, Robb faced his pursuers, struggling to contain his anxiety.

"Uh, are you calling me?" he queried. Up close, the two towered over six feet in height. Of lanky build, each moved easily with a springy gait. The speaker was topped with a red flame of abundant hair and had very light skin, his silent partner possessed dark locks, high cheekbones, almond eyes and tanned, olive skin, but they were not adults. They were adolescents, sporting unkempt, squirrelly facial scruff. Each exuded an aura of rebellious boredom. Hooligans.

"Yes," the redhead answered, reaching for his back pocket. The other stepped in closely, menacingly. Robb stiffened for an assault.

"You dropped this back there," the youth said politely, handing over a black plastic disk. It was the lens cap from his camera.

"Huh...? Uh, thanks," Robb replied, warily.

"No problem, eh?" Adroitly, the teens turned, nimbly striding back toward the park.

Shocked, Robb hesitated, catching his breath, slowing his palpitating heart. After a moment, he carefully replaced the protective cover over his lens, purged his fear-induced paralysis, and began walking toward the downtown.

He needed relief and was no longer held at an impasse from the bar, Robb headed for its comforts. He covered the short blocks briskly, somewhat anxious the two youths would return offering less than benevolence. He need not have worried. Without incident, he made his way to an empty barstool and ordered, intending to rebuild his courage in liquid.

An hour later, finishing a second lager, his fears were doused. His mood sublime, he took stock of the swelling crowd, noticing the assemblage of thirsty miners. Rough-hewn men, coarse in language and appearance, many owned brutish faces furthered marred by scars, broken teeth and broad backs. To a man, they were coated with a layer of grime no half hour of vigorous scrubbing could remove.

Vulgarity sallied across the room. The intensity of macho insults seemed proportional to size, strength or the combination of rank and fitness to back up the jest.

By contrast, he was puny, soft and unblemished, living a refined life limited to stresses of a mental sort. He exhaled slowly. His back was straight and not bent. It was preferable to kick and claw against cerebral challenges, even if politically or academically charged, than risk breaking his body.

A toothless old man, tottering with drink, tripped over his failing legs and stumbled into a much younger man.

"Hey, watch yourself!" The old man slurred his admonishment.

"Be careful," the young man replied dubiously, but somewhat amused.

"Kiss my ass," the grizzled miner groused.

"Just walk away," the young man cautioned.

"You want to fight me?"

"No, go on your way."

"Chicken shit little punk," the old man goaded. "I'll kick your ass." As his voice rose, the bar hushed, all eyes riveting on the altercation.

"Hammer him!" A gruff voice demanded jocularly.

The younger man gently took the geriatric by the shoulder, leading him toward the door.

"Take him outside!" Another jeered. "To the parking lot!"

"I'm not fighting you," the younger man assured, incensing the old man greatly. Fluently cursing, he volleyed obscene epithets, much to the merriment of the bar. A manager materialized, grabbing the opposite elbow firmly, and the trio exited to the street. The forcible eviction was having zero impact in placating the inebriated elder.

As the door closed behind them, the bar cackled with mockery. Patrons voiced sordid conclusions and returned to previous attentions. Pensively, Robb considered his own appointment.

The beer was having another effect, inducing a ravenous hunger. As he prepared to order a meal, a short blast from the train sounded, reminding him to check his watch. He sighed. There was no time to sup away from the train. Instead, he would have to wait and dine aboard this evening.

Taking his leave, he settled the check and hungrily departed.

Crossing the street, he heard the old man still cursing grievously, goading someone, anyone, to fight his miserable soul. Staggering drunkenly, he yawed against parked cars and stumbled into signposts, his fists balled in impotent rage. In the backdrop of his piteous ranting, Robb resolved he would not turn back.

Boarding the train, Robb bypassed his seat for the dining car, intending to secure an early placement on the reservation queue. Upon entering, he was pleased to find the dinner service in progress with open tables available.

Apparently, the libations across the street were a strong draw.

Choosing a seat overlooking the station platform, he perused the menu, a laminated fold-out casually stashed between shakers of salt and pepper. It was replete with unusual entrées, described as 'local faire.' The spicing of choice items was foreign to his palette, but the descriptions were appetizing.

A hostess appeared, and Robb smiled broadly. This meal would be an adventure, one he would welcome heartily.

Ordering a final *locally produced* listing, this time a Saskatoon berry aperitif, a satiated Robb picked up the resonant voice of the conductor approaching the dining car. The meal had been sensuous; lightly breaded, pan-fried pickerel powdered with spices whose savor subtly diffused into the tender, white, flaky meat. Alongside, freshly picked hothouse green peas, blanched baby carrots, and butter-slathered baked potatoes, sans skins, had been delectable.

Halfway into dining, the train shocked awake, a jolt cascading through each car. In his half-filled goblet, Robb watched the water shimmer; a lazy wave rolling around the perimeter, mirroring images of the car's interior.

The simple phenomena seemed strangely relevant. He studied the glass intently, but drew a blank. It was irksome. There was a connection in the water's undulating motion. Slowly sipping his beverage, he wrestled the nagging thread which now threatened to fray his evening.

Before Robb could resolve anything, the conductor entered the car. As indicated in Winnipeg, he was releasing unsold sleeping berths to all classes of passengers on a first-come, first-served cash only basis. Without hesitation, Robb solicited and secured a solitary cot.

The discounted price was negligibly higher than the ticket agent had foretold.

As they settled the transaction, a pair of thirty-something men quietly entered the dining car. The lead man, swaying with the train's movement, repeatedly brushed his shoulders against the narrow foyer walls. Not having found his train legs, he might have been among the few that recently boarded.

The second man tottered a careful distance behind, similarly unable to navigate an accelerating train.

Anticipating a sound night's rest, Robb discarded his fruitless remunerations and sopped the last buttery morsels of breaded crumbs from the white bone china.

His intuition needled again, this time suggesting a second glance at the men he was ignoring. Lackadaisically scanning the dining car, he gathered that the pair were moving closer and occasionally glancing his way. Catching the hostess' eye, Robb indicated a desire to make an additional order.

The ruse gave him an extra moment to observe.

The pair selected an adjacent table, slipped into their seats, and silently beckoned for the hostess. She bustled over, but bypassed the newcomers, hastening to Robb's side. Asking for a suggestion, he dutifully complied and ordered Saskatoon pie á la mode.

After she left, Robb harvested first impressions.

They were drifting casually below the radar, skilfully blending into the paneled woodwork, showing no interest in their fellow diners. While they conversed privately in muted tones, their eyes examined the car. The subtle body language and orchestrated reconnaissance choreographed a militaristic protocol with classical superior and subordinate undertones. It was oddly misplaced.

During the thousand kilometers he'd traveled since the border, he'd not seen any armed forces. It was possible the two men were a show-of-force safety detail protecting the passengers. Undoubtedly, the mining town defined an informal border between civilization and the northern frontier. It would be wise to project a last bravado at keeping the peace as the land transitioned into the wild frontier.

His wishful conjecture could not withstand the simplest scrutiny. The two were sitting down to eat, not strolling through the cars. And, their demeanor was oddly ajar. The other travelers were mainly miners and farmers, humble folk possessing bearishly strong, calloused hands and ruddy, coarsened faces bespeaking a lifetime of strenuous labor and outdoor exposure. Instead, creasing the corners of their eyes were deeply crinkled crevices revealing a lifetime well stirred by good humor. Their smiles were warm, encompassing, untempered by anger or regrets.

While Robb clearly was not of that ilk, neither did his persona decry mischief. These two raised alarm bells.

For a moment, he studied the other occupants anew. The iron-bodied locals were lighthearted, blue collar folk. Their hearty laughter rose above and drowned away the endless, rhythmic clacking of the steel wheels. Their language, mainly English, was flavored with a strange accent, and frequently spiced with phrases of a foreign tongue.

Ah, they're Ukrainian, Robb deduced, recalling the ornate Orthodox edifices he'd seen a few hours earlier. Concurring with his conclusion, their strong sounding utterances were akin to the phonics of a Slavic language.

And so is Trakalo, he remembered, connecting the dots. The remnant of a Gregorian culture he'd recently read about was actively surrounding him, but he had little time to observe or absorb. Instead, Robb warily watched the twin outsiders order their meal, balancing discreteness with a desire to placate his concern.

They appeared disharmonious. At times, the junior man was tense, agitated, snapping his lips, as if emphasizing some point of discord. His flashing eyes underscored frustrations, but with restraint, he tempered his bodily gestures and kept his volume below Robb's cognition. For all Robb could hear, the argument might be simple bantering over sporting loyalties.

With parabolic ears, Robb strained to listen in on their conversation.

By leaving Flin Flon they were entering land almost devoid of human habitation—it was disturbing. He needed to allay his worry, but the merciless noise of an accelerating train had no regard for his anxiety.

Using a plate glass window as a mirror, Robb watched the silent activity, slowly nursing his berry pie. The fray was escalating. The senior man repeatedly parried the junior's verbal jousts, annoying his subordinate, whose composure was steadily eroding.

Without provocation, the agitated younger man slumped in his seat, his head falling forward perceptibly, as if briefly losing consciousness. Instantly snapping back, he regained alertness and composure. With unmistakable brevity, the junior man leveled a glance across the table at his companion, but it was non-threatening. The argument ended. The contrast between warring warriors and peaceful passengers was surreal. The youthful associate's demeanor had transformed—now, his body language portrayed only bland compliance.

Robb wondered, but the new *status quo* was no illusion, there was no return to the bellicose state.

The junior man was compliant, seamlessly initiating another topic. The argument had been abandoned, even forgotten.

In thoughtful silence, Robb finished dining, the evening's plastic charm shattered. After organizing his cutlery neatly on his plate, he alighted, settling his bill with the cashier. While paying, he couldn't resist stealing another glance across the car. It was a festive tableau; his fellow diners were escaping the everyday mundane, feasting on choice food and delicious conversation. Robb could not mistake their gaiety, nor fail to draw the obvious conclusion.

They hadn't noticed a thing.

Overhead, the skylight windows were aglow in sunset's full palette. Dusky reds, shadowy oranges, and turbid blues diffused through the translucent dome, bathing the rounded roof with a display worthy of the mood.

Robb sighed, coveting their cheerfulness, desiring to join in their blissful furlough, unencumbered by what he had just observed. Or thought he had observed. It had happened so speedily, he doubted his recollection of the scene.

Robb continued his surveillance, using the dark window panes as a looking glass. It wasn't a perfect mirror.

At brief intervals, ghostly images of thick foliage loomed through evening's haze. For the next several hundred kilometers, the speeding train would be overwhelmed within a boreal forest of stunted pine and tamarack. It felt confining. Isolated. Here, one could walk in, disappear and never be seen again. Here, a man mattered little.

Wearying from his extended travels, his body aching, Robb's mind would not quell, instead navigating the latest conundrum of an odd couple and their bizarre behavior.

Forget about it, Robb, he chided himself. *Get some sleep. You're jumping at shadows again.*

He turned to leave.

At the end of the car, polished steel doors barred his passage. Confused, inebriated with fatigue, Robb searched for a mechanism to release the barrier. There was none. Again the interplay of light and mirrors intervened, reflecting an image of the busy dining car on the polished windows. In full frame view was the odd couple. Having abandoned their culinary fare, they stared, malignantly, in his direction.

How long have they been watching? His intuition tolled softly, a rustling wind chime in a whispering breeze, but it was enough to arm his instincts. Turning on his feet, he glared at their faces, forging eye contact. Instantly, he was dumbstruck. Their black eyes salivated, glistening with hunger before a facile kill. Losing his nerve, Robb averted his eyes and stepped backward.

Hissing sharply behind, the automatic door opened. Escaping, Robb stumbled through, the disturbing full color image emblazoned within his thoughts. Sighted within their murderous crosshairs, Robb's anxieties resurrected, an unrelenting, ponderous warning bell urging him to flee.

There was no place to hide aboard a speeding train.

With a pneumatic hiss, the doors slid shut, disarming the spell. Shrugging his shoulders, Robb shivered. Collecting his thoughts within the cold, damp baffle, he suddenly felt very unsure of his own premonition. His indecision was brief. Gathering his composure, he shelved his doubts. These two were plotting mischief. He had to assume they knew where he was sitting and that they would seek him out later during the long, uncomfortable hours of the night.

Ha! I won't be there. He was no longer occupying his coach class seat. Neither could they easily find where he'd moved. He'd paid cash, off the books, to the conductor, inadvertently erecting a buffer of protection.

As he stood, relief welling, the sliding door behind sensed his presence and opened. He backed through into a coach car. As if greeting him, an infant cried out irritably while its mother softly fussed and cooed. Across the narrow cabin, the conductor looked up and recognized him.

"Right this way, young man," he smiled, beckoning Robb to follow. "Your berth is this way."

Leading Robb to the sleeper car, he paused in front of a paneled door, "I trust you will find yourself in comfort."

Unlocking and opening the door, the conductor waved his hands importantly, pointing out luxurious accoutrements and narrated the operation of the Pullman bed. When Robb indicated his acceptance, the conductor presented a key, placing it in Robb's hands. Turning on his heel, the official strode toward the dining car, presumably to chauffeur the next passenger's arrival.

Robb locked the door and bee-lined to coach hoping to see if he was garnering attention. No one even looked. Quickly securing his personal belongings, he returned to the berth. Stepping inside, he locked the door, putting a solid barrier between himself and the wretched diners. For a moment, he held his breath and listened through the walls. All was silent.

What the hell did I see in the dining car?

Half the night Robb was flipping restlessly on the bunk. Staring into the murk, he puzzled, frustrated, unable to exacerbate his visions. His active mind would not allow him to sleep. Counter-productively, earlier exhaustion was now enhanced by furor.

A minor disagreement? Perhaps a muted act of resistance, but the peacemaking process was swift, severe, non-conciliatory. The man in charge simply looked across the table and tilted his head. The singular gesture had a profound effect, instantly squelching the junior man's waywardness, replacing it with a brainwashed quiescence. Having witnessed the sequence in real time, it was still fantastic in recall. A nervous twitch, the momentary loss of faculty, his ruddy face blanching to pallor, the rapid recovery, with his attitude suddenly back in line.

The behavior was more than odd, it bordered on paranormal, but Robb's trained mind rebelled, not accepting any ethereal basis for this vaudeville. Yes, there was mental-behavioral manipulation, but it had to be induced by something real, a switch he had not surmised.

Eerily, the event was reminiscent of Shaparell's murder. Having viewed the death footage endless times, he could recall the video frame by morbid frame. There was something similar in the way the men's faces had convulsed. Again, Robb perceived a connection he could not prove.

"What was the trigger?" He speculated wildly, "...mind control with the power to kill?"

He thought it all farcical. Who would discipline a wayward peon with a power better suited for political leverage? Robb tempered his earlier conclusion with skepticism, but his intuition pegged them as Americans.

Behavior modifying drugs? This argument had gaping holes. Logistically, a companion's meal could be surreptitiously laced, but poisoning a well-guarded Shaparell would require a large, complicit team of perpetrators.

A whole team of people...a torrent of questions were further unleashed.

What happened after Mexico? Was Shaparell fully screened? X-Ray, NMRI, whatever? He should have been. If not, why not? How many people knew? If Shaparell was inoculated with death, how was it activated?

Was someone in the audience close enough to trigger a release mechanism? If so...who?

Robb sighed. He was chasing a red herring, hyperbolizing into morbid fancy an inattentive observation from the dining car. He needed a reality check, beginning with chemistry.

Could a liquid injection be remotely activated? An embedded capsule, a deadly elixir not easily exposed by medical imaging devices. That was a possibility. Shaparell's kidnapping happened only weeks before he was killed: it was ludicrous to reject the idea that the two events weren't connected.

Yet, when Robb had presented the notion to Ottley, his boss had become unglued, harshly chiding his *sophomoric* suggestions. Beneath the apoplectic response, Robb had instantly quelled, accepting his apparent naiveté. With disgust, Robb realized it had been a bullying tactic and that he'd allowed Ottley's bluster to undermine his common sense. He was the science expert, not Ottley. The bad tempered ex-boss was a bureaucrat, not an analyst.

Robb remembered the rest of his hypothesis—with some chagrin— triggering a capsule's explosion wouldn't require an IR signal, the human body is opaque to IR. He put the idea on hold, unable to marry the ex-president's death to the odd couple on the train.

Unable to squelch his anxiety, Robb studied his sleeping quarters. Recessed along the train wall were two switches, protected in a lacquered, tiger-grained wooden console. Above his head, a pecan-stained panel ceiling reflected amber spots of the emergency lighting strip on the floor below. Outside, violet moonlight shone over a steel horizon of dark foliage. The night was unbearably long.

Accidentally flipping a console switch, Robb blasted his night eyes, staring directly into an overhead reading lamp. Half blinded, he fumbled at the switch again, this time engaging a servo-motor. Through befuddled eyes, he saw a small TV panel rotating toward his head. The screen brightened to life to a muted news anchor woman mouthing sensational words. Behind her, a young girl dressed in blue jean coveralls stood in front of a narrow stall housing a Holstein calf.

The pretty girl beamed proudly, displaying a blue ribbon. *4H...that was a long time ago,* Robb reminisced, fondly recalling a quaint image of a young boy, chest inflated to full bore, displaying his prize for showing a ring-tailed feral cat he'd somewhat tamed in a miscellaneous category.

Now my life is filled with 4f.

At lightning speed, ideas coalesced.

The water...the waves...4f...that's it!

Retrieving his laptop, Robb booted it to life. *Why didn't I think of this sooner?*

The midnight minutes tolled laboriously as the immobilized operating system refused to resurrect.

"C'mon," Robb bullied to no avail, the necessary drivers quickening reluctantly one at a time. When his system booted, Robb hastily clicked for the internet. Nothing happened. *Don't crash, don't crash!* He begged, his computer stagnating while the virus checker blocked his keystrokes.

"Don't start a full scan now, you worthless piece of...," he threatened, punching an icon, killing the scan. The internet connection tarried, uncustomary shyness as hardware greeted the wireless server, a skittish process of verification, synchronization and authentication as opaque as it was long. Tonight, it seemed especially protracted.

Am I being tracked?

Finally, with the electronics on speaking terms, he opened his browser to its familiar homepage. Oddly, the front page headlines were local to an unfamiliar town, Chantilly, Virginia. Robb grimaced. The city housed the US National Reconnaissance Office.

His internet usage was under surveillance.

Ignoring the implication, Robb impatiently connected to his favorite scholarly browser. In the wee hours, the network traffic was minimal and the download speed was suddenly fast, almost keeping pace with his rapid fire thoughts. His first query returned a short list of out-dated titles nearly a century old. Intriguing possibilities.

What's in them? In moments, he was downloading the obsolete papers which suggested a Rare Earth-based compound so strange it'd first been regarded with universal skepticism, but the paradigm had shifted, technological advances were demystifying the historically fanciful ideas.

Switching to recent published works, Robb honed in on the theme of experiments from a strange and macabre vein. He felt a growing sense of mortification. The ideas were cogent and lethal. His electronics hypothesis had been shortsighted and naive.

There was far more to the Rare Earths' potential than high tech electronics. The ultimate utility resided outside his field of expertise, alien applications capable of affecting life and living tissues, not just the electrons and photons of communication.

The devices in Ottley's makeshift lab were useful tools in this new genre. How his former co-workers, Yakov and Shaparell fit together, and whether he could convince anyone of his reasoning were bigger issues, knotted questions that might unravel with answers at Churchill.

*   *   *

The early scientific studies of Rare Earth elements called REEs aroused considerable intellectual curiosity, but generated little substantial attention from the industrial front. REE metals do not exhibit superior properties for construction, such as hardness, ductility, malleability or electrical conductivity. They cannot supplant iron, aluminum or copper. And empires are not built exploiting eccentric minerals.

Instead, their allure and intrigue cultivated interest in the academic domain, for a comprehensive description of their unusual material properties was elusive. Just over a hundred years ago, the physical sciences were quite new.

Physicists had only recently proven a rudimentary, three particle structure of atoms, that of tiny electrons perpetually orbiting a core of protons and neutrons. Yet, with that breakthrough understanding of the foundation of matter, knowledge was exploding.

It soon was understood that atoms bind together to form compounds, the basic building blocks of the matter that we sense. By selectively blending, mixing and heating these compound soups, one could vastly improve old products while reliably fabricating them in quantity.

The science of chemistry toddled past infancy and the discipline of chemical engineering was born. It was inevitable that substances not found in nature would be cleverly invented. With the formulation of Bakelite, the science of plastics and polymers was launched.

With rapid fire progress in applied knowledge creating work-a-day products, advancing theories of physics captivated the public readership, especially the increasing number of high school and college degree wielding graduates and students.

It was intoxicating to realize that there was order in the invisible world, and it could be predicted, manipulated...and controlled.

The 19th Century Russian scientist, Dmitriy Mendeleev, had first correctly ordered the atomic elements, constructing a *Periodic Table of the Elements*, arrayed by increasing atomic mass. With the atom's superstructure unlocked, Mendeleev's work was better understood and expanded.

Each row represented the construction of a spherical shell incrementally filling with electrons, beginning with a single electron and ending, seven columns later, nobly filled with eight. The next row built over the previous shell. Most illuminating was the observation that atoms in the columns had similar, but progressing properties, from top to bottom.

By the third or fourth row, depending on the reckoning, the patterning wasn't so predictable. After the second atom, the orderly progression of characteristics stalled, transitioning through eight elements until familiar characteristics reappeared on the right hand side. The pattern repeated on the next row and this table within a table grouped the common industrial metals. The theory was modified to accept an additional grouping of eight electrons within the outer shell of eight, but the electrons were getting crowded.

For the next two rows, a pair of lines counting fourteen specimens split the metals. These squatters, the Rare Earths and Lanthanides, are only partly metallic. It was supposed that they, too, possessed additional electron orbitals residing inside the outer shell, and that their unusual properties originated from the deviating configuration. The changing rules challenged the theory, although the general explanation is mostly correct. However, it would take decades to re-write the theory and prove its usefulness by inventing industries that manipulate the phenomena.

Public interest, however, centered on the concept of order. An analogy comparing electrons in orbit to the planets revolving around the sun was too obvious to avoid making. At first glance, the disparate systems size together like a *Matryoshka* doll, a microscopic world nested inside the macroscopic, each atom an analog of the solar system, which in itself is a template for innumerable suns orbiting the galaxy center.

The symmetry was compelling.

The ideas influenced political, religious and social models. Some were dangerous extrapolations, like eugenics, nationalism and race supremacy, but over time, public interest waned, no doubt influenced by social unrest, economic failures and international wars.

The science moved on, discarding the notion of prescribed order and replacing it with a nebulous concept, a probability-based occupation of space. In the refinement, only a few electrons live in shells. Other electron domains are far different, form-factored like hour glasses, dumbbells and even more bizarre shapes.

For a time, the scientific community divided, most notably splitting over the notion that probability was involved, resulting in Einstein's famous declaration, "God does not play dice." But the newer interpretation was even more powerful, propelling into existence the fields of optoelectronics and nanotechnology.

The learned rift healed.

Even in the early days of discovery, the Rare Earths were realized as transcendental. And it is the oddly shifting electrons, the fourteen wide group humbly dubbed "4f", that imbue them with chemical and physical idiosyncrasies that some researchers overstated with rampant speculation. They were sometimes considered as potential building blocks to forming the large, complex molecules critical to the appearance, development and sustenance of life.

Rare Earths might even assemble into entirely new biological compounds, forming protein analogs alien to the carbon-hydrogen-nitrogen molecules humans possess, yet equally capable of mediating the functions of organic living tissues.

With his new brainstorm, Robb re-engaged his forte, an active scientist, not merely a disoriented novice on an intelligence team. Lying back in his private berth, he assembled peculiar and wondrous quantum mechanical building blocks into strange, new compounds.

With his mind thus occupied, he let his guard down, conjuring a myriad of increasingly illogical invention. Slowly detaching from reality, his mind plummeted into nonsensical vignettes of Hermitian space. In the twilight of creative detachment, he softly succumbed to an untroubled slumber.

Chapter 20

Churchill

Morning dawned over a glistening landscape abundantly slaked in dew. In a verdant heather, a solitary, velvet-tined buck grazed, nonchalant about the iron monolith whistling by. A dozen kilometers and ten minutes northward, the iron rails bisected an expansive, steaming bog littered with the preserved carcasses of dead trees.

Through the murk, a brutish moose wallowed in the shallow slough; its head plunged to his neck for underwater greens. Sensing the train's vibrations, the animal startled, lifting his head in panic. Shimmering water cascaded from a bowl-shaped rack as he righted his concerns.

Saturating Robb's senses, the scenery had become monotonous, a thousand kilometers of repetitive sequences of small grass prairie, peaty marsh, scrub forests and oversized wildlife. Twenty tedious hours from onset, the steel boxes escaped the untouched world, descending the continental plateau onto the Hudson Bay lowlands.

Nestled into its western shoreline lay Churchill, a hard-working village sometimes renowned more for harboring polar bears than as a strategic shipping port for the northern Canadian frontier.

Absorbed in fresh ideas, Robb ignored the changing geography, instead sending emails to colleagues and scouring the search engines digging into a fresh angle of Rare Earth science. With a night's rest under his belt, his midnight suppositions were already losing their certitude.

Practical realities were infinitely more complicated.

His starting premise, perhaps the weakest conjecture, was the hypothesis that his summer hiring had been prearranged. He might have been recruited for his expertise or, equally likely, by happenstance, *discovered* after the chance encounter with the thieving woman. Well versed in the Rare Earth science, he was an ideal candidate to fill the role as a coal miner's canary—and just as expendable. Fully versed in the electronic applications, he'd never delved into the newer, biological advances, such as synthesizing inorganic protein analogs.

This human aspect was most chilling.

First, could Rare Earths be fashioned into pharmaceutical poisons, a hodgepodge of chemistry that could more easily kill than cure? Normal CHN biology would be defenseless. Second, was it possible to clone a person's DNA from a template that precisely identified each of the code's four proteins without having to decipher the structured riddle?

Moreover, did Ottley possess the capability to be involved? He had access to information of all sorts, scientific and business, classified and clandestine, and an extended reach into the most sophisticated government-sponsored projects that would provide awareness to projects, peoples, and events inhabiting the cutting edge. Apparently, he'd assembled equipment, too, but how or who he had using them was unknown.

On the other hand, the geologist was a pawn of contracted employment, a strategy that might have been similarly useful for technology acquisition. Most of the hardware Yakov had mentioned was not bleeding edge development, but could be acquired on the open market, albeit, for a dear price.

Was there a wild card connection to Ottley? There was the bow hunter that Trakalo had described, badly injured, stumbling over the ore body, and recognizing the value, inadvertently confirming the location that Yakov had vaguely confirmed, but also according to Trakalo, Moe wasn't a corporate sleuth, anxiously obsessing that his employer would jump his claim by prosecuting him for a conflict of interest. His involvement was purely stochastic. No malice, no intent, no obvious connection other than bad luck and coincidental timing, but the corporation employing Moe might be playing, pulling strings to acquire a hunt for the unwitting engineer.

Were they also bankrolling some of Ottley's endeavors? This was a possibility to discuss with Trakalo.

Interrupting his analysis, a long, exuberant whistle announced the homestretch. Subtly, his inertia shifted. Subconsciously adapting, he leaned forward, compensating for the change, continuing to work while the train coasted through slow down.

Ten minutes later, to the complaints of hydraulics, pressure venting and brake pads, the train rocked and swayed, shuddering to a halt. It was late morning, the sun shone warmly; the salt air was cool and fresh.

Disembarking, Robb sought a nearby hotel, following a route memorized during his online mapmaking. Outside his cozy berth, alone in the town, he felt exposed.

Churchill's downtown was a eclectic blend of old and new. It was a commonplace design, similar to each western Canadian business hub sampled during his journey. Diagonally facing the train depot, a block row of multi-storey businesses tendered goods and services on the ground floor, capped by proprietor residences. What made Churchill different were two things, it was larger than any place he'd seen in a day, and it had beachfront.

Actually, two beachfronts, if one counted the river delta.

At the far end of the first block stood a four-storey brick edifice adorned with a vertical, pink neon sign modestly scripted as *Hotel.* The balance of the frontage comprised necessity boutiques; convenience, drug, cafe, tool repair and hardware.

Farther down road was a grocery store trimmed in rows of dusty vehicles at rest on a crumbling asphalt lot.

Robb hastened toward the hotel, mildly disappointed that Trakalo had not met him. A useless regret. He'd not informed the cop of his arrival time.

He checked in at a humble wood and plaster front counter, requesting a weekly rate from the clerk, a young lady with a beaming smile. Being out of season, the lower rate was immediately granted. Paying with plastic, Robb chuckled at the price. It would cost less to live here for a week than to rent his hovel for a day in DC.

"Do you have cable and internet?" he asked.

"Yes, we do," she smiled, amused by his polite concern.

"Wireless?"

"Of course, it's all by satellite."

"What's the wall voltage?"

"You from the US?"

"Yes."

"It's the same. Perhaps even better," she flirted.

"Thanks," Robb mumbled, his cheeks flushing slightly with embarrassment.

"Call the desk if you need help," the girl smiled, handing him his card key.

"Thanks," Robb muttered, flustered again.

The remainder of the first day was uneventful. Just before noon, Robb called Trakalo's number, whereupon he was informed that the cop was out of the office but would return later in the afternoon. He could leave a message. Robb did, blandly requesting a return call to his hotel room. His cell phone battery was spent and he'd neglected to pack a charger.

Needing the electronic godsend, he would shop the business alley after lunch.

He dined in the barroom, ordering his new favorite food, *chips and gravy,* a concoction of shoestring French Fries slathered with rich, brown beef stock gravy. *Heart disease down to an art,* he chortled, assessing the artery-clogging multiplicity of deep fried starch and animal fat.

Stepping out of the bar onto the sidewalk, he stopped fast, disgusted, realizing he'd cornered himself. He could not take the Mountie's return call and solve his communication quandary. Regretfully, he turned back, returning to his room where he caught up on the internet news, sent communiqués to colleagues and friends, and unwound.

Unaccustomed to heavy food, he wilted, feeling like he'd been slugged in the gut. The deep fried food knocked him out and he slept heavily.

In mid afternoon the phone rang, perturbing his ponderous slumber. Groggy, perspiring and disoriented, Robb awoke in time to perceive the last ring. Fumbling for the cradle, he lifted it from the dock, hearing background voices chatting in a busy room before the harsh disconnect.

"Shit!" He cursed. Quickly calling RCMP HQ, he was updated that Trakalo was out of town for the day.

Now, at least, he could take care of his cell phone. Passing the check-in desk, he sought the advice of the pretty clerk, disappointed that a gray-haired matron was occupying the desk. With practiced disapproval, she directed him to a nearby convenience store. Here, the financial ledger reversed. The tiny power pack cost an exorbitant sum, totaling over half of his hotel's weekly rate.

For the balance of the evening, he stayed within his room, only venturing out for a light supper in the barroom below. Still fatigued from his long travel, he turned in early and slept soundly.

The second day was little better than the first. In fact, regenerated with a night's rest, it became significantly more difficult to remain idle. At breakfast, resolving to eat better, he ordered light fare; coffee, toast with preserves, no butter, scrambled eggs from an oil-free pan, washed down with water.

Afterward, he endeavored to take a brisk, exploratory walk, adding momentum to his health conscious agenda.

It helped—for a while.

By mid-morning, his energy and ambition outgunned the novel targets to visit. Exploring both the seashore and the river delta, he looped a perimeter around the town, passing by European tourists, a documentary film crew, and a battalion of bird watchers outfitted in the latest Audobon paraphernalia.

The waterways were awash with scores of birds, terns, gulls, dippers, puffins, plovers and others, most in transit to the Arctic for the short summer season.

As lunch time neared, he explored the town, locating the police station minutes before noon. It appeared a diminutive, red-bricked, two-tiered schoolhouse. To his surprise, it was locked, a door sign suggesting that it would re-open in ninety minutes.

Returning to his room, by way of a *Co-Op* grocery and dry goods store, he parked his body in front of an ancient CRT television and slowly savored his deli lunch; sliced roast beef on thickly cut, dark rye bread, decorated with sliced tomatoes and whole cucumbers. To spice it up, he'd layered a horseradish sauce, recommended by a petite and curvaceous server, over the baked grain staple.

She had first eyed him with a mixture of interest and suspicion, as he must have looked every bit the outsider he felt, but to her credit, the sauce was a hit—in moderation. The first bite had nearly seared his tonsils.

The noon hour local news was of little interest, although amusing. Smiling, talking heads inanely expressed local concerns interspersed with dry humor advertisements. The region's tepid political topics were out of his context, except a detailed report on the unrest in his homeland over the slaying of Shaparell.

The latter vignette was all the more surprising considering the ex-president had not been well-liked by his neighbors to the north.

For a moment, he felt snotty. In every community he'd traveled, it was the same. From an outsider's view, local concerns and mannerisms were distinctive, even unusual. Looking past the veneer of idiosyncrasy, however, people were consumed by similar issues and interests, even if the prism was pigmented differently.

As the Shaparell clip ended, Robb bit into a second sandwich. Suddenly, a familiar face broadcast onto the screen. It was an image of a colleague from Paulina's lab. Dumbfounded, the hair on his neck prickling, he stared.

What the hell?

Confidently, the voice-over asserted that the accused, a graduate student, one Wei-Ahn Lu, at a prestigious US university had been caught engaging in espionage. After the standard investigation by the usual undercover agents, the alleged had been ensnared and arrested in an apparent sting operation. He was charged with multiple crimes, including tax evasion, the theft of high tech equipment, and the sale of strategic, technological secrets to foreign interests.

Underscoring the drama, a collection of lab instruments, moth-balled in a crowded evidence compound, briefly flashed across the screen.

Robb's eyes bored through the images. At least one item was familiar. Included in the midst was an AFM, similar to the one he'd seen in Ottley's garage.

The hype was convincing, but any damning facts, if they existed, were not expressed. There were no hints on who was buying secrets or how the information might have been sensitive. Fittingly, the connection to the IRS was left unexplained.

The IRS? That's nuts! He's a grad student. He doesn't make squat, Robb argued in his head, puzzled by the accusations. *Besides, what spy makes himself an obvious target by shortchanging Uncle Sam?*

The proximity to his personal life was unsettling. Neither his advisor, nor the school, could withstand the public glare if trusted students were accused of treason. While the institution would openly claim neutrality, associated personnel would be quietly isolated. His advisor would be unwise to differ.

The pressure had been ratcheted a single notch, the singular objective was not his arrest, but to ruin him long term, professionally. Even if ultimately exonerated, its message was clear: he was near the precipice wherein a careless comment or a clever innuendo was all that was needed to implicate him. As he was out of the country, physically untouchable, but unable to defend himself, the pattern all fit together nicely.

There would be carnage before he could return.

Prudently, Robb passed the afternoon in his room, occasionally calling the barracks and reading related internet news publications. By late evening, hunger and boredom surfaced. He ventured into the hotel's pub for a quick bite and a tall, ice-cold mug of *Molson*. As the beer worked its magic, he relaxed. His mind began to sort the day's salvos.

If anything, Ottley's cadre was not idle. Though the two from the train had not reemerged, a colleague was now accused. A close strike, but not on target. Ottley was not incompetent. Instead, he was driving him, goading him to rash action.

They needed him to make a move. Otherwise, he would never have been permitted the freedom to leave the country. Even now, he was sure they were watching, keeping him on the short leash, hoping he'd lead them into something they desperately desired.

But what? He was sure the Mountie and the fugitive Russian were holding the key.

Maybe there was no immediate hurry to contact Trakalo. The longer he waited, the more he assured his survival. His biggest concern was his dwindling credit limit. He had but a few weeks of comfortable living left.

Convincing himself that his life wasn't in imminent danger, the overwrought scientist relaxed, returning to his room. He crawled wearily into bed and slept soundly.

On the third day, Robb purposed to explore, less of a decision to remain active than a compelling need to topple his tedium. Secluded within his hotel room, waiting for a laryngitic phone to speak, was wasting his resolve.

He elected to visit the world-famous polar bear grounds after all, somewhat chagrined that his bored malaise had elevated the level of a cheesy attraction to top notch.

Outfitting his camera bag for game, he shopped the *Co-Op* for a half-day's worth of rations: a liter of water, a cheddar cheese and bologna sandwich and a package of *Old Dutch* potato chips.

His recent diet had lasted but a day.

From the market, he hurried to catch the *Northern Safari* shuttle. The staging point was disconcerting, a decrepit wooden hut on a grassy lot ordained with a hand-painted sign advertising the entrepreneur's write off.

Open to the sea and the north wind, it was brisk and chilly. Robb shivered, preoccupied with thoughts from a different dimension.

Before departing the hotel, he'd emailed a carefully worded communiqué to Trakalo outlining his findings in Ottley's garage. He needed to allay any suspicions generated by the news piece and, with upfront brevity, describe his association with the accused. *It's not likely he'll believe me,* he lamented internally. Based on the footage, the damning evidence might have been relocated and retrofitted to frame his associate.

Sightseeing was more than a good idea. It was a clever way of disappearing for a few hours, letting the electronic gremlins diffuse and begin their dirty work. Having sent the anecdote, he felt a mixture of relief and trepidation.

Joining him at the depot were the usual folks, middle-aged men with bulging stomachs and shining palettes. Close by, gaggles of their obese, obnoxious wives. Some spoke English while others tittered exotically. With a small measure of satisfaction, he gloated that Americans no longer reigned supreme in the *super-sized* tourist category.

Quit being so snotty, he chided himself, realizing that his own presence placed him as a wild-eyed, fanatical youth Eco-tourist, suitably equipped in high-priced hiking boots and carting an expensive digital camera. They boarded the bus, a converted AWD yellow school bus that could easily hold triple the number of passengers.

Robb selected a seat near the back and hid.

A few thrilling hours later, the all-terrain vehicle bounced over uneven ground kilometers beyond the outskirts of the village. The day had not disappointed, having chanced several sightings of the massive white bruins, but none sufficient to photograph as anything more than insignificant snowballs.

The *piece de resistance* was nigh. Heading into the town, a noxious stench descended upon their meandering journey that raised Robb's bile enough to irritate his throat. Older passengers murmured, involuntarily expressing dismay. As the foul odor sharpened, discord bristled.

The town's dump, Robb realized, recalling that nearly every website made reference to the bears co-existing near human refuse. Unusually, the solitary mammals tolerated each other at the food trough, disgruntled denizens to a daily banquet at the city's slag heap. The stench from a winter's worth of putrefying scraps nearly made him retch.

"Normally, at this time of day, the winds carry this fragrance out to the Bay," the driver's voice quipped over the vehicle's intercom, as if it really mattered to him.

"He can't smell anything," Robb groaned aloud. *After years of exposure, his adenoids are probably burned to a crisp.*

The excitement buzzed meekly, well-tempered by queasy stomachs and the nausea of a jostling ride.

"There's one!" Shrieked a plump, pallid face. Ringlets of red-tinted, tightly clenched curls bounced collaboratively with her jowls as she pointed out the opposite window. In unison, all eyes followed to where a mother and year old twin cubs were browsing through rubble, bursting apart cardboard boxes for examination.

Briefly, Robb looked at the spotter. Her nose was tightly crinkled from the stench, but for the moment, she stared unwaveringly at the cubs frolicking through the garbage. She won't hold out much longer before puking, Robb decided.

Her face was green.

The vehicle climbed a small rise. Robb saw a much larger specimen opposite the sanitation field. Its massive shoulders were rippling powerfully, pawing at an object beneath his forelimbs. His fellow passengers, riveted on the first sighting, failed to notice the new bear.

Nearly blurting his finding, Robb instead checked his tongue. For now, *his* bear finding was a dull alternative to the maternally led trio foraging inside piles of fuming garbage.

The vehicle crawled along the dirt track slope, the driver prudently providing unhurried viewing time to his customers. Robb turned back to his private showing. From the top of a small knoll, he could see the bruin distinctly. Outside the landfill perimeter, the massive beast was lazily foraging over a blackened carcass. He watched it sink its teeth deeply into the carrion, effortlessly pulling free a portion of pinkish flesh. Holding the torn prize above its head, the bear relaxed its jaws, showing a brief flash of the lethal interlocking fangs, and swallowed. In slow motion, the morsel vanished into a cavernous mouth. Shrugging his shoulders, a wave of matted fur shivered over powerful muscles.

"Flin Flon was much safer than this," Robb muttered, awestruck by the carnage. Dismemberment of an animal body was being trivially accomplished. Two convulsive gulps and several pounds of meat efficiently disappeared into the bear's wide open maw, but not everything had been consumed. A small flap of charcoal gray material remained suspended from ivory canines.

What is that? Robb wondered. *It looks like an oily shop rag.*

Positioning his camera at the bear, he slid the lens barrel outward, adjusting magnification to full power. The powerful optics worked the light, enlarging the object eight times larger than life. Back-dropped against the pebbled, pink tongue, the material was easily identified. It was a piece of soiled cloth, bloodied and ragged. Now dissociated from flesh, its tasteless texture no longer appealed to the bear, who shook his head, working to rid itself of the limp fabric. The tatter refused to yield. Finally, rubbing his head back and forth against the ground, it released the garment onto the trampled earth.

With the bear preoccupied, a line of sight opened to the carcass and Robb peered intently.

"No, no, no...," he mouthed, a sense of horror overwhelming his macabre wonderment. The carrion was not a four-legged mammal. Barely visible through a cloud of swarming horseflies were two long, parallel bones, one straight and one gently curved, jutting upward from the ground. The upright pair terminated at a knurled joint, connecting to a fin-like spread of five spaced digits.

At first glance, the skeletal outline was so commonplace, a benign image often displayed in medical supply catalogs and annual costumes, it had not registered, but once perceived, he could not mistake its meaning.

It was a human hand.

Sweat beads sprung from his brow. He traced the twin limbs downward to another segmented joint. It was unmistakably the protruding arch of a human clavicle.

Suppressing simultaneous urges to vomit or exclaim his disgust, Robb stole a glance at his fellow tourists.

None returned his gaze. To a person, they were looking away, enthralled by the playful antics of the exuberant cubs with their vigilant mother.

Mesmerized, Robb purveyed the damaged remains of a human head, a skull covered with skin, stretched and intact. It was uncommonly filthy, making it impossible to recognize distinguishing features, even if he could hold the powerful telephoto lens still. The dead man's color was freakish, an unnatural, gray pallor that jetted a fresh surge of bile within Robb's gut. Steadying his lens against the window frame, he examined the body minutely through the lens. A growing curiosity demanded that he discover who the man had been.

A fellow tourist, an unfortunate local, or the victim of crime? He considered, dispassionately. With a start, Robb associated on a more personal level. *Could it be the non-existent cop?*

Leaning forward through the window, Robb unfettered his view from the edge of the window. The breeze rustled his face. Vaguely, he heard a disconcerted murmur of appalled voices behind him. Lurching hard, the tour bus stopped suddenly. Robb slammed against the aluminum frame. He felt a jabbing pain beneath his ribs, but he did not cease in his analysis.

Dragging the corpse towards its body, the bear pawed it onto a small dirt mound. Conforming to the ground, the back arched and the lifeless head twisted sharply, flimsily flopping against the bones of an exposed shoulder.

Even dead, the inhuman treatment of the unfortunate soul affected Robb, creating a phantom pain in his neck. Involuntarily, he cringed.

The unorthodox motion of the body had another, unexpected effect. The disintegrating black insect cloud of flies plumed upward. Disgust trumped his sympathies. In unison, the startled insects rose a meter into the air. Hovering a moment, they collectively assessed their options, deducing there was little danger. But Robb was not watching the coordinated sequence; he was examining details of the body.

It wasn't the lens after all.

The winged cloud descended hungrily. Alighting anew, they immediately coated the half-consumed body, obscuring Robb's clarity again, but in the brief interval, Robb had recognized a familiar face.

It was not the cop. Rather, the dead man on the ground was the insubordinate junior he'd seen on the train.

I have to find Trakalo.

Another anxious thought gripped him.

Is the cop already dead, too? Is this why I've had no contact with him?

Robb imagined the Mountie, lying above the ground in another forgotten location, slowly putrefying as a half-hidden corpse whose final fortune was satiating the voracious appetite of a bear visiting during a spring forage.

Is Yakov alive? If Trakalo was gone, the Russian would also be gone.

Shuddering involuntarily, a final, chilling thought took hold. *If they're dead, how long before I join them?*

The fear of death broke his fixation, returning him to reality with an unforgiving force. His side hurt like hell, his ribs digging against the unforgiving window frame. Realizing the bus was still and he was precariously hanging halfway out, Robb wormed his way back onto his seat. He was probably making a spectacle of himself.

Not surprisingly, the other occupants were transfixed, but not with his antics. They were still staring out the opposite windows. An intriguing contest was brewing amongst lesser rivals. An angry, snarling young male was bullying the mother and her cubs, attempting to purloin the family's picnic table.

Robb was stunned. He was still the only one who'd seen the gruesome spectacle. If the mother-bachelor fight for life continued engaging the bus party's attention, nobody would confirm his discovery. In a flash he realized it was better this way. He could discretely document the scene and relay the evidence to the RCMP.

Leaning out the window, he aimed carefully, methodically snapping a dozen shots in rapid succession. At this distance, they would be of poor quality, but it would not be impossible to digitally discern the important features.

His timing was fortuitous. Within hours, no flesh would remain on the body. His squalid images might be the only evidence establishing the identity of the dead man.

Quickly finishing, he pulled himself back into the bus, stepped across the narrow aisle, and half-heartedly clicked a few obligatory photos of the fierce spectacle.

"Nearly forgot your camera," a woman chuckled.

"Yeah," he replied, "I don't know what I was thinking."

But he could not quit thinking. The return journey was unnerving, and Robb carefully considered a number of next-step scenarios ranging from reporting the homicide to simply packing his bags and escaping. This far from his homeland, in a remote civilization, he felt trapped, surrounded by dubious friends and vicious enemies.

He would need help to leave safely.

An hour later, in disturbed solitude, Robb trudged toward his hotel room. Fully convinced he needed to flee the quaint village, he still struggled to determine how.

Reluctant to depart by train, he knew of few other options. One thing was certain, he would not charter a flight out. The last bush pilot whose services he'd employed was a lunatic, an eccentric bastard who was cavalier with the upkeep of his Cessna. The plane was an easy target for a half-skilled, homicidal saboteur.

Robb shuddered involuntarily, imagining a final, uncontrolled freefall on the stodgy deathtrap.

Perhaps he should disappear into the wilderness until the furor receded, but that was foolish thinking. He was no outdoorsman; he wouldn't last a season.

Could he simply walk into the police station and begin talking? Would anyone except Trakalo believe him?

If he started toward the brick building, would he even make it? The dead man he'd just photographed was deemed a dangerous enemy, yet was trivial enough to be ruthlessly discarded. A few moments earlier, at the *Safari* drop-off, Robb sensed he was under scrutiny.

He felt caught in the crosshairs, a stenciled target in a deadly cat-and-mouse game. Until now, holding fortress at the hotel room might have kept him out of range. Sending the email to Trakalo changed the game's trajectory, placing him even closer to the swath of fire.

Repeatedly, he cursed himself for his foolhardy gambit.

Unless he spoke to Trakalo, this seemed as foolish as it was facile. He pictured himself committing the fatal mistake, relaying a midnight message over tapped phone lines and being bloodily butchered before help arrived.

What if he stayed? The question vexed him. Even in the best case scenario, one where his sophomoric suspicions were correct, it might be months before he would be allowed to leave.

He needed time to think, but wasn't prepared for the isolation of his room. Entering the grand foyer of the century old hotel, Robb hard-heeled the well-worn deep pile carpet path into the bar. Although he was hungry, a *whiskey neat* called louder.

Searching for seclusion amongst the crowd, he selected an empty, rough-hewn oak table at the rear of the barroom. Squeezing behind the sturdy frame, he set his back against the wall, securing an unobstructed view of the entire room. The grained tabletop was a well-carved epigraph, inscriptions scarred every square centimeter with doodling ranging from simple block initials to cursive, risqué petroglyphs. A hundred years of loneliness and teenage fantasies recorded in shellacked cellulose.

Robb ignored the yelping. He was covering his back—figuratively and literally.

Waiting for a server to notice him, he nervously watched a couple of locals drunkenly taunt each other before a game of billiards, relaxing slightly as he realized it was only posturing between pals. One man racked and broke, the cue ball propelled balls randomly about the table. Two dropped, one striped and one solid.

The opponent cursed, the shooter crowed.

You make your own luck, Robb observed, welcoming the competitive diversion.

"Two *Labatts*," he heard a man order, "and please bring them to the table next to the back wall."

The man's voice was easy going and cheerful. Robb paid no heed. He chuckled as the first shooter gaffed the follow-up, a short tap in, too drunk to finesse the deceptively easy shot, but the opponent fared no better, falling onto the felt top as he leaned too far into a cross-table setup.

Scratch, Robb scoffed, without pity. The amateurish contest was becoming boring. His mind riveted onto his at-hand perils, obsessing on one simple goal: He had to find Trakalo.

The heavy fall of approaching footsteps startled him. Anxiously, he glanced upward. In front of his table was a formidable figure—tall, muscular, displaying a countenance of dead seriousness. In his massive hands was a curious object, a telescopic walking stick, thickly banded by a trio of silver foils. The pointed pole seemed poised for striking.

For a moment, Robb imagined a bladed bayonet emerging from the tip. His demise would be a brutal stabbing in the wayward corner of a tired bar in a barren northern land, far from his home.

"What can you tell me about this, Robb?" The voice was familiar.

Robb looked up in surprise.

It was Trakalo. Standing behind him was an exuberant barmaid, hands laden, bearing a pair of blue-labeled beer bottles, decorated in droplets of beaded beer sweat. A cheery smile lit her cherubic face. As Trakalo took a seat across the table from him, she set the bottles and departed. Relief seeped through Robb's soul.

"I didn't know if you were still around," he blurted.

"Yeah, that's another story, which I'll save for later." Trakalo was all business. "Right now I need your undivided attention."

"Yes, of course, and..."

"Answers, not questions, please."

"And the beer is for...?"

"A loose tongue."

"Okay," Robb agreed dubiously, but Trakalo's tone was commanding. Focusing on the elongated object, he instantly snapped to attention, asking, "So, what do I have here?"

"It's an ultra-light carbon fiber walking stick, often used by hikers, adventurers, sometimes—even prospectors."

"I see."

"But there are a few add-ons."

"It's been accessorized?"

"Something like that."

"In what way?"

"Take the foil bands, they're not Mylar, they're solar panels. We haven't determined the manufacturer, but they were intended to power a two-way tracking device."

"Solar?" Robb's mind jump-started at full throttle.

"You know something about this?" Trakalo paused, noticing Robb's reaction.

"My first assignment in that group was researching an industrial espionage complaint from a thin-film solar start-up."

"What did you find?"

"It was an inside job. An employee on an H1-B visa had sold the technology to a foreign competitor through a well-heeled embassy official from his native country. They immediately started a competitive brand, making just enough modifications to complicate an international patent infringement lawsuit."

"Did you prosecute?"

"Pointedly, no," Robb admitted, "I was told that our interest was leverage."

"Hmm," Trakalo frowned, "interesting." For a moment he withdrew, sitting against the hard wooden back of his seat.

While the cop contemplated the nuances, Robb examined the object in detail. Curiously drawing the metallic bands toward his face for a closer inspection, he noticed subtleties in its manufacture, rough edges seaming the foil and carbon fiber.

It had been assembled by hand. It was custom made, a one-off device.

"It must have cost a pretty penny," he concluded under his breath. It did fit the profile from his research project. Without thinking, he mused. "The company's idea was to build a solar panel from the bottom up, rather than a top-down approach."

"I'm not following you, Robb," Trakalo chided.

"Most solar panels are made on silicon wafers. Actually, the first layer is made in the wafer's surface."

"Why?"

"There are many reasons; purity, material strength, crystal structure, higher efficiency, but the advantages come at a price, the largest being increased cost."

"Cost of what?"

"The starting material. The single crystal wafers are pricey and each layer exacerbates the cost. Stratifying costs squeezes the potential margin."

Trakalo stared, "I have little reference to anything you're saying."

"Quick comparison," Robb scrambled, "a computer chip company integrates over a million dollars of gross revenue per wafer, but a solar company realizes a paltry fraction—in the tens of dollars."

"Yeah, but don't the chip makers do more?"

"Of course," Robb agreed, "but they also get more, and have more room for improvement. Double the transistors every eighteen months, double the power, but for solar manufacturers, a top down approach leads to only marginal improvement, a percent or two of efficiency gain, not enough to offset the increased expenses."

"Since material costs are prohibitive, manufacturers are constrained to use the lowest cost processing techniques. There's no profit in using expensive, high tech, precision equipment."

"Then the obvious..."

"...is not so simple to make," Robb halted, closing his eyes his fingertips sensing the foil's edge. As expected, a thin trim bordered the smooth, reflective material. He opened his eyes to inspect the boundary. It looked a little like silver bands, nearly too small to perceive.

Trakalo accepted the eccentric pause.

"What's the width of this conductor?" Robb asked.

"I don't know, why do you ask?"

"Some of the newer, bottoms up companies are pursuing a nanotechnology approach to fabrication. They buy or make nano-particle inks, print them in place, and fuse them together to build ultra-thin cells that are less efficient, but cheaper to make. If done right, these cells are also more flexible than wafer-based modules."

"I could have someone check. It'd be a day or two before we'd get an answer."

"That's too bad."

"Not quick enough? What are you thinking?"

"A company I researched *was* making ultra-thin electrical connections using silver nano-particles. It was an experimental approach, meant to displace the state of the art silver flake process. None of the big players were willing to invest time or money to perfect it. So these guys were jetting around the world looking for development partners. As you can imagine, suitors were hard to find, even though the company claimed significant advantages in conversion efficiency."

"Was it just a load of BS?"

Robb continued, "No, the gains were real, but not well understood, and inconsistently reproducible. So they took a different strategy, hoping to create a foothold in the marketplace by finding an inconsequential partner willing to invest in a sexy *nano* approach. While the first alliance might fail, the results would percolate through the community, garnering the next joint development partner. If they hit a homerun, they could sit back and play hard ball, striking new agreements with those who'd spurned them, and collect huge profits while the giants caught up."

"They offered exclusivity agreements to their primary partners, intending to leverage the strategic advantage when the major industry followed suit. They weren't entirely cutthroat, they were willing to share some reward for jointly developing the risk, but only if a partner joined long before industry adoption."

"I'm not interested in the business side," Trakalo guided Robb back on course, "Are you saying that if these *contact* lines are narrow enough, we have a limited set of companies to investigate?"

"Exactly, maybe even only one or two."

"That's very helpful. Anything else?"

"Yes, this company I researched wanted to sell their technology to other, more rudimentary, industries, such as construction. It's a big idea, flexible solar sheets making things like shingles, siding, car panels. Generating energy anytime and anyplace the sun's rays hit."

"Good ideas, not unique, but how does that apply here?"

"It's relevant," Robb assured. "These guys were quite ambitious, co-developing another product. Not unusual for a start-up, of course, but they stood apart because both ventures were huge undertakings."

"Biting off more than they could chew?"

"Maybe, yet each line had commercial viability, and, if either failed, could be parsed and sold independently. The ultimate goal was a synergistic approach, the sale of the solar diving demand for the other business."

"Which was...?"

Robb sat back for a moment and thought, "I didn't pay much attention to it since it was outside my scope, but give me a moment to think it over. It'll come to me." He closed his eyes and thought.

Trakalo waited patiently, but his alert eyes constantly swept the room. Robb had not noticed his agitation.

"What would anyone do with all the energy?" Trakalo wondered aloud, scanning the nooks and crannies around the barroom.

"Of course!" Robb exclaimed, "it was a nanotech approach to battery materials."

"A new type made with Lithium Nickel Oxide," Trakalo commented.

"Yes!" Robb stared at the cop in amazement.

"That's the battery that the Force's lab found inside the stick," Trakalo explained. "Maybe it was no coincidence that this espionage case was your first assignment."

"Meaning what?"

"You were supposed to draw an obvious, but misled, conclusion."

"Yeah," Robb muttered, reluctantly grasping the implication.

He kicked himself in frustration. "The data was all fed to me, I didn't control the data-mining. I read *weeklies* and assembled conclusions. I trusted that the raw data was collected independently, naively rejecting that it could have been filtered and skewed." Robb grimaced, "Neither did I perform novel, independent searches. I had little access to the sieving process. Huh, I wonder what other information was held back."

Thinking hard, he pondered for a moment, then sighed in resignation, "Even though I analyzed it thoroughly, I always thought the synopsis was too straightforward."

"You thought it was so obvious it should never have gotten to your desk, eh?"

"Exactly, the information all suggested an insider connection, a recent member of the technical staff who left their employ rather suddenly. Incidentally, his involvement in the theft was a correct conclusion, and he was paid a pittance for siphoning away secrets, but his underwriters may not have been a foreign government, rather, it might have been someone in North America, a company, competitor or even a fringe group within my own organization."

"Yes."

"At the time I would never have suspected my own agency," Robb made his excuse. Then, less defensively, "Or rather, a rogue group within my department."

"And now..."

"Now we crush them."

Chapter 21

Bloodied

"That's what I was hoping to hear," Trakalo's teeth flashed, but his lips were pursed.

"I'm not being entirely objective, you know," Robb admitted.

"Because you're a fugitive?" Trakalo dropped the bomb.

"What?"

"Courtesy of your old outfit, I suppose," Trakalo suggested. "It came via satellite this morning."

Handing Robb a pair of black and white high definition images of Internationally Wanted posters, the first presented profiles of Robb taken less than three months earlier. Robb grunted, they were his office ID badge photographs.

Stenciled beneath snapshots was a scathing description of his criminal past and intent. The montage of fouls included espionage, robbery, and, most damning, collusion with agents from restricted foreign sovereignties. The second leaf was equally stunning, a similar depiction of his friend from the grad school lab. The two posters were complementary.

"Bullshit!" he muttered.

"Yes," Trakalo soothed, "but I think it's a good omen."

"What do you mean?"

"Someone is overplaying his hand. This kind of activity is traceable."

"Oh?" Robb pondered for a moment, not daring to agree. His freedom was at risk.

"Speaking of traceable, where have you been the past few days?" He asked the cop.

"Spying on you."

"You didn't trust me?"

"On the contrary. In this farce, you've been the only honest crook," Trakalo laughed. "I hoped that the publisher of this fabrication," he pointed to the poster, "would also be stupid enough to be following you."

"They were on the train," Robb replied.

"How many?" Trakalo instantly tuned in.

"At least two."

"Yes, we know, but we can't seem to find one of them."

"You won't," Robb remarked carelessly, instantly regretting his certainty. It sounded like a confession. Suddenly suspicious, Trakalo looked the young scientist in the eye.

"What have you done?"

"Not done," Robb backpedaled swiftly. "I saw. Look, it's here in my camera."

Pulling out his digital SLR, he navigated to the image library and began thumbing through his day's photographs.

"How did you know...?" Trakalo asked suspiciously.

"I...I didn't," Robb stuttered. "Before I left the hotel this morning, I left you an email hoping to find you, wanting to provoke a response. It was a stupid move, but I was running out of options. After I sent the message, I hid."

"I took a polar bear tour. I've been going stir crazy. I reasoned it would be a good way to escape while remaining somewhat public."

"Why?"

"Not having heard from you, and having been followed on the train, I feared you had met ill will or rejected my offer. If you were waylaid, I had no doubt about my chances. I had decided to leave town, but suddenly, I wasn't sure how to get home safely. So, in short, I had to give it one more try."

"And the body?"

"Dumb luck. Nobody else saw it except me. Everyone else was watching something else, a mother bear defending her cubs on the other side of the bus."

"How convenient. Do you expect me to believe that?"

"What?" Robb felt alarmed.

"It's very coincidental," Trakalo repeated.

In a flash, Robb found a way out. "You've had me under surveillance, right? Did you have someone on the bus?"

"No, just a moment." Trakalo got up, walked by the bar, and politely delivered an order to the bartender before stepping outside. A moment later, the waitress reappeared in front of Robb, a fresh pair of filled beer mugs in her hand.

"Ready for another?" She beamed.

"I might as well," Robb sighed, accepting and sinking his face into the beverage.

Halfway into his glass, the cop returned.

"Your story corroborates," he admitted. "Sorry I doubted you, but the likelihood of you finding this body is just..."

"...patently obscene," Robb agreed.

"I need to trust you, Robb," Trakalo's eyes bored into his own.

"I've nothing to hide," he staunchly defended, unwarranted guilt rising in his gullet.

Brusquely clunking, metal jaws snapped in the walls all around them, quenching the lights and plunging them into pitch blackness. From across the pool table, a startled shriek pierced the vapid air, unbridled fright from a sightless, drunken patron.

"Get down," Trakalo hissed. As Robb complied, he heard the double thump of doors being kicked open and slamming to a hard stop against a solid wall. The brittle wooden casings must have shattered under the blow, its dry wood crackled harshly. Heavy footsteps scrabbled the hardwood floor, moving closer, but suddenly were arrested in muted thuds as bodies collided and elbows met chests. Pained gasping erupted, the wind driven from their owners' breasts.

In an instant, shouts of anger turned to alarm as a client panicked, his terror igniting a cascade of fear, amplifying virulently as the contagious sentient spread.

"Follow me," he heard the cop command. He felt a vise-grip clenching his shoulder, pushing him downward from his seat toward the floor then pulling him toward the bar. Propelled by the rough treatment, his unseeing head brutally slammed against a ledge, nearly knocking him senseless. The warm sensation of blood wetted his temple, a creeping, hot flow slowly rolling down the side of his face.

"Aaah," he gasped.

"Quiet!" Trakalo hissed, unmercifully pulling him along in flight.

Behind him, silenced gunshots punctuated the darkness, echoed by the dampened thud of leaden slugs embedding into wood. Shell casings clattered onto the floor, rolling in grinding spirals before halting. Screams of terror catapulted again, dousing the metallic fury. As the blatant threat of death was unleashed, pandemonium ensued.

Robb and Trakalo were already gone, shielded behind a protective barrier of thick walls, having fled underneath a closed saloon door into the kitchen. Here there was dim light, an overhead emergency lamp weakly illuminating their way.

How the hell can he see anything? Robb wondered, but Trakalo either knew where he was going or had a route in mind, unwaveringly moving toward an unseen portal. Struggling to keep his balance, Robb barely kept up.

A moment later, he heard metal grating as Trakalo twisted an ancient door handle. Hinges creaked stubbornly as the unseen portal swung open. Robb stepped through into a dark passageway, blood dripping from his face, and Trakalo noisily secured the door behind. There was quiet once more.

"We're inside the hotel," Trakalo whispered in explanation. "Now keep up!"

Back-up interior lights, battery-powered, were awakening from their slumber, feeble rays of guidance for the escaping pair. Above their heads, exit signs glowed radioactively, pointing a ghostly way out, but the cop headed inward, toward the shadowed maw of a carpeted staircase.

"We need to go up," he commanded. In silence and confusion, Robb followed. Behind him, an angry commotion was building again. Evidently, their pursuers were moving, closing in.

How the hell do they know we're here? He wondered, his knees growing weak.

Reading his mind, Trakalo answered. "They're wearing infra-red goggles. We can't hide easily, even in a blackout."

"Can they see blood?" Robb asked.

"Yes, dammit," Trakalo admitted. "Take your shirt off and cover the bleeding. Sorry about that." The Mountie paused for a split second allowing Robb to address his wound.

"Where do we go?" Robb spoke, his voice eerily displaced in the darkened hollow, reflecting vacuously off a wall a few feet away.

"Fourth floor, over the roof, onto an adjacent building," Trakalo answered. "Don't lose me."

He turned and darted up the stairs. The younger man needed no additional encouragement.

Opening another half-frozen creaking hatch, they crawled through a narrow square, emerging onto an asphalt rooftop. The moonlight illuminated a dusky path through vent sticks, skylights and ceiling fans across the spongy flat surface, which Trakalo followed to the shadowy rim of a meter high parapet. It was a precipitous drop to the adjacent rooftop—almost two stories of freefall.

"Do we jump?" Robb asked.

"Hell, no," Trakalo laughed, "we'll use the stairs." Hugging the wall over the ledge was a rickety iron staircase, a rusting egress to the level below.

"Don't cut yourself again," Trakalo warned, "and give me a moment to get ahead. I don't know how sturdy this thing is."

"Yes, sir, Dad," Robb grunted as Trakalo dropped from view. Then it was his turn.

Gripping the rusted iron, he stepped over and began his descent. Screeching loudly, the staircase betrayed him. Roughly scouring his hands, the coarse metal chewed through the skin of his soft hands, discouraging speed, but the idea of being exposed on the open iron path prevailed and he refused to slow down.

"A meter to go," Trakalo whispered, the ladder disappearing beneath his feet. Robb slipped off the rung and slid the last length, sandpapering his palms and drawing blood afresh.

"Shit," he cursed, stifling a stronger cry.

"No time," Trakalo demanded, darting across the flattop toward a rooftop door. As they approached, the door swung open, accompanied by yet another piercing metal shriek. Robb's heart sank, but Trakalo was not in the least bothered.

"Good to see you, Sergeant."

"We're ready, sir," came the affirmation.

He expected this! Robb ascertained. Their flight was not an improvisation, but had been adroitly predicted with an escape route expertly organized and planned.

Descending a short staircase, they entered living quarters modestly decorated with modern furniture and appliances. Double-paned windows overlooked the railway frontage, but the dark interior and drawn draperies fortuitously concealed them from onlookers. Strangely, at this hour, the flat was deserted. Without pausing, they continued through its apparent abandonment and down the next flight of stairs.

At ground level, the three entered the dimly lit gallery of a pool hall. The room was long and narrow, housing a succession of official snooker tables. Framing one wall, a double row stadium of aluminum benches faced the slates, throwing imposing shadows onto the floor. The opposite side was barren.

Past the tournament theater, between benches and a canteen, a familiar glow emanated from two video game consoles, circa 1980. Alive and ready, their obsolete electronics chirped constantly, an invitation to customers that wouldn't arrive for another dozen hours.

At the farthest end of the corridor, a translucent view of vacant pool tables bounced back from plate glass windows.

"Shit! They've cut the power. We're visible." Neatly obscured behind restroom walls, the backdoor beckoned.

Overhead, an exit sign shone, weakly proofing a paint-peeled portal.

Trakalo grabbed his shoulder. "Stand still against the wall," he warned Robb. Pivoting his head, he commanded firmly, "Find the door."

"Yes sir," the sergeant replied, donning headgear. Walking astride the benches, he reached over, gently touching the wall above the top row. At the video consoles, he stopped.

"It's here," he announced.

He's wearing IR goggles, Robb surmised, this time correctly.

Trakalo and the sergeant sprung into action, silently sliding the two meter box frame aside. Partially recessed into the wall behind was a meter high trap door, securely shut but unlocked.

The sergeant released a latch, opened the door, and peered inside, using thermal rays to survey the void below.

"All clear," he proclaimed and crawled through, bidding the others to follow.

"C'mon, Robb," Trakalo called, disappearing from view. As Trakalo dissolved into the dark, he grinned over his shoulder at Robb.

"The hotel used to be a brothel," he chortled.

Robb stepped inside. The corridor was confining, originally sized to let shorter men pass through. The three of them were tall, needing to stoop their shoulders and stand sideways to avoid contacting either wall.

"Sir," the sergeant requested, "shall I head back and cover the door?"

"Yes, of course," Trakalo agreed. "I will manage from here."

The younger man slipped past his superior, brushing against Robb, nearly knocking him senseless.

"Sorry," he apologized curtly.

"It's okay," Robb grunted. "Geez, the guy's made of bricks."

Momentarily, the hidden door swung shut, eclipsing the gloomy light, but Trakalo was prepared, brandishing a flashlight from his belt.

Switching on the LED beam, he explained, "I had to wait until we were out of sight."

"Understood," Robb agreed, "how far can we get in here?"

"The whole block is connected underground. I don't think many citizens younger than fifty know about it."

"The trade's been closed down here for at least a half century." He chuckled. "Of course, these passageways never appeared on any official blueprints."

"Remnants of the wild west?"

"And more," Trakalo smiled reminiscently. "I considered asking the town council to have them sealed off, but I didn't have the guts. In hindsight, that would have proved unfortunate."

"I'm glad you didn't."

"Yeah, once it hid the sinner and politician alike, I wonder where we fit in?"

"I'm neither a politician nor a proven reprobate," Robb quipped. "Ironic, isn't it?"

"Indeed. Now I believe I'll ask the town council to put it on the historical preservation list. Have them investigate its origins, drag up some dirt. It'll be a wonderful scandal."

Fifteen minutes later they emerged onto a dark street a block away, well separated from the barroom. Immediately, Trakalo doused his light. Behind them, a commotion was in progress, anxious patrons standing in disheveled masses outside the hotel's front door. A pair of uniformed RCMP officers, including the sergeant, dutifully accepted their statements. The intruders had vanished.

The night air was cool and damp. Pressing their faces, a putrid oil and saltwater wind breezed in from the bay.

Overhead, a mercury vapor street lamp flickered weakly, struggling to strike a new plasma, buzzing ominously.

"This way," Trakalo tugged his arm and they hustled away from the business district toward the bay. A few blocks later, they paused in the shadow of a large maple tree in front of a vacant lot. Crickets chirped slowly, measuring and reporting the night's chill. From out of sight, crooning frog voices resonated at intervals, and a rising rhythm of surf tumbled from the beach.

A high-pitched humming resounded above his head. Looking up, Robb saw a flurry of gray bits silhouetted against the pallid cloud light. Mosquitoes. They hovered in numbers that caused him claustrophobia. Darting from the frenzy, the most famished landed on his neck, searching his exposed skin for an easy meal. Suddenly anxious to leave, he glanced over at Trakalo. But the cop was gazing resolutely at the bay.

Far off into the harbor's thin mist, ghostly framed lattices stood erect above an array of hulking shadows, enormous freight ships anchored at dock. Berthed beneath tall skeleton cranes, the massive iron frames anxiously awaited the commencement of the busied day, unmoved by the tide's gentle swell.

As his eyes adjusted to the darkness, closer objects became visible. The nearer, seagoing shapes were huddled together in a humbler harbor, shrinking in size but advancing in age.

Kilometers away, across a wide stretch of water, city lights populated a short hillside. In the heavy, humid air, their yellow eyes twinkled, regularly scattered by moving tufts of air.

"Now we wait," Trakalo explained, "hopefully, not for long."

"Where are we?" Robb asked.

"Near the docks," he answered vaguely.

Before Robb could complain about the bugs, or decry their human pursuers, Trakalo suddenly craned his neck toward the nearest vessels.

"There it is," he announced. With a start, he took off, trotting toward the night shrouded shore.

"Where are we going?" Robb jumped into action, quickly catching up.

"My makeshift safe house."

Hustling downhill to the bayfront, they exchanged the concrete path for a coarse-grained, sandy strip, heading toward a battered, unused wooden dock. Built almost a century earlier, the ashen timbers were seriously decayed, slowly succumbing to the forces of wind and water.

Climbing a bloated, barnacle encrusted ladder onto a warped, slatted surface, Trakalo homed in on a levered, grate gangplank, lowered in welcome for their arrival. Atop the levered portal was a metal fortress, the rusting carcass of an abandoned ore carrier.

Inside the ship, it was cold and dank, still air reeking with a peculiar vintage of salt, oil and guano. Fortunately, neither were smokers. Descending vertical hatches and treading narrow corridors, they found and entered the captain's quarters, a tiny room, stark and comfortless.

Outside, waves funneled the hull, creating the effect of a sound booth inside the ship—a silent zone from the modern world. Not a noise from the town penetrated. For better or worse, there was no cellular signal. It was like stepping out of time.

The craft rocked in the strongest surges, lifting minutely, creaking and groaning, before settling back noisily onto the small rocks and mud beneath. For a moment, Robb worried that the fatigued hull might not withstand another battering night and that it was fated to split open before the morning. Shrugging off the nonsensical concern, other questions needed answers.

"How did you arrange this?" he began.

"I...I, uh, can't say for sure," Trakalo confessed. Too hastily, he expanded, "I'm afraid I may have divulged the location of the ore body to a local mining company."

"You told someone where it is?" Robb complained, forgetting his other concerns.

"No, I told them I'd heard wind of something big, but I needed a place to lie low and preserve it from foreign interests."

"Is that illegal?"

"Technically, no. I spoke nothing but speculation. But, now that I'm faced with the consequences, I will be reporting a conflict of interest in this case."

"When did this happen?"

"Earlier today, after I got your email."

"I see, but you're still here..." Robb smiled, beginning to comprehend Trakalo's dilemma. His last ditch effort had forced Trakalo's hand, albeit prematurely.

"I have too many people depending on me not to screw up. Besides, I couldn't tie down loose ends any sooner."

"And now?"

"Your life is in danger. I'm sworn 'to serve and protect,' eh?"

"Thanks."

"It's my duty. If not by the letter, then by the intent."

"Now what?"

"We'll spend some time here, get some rest. In the morning, we move."

"Where?"

"Out into the country," Trakalo answered vaguely.

"Why?"

"To spring the trap you asked me to set."

"I knew you understood."

"Indeed."

In the morning's wee hours, after a restless night endured on a musty cotton cot, Robb awoke, ready to depart.

Trakalo had advised him to prepare for rough travel, not to stray above deck, and to conserve his energy for a lengthy hike. The Mountie was pensive, but not about his previous night's professional *faux pas*, rather he seemed to have lost reassurance in something important, a detail he refused to discuss.

"Ready to go?" Trakalo asked with no small measure of anxiety.

"Of course," Robb answered. There would be time later to ask questions.

At dawn, they left the iron tomb, briskly re-crossing the brown sand toward a four-wheel drive pickup parked on the vacant street front. Surprisingly, the truck was idling, having been dropped off by an unseen accomplice of the Mountie. The cabin was spacious, but its bed was half filled with a molded, black plastic container concealing some kind of optional equipment.

"What's underneath the hard top?" Robb asked after they were underway.

"Extra fuel," Trakalo answered, without explanation.

Accelerating the truck, he sped through empty streets, heading west. In a few minutes, without fanfare, the structured rows of houses abruptly ended, giving way to wilderness. Engulfed within the endless parkland, the paved ribbon of road wound constantly, never offering more than a kilometer of visibility.

After a succession of widely spaced, peripheral villages, the asphalt highway halved into a less amenable conduit, a narrowed, single lane hard top. A few hours later, it transitioned again to a graveled grid, which was, apparently, still too luxurious to last. At last, the road terminated into a worn, dusty dirt trail, which wormed around soggy meadows and within taiga forest for kilometers.

After each change in venue, Trakalo stopped and refueled the vehicle and religiously maintained the truck's vitals; tire pressure, suspension, belts, and engine fluids. This was no place to become stranded. Along the way, he began unwinding, expressing his pent up thoughts.

"Does it make any sense to you how easily we got away last night?"

"Easy? Nothing easy about it," Robb argued.

"Not at first," Trakalo agreed, "but once we hit the street, we weren't followed."

"But you said..."

"The passageways were secret? Yes, but why there was no back-up along the block's edge is mind-boggling. They weren't stupid, nor ill-prepared, so there must be another reason that the entire block wasn't fortified."

"Meaning?"

"When they couldn't take us at the pub, they went into reconnaissance, observing where we went."

"Why wouldn't they attack?"

"We spent the night in a metal box. We were well contained."

"Should have been easy pickings."

"Yes we were, but they didn't come after us. Why? Perhaps we are more valuable alive then dead."

"Are they following us, now?" Robb craned his neck, surveying every direction. The rolling terrain made it difficult to see. Billowing behind their spinning wheels, airborne dust unleashed an unmistakable tell-tale for a pursuer to trail. Someone could leisurely remain miles behind without being detected.

"No, now we're catching up."

"I'm confused."

"I'm pissed," Trakalo confessed, "but mainly at myself."

"Why?"

"Last night, as we discussed our plans, they were listening in."

"Huh? How?"

"The ship is metal, nothing more than a giant sounding board. Whether they bugged it previously or had a diver equipped with a listening device, I don't know. It doesn't matter anyway. They know where we're going. And, being forewarned, they got away quicker." He snorted derisively, "In fact, I suspect they used the same trick twice."

"When else?"

"The first time was when we were talking in the bar. The hotel is old, full of metal pipes, obsolete remnants from an abandoned steam-heating system. Some half decent equipment and a digital recorder could pick up every conversation from the boiler room."

"It would take time to sort them out."

"Just some good software," Trakalo fumed, not accepting the technical obstacle as being significant.

"Excuse me?" Robb asked, still not fully following Trakalo's rant.

"A few minutes of signal de-convolution and, presto, individual conversations are as clear as a bell. Hah! And I thought I was being clever using the hidden escape route."

"Then why aren't we changing our plans."

"Because it concerns Yakov."

"In what way?"

"After your phone call last week, I had him transferred."

Robb understood the semantics, "to where we're going?"

"Yes," Trakalo answered grimly.

"Why?"

"With the firepower moving into town, I thought he'd be safer a long way from the jail. HQ wasn't mobilizing quickly enough to help." Wistfully, he added. "Besides, he's slowly going to pieces behind bars."

Robb shrugged off the humanitarian lapse in judgment, in turn consoling the cop. "No, moving him made sense. Where did you send him?"

"Sorry, I can't say."

"What's so important about Yakov?" Robb probed.

"I'm still not sure," Trakalo replied. "I'm hoping you can help me figure that one out."

Nearing sundown, Trakalo stopped the pick-up for another roadside fueling.

"Do we have enough fuel to get back?" Robb asked.

"Of course," Trakalo replied. "It's when I'm hauling my snow machine that I start to worry. There's less room in the bed for a large extra tank then."

Astonished, Robb asked, "You travel out here in winter with something as unreliable as a snowmobile?"

"Of course," Trakalo replied, "it's my job." Quickly, he turned to business, "We're close to the outer edge of my territory now. We're not entirely alone, you know, we're only a few kilometers from a small, Inuit town on a reservation."

"Out here?"

"It's never been any other place," Trakalo quipped.

"I meant, why live out here?" Robb reiterated. "No offense."

"It's a simple life," Trakalo replied sagely. "There are those who prefer the sublime."

On cue, the sun slipped below the horizon. The evening sky erupted in magnificent theater. Choreographed by the ancient, atmospheric prism, the ballet commenced with a dance of fiery orange and red before relaxing into softer and subtler hues. Spanning shades from crimson to purple, the promenade of progressing pigments gently transformed the unremarkable summer sky from blue to black. It was graceful and peaceful.

Reverently, Robb stared, not noticing Trakalo's driving speed had, of necessity slowed, becoming deliberate because of the fading light. As full darkness descended, they stopped. Some distance northward, a drifting cloud glimmered, reflections of a village's lights on an star studded, inky sky.

"From here we go on foot," Trakalo announced.

"Sure," Robb replied dubiously, wondering when the cop would rest. He seemed to have only two speeds, *Stop* and *Go*. Thus far into the nonstop day, he hadn't seen much of the latter.

Hearing the younger man's doubtful tone, Trakalo assured. "We can rest for a few hours. The moon's not out."

"Where are we going?"

"To the trapper's cabin."

Moonrise.

An hour later, the eastern horizon lightened, far sooner than Robb desired. With less fanfare than the sunset, the humbler, diffuse glow intensified into a singular provenance, focusing strength until the patterned, celestial mirror edged above the earth's rim. Immersing the land in cool blue, the monotone effects were, nonetheless, remarkable.

Receding from sight, the bright pincushion of stars dissipated. Vespered shadows loomed, pillowy silhouettes of cumulus clouds slowly shuffling along endless, uncharted journeys. Imperceptibly swelling, they were enriching on the day's spent moisture, promising the return of rain.

Farther overhead, shredded silver wafted westward, tightly tethered on invisible pulling strings. Sailing convective crosswinds, they tore easily into tattered, dissipating wisps. Clinically, Robb regarded them as evidence of fierce high altitude winds roughly a kilometer overhead.

On the ground, the backdropped light enhanced amorphous forms, which slowly resolved into ghoulish shadows of hills, trees, and rocks. Their dark casts cloaked long stretches, creating black voids of uncertain terrain.

Shortly, the moon floated above the knoll tops, brightly illuminating hints of color in the foliage. As Robb's eyes adapted, his confidence to travel was renewed. He felt a gathering impatience with Trakalo's lack of activity. The stuffy air inside the vehicle was sapping his wakefulness. If the cop didn't mobilize soon, fatigue would prevail.

Rolling the passenger's window down to gather fresh air, a strange chorus of night sounds greeted him.

Soft winds rustled the grasses, hissing through the shivering trees. Deeply hidden within recessed branches, owls hooted before softly alighting to hunt. Field mice scurried beneath sheltering blades of grass, abundant sustenance to feed the fledgling owlets.

At intervals, human voices carried across the nocturnal plains. Robb looked up in alarm.

"The natives' village," Trakalo explained, pointing toward the area where Robb had earlier noticed reflected lights. Embarrassed by his startled response, Robb said nothing in reply.

Beneath the grass carpet, crickets chirped and grasshoppers droned. Frogs croaked, whispered taunts preceding jousts, their arguments rapidly inciting rivals further away. Within moments, collective voices dueled, proclaiming individual might, strength and virility. At full volume, the resulting cacophony overshadowed all other sounds, whereupon a night bird would silently swoop and harvest the exposed and foolhardy. Every few minutes, the night wind gusted sharply, timidly quelling the outburst. Quieted for but a moment, the rivals would call again, bravado afresh.

Other noises were less constant. Field mice, rats and moles rustled the grass, rushing headlong on hungry quests to find tidbits of sustenance before the whispering owls found and fed on them. Mournfully, a coyote howled, resonating at length before its soulful tome faded. The call was immediately answered, excited yips from a pack of playful pups. Fear pulsed through the smaller game, stilling them in their tracks. It would be several minutes before they ventured forth again.

Fresh scents of green grass and field herbs, brome, chamomile and clover drifted over his palette. Finding their soft fragrances relaxing, he absorbed the pleasant nuances. They were uncommon to Robb, exuding the strangeness of his present location. Like a switch, the aura of peace vanished. He felt cut off from civilization, adrift and isolated. Alone on the prairie, astride the manmade metal fortress he lost his sense of security.

Robb was no longer certain whether he liked being where he was. Perhaps they should just get on with their plan—whatever it was. An anxiousness to act, to just do something was festering, dovetailing neatly, but in contrast with his exhaustion. Impatiently, he checked his watch.

1:00 AM.

He sighed. Too early for the day to begin.

Trakalo smiled, "I agree."

"What are we waiting for?"

"Two things, both quite dangerous."

"Which are?"

"I'm sure we've been followed, but except for those sounds from the natives' village, I haven't ascertained anyone else's presence."

"If someone is following us, wouldn't they also stop for the night, or else they'd risk running over us?"

"Usually, yes, but now I'm thinking they've gone around us."

"How?"

"About fifteen kilometers back there was a fork in the road. It wasn't much to look at, so you might have missed it. It leads to the natives' village and from there turns into a walking trail which winds for kilometers before crossing the main river. At this time of year, the water level is high, but it may be passable with a four-wheel drive truck. A few weeks ago, the river was impossible to ford."

"Where would they be going?"

"Taking a shortcut to where I believe the mineral deposit lies."

"So they already know where we're going?"

"Yes."

"How would they know that?"

"Any number of ways. Besides listening to our conversation aboard the wreck, they might have eavesdropped in the bar. Put enough information together and they could have already guessed." He neglected to mention the Russian. "I think it's a given for us to assume that they know."

Robb pondered, chewing on the certainty of his assumption, but there was the other nagging question, "what else is so dangerous?"

"The night life. This isn't exactly the city, eh?"

"It's a good night to be hunted?"

"Yes, but most game animals aren't out on a bright night, which it will be soon. They are leery of being detected in the light and hide when the moon rises. The wolves and bears, however, spend some time searching for stragglers. Although the pickings are slim, the success rate is good, but they'll give up after an hour or so."

"How much longer do we need to wait?"

"At least another hour. Get some rest."

"You don't have to tell me twice," Robb smiled, closing his eyes. Within moments, he passed out, embracing an ephemeral peace.

At 2:30 AM, Trakalo shook him awake.

"It's time," he announced. Overhead, the moon shone brightly through the truck window. Mercifully, Trakalo had tarried longer than necessary to allow Robb additional time to rest.

The short slumber was refreshing, but insufficient to regenerate his body. Feeling drugged, Robb stiffly unfurled from leaning against the truck's door. Sorely, he half crept and half fell out of the vehicle. Upon his feet hitting the ground, he reached his arms skyward, stretching, forcing the numbing icicles of fatigue to flee his flesh.

He was standing knee high in a thick, grassy heather, deathly still in the early morning calm. Not an iota of human civilization lay within in sight or earshot. It was an alien landscape. An odd urging awakened, demanding he immediately return to the herd.

Trakalo showed no such frailty. In the crisp, violet light, he mobilized a bag of provisions, assembling water, dried food, some chemicals and ammunition. The truck was a mobile arsenal, pantry and communications center.

"Is there anything I can carry?" he asked.

"No offense," Trakalo replied, "I'd prefer if you're only lightly burdened. Conserve your energy, because you will need it."

For the next two hours, Trakalo hiked at a pace that was relentless. Robb struggled to match him. Altering his gait from a very fast walk to scrambling, he frequently lost ground, falling meters behind until Trakalo paused for him to catch up. The uneven ground and the dark of night made it an extremely hazardous jaunt. Robb was grateful there were no steep climbs to conquer in the dark, but the flat terrain offered other treacherous pitfalls.

Groomed by the atmosphere and generations of subterranean sculptors, its scars were frequent and bone-rattling. Abruptly walled washouts, overgrown, mossy mounds, and hidden, thirty centimeter entrances to underground burrows formed a litany of obstacles that threatened to tear his ligaments and fracture his bones.

This land had never yielded to an iron plough, its ilk similar to the ground traversed millennia earlier by the first humans.

Unable to distinguish hazards beneath the wanting celestial light, Robb moved tentatively. He was more concerned with avoiding serious injury than rectifying his laggardness. At the last second, he recognized and sidestepped a deep, dark hole materializing underneath his feet. If he cared, he would have noted that it was the burrow of a large rodent, a rabbit or badger, but the impact roughly wrenched his knee and jarred his hip. He cut his speed, gingerly walking off the discomfort. The journey was degenerating into a nightmare.

Sensing the resolve eroding in his younger companion, Trakalo mercifully slowed his torrid pace. Over the next half hour, he purposefully maintained a slower gait, pointing out hazards, which Robb gratefully avoided while keeping up. The time passed without serious incident.

As the moon set slowly on the western horizon, darkness consumed the world. The fabled starlight was insufficient for navigation. No longer capable of walking safely, Trakalo signaled a halt. Robb collapsed in a heap, his legs rubbery with exhaustion.

"Don't lie on the bare ground," Trakalo counseled, "you're soaked through with sweat and you'll chill. Here, take this."

He offered a thin woolen blanket, stashed within his backpack. Dubiously accepting, Robb wrapped it around his body, covering his shoulders and torso. Too small to protect his legs, he huddled inside the cover, sitting in the standard fetal position on the grassy turf. He longed to lie down, but heeding Trakalo's warning, he dared not prostrate himself on the cool earth.

"Put the blanket on the ground," Trakalo suggested.

"But you said..."

"Wool insulates in spite of the damp. You should know that."

"Yes, of course." Robb agreed, then apologized. "I suppose that's the difference between book smarts and being practical." He sighed, tightening the blanket around him before reclining onto a patch of short grass. It was refreshing. Beneath him, the thick, dew-drenched grass crumpled and rustled, agitated and loud. Yet the bladed bed was soft and yielding, a suitable comfort.

Straightway he relaxed, sensing the blanket gathering moisture. As Trakalo had promised, the wool fiber continued insulating, keeping his torso warm, but no matter how tightly he tucked his knees to his chest, the fabric barely covered his legs. Contacting the grass, his shoes absorbed the heavy dew until his feet were soaked. Their wet chill was insufficient to keep him from sleeping and the heavy burden of deep fatigue descended.

He drifted into sleep, his mind awake with rapid fire dreams. In one, he was running in panic through urban clapboard rows, overwhelmed by oppression from an anonymous adversary. In the next, he was also fleeing, this time eluding an unknown enemy by choosing to traverse dangerous, mine-filled, remote terrain. Juxtaposed, the visions were disconnected, nonsensical, although haunting illusions. Every few minutes, his terrors crescendoed and he awoke, disoriented but relieved to find it wasn't real. Groggily reorienting, he'd shift positions and seek unconsciousness, whereupon the same nightmares would sequence anew.

But dreams merely mirror waking predilections, and Robb could not escape his troubles, not even in slumber.

Mercifully, the intensity of his delusions slowly dulled, his restless mind sorting and filing away the grievous day's stresses, until finally freeing himself, he slipped benignly into slumber.

When he woke again, perhaps only minutes later, he felt refreshed. The eastern sky was graying. Trakalo was dozing, exhaling softly, seemingly at peace. Not anxious to start another exhausting hike, Robb let him sleep.

With daybreak undoing the night's canopy, Robb quietly exited his blanketed bed and climbed a small knoll to become acquainted with the surroundings. To his surprise, they had adjourned within spitting distance of a wood-framed cabin. Silhouetted by the dawn sky, a dilapidated, log structure stood roofless and decrepit, condemned between a state of human abode and natural decay.

A light breeze stirred, morning's early breath caressed his face. It bore the hint of smoke.

Who else is out here? Robb wondered, hurriedly looking upwind for evidence of his pursuers, but there was nobody else in sight. Once again, he glanced toward the cabin. Sensing something wrong, he instinctively stepped closer, as if a few meters would clarify his view. Instead, the daylight pulsed brighter and Robb instantly surmised that the outpost was only recently destroyed.

Turning around to go back and awaken Trakalo, he found the cop, ashen faced, standing a few meters behind him. Binoculars set to his eyes, the cop metallically stared through him, hard set on the damned domicile. Aghast, Robb understood that this was where Yakov had been sent.

Halving the horizon, the sun cast an apocryphal glow, saturating the cabin in bloodied hues. The cabin had been set ablaze, a fire quickly quenched by rain, leaving half burnt log walls reduced to charcoal fingers. Several embers were still alive, orange eyes glaring within slivered crevices. Puffs of steam breathed, jetting and hissing, a tepid dragon that smoldered too weakly to burst back into flame.

Unmarred at the center of what was left of the cabin, Evan's potbelly stove sat, stolid, cast iron legs buried within a layer of ash. Jutting skyward, covered in char, an exhaust pipe aspired, unmarried from a nonexistent roof. Alongside, blackened stovepipes lay jumbled amongst cold cinders.

Ten meters away, razed but not incinerated, remained Evan's pelt shed. Through a thousand sparkling perforations, the morning light testified that nothing large within would be alive. Feverishly, Trakalo ran down the hill and tore through the slat boards, flinging them aside like matchsticks until convincing himself it had been unoccupied.

It was a harbinger of change. Five generations of trappers had worked the hinterland, for two centuries surviving the harshest of elements, the hungriest of predators, and the inanity of petty feuds amongst their dying breed, but never facing a force as instantly lethal as their own, technologically enhanced, modern brothers in kind.

"Shit," Trakalo cursed impotently. After exonerating the hermit's checkered history, he'd grown to admire the resourceful trapper. He was downright chilled. Losing Evan was an irreplaceable, unforgivable loss. The man's character had been reformed, even tempered, not by social customs nor monetary pursuits, but by primeval tribulation, a process borne of painstakingly eking his survival from forces far superior to himself. Unlike a belittling human taskmaster, the north's granite and ice edges merely humbled, they did not sap his spirit. In rising up to challenges, Evan had forged respect for himself, his fellow man, and most surprisingly, common social customs. The compressive angst of his youth had been relieved, uncoiling a resolve to salvage his present.

Having witnessed the social reclamation, Trakalo had pardoned the trapper, albeit against his superior's intolerant reticence, but the junior officer had many valid reasons. Needing the trapper's eyes, ears and expertise, he had pragmatically recruited Evan as an ally against foes considerably more dangerous than other, emotionally marooned hermits squatting the sub-Arctic, fur bearing plains.

For the next half hour, Trakalo and Robb hesitantly searched the rubble for clues, fearing the macabre, but the most sinister discovery was broken bottle glass, implying that a petrol bomb had been employed to start the blaze.

There were no charred corpses.

Widening the investigation to include the surrounding meadow, Trakalo soon came upon a trampled swath of grass leading to and from the outpost. It could easily have been made by a half dozen men. Without delay, they started along its vector, but within a quarter hour, the trail vanished over hardened ground.

Trakalo sighed, an expression not borne of futility, assuring Robb that he most certainly knew the destination. He pointed to the tell tale indentation made in late spring by a snowmobile track.

"Where do we go now?" Robb asked, not comprehending it significance.

"They'll have gone to the deposit. Everything is pointing in that direction."

"How far away?" Robb asked excitedly, but as the words recklessly slipped his lips, a sense of foreboding formed in the pit of his stomach.

"It's a few hours," Trakalo understated.

"Do we need more supplies?"

"No," Trakalo determined, "we have enough provisions." He turned to face Robb, analyzing his fitness. "How are you holding out?"

"Better than expected," Robb resolved. "I was pretty beat earlier on, but I'm fueled by adrenaline now."

"You'll need it," came the grim response.

"Let's not waste time," Robb plied in return.

Hiking at steady pace again, Trakalo regularly pointed out shreds of corroborating evidence, indentations of rifle butts, unmatched boot prints, fragments of shed cloth and metal. The preponderance of clues quickly confirmed the recent passage of a large party. As they drew terrain underfoot, Trakalo grew hopeful that the wily trapper was alive. Dead men would be discarded, but a live man could disappear. But for the geologist's fate, he could not assuage his conscience. Since the infrequent tracks were leading toward the mineral bed, the inescapable conclusion was that Yakov was captured.

From his backpack's side pocket, Trakalo retrieved a black, rubber coated two-way satellite radio and headset. Selecting an encryption scheme, he transponded a short, terse communiqué. After receiving the first response, he fell silent, but did not remove his headset.

"I'm asking for recent satellite images from this area," he explained.

"Asking who?"

"At first, my HQ, but they deferred. Now I'm being patched through to CFB Moose Jaw."

"Is that good?"

"I don't think it's good or bad. If the air force were deploying, I think they would inform us."

"Do you think they have a fix in place?"

"By 'they,' you mean..."

"Ottley's my first choice. At the very least, he is connected. I suspect he runs the operation, but is bankrolled by others."

Trakalo raised his eyebrow in question.

"Whoever provides the money is an unknown, completely beyond my pay grade, but their affluence seems limitless. Perhaps they have..."

"Probably not, there's a thousand, more practical, reasons delaying a response," Trakalo cut him short.

"Logistically, the air force monitors a million square miles of territory. We Mounties help, patrolling our local districts and passing suspicions up the chain. Most times, our concerns are well below their radar, and we decide whether to investigate."

He sighed, slight exasperation, before continuing. "The armed forces need tangibles before concentrating resources. In my opinion, we haven't provided much proof yet."

Robb winced, bearing the burden of personal failure.

"Perhaps," Trakalo continued, "Churchill's events are what they need to start paying attention. Even so, it doesn't happen overnight."

"Then we're on our own," Robb concluded. "What help will I be?"

"Hopefully, you can hide well," Trakalo warned. "In my original master plan, you weren't supposed to be here."

"Yeah, sure," Robb responded, dubiously.

"Look," Trakalo soothed, "I'm pulling your leg. There's only two of us, we're not going to provoke a confrontation."

"So, what are we doing?"

"Fact finding."

"What about Yakov and this Evan?"

"They're compromised. As yet, we're not. As much as I hate saying it, I'd like to keep it that way."

Chapter 22

Insubordination

The sun hovered steadfast, fortifying at a mid-morning height, while gathering steam to sweep an arc across the sky. The soft, dawn breeze had grown bitter, bristling into a brisk, damp wind, cold and penetrating. With each broadside buffeting, pliant grass carpets bowed in unison. The dank air suggested rain and the fields prudently paid homage for the wind's promised blessing.

Along the northwestern horizon, storm clouds assembled tumultuously. Tumbling and twisting, the pallid pillows darkened into a billowing, charcoal rage, consuming the distant turquoise sky. Then the winds altered, vectoring the storm front toward them. In little time, a ponderous gray cover swept beneath the brilliant sun, plunging the land into a depressing, daytime dullness.

Pilfered of radiant warming, the humid air cooled rapidly. Throttling harshly, frigid winds persuaded the vulnerable inhabitants to seek cover, either below ground or in the trees. Shivering, Robb determined to join them, longingly seeking the nearby ravine. Before he could make his request known to Trakalo, the zephyr abated. An eerie quiescence ensued, unperturbed by the common calls of birds or rodents, now accompanied by the sounds of their legs swishing through the short grasses.

Overhead, the summer squall marched closer. Blinding, lightning fingers singed the air, presaging ricocheting thunder that bounced between cloud layers. Robb unconsciously marked the time between explosions, gauging the storm's distance, yet neither he nor the driven officer would be deterred by the worsening weather. As each was preoccupied with personal dilemma, immersion in a bone-chilling tempest seemed trivial. For his part, Robb quietly debated his hypotheses, but without gain. The mysteries outweighed what he knew. He needed to unlock and retrieve the knowledge inside Yakov's head, but the opportunity to speak again with the Russian might well be permanently lost.

Trakalo wore his headset, anticipating Moose Jaw's reply, although the receiver remained silent. In deference to Robb's fatigue, he'd slowed the pace. Having lost Yakov, he was under a cloud. He'd gambled and lost and his future was uncertain, no matter how prudently he had assembled his logic. Would his politically constipated superiors understand that he'd chosen the lesser risk, a course of action that had been justified by the previous night's assault? Or would his failure cement his fate?

Robb welcomed the less taxing effort, although his lack of fitness was doing him in. Since dawn, his legs had slowly deadened, inexorably sapped by sustained walking. He walked clumsily, lactic acid in his legs left him unsteady as they travelled over the rough ground. His calves began to twinge with each step, warning the onset of muscle spasms. Stopping to rehydrate, Trakalo paused and handed the young man two tablets of Ibuprofen. Almost immediately, the fluid and analgesic aided, reducing the inflammation. With little time to rest, it was advantageous to mask exhaustion's symptoms than address its causes.

Unable to resolve his own pondering, Robb considered the cop's burden, specifically that the radio call was not answered. At least thrice, the officer had reiterated his request, only to be rebuffed by a tight-lipped admonition to stand by. Worse, Trakalo was losing his calm demeanor, appearing harried, although he did not express his concerns. Robb accepted Trakalo's discretion. When Trakalo wanted to vent, it would be on his own time and, presumably, at his own professional risk.

Overhead, the storm clouds continued roiling but refused to rent. Optimistically, Robb wished the squall would pass by. He was not the only nervous soul. A hawk's shrill cry shattered the pre-storm quiet. Robb looked up, quickly sighting the bird flying a circular pattern, smartly searching for the impatient field mice fretting to return above ground.

A wind rebuilt, strong, but with less bellicosity than before. It kept them cool, saturated in the fragrance of struck lightning, reminding them of worsening conditions still to come. The next hour was uneventful, doggedly treading several kilometers over undulating, grassy knolls. Surmounting a final rise, they stood atop the upper edge of a wide, hollowed plain, a bowl-shaped width stretching to the opposite horizon. Bisecting its midline was a green ribbon demarcating a large, central river valley.

Over the gently sloping, open plateau, the wind blew fiercely. It must have been a frequent and constant force, taking a toll on the inhabitants. Exposed to blasts, the vegetation changed, abruptly becoming shorter, hugging the ground. Rising above the ubiquitous short grass, bristling, meter-high rosehip shrubs and stunted thickets of poplar trees dotted the flat.

A half kilometer to the north, a frontage of evergreens, tamaracks and pine peered over the edge of the grassland, marking the location of the ravine. The tree line stretched eastward, descending until merging with the river below. Across the river valley, several similar drainage clefts forked at intervals, each tine draining the upper plain and feeding the river.

They were close.

In deference to the wind, Trakalo headed northeast, toward the evergreen forest. Approaching its sheltering trees, Robb realized that, like most other features in the vast landscape, the wide open perspective diminished the watershed's enormous size. In places it appeared to be extremely deep but not uniform, sometimes sloping gently and other times scarred by blunted, rocky outcroppings. Neither was the foliage homogeneously composed, pockets of deciduous, poplar and birch, textured amongst towering conifers.

Kilometers east, where the ravine merged into the river valley, the bottom was perhaps a hundred meters below the topside plain. Along the watery base, a densely packed, deciduous forest grew, a mottled carpet of thick leaf tops.

Shining through leafless gaps in the cover, a silvered surface dully reflected pinpoints of the overcast sky.

Tracing a serpentine path, unslowed by oxbows and open plain, Robb was surprised to see fast water raging. The land was draining its winter feed.

"There's the ravine. Once we get into the trees—we'll be out of the wind. Inside, we can navigate downhill towards the river," Trakalo explained, pointing toward the turbulent liquid ribbon. Although Trakalo made it sound easy, their destination was kilometers away.

The expanse of the landscape unnerved Robb. He was accustomed to urban sprawl, city neighborhoods engineered within architectural plans, artificial inkblot parsings forged by iron scythes into laminates of domiciles, businesses and open space. Here, the land was vast, untamed, infinite. They were insects, crawling over the thin layer of its ceaseless expanse. It felt harsh, unrelenting, and foreboding to human habitation. Here they were insignificant. Here it was easy to be beaten.

Diverting his mind from its depressing volume, Robb turned academic, analyzing the geography. It was only a waterway on an alluvial plain, with spurs of craggy drainage radiating from the main channel, a natural environment of erosion clefts cut through rich silt and clay.

Kilometers upstream from the river, at the limits of his eye's discernment, the watersheds lost elevation, gently melding into an opposing plateau. Densely vegetated at their nether, the zeniths differed discretely in appearance, characterized by a loss of vegetation and a shallower hill-side gradient. From Robb's vantage, it was clear that the river's force had, over the recent passage of time, cut its deep gouges into what had once been a shallow glacial lake.

Since the last Ice Age, as the glaciers slowly melted, untold volumes of liquid had scoured the soft till. Under gravity's forcing, water eroded a network of remarkably similar valleys housing more than green flora and hardy fauna. Beneath the lowest course where the main silver thread tumbled, slicing, pulverizing and carting rocks a billion years old, the telltale shards of concentrated minerals deposited by forces long extinct was being exposed with the passage of time and the forces of nature.

Here Robb would witness something amazing. The scientist felt his excitement building. In the midst of that chasm, long harbored beneath the earth, was an ancient treasure, a modern repository of high tech gold.

Without warning, the wind blasted, flattening the grass and bringing shivers to the trees. The leaves ruffled noisily, then lingered softly before dying away.

"Here it comes," Trakalo announced, "let's get into the trees. Now!"

Underscoring his warning, a lightning bolt pegged the earth, setting off a blaze of sparks that quickly quenched into smoldering strands. It would not burn any longer. Seconds later, rolling thunder rumbled, urgently lifting its volume, sharply cresting with a stupendous clap. Instinctively, Robb covered his ears. As the echoes reverberated over the plateau, he felt like he'd been slugged. It was damn close and louder than anything he'd ever experienced.

"Half mile away," Trakalo deduced, "we'd better hurry."

"Eleven hundred feet per second..." Robb began, still too much in awe to consider the practical.

"Two and half seconds from bolt to sound."

Another fierce gust pressed against them, halting their progress, nearly tilting Robb from his feet. But, unlike the dry first blast, this one came loaded, propelling small, stinging pellets of rain into their unprotected faces. Accelerated by the driving convection, the droplets of water impacted his skin like hardened hailstones.

Trakalo broke into a trot, leaning into the wind to cut the resistance. Needing no encouragement, Robb sprinted to catch up. Gale force gusts clobbered the grass, mercilessly twisting corkscrew patterns in the pliable blades. Briefly stationed for a few seconds, an invisible vortex danced haphazardly, leaving behind a flattened spiral tangle that did not quickly rebound upright. Robb ran hard, head tucked beneath his forearm to protect his face, his disbelieving eyes watching the snaking trails from the ghostly funnel tearing uphill through a hundred meters of grass, ripping the tough blades from their embedded roots and flinging them outward as clumps of green debris.

Then, equally eccentric, the funnel disappeared.

As the squall's initial onslaught moved away, the pelting rain weakened its fury. Larger droplets struck them with less intensity, but delivered improved wetting power. Before they reached the tree cover, the two men were soaked to their skin.

"Didn't quite time that one well," Trakalo grimaced.

"Where the hell did this come from?" Robb exclaimed, still in awe as the intense thunder and lightning show continued.

"You're not used to this?" Trakalo questioned wryly.

"Not at all," Robb responded. "We don't get weather like this in So Cal."

"For sure," Trakalo agreed, "but we don't have quakes, you know."

"It's a fair trade then," Robb laughed.

Retreating beneath the trees, they took reprieve. Selecting a game trail to follow, Trakalo descended a dozen vertical meters before halting beneath a stand of tall tamaracks. The ground beneath them was spongy, littered with coarse, brown pine needles, through which mushrooms were growing. Trakalo paid the wrinkled gnome hats of the fungus no notice.

In concert with the odd texture, the needle bedding crunched each time Robb stepped. It was still dry. Raindrops were rarely reaching the ground, intercepted by the thick growth overhead. Another oddity, the lack of ground cover provided long lines of visibility.

The air was fresh, a pungent olfactory experience of pine, ozone enhanced from lightning surges. The aroma was completely unlike the cheap industrial cleansers with which Robb was too familiar.

"Are we in any danger?" Robb wondered, as the trees frequently flashed daylight bright during lightning pulses.

"Probably not," Trakalo assured, "this grove is well below those trees on the upper ridge."

"Not quite the tallest lightning rods, then."

"Let's hope."

"You're taller than me," Robb teased.

"That's why I ran so fast," Trakalo quipped in return.

Thirty minutes later, the storm abated. Rainwater slowly trickled through the pine fronds, collecting, melding and slipping from bough to bough. Splattering onto the ground the rare droplet ended its disjointed fall with an unceremonious, unseen drip.

As the storm moved further southward, flashing lightning no longer blinded and the deafening thunder declined.

The tempest, although strong, was brief.

Trakalo busied himself to return to the plain. Pointedly, his radio calls remained unanswered. He geared up and stood, jaw set in determination, eyes creased with worry.

"Let's go, Robb," he requested, "before we lose our daylight. It's a hard trek and a long way back."

"Shouldn't we travel through the trees?" Robb queried.

"No, it'll be easier along the tree line."

Scrambling to keep up, Robb ascended the ravine wall. It was decidedly more difficult to get out than get in, now especially when the ground was wet. Slipping and tripping, he propelled himself using handholds from the perimeter bushes, until he emerged onto the plateau.

The difference was surprising.

The land looked devastated. Pockets of formerly upright grasses lay in fallen, crushed heaps of tight, braided piles on the ground. Those that remained standing were soaked through, lonely sentinels ready to snap should the wind rear again. Scrub bushes lay splayed over the ground, their slender stems bent obscenely as if stepped on by a massive, crushing foot.

"What the hell happened here?" he asked.

"Don't worry, it's normal," Trakalo answered. "In a few hours, you'll never know a storm was here. This will all bounce back, but if there had been hail, it would be a different matter. For us, too." He grimaced.

Looking southward, Robb watched the profusion of purple clouds churning the upper plateau, pursuing their next unassuming target. Through the light drizzle, an occasional jolt of lightning still shot back, but the answering thunder was taking longer to reply.

Trakalo's radio crackled. Quickly responding, he answered its tardy call, but to no avail. Electrical interference from the departing squall made it impossible to transmit and receive. One thing was unmistakable, however, the sender's voice was urgent and his tone ominous. He seemed to be delivering a warning.

"We'll have to wait a few more minutes," Trakalo groused.

"How long?"

"No more than an hour."

"We'll keep going?"

"Absolutely, there's no time to waste."

The gray skies trembled, a distant thunder roll that lolled over the horizon, refusing to die away. Cloaked within the inclement weather, the tremoring crept nearer, advancing in power, escaping their cognizance.

When the humid air shuddered, Trakalo stopped to listen. The percussing was unnatural, incongruous with an atmospheric squall. It had to be man-made.

No longer drumming beneath his radar, Trakalo frowned, turning to Robb. In an instant, the vibrations altered pitch, popping violently from deep-throated rumbling to high-pitched shrieking. The effect hijacked Robb's attention. He stood, mouth open, his eyes riveted upwards, peering into the overcast sky, waiting, wondering, fearful.

Banking through a circular overpass, a squadron of fighter planes dipped beneath the cloudbank, no longer hiding in front of their own shockwaves. Diving toward the ravine's mouth, they discharged a hail of fire, leaden lances of fury.

Instinctively, Trakalo and Robb dropped to the ground. The ground throbbed, betraying their vulnerability. Rolling into a tight, fetal ball, Robb sought the protection of an overhanging tree branch. Trakalo dived into a shallow depression in the grass. Covering his face, he, too, shielded himself from the explosions. But the cop quickly deduced the origin of the air attack. Fighting his impulses to cower and hide, he regained his feet, nonchalantly standing and observing the aerial onslaught. He realized that they need not worry about the razing rounds. They were nowhere near the intended targets. Seconds later, his radio vocalized, affirming the attack.

The victims fell quickly. While most projectiles missed their mark—enough struck home. Dying instantly, the men departed in shame, expressing little more than wails of anguished agony. Forfeiting their lives in a nameless battle, with little fanfare, vitriol welled in a few, nihilistic souls.

They died cursing and raging, angrily twisting beneath the barrage of piercing lead.

Robb felt little sympathy for the fallen. Although they wore the uniform of his country, they had long ago ceased to be patriots, having allied themselves with the forces for ideological subversion. They were little more than zealot traitors, rogue elements occupying an abnormal extreme of a maddened political spectrum.

Tearing into the sky, the fighter jets completed a screaming about-face and departed. In mere seconds, they rumbled beyond earshot, leaving little aerial evidence of their intrusion.

On cue, the heavens poured open again.

Draining in sheeted, down-swept intensity, the rain restarted at a downpour, instantly soaking them through. Within moments, their skin was chilled and numbed, forcing them under cover again within the wooded ravine. This time, they elected to keep moving, descending below the ridge top conifers to mid ravine height. Here Trakalo predicted they would find the game highways again, running parallel to the seasonal water flow, leading to the main river.

Unfortunately, the trails were of little navigable use. Saturated and muddy, they'd become nearly impassable. With each step, their feet sunk deeply into the rich gumbo ground, caking their boots with heavy, thick pads of sludge that clung heavily onto their soles. The added burden quickly fatigued them both.

Underneath the brown leaf litter, rivulets of water trickled down the steep slope.

By mutual decision, they stopped beneath an ancient, massive poplar tree. The giant boughs spread overhead nearly a dozen meters in every direction, arresting the deluge. Sitting beneath it against soggy bark, they waited through the heavy downpour, chilled and uncomfortable. Rain dripped continuously through the leaf cover, a steady rhythm spattering onto fallen leaves. It might have been calming if their clothes were dry— they were soaked to their bones.

Optimistically, Robb gratefully ceded that the incessant insect activity had abated. But not for long. Breeding vociferously through the short season, the mosquitoes used the pools as nurseries.

Needing a quick shot of regenerative sustenance, they found their way out of the dank and damp hiding places, stalking the scent of mammalian perspiration. Homing on the chemical cues, they gathered in clouds, shrilling wings circling and diving as they sought a blood purchase. It drove the two men away from their still repose.

Soundlessly, they slipped and climbed the thirty vertical meters back onto the grassy plain. There was no straight path, but Trakalo ensured their overall progress was both upward and toward the river. An exhausting hour later, they exited the ravine—once more breathing heavily after ascending the steep walls of their sheltering safe zone.

To Robb's surprise, they were only a few hundred meters from an encampment.

"How did we miss this?" he blurted.

"The rain was too heavy. From overhead, the trees form a protective semi-circle of cover," Trakalo breathed, unfastening his sidearm from his belt holster.

"Is there anyone here?"

"Unlikely. It looks deserted, but it won't pay to be wrong, will it?"

They searched the temporary quarters cautiously, but not a soul had remained at the camp. With their fears calmed, Robb and Trakalo turned their attention to examining the abandoned personal effects.

Poring through others' private belongings was troubling to Robb, doubly so as the owners were recently deceased. He kept reminding himself that his freedom was at stake, and while investigating the camp of the dead was disturbing, he could not intuitively sympathize with their departure any more than their political cause.

A dozen small, one-man, silver *Mylar* tents remained as temporary memorial headstones to the fallen invaders. Staked to the ground with metal clamps, the walls spread open and were held wide apart, flapping in the breeze, over stiff corded seams. The tents were extraordinarily functional, not requiring external support to maintain their upright posture, not even lightweight fiberglass poles.

Inside one man's tent, assuming it was a man and not a woman, Robb found a waterproof journal. Thumbing through several pages, he searched for details, a name, a date, some trivial confirmation of the man's origins and duties, but there were few illuminating details. The entries were in English, but the text detailed nothing of the man's occupation. Most pages read like a diary, semi-daily attestations of thoughts, feelings and ideological sympathies.

It was the cause that gave Robb pause. He read more closely. Once each week, the journaling changed themes, extended rants praising the virtues of a well-ordered, work-a-day society, contrasted with abundant criticism levied against the decadent liberalism that he felt was pervading his country.

The man was a fanatic.

The more he read, the less Robb found himself able to sympathize with any iota of the dead man's religion. Tersely skipping through the journal entries, he ignored the vitriol, instead seeking dates, place names or contacts. Unfortunately, there weren't any clues forthcoming. The man's origins, cause, and current mission were framed in hate.

"Robb!" he heard Trakalo calling.

"Yes?"

"Got anything? You've been in there awhile."

"Hoped so, but nothing significant—except a litany of hate literature."

"That's not too bad," Trakalo surmised, surprising him. "I've got something you might be interested in."

"Be right there."

Robb wormed out the entrance on hands and knees, keeping possession of the handwritten journal. A moment later, he joined Trakalo, who was proffering a similar notebook. They exchanged finds.

"What's this?" Robb asked.

"Look at this page," Trakalo requested, holding the bound volume open at a chosen location.

"Sure."

Viewing handwritten scribbles on the paper, Robb discerned numbers that indicated measurements of mass and volume, some acronyms and a mathematical formula. At first glance, they had nothing to do with the technology of Rare Earths. They looked more like medical journal entries.

"Does it make any sense to you?"

"Not much," Robb admitted, "it's certainly not electronics."

"Don't tell me what it isn't, please," Trakalo urged. "Fathom a guess at what it might be."

"Of course," Robb agreed, "as long as my ass isn't on the line if I'm wrong."

"Your ass is already torched," Trakalo reminded him, "how's a bad guess going to make that worse?"

Robb shot him a wary look, but said nothing. Trakalo's face was creased in an ironical smile, humored and compassionate, not malignant.

"I think it's a dosage calculation, maybe an injection aliquot," Robb ventured. "This number, *80 kg*, is a mass roughly equivalent to an adult man. Over here, a concentration, *100 mg/L*, and a formula that seems to be calculating a volume, *10 cc*. He traced over a pair of four-letter alphabetic strings, pointedly capitalized. Perhaps these letters are acronyms that indicate a drug or a pharmaceutical."

"Any drug you recognize?" the cop queried.

"Not at all," Robb answered, "wouldn't this be more in your arena?"

"Yeah, it is," Trakalo agreed, "but it's not one I recognize. And frankly, I think it should be. My profession requires that I keep up to date on that line of merchandise." He sighed. "What a change in twenty years!"

"Huh?" the introspective comment caught Robb off guard.

"When I started in the force, the illegal substance was alcohol. In my districts it was mainly a bootleg trade or packaged in diluted, secondary forms like mouthwash and vanilla. Now, even here, the illicit trade has been modernized and industrialized."

"It's not just old wood-fired stills hidden in piles of pig manure. Now it's chemistry—labs, glassware, distillation columns and refluxers. The contraband is constantly evolving and the equipment is more sophisticated. Those involved are ever more dangerous, but this isn't drug running. This outfit is well trained, a professional paramilitary. So this entry could stand for just about anything."

"If it is a pharmaceutical, these symbols could code an experimental formula," Robb suggested.

"Yes, it would seem so. My hunch is that it was something intended for Yakov," Trakalo replied, grimly. Then, unusually, he thought out loud, "how do we make sure?"

"We'll find him down there," Robb pointed to the ravine.

"Yes, of course," Trakalo agreed. "But, just a moment, let me get permission. With the Air Force having struck, I probably no longer have jurisdiction."

Calling on his radio to his HQ, he relayed their desire to investigate. As before, his request was ambiguously re-routed up a ladder of command. This time, however, they did not have to wait for several hours for an answer.

Fifteen minutes later, their request was emphatically denied.

"Absolutely not," Trakalo relayed. "I'm not to venture into the area."

Robb swore, "Why not?"

"With the military involved, I'm required to keep a *safe*, translate, ignorant, distance."

"Do they know what to investigate?"

"Who knows?" Trakalo fumed. "Most likely they don't, but if they do, it'll never be shared with me. I'll never find out what's happened, who's behind it, or what I can do to stop it next time. It'll be classified. Worse, if Yakov is alive, I'll have lost any bargaining chip I have to secure his freedom."

"Is the air force there now?"

"Not at all," Trakalo replied, "those fighter planes are built for attack and speed, not parachute drops. It'll take a few hours for a transporter to arrive."

"Then we have some time," Robb tempted. "They couldn't have expected us to be up here, otherwise they'd have radioed a directive sooner."

"No, this would be illegal," Trakalo retreated.

"Not you," Robb answered, "Me. I'm already on the shit list. What difference does it make to me?"

"How do you propose to get away with it?"

"Play ignorant. You and I were separated, I wandered in before you could tell me to stay away." Trakalo's eyebrows raised, but he said nothing. Undaunted, Robb blustered, "how the hell will they know?"

"Hah!" the cop scoffed, "that's so obvious. And dumb enough we might make it work."

"Tell me what to look for."

"Not so fast, you'll be visible by satellite."

"Not beneath this overcast, remember."

"Of course," Trakalo chuckled, "I can't fool you that easily." His tone sobered. "Can you hold yourself together at the sight of dead men?"

"I don't know."

"Fair enough. It'll be brutal, bloody gruesome, to say the least. But that's not the least of it. This is real, not made for TV. The sights, sounds, and smells will be repelling." He paused, a nowhere visage on his face. "Torn open bodies, the stench of blood, odors of excrement and half digested foods. If you're lucky, it'll only make you queasy."

He stared at Robb, unrelenting, until the young man flinched, averting his eyes. "Try not to look at the faces. The hollow expressions of vacant dead eyes will haunt you through. If you have half a conscience, it will get to you."

Robb put up his hand, requesting that Trakalo cease the ghoulish pep talk, but the Mountie refused, needing to prepare him.

"It's possible you'll react before you even smell a thing, that your brain will pick it up. Suddenly, you're legs will give out and you'll retch. And you'll want to run like hell to get out of there. You might even find yourself feeling confused, delusional, and going into shock. If you do, you'll have a hard time putting yourself together again. If you fall, crawl out. If you lose your head, walk away. Close your eyes, pinch your nose, pick a line and go. After a few minutes and some distance, the effects will fade."

"What are you talking about?"

"No one is prepared to face his own mortality, especially the aftermath of human inflicted violence. Just don't go into shock."

"I understand."

"No, you don't."

"You're right, I don't. I'll face it when I get there."

Descending from the broad plateau toward the wooded river gorge, Robb fought against the reservations Trakalo's encouragement had fostered. He half wanted to turn around passively and deal with whatever legal troubles awaited him, but a quiet, urgent voice confronted his inclination, sanely reminding that he must assert his own future. So onward he pressed.

He was unarmed; except for a razor sharp, sheathed hunting knife the Mountie had supplied him. The blade was from the trapper's hermitage. Carrying a weapon had risks, particularly if armed forces arrived during his jaunt. Worse, it might implicate Trakalo as complicit. Losing Trakalo's testimony would death knell his legal defense. The knife, of course, could have been lost by the trapper, and Robb could argue a plea of self defense.

Unable to thwart his troubling thoughts, Robb unsheathed the knife and held the carved, wooden handle firmly. Trakalo's descriptions had been disturbing, and he could not clear his mind. Balling up, his stomach apprehensively twisted, curdling knots began to develop in his gut.

I must be going nuts! He deprecated, chastising his mental state. It had seemed necessary, but he now regretted the decision to visit the killing field.

Ottley can't have pissed me off this badly, he reasoned, and it was true. His motivations were changing. No longer driven by the original vendetta, his propulsion now was a quest for self-justification, turbo-charged by his old self, his unrelenting, unrequited curiosity.

Frequently checking his watch, he soon had another worry. Time was passing quickly. Allotted a scarce ninety minutes to complete his searching, twenty had passed without drawing significantly nearer. Doubling his pace, he broke into a hurried, downhill trot, the short blade flashing wickedly as he pumped his hands. The grassy ground was broken and uneven, threatening to trip him onto the dangerous edge, but he began discerning a thin, worn trail running parallel to the tree line. Along this smooth track he ran.

Not grasping the significance of the game trail's connection to the man he sought, Robb nonetheless appreciated the efficiency gain. Closing on the river valley, the path effectively skirted the sharp drop of the ravine on his left.

The ravine floor was dark and foreign, full of mystery and danger against which he was unsuitably armed.

Twenty minutes later, he halted, catching his breath. From beyond the river valley's edge, a few dozen meters into the foreground, the earth dropped away steeply. A monophonic murmur welled over its hidden depths, the constant pouring of tumbling water. A half kilometer across the divide, he saw the bare earthen walls of the opposite embankment.

Carefully stepping across the soft, unstable ground, he searched for an egress. In short order, the game trail led over a small knoll and angled a path through the ravine leading straight toward the river's edge. Peering through the trees, he got his first view of the landing below. The meeting of the two waters had opened up a broad meadow several hundred feet beneath his feet.

From his elevated perch, Robb stopped and surveyed the scene. It was ghastly, an otherworldly visage he'd never experienced, only flatly glimpsed from sensationalized two-dimensional newscast footage of guerrilla battles.

Crisscrossing the meadow, aerial gunfire had scythed twin rows through two meter tall, reedy bulrushes. Along the parallel paring, shattered stalks protruded, revealing splayed open cores glistening white, their stems splintered and frayed. Strewn about the shredded meadow were the slumped over, punctured bodies of men, steadfastly immersed in stains of ruddy crimson. Lifeless limbs projected impossibly, unable to move again. At random, an arm or a leg lay in discard, motionless, savagely dismembered from its lifelong partner.

His stomach began to suffer spasms forcibly and Robb vomited, convulsively and repeatedly. "I'm such a wimp," he scolded himself, acknowledging that he hadn't even entered the mortality zone.

Several times he attempted to step along the path over the valley's edge, but his legs were palsied, their synapses locked out in neural disobedience. The conveyance concerted with a stronger instinct—survival.

Thinking furiously, Robb elected to survey the scene, looking for someone who didn't fit in, an aberration of clothing or hairstyle or some trivial detail that did not blend, but all the men were commonly outfitted, and now were homogeneously dead, having anonymously expired in blood-stained, khaki green camouflage. From his vantage, the dead were indistinguishable from each other.

He searched for movement. Nothing was stirring.

"You've got to go down there, Robb!" he commanded aloud, as speaking would drive his legs. With great reticence, he pushed a foot forward.

A twig snapped. The fracture was close by, behind him in the trees.

In panic, Robb froze, his gaping eyes boring holes through the tree line, straining to see the sound's origin. A dull thud followed. Robb's legs fearfully gave way. It was fortuitous. Screaming through the air, a bullet whizzed over his head, tepid lead boring a heated trace above his skull. Silencing the forest chatter, the single volley's report crisscrossed the valleys.

Hitting the ground, Robb shook, his heart racing in terror. Anxiety impaired his mobility. Behind him, the open plain beckoned dangerously.

He resisted. It was sure death. An unarmed runner could not elude a covered sniper.

What do I do now? Who the hell shot at me?

Laying low in the tall grass seemed to offer a small, if temporary, measure of protection. If the assailant moved closer, he'd be able to gauge the attacker's direction and dart away into the bush cover.

From a few yards away, he heard a gurgling noise, followed by wheezing and the scuffling of footsteps treading through damp leaf litter. Robb froze, a deer in headlights, unable to command his body to flee.

Get up! Get out! He commanded his body, but his legs refused to obey.

The gun barked again, and Robb closed his eyes in terror, a montage of color coursing through his mind, heralding the blackness of eternal night to follow.

Shit!

The inevitable did not materialize.

A half-choked scream gargled from mere meters away, grotesquely chilling Robb's blood. Stifling a panicked reply, he held his breath, Another thunderclap, the third shot, sounded, accentuated by line of sight proximity, but its projectile did not pass near the young scientist. Instead, the nearby bushes shivered, roughly loosening a rustle of rain-soaked leaves from the top boughs, hissing foliage blading chaotically to the wet ground below.

Out of sight, thrashing persisted, skirting the perimeter of bush along a random, haphazard path. Strangely, it suggested that the attacker was trapped, unable to find a clear way through. Near the tree line, the bushes grew densely, forming a tight barrier against the plain.

Inefficiently stumbling through the tight bramble, the assailant bulldozed ineffectively, snapping small stems and bending saplings which Robb heard thudding against his body. Incredulously, the attacker seemed suddenly spastic, flailing in ineffectual rage against networked barriers into which Robb could not see.

For a moment, motion ceased, perhaps brought on by entanglement within grasping limbs. Then the struggle began anew and in earnest. Writhing against the bended branches, the unseen soul twisted and jerked constantly, but with less ferocity. His futile efforts were unable to free him.

And then, Robb understood. Seized not by the trees, the doomed soul was scuffling, wheezing and gasping, against the jaws of his death throes. After a shortened struggle, there was a quivering pause, then the terminal, violent shiver of branches which suddenly ceased.

The trees stilled and silenced. Back-dropping the fatal calm, the constant, dull roar of rushing water permeated Robb's senses once more.

From high on the plateau above, Robb imagined hearing a faint call of alarm as Trakalo responded to the gunshots' reality. He pictured the cop sprinting into action, ignoring orders, and dashing down the long slope to Robb's aid. Even at top speed, the journey would take too long. He'd probably be too late in arriving. A killer was still in the ravine.

Amplifying his fears, a man adorned with a very thick beard emerged from the bush, clothed in torn, unkempt rags. His shirt, a checked green tartan felt, was ripped open at the elbows, exposing a dirt-encrusted, lacerated elbow and bloodied hands. His jeans were soaked and soiled with mud. On his head, dark hair drooped matted and greasy, but it was the face that commanded Robb's attention. The man's eyes were pained and bloodshot, strangely offset as if focusing in different directions. One pupil had narrowed, intent on seeing on every small detail, but the other was incongruously wide, dilated, drifting lazily along a different plane. He looked like mud-stained hell, struggling to hold himself together. Flies buzzed over an infected gash on his head, a singsong, throbbing, unceasing chant.

Peering past the veneer, Robb perceived a soul hovering precariously over an abyss, untethered to reason's stanchions. The humblest nudge would be sufficient to commence the plunge, a headlong free-fall over the brink into madness.

It was Yakov.

"*Xkodeh! Xkodeh!*" The Russian barked, gesticulating frenetically, ordering Robb to follow into the trees.

Hesitating, Robb refused, a knee jerk response. *Is he threatening me?* Frantic for options, Robb failed to reason why he should delay acquiescing, other than an overwhelming preference to avoid nearing the Russian until armed assistance arrive. He feigned ignorance, the most passive of resistances, a defense easily constructed against a language barrier—Yakov could not be dissuaded nor derailed.

Closing the ground between himself and the frightened scientist, he grabbed the young man's forearm and pulled hard, dragging him down the slope toward the river.

Seized in the bear paw grip, Robb winced, feeling rather than comprehending the commanding request.

"*Proshou, xkodeh!*" Yakov pleaded, not releasing his iron grip.

Robb relented. If the man wanted to kill him, it would already be accomplished, but even if Yakov wasn't intending harm, Robb remained wary, having caught sight of the unhinged conflict raving inside of Yakov's mind.

With no time to debate, he ran to keep up. The forest floor declined steeply into a shadowy chasm. Staining the charcoal void, a trail of blood commanded his attention. The dark splatters led him through a thicket of tangled bushes to a stand of young poplar. At the barrier, the blotches terminated beneath a tangle of broken stems. Above the clutter, a uniformed body hung limply against the spindly trunks.

Dressed in a blood-soaked uniform shirt, the dead man slumped, his elongated neck snagged between a 'V' of diverging branches. Lifeless and limp, his head sagged impossibly over the crook. Flies buzzed about the corpse.

In perpetual frenzy they swirled, circular approaches abruptly ending in swift descents, whereupon they suckled and alit. After countless bites, the corpse's face was sugar-coated with his own coalesced blood.

Discordant against the crimson death trail, the bush was alive with the spring season, speckled with clusters of miniature flowers, shockingly white against the bloodied backdrop, but Robb had no time to assess the expired fanatic.

From forty meters away, an agonized groan quelled the droning flies. Instantly, the blood drained from Robb's face, and his knees buckled weakly.

How many more are here?

But Yakov was not alarmed. Spurring to action, he dragged Robb toward the moaning. In an instant, Robb perceived the reason for Yakov's persistence, and he broke free from the Russian's grip, hastening toward the injured man.

Folded into a crumpled heap the trapper held himself upright, a fractured femur protruding through his dark stained jeans. His skin was ashen, having lost several pints of blood before applying a tourniquet. He was wedged against a fallen tamarack trunk, one foot dug stolidly into the splintered remains of a root.

His left arm slung over his waist, bloodied and useless, tucked tightly with a makeshift sling. In his right hand, he clutched an semi-automatic rifle in a pistol grip. The gun now pointed skyward, but moments earlier, had threatened the two scientists until the bearer recognized the Russian. Even so, unsure of Robb's allegiance, he remained wary and vigilant.

"Are you Evan?" Robb asked.

"Yes, who are you?"

"I'm Robb. I'm here with Trakalo."

"Where the hell is he?"

"About a mile away."

"You're American?"

"Yes."

"They were American, too," he spat, and passed out.

Springing into action, Robb pushed the rifle aside to examine the wounds. The extent of damage was mortifying. Evan was bleeding to death through the punctured skin in his leg, alive still only because of the leather belt tourniquet.

The injury to the trapper's arm was a mystery until a blot in the jacket fabric led Robb to a small caliber bullet wound. The lead had bored through Evan's soft tissue cleanly, partially cauterizing the openings. Robb pulled him forward to examine the exit wound.

The mere sight was unpalatable. Clustering on his back, tiny black ants were streaming fearlessly at the singed flesh. Every moment, a few minuscule heads emerged from within his body, each bearing a tidbit of pink between clenched mandibles and transferring the booty to the transport group clamoring about the perimeter.

Evan was being consumed from within. Incredibly, he had shook off the pain and maintained guard over his troubled companion.

Squelching the urge to vomit again, Robb feverishly brushed away the insects. Attacking their approach line, he dragged his feet through the leaf litter, displacing and disorienting the skittering horde. At best, it would keep them at bay for only minutes.

Away from the trapper, he couldn't hold his stomach, letting loose with the last of his alimentary fluid. Embarrassed, he wiped away the lingering viscous strands and returned to the trapper's side. Evan pretended not to notice or, more concerning, he was slipping into a deep, numbed shock from which it would be difficult to return.

Robb was suddenly aware that Yakov was nearby. In alarm, he looked up. The Russian was staring at him, quizzically, a hint of frustration flashing in his eyes. Perhaps he'd expected Robb to be capable of more.

"*Voda*," Yakov grunted, pointing away, toward the dead man, and an object slung over the ensnared man's shoulder.

"Yeah, sure," Robb agreed, not understanding.

Yakov rushed over to retrieve the vessel, his movements stilted and jerky. Handing a carbon composite canteen to Robb, he again watched him keenly, that ever-present tinge of madness bleeding from his pupils.

Confused by the man's expectations, Robb reacted slowly. Too slowly for Yakov.

"*Voda!*" He demanded, pointing at Evan's mouth.

Of course! Robb finally understood. He needed to replace vital fluids to slow the onset of dehydration or shock. Unscrewing the cap from the canteen, he poured the fluid into Evan's lips. Most dribbled over his face onto his cheeks, spilling uselessly onto the ground below, but a small amount got through. Reflexively, the semi-conscious man swallowed, ingesting the precious fluid. Robb was encouraged to try again.

Why the hell isn't Yakov doing this? He wondered. He obviously was better skilled in administering survival aid, but oddly, was holding back. He seemed to be going out of his way to avoid contact with the battered trapper, scrambling and scurrying about nervously, unwilling to sit still. Glancing over his shoulder, Robb saw the fugitive trembling in place, his behavior bordering on deranged. Clearly, the man was straddling the threshold of sanity.

He could be sick or mad, Robb softened his judgment, recalling the undecipherable journal entries, *but he's not crazy enough to forget to ask me to help.*

Pointing at Evan's leg fracture, Robb traced the outline of long, thin supports, implying that Yakov should locate material for splints. Immediately grasping the gesture, Yakov darted unsteadily toward the upper bush line.

Moments later, the telltale thrashing and cracking foretold the search, selection and harvesting of makeshift supports.

The woods fell silent. Yakov was nearby, only meters away, yet Robb could not spot his form. He listened for footfalls, but it was quiet. The geologist had melted into the forest.

"Yakov!" Robb called, but there was no answer. His irritation flashed hotly. Something was definitely wrong with the man's state of mind. He was not the same adventuring soul Robb remembered meeting only weeks earlier. The man was consumed with eccentricities.

"Yakov!" He shouted again. The call fluttered across the ravine and echoed once before dying in the trees. The forest hushed. Fear rose in Robb's gullet, displacing his agitation. He scanned his surroundings warily. Behind Evan and himself, the thick trunk shielded them well, but the cost was zero visibility. Robb was partially relieved.

Even with a rifle at hand, hiding was the better of choices.

Softly scrambling on hands and feet, he scurried away from the unconscious trapper along a fallen trunk, the damp pine needles silencing his movement. Selecting a viewing slit behind his wooden fortress, he surveyed the ravine upstream.

At a distance, he heard the characteristic sounds of a large animal foraging, noisily picking through whipping brush. Its lack of stealth betrayed an unchallenged brawn. At intervals, the animal quieted, treading sparsely covered ground, falling silent except for padding footfalls. As it neared, the creature scuffed a bush and paused, sniffing roughly. Robb heard its nostrils flaring as it expelled breath.

On cue, a drumbeat of horseflies droned, heralding the intruder. The vibrant volume collectively elevated to an annoying hum, alternately pitching highs and lows as individuals swirled around their carnivorous companion.

Quietly, Robb crept toward the rifle.

Halfway to the weapon, a double thud hammered the damp earth.

Robb stopped fast.

Branches whipped and timber splintered, as ground fall was destructively shoved hither and yonder. Again, the shuddering stopped, replaced by punctuated sniffing as the cautious animal constructed an olfactory image of its environs. Enticing scents must have been wafting, for the rasping continued unabated for several interminable minutes. Robb crouched, deathly still, afraid to sweat or breathe and broadcast his presence.

After the long moment, Robb peered through his tree shelter, stealing a first glance of the animal's back. It was a full grown black bear, curiously standing erect on hind legs. The body swayed back and forth in constant motion, a pointed head sampling a wide range of odors. Although the bear's body color blended neatly with the dark trees, the head was easily visibly, especially the perimeter of its pink nose's dancing and bobbing.

The bear was most interested in an easy meal, the human carcass hanging from the bushes. With caution uncharacteristic of its unmatchable strength, the bear deliberated its sensory reconnaissance. At long last, deciding that the nasal remnants of gunpowder were too dim to be of consequence, it ambled the few remaining steps toward the hung body.

With a single swipe of a broad paw, it bludgeoned the body free. Released from the bush's tendrils, the carcass fell stiffly, paralyzed with *rigor mortis*, and landed feet first. Momentarily, it looked alive, startling the bear. Instead, slowly cambering, it pivoted into the bruin's legs.

The bear snorted in surprise.

Gunfire boomed, shrilly renting the still air. The bear whined in disapproval. This interruption was not expected. Echoing the report, the torn air sheared across the ravine's divide, but the beast did not tarry.

Wheeling halfway towards Robb and Evan, it dashed into the deep woods assaulting the ground cover intersecting its flight. With a cacophony of fragmenting vegetation, it annihilated the unfortunate foliage.

Robb ducked low, pressing himself against the trunk, fearing he was not well hidden from either the fleeing bear or the new threat of a gunman's sight, but he need not have been concerned.

A moment later, the Mountie appeared, warily surveying the grisly scene.

Evan groaned, slowly gaining consciousness. Glancing around for hidden dangers, Trakalo rushed toward the prostrate man.

"Jesus," Trakalo breathed.

Robb stepped out.

"Can I help?"

Briefly, Trakalo raised his gun, but recognition of the voice stopped him.

"Of course."

"Yakov is getting splints for Evan's broken leg," Robb conveyed. "Well, he was before the bear scared him off."

"Yakov is alive?"

"Yes, somewhat," Robb answered, allowing uncertainty to communicate his concerns.

"Any opposition?"

"No," Evan croaked his first words, "they're all dead now."

* * *

"I've found this," Trakalo understated, handing Robb a journal with an outward form similar to the one he'd found earlier. It was open to a page of names and phone numbers. Robb's eyes locked onto the most important moniker, *Rolfe Ottley.*

"Thanks," he mumbled.

"You never saw this," Trakalo promised, "and you'll never see it again."

"Huh?" Robb questioned, but Trakalo had moved on.

"We've a lot to do in a short time, let's get busy," he called over his shoulder, double-timing toward the trapper.

Within an hour, as Trakalo had predicted, a transporter droned overhead, delivering a paramilitary troop, armed and lethally prepared. The men floated gracefully, suspended beneath billowed skins, rippling and flapping, into the river valley.

Alertly, Trakalo advised the descending warriors of his earthbound cadre, communicating their position, numbers and medical needs.

With soldiers arriving, Yakov began trembling, fidgeting, unable to hold still. As Trakalo concentrated on rendering first aid to the trapper, the Russian's nervousness grew until, without comment, he bolted headlong into the downhill trees, muttering unintelligibly. Trakalo didn't lift his head, engrossed in cleaning the bullet wounds and dressing the fracture's puncture.

Running short on gauze and antiseptic, the cop left Robb holding a compression bandage over the trapper's leg while he secured additional supplies.

Several moments later the geologist reappeared, wild-eyed and fearful. His shirt was torn and his cheek was bleeding, a fresh wound undoubtedly suffered during his rampant rush. He approached Robb, eyes alternating between menacing and pleading. Alarmed and unsure, Robb kept eye contact, stood up, walked backwards and left the injured man with the deranged geologist, electing to find the cop.

Finding Trakalo descending into the ravine carrying medical packs bearing red crosses, Robb blurted the tale of Yakov's strange behavior. Suddenly ill at ease, Trakalo brushed past him, darting back to the injured man.

Yakov was calmly attending to the wound, applying the compression Robb had relinquished, administering pressure above the broken bone exactly as Robb had been moments before. Without a word, the cop took over, motioning his helpers into position. With gut-wrenching efficiency, they reset the broken bone. Yakov held the trapper's shoulders and

Robb sat on the unbroken leg. Evan clenched his teeth in white knuckled pain, unwilling or unable to find solace in unconsciousness, while Trakalo stretched and realigned the damaged appendage.

When it was over, Evan lay sweating alongside the broken tree stump, groaning in diminishing discomfort. Trakalo applied a splint, lashing both legs together for support. It was crude and ungainly, but the field dressing would be effective. More importantly, help had arrived.

An hour after the military's arrival, summoned by Trakalo's request, a helicopter hovered overhead. Its timely presence indicated that the military strike was only part of a coordinated sequence of activity. Perhaps Trakalo was correct. The street fight in Churchill had been an awakening.

Removing the wounded trapper, the chopper airlifted him to urgent care, pain mitigation, and the vital fluids he desperately needed.

Then Trakalo was summoned. The ledger disappeared.

Sidelined to insignificance, Robb loitered along the tree line. The reprieve from fear was a welcome relief. His adrenaline ebbed, extricating from the reality of the mortality below, and settling his mind onto a substrate of shock.

With little to do but wait, all his problems unburdened. At present, the dead were not his concern.

The thrum of cascading water welled softly, peaceful and calming.

With only his thoughts for company, Robb slowly unwound. It was consoling to know he'd been right. The fanatics had been dealt a serious blow. He would probably never know the final outcome. Justice would be administered, probably through a clandestine policy of leverage, the unseen resolution between governments that make officials appear scatterbrained and clueless, but frequently settle other unspoken scores and effect small measures of peace.

A hundred meters away from him, it was anything but peaceful. Resolutely, Trakalo faced and answered a thousand suspicions. At first, the tone was confrontational, condescending and heavy handed. Robb was certain the Mountie would be incarcerated. But the bodies of evidence, a badly damaged hermit and the shaken scientists ultimately weighed the tilt in his favor. Besides, not abandoning a wounded man held valor.

As the day lingered, late afternoon's cool descended until Robb found that sitting on the damp ground was chilling.

Overhead, the dark rain clouds frayed.

Then it was Robb's turn. Taking his place before a commanding officer and a radio link to Moose Jaw, he weathered his own inquisition. Naively and skillfully, he answered the questions as a scientist should, avoiding exposing personal motives or incriminating himself by establishing ideological connections with the intruders.

Underplaying his links might have been strange had he been found in the killing fields alone, but his involvement with Trakalo had already been verified. Sticking to his technological guns, Robb impressed, sidestepping scrutiny by displaying his true talent, an unabashed excitement at the mine's potential. Not that he was fooling anyone, his history with Trakalo would be scrutinized many times over in the coming hours.

Fortunately, he did not have to face the tribunal in solitary. Flanking support was provided by a surprisingly composed Yakov and deeply disturbed Mountie, each shoring Robb's innocence.

The commander withdrew for a moment, receiving an urgent radio communiqué. When he returned, he shot Robb an inquisitive look.

"Robb, answer me truthfully. Are you with the CIA?"

"No," Robb answered with conviction. The CO accepted the presented truth. It was obvious he'd been apprised of much more.

After Robb's briefing, all three were granted their leave, but not their peace. An aura of suspicion hovered and it was suggested that they should disappear. The investigation was continuing without their input and would emphatically not require their services.

Shortly after being dismissed, a chopper transported them to Trakalo's pickup. While the vehicle was intact, the contents of each lock-box and storage bin lay strewn about the ground. The lack of subtlety of the searchers was disturbing. To the cop, the evidence was foreboding.

"There's still hell to pay," Trakalo muttered. "Let's get back to Churchill."

The road trip to Churchill started sullenly. Trakalo drove firmly, while Yakov stretched across the rear seat in the crew cab, exhausted and sleeping. Robb was bored, sitting in the front passenger seat, and leaning against the door. The metal was cold but the heater was on.

"Why did they need Yakov?" he asked, breaking the silence.

Trakalo exhaled sharply.

"It's most strange," he mused under his breath, concentrating on navigating the winding dirt road. Illuminated objects threw shadows that stretched into the seemingly infinite void. At times, they couldn't see more than a few feet away.

"Don't tell me you can't say," Robb complained.

"No, no, not at all," Trakalo laughed. He looked over his shoulder at the slumbering geologist.

"I'm surprised the military didn't take him into custody," he answered.

"Why didn't they?" Robb accepted the digression.

"He isn't out of reach," Trakalo answered. "A deployment is conducting an investigation in Churchill."

Robb looked dubious.

Trakalo chuckled, "I suggested to the CO that there might be an experimental drug connection. It was unsettling news to him. He conferred with his superiors and Yakov was allowed to travel with us. I don't think he wanted anyone to get near him. If what we suggest is true, no one knows what to expect."

"Yakov isn't virulent," Robb answered. "If he is, their operators were at risk."

"I didn't point out the obvious," Trakalo grinned. "I worked his imagination a bit, eh."

"Okay, but what else was so strange?"

"It was a damn bird."

"Huh?"

"Before Yakov escaped last month, he was tagged with GPS trackers in his food. He didn't know about it. By luck, he vomited and expelled one a day early. Apparently a bird, a crow or a raven, I'm not sure which, picked up the device and flew it to its nest. The fanatics followed up on the signal, which of course, was miles away from the lode. They had no choice but to fan out their search from there. It was unsuccessful."

"How did you learn this?"

"Evan told me. Between his Russian and Yakov's English, I got the gist."

The cop shot Robb a hard look, "Ottley didn't know Yakov was alive until you called me."

"I did not realize that," Robb protested. "I'm not a very good criminal."

"I'm just messing with you," Trakalo laughed. He turned serious again. "Once they realized he was alive, they pulled him in. They needed him for a few days longer." He paused. "And not much more," he finished bitterly.

Chapter 23

Templates

A few days after arriving in Churchill, Yakov occupied an open-door cell in the tiny lock-up. He was free to move about the small building, merely under a house arrest of sorts, while his life sentence worked its effects. Although he had no recollection of being administered any dosage, Evan witnessed that he had seen Yakov unconscious shortly after being captured. Yakov's health and mental stability were deteriorating. Palsy gripped his central nervous system. When no one else was present, he would tremor gently and constantly.

The military was observing him from a safe, glass-lined distance. A military doctor and psychiatrist had been promised, but their presence had not materialized. The hospital had refused to admit him. There was extreme reluctance to examine his incomprehensible infirmity. Until anyone understood what ailed him, he was a biological pariah.

The same courtesy was gradually being transferred to Trakalo and Robb. Conversations with officials were no longer face to face, but were sanitized by technology.

There was little news confirming the takedown of Ottley's organization. The Canadian military was mum about their findings at the river. The networks and web were silent. Using internal sources, Trakalo learned that Ottley and an associate were in custody and were invoking secrecy acts. The paper trail of his financing and operations was cloistered within layers of dummy corporations whose characteristic signatures were post office boxes.

It was taking time to drill through.

Ottley had been most effective in covering his tracks. He had cleaned house earlier, perhaps a precautionary move following the bungled skirmish in Churchill. If records and equipment were non-existent, his army of mercenaries or double agents had simply dissolved into the shadows.

It was an impossible Houdini for one man—and most unfortunate that the journal identified only the *field general.*

An invisible machine worked the vagaries of politics. The accusations were too fantastic. There was nothing to support a link to Shaparell's murder. Naming a government official in a fanatic's document was not indicative of complicity. The *brouhaha* was merely a failed, high stakes mineral grab.

Trakalo took it in stride. The backlash was having a calming effect, something needed in the undertow of a major tidal force. A complex organization would resist, yet one fact was immutable. Ottley was not being released. It was theater.

Robb grew increasingly restless, motivated by a burgeoning impatience to return to his scholastic life. He needed to get on with his life. Laying low didn't suit his personality.

Requesting an audience with Yakov, Robb summoned the geologist to the barrack's interrogation room. Yakov arrived early, sitting on a plain wooden chair, vacant eyes addressing his image in a two-way mirror.

His mannerisms continued being listless and detached, but his torso quivered without respite.

"Hello again, Yakov," Robb initiated, wondering if his words would be heard.

"*Dobre dehn*," came a feeble response.

"Can you talk?"

"Da."

"How are you feeling?"

"I am intolerably saddened."

Robb held silent, unsure, unable to venture a meaningful response.

"But it is not your beautiful country, it is my heart," Yakov continued.

"I'm very sorry."

"...my heart," Yakov sighed, and then he willed himself into sobriety. "How can I help you today?" He no longer shook.

Robb watched the transformation with a measure of respect. "I need to ask you some questions about your ordeal."

"Of course."

"Do you feel strange?"

"I feel like shit."

"No, no, no," Robb stumbled, "that's not how I meant to say it. Are you having any unusual mental symptoms?"

"I am not myself. I am ill."

"Yes, I'm trying to understand how and why. When did it start?"

"Months ago..."

Robb sighed, "do you feel forced to feel or think or act a certain way?"

Yakov looked at him disdainfully, "what the hell do you mean? I am worried and I am homesick."

"You're afraid...?"

"No, what the hell is wrong with you?"

Robb sighed, his hypothesis was all wrong.

"Just leave me alone," Yakov continued, working himself up.

"You're not squaring with me," Robb retorted. "What are you hiding? You need to let me know."

"Who the hell cares?" Yakov mocked, "I've been through worse. I did what you wanted. I was bait, but for what? To die like this? If I survive, I am never again safe. Your foolishness injected with this death sentence!"

"That it did," Robb confessed, "but I'm trying..."

"What do you care?" Yakov badgered, refusing to let him off the hook. "You'll walk out of here, go back home, no problem. I'm just a prisoner, no future, a stupid pawn..."

Damn! He's not letting up. Robb wondered where Trakalo was. Should he should signal for help. If there was a time he needed expert assistance, it was now.

Or is it?

Yakov's outburst was distantly familiar. Recalling the subtle gesture he'd seen on the train, Robb cocked his head, flared his shoulders, and stared Yakov directly in the eyes.

Nothing happened. Instead, Yakov read the posture for what it was, an unmitigated threat.

"*Ach, te khouyou!*" He swore, rising in his seat. Red faced with vitriol, the veins on his temples distorted his skin. It was as far as he got.

To Robb's amazement, the geologist suddenly withered and slumped, his head falling toward the table. An instant before it made contact, he regained consciousness and lurched upward. The red-streaked whites of his eyes showed, an aperture into a tortured mind. Robb stared hard at the grotesque image of panic. Yakov blinked, and the portal closed. When he re-opened his eyes, they were placid and untroubled. But his fingers twitched repeatedly.

There is a trigger.

"I will heal," Yakov spoke, exuding conciliation. He was beaten.

Robb scarcely acknowledged the olive branch. His mind was racing. In Yakov's blood was the physical evidence he needed to obtain.

"How are you mending?" Robb asked, breaking the ice. Evan reclined against an angled hospital bed, his arm and leg immobilized under plaster. His face was unshaved, his skin was jaundiced, an unbecoming cast enhanced by the warm glow fluorescents. The window drapes were wide open, but the sun shone weakly through an afternoon drizzle. Trapped beneath the tube lighting, the frontiersman appeared more ill than injured.

"I've been better, I suppose," he grunted.

"How long before you can leave?"

"At least a month, this leg will take some time."

He shifted slightly to face the scientist, wincing in discomfort. The pain flushed the pallor from his skin.

Robb moved to a more amenable position.

"It doesn't hurt as much as yesterday," Evan lied.

"I never got a chance to thank you," Robb said.

"I was saving my ass, not yours," Evan challenged, but Robb failed to see the mirth in his eyes.

Shifting nervously on his feet, Robb changed the subject.

"I've got some questions about Yakov."

"I've got some questions about Yakov," Evan parroted, laughing heartily. A second voice joined in the mirth. Trakalo was standing in the door frame.

"I thought I might find you here," the lieutenant quipped.

"I'm not going anywhere soon," Evan deadpanned.

"No doubt," Trakalo agreed. "How are you doing?"

"Healing slowly."

"Can I get you anything?"

"Two fingers of a good tonic, my tongue's dry."

"Will you settle for a cup of water?"

"Of course."

Trakalo departed, leaving Robb to initiate a conversation a second time.

"So where did you learn to speak Russian," Robb started cautiously.

"My grandparents were immigrants," Evan answered. "They taught me when I was a child."

"And your parents?" Robb continued with the small talk.

"They refused to speak it at home. When my grandparents died, I forgot most everything. It's coming back a little at a time."

"Good, what can you tell me about Yakov?"

"They did something to him."

"I think so, too. Did he tell you what?"

"No, after he was taken, I..."

Robb's eyes opened wide in amazement.

"...I was never captured," Evan addressed the cue. "They would have killed me on the spot."

"Of course," Robb agreed, "so how did you avoid...?"

"Simple, I wasn't there. I left Yakov at the shanty for a few hours while I picked Morels—they're a spring mushroom. When I returned, he was gone. My place was demolished."

"I saw it," Robb said quietly. "Only the stove was standing."

"It needed upgrades," Evan spun awkwardly. "But, I couldn't stay, I wasn't sure if anyone was hanging back, waiting for me. If there was someone, I guessed he'd be between my place and the Native village. So I went after Yakov, thinking I might be able to get him back. I had my gun."

"You took your gun to pick mushrooms?"

"Of course," Evan laughed. Robb felt foolish.

"I know the land well so I was sure I could get there without being seen. I sure as hell wasn't going to let him be killed without trying to help."

"You know where the minerals are?" Robb asked.

"I've known for years—so do the natives. Nobody out here thinks they're special."

Evan paused, a troubled silence, eyes narrowing beneath a furrowed brow. Robb glanced over his shoulder for a nurse. The pain medication was wearing off.

"The land will be developed. I can't trap there anymore," Evan added softly. It wasn't physical pain he was experiencing.

"What will you do?"

"I'm not sure, yet. I sure as hell can't farm out there."

Trakalo returned, bearing a plastic pitcher of water and a half-filled Styrofoam cup. He seemed to fill the tiny room. He handed the beverage to the trapper.

"We'll talk about that later, Evan," he said. "What changed in Yakov?" He'd been eavesdropping from the door again.

"I was beneath some trees in the ravine watching him. He was being guarded next to the river while the men picked stones and surveyed the valley. Yakov wouldn't sit still; he was rocking back and forth on his feet. They were making fun of him. Finally, someone hit him and knocked him to the ground. He lay there unconscious, but he couldn't stop shaking. It looked like he was having seizures."

Evan was sweating. Trakalo prepared another measure of water.

"I think he was still unconscious when the jets arrived. The noise scared the hell out of everyone, including me. I dove into the dirt underneath a tree. The shooting began immediately."

One hand gripped a metal bar astride his bed. The knuckles were white.

"From the ground I could barely see Yakov through the underbrush, still lying where he'd been beaten. My ears rang like hell and I couldn't hear anything, but his guard was injured and was reaching for his gun. I don't know if he meant to shoot at the fighters or Yakov, but I reacted."

His voice broke and he paused. His face was ashen.

"Then I was sick. The jets came back for a second pass. The screaming filled my head and I couldn't think. I thought my head was going to explode. Something slammed into me, huge and immensely strong, knocking me over. It hit me like a one ton truck. My leg snapped. When I looked up, I saw a buck running madly through the brush. At first I thought he was spooked by the jets. But then I saw his hindquarter was ripped open. He'd been hit. I saw shredded flesh through the wound. He was dying. Then the pain knocked me out."

Evan drained his second cup. Trakalo instantly refilled it.

"Sometime later I awoke. The fighters were gone. The buck was gone. My leg hurt so badly I could barely move. Through the branches, I saw Yakov staggering about the field. He looked unharmed. I called out to him, asking for help, and I thought he heard me, because he started toward me. I lost sight of him as he entered the bush. I waited for a few minutes, but he didn't appear. I pulled myself to my feet—the pain was awful—even with the rifle as a crutch."

"It was a stupid thing to do. I heard a gunshot and the tree behind me shattered. I spun on my good leg and returned fire. A man screamed. If I hit him, it was pure luck. But I couldn't move fast enough again and the next bullet hit my shoulder, sending me to the ground. Then everything went quiet. There was only the sound of water moving."

"A few minutes later Yakov worked his way up the ravine. He must have been hiding from the shooter. I could see right away that he wasn't himself."

"In what way?"

"He got close to me and then he backed off. His eyes were wild and he was apologizing. He said something strange..." Evan thought for a moment, "...he said, 'Sergei, you're bleeding. I can't help you now.' He was frustrated, yet he seemed to be grieving."

"Sergei?" Trakalo asked.

"I don't know who he meant," Evan answered. "My leg needed a tourniquet. A moment later, Yakov took a shirt off one of the dead men and just tossed it on the ground beside me. He refused to help tie it."

Evan closed his eyes, picturing the scene.

"He was really jumpy. Sudden sounds kept his neck swiveling. Even the water dripping from the trees made him edgy. At the time, I thought he was nuts."

"Could he have had a nervous breakdown?" Robb asked.

"I don't think so," Evan considered, "he knew we were being stalked. His instincts were crystal clear, but his behavior was inexplicable."

"Hah!" Robb snorted.

"You disagree?" Trakalo queried.

"No," Robb answered, "I thought the same thing. Yakov demanded that I supply first aid to Evan's injuries, but he stayed away. He acted like he was a poison."

"Exactly," Evan agreed.

"Did he say why, Evan?"

"No."

"Then he doesn't know," Robb concluded.

For the next hour, Evan recounted his involvement, but shed no further light on Yakov.

When Trakalo and Robb took their leave, they trod the short hallway in silence. At the entrance foyer, Robb halted.

"I forgot my bag."

"I'll wait, I need to talk to someone," Trakalo responded, seeking out the desk nurse.

Returning to Evan's room Robb knocked on the door.

"Who is it?" he heard.

"It's Robb, I forgot some stuff."

"Come on in," Evan invited. "Where's Trakalo?"

"Chatting up a nurse," Robb smiled.

The trapper was now sitting upright on his bed, reading and smiling, a cheerful demeanor on his face.

Robb stopped in his tracks, aghast.

"You might want this," Evan offered, closing the book and extending his good arm.

"What's in it?" Robb jumped across the room.

"A lot of symbols. I can't understand much of it."

Robb opened the book and flipped through several pages. It was filled with incomprehensible code—except for the chemistry.

"Why didn't you mention this when Trakalo was here?" Robb asked, still not believing his eyes.

"He's a good man," Evan replied, "but if he is accused of withholding evidence..."

"Better my neck than his?" Robb asked.

"Destroy it then."

"I can't."

"Don't ruin him."

*   *   *

"I need to draw a sample to send to an analytical lab," Robb stated.

"What are you looking for?" the cop questioned.

"A sub-monolayer assembly of REEs on SWNTs."

"In plain language, please."

"Single wall carbon nanotubes partially coated with minerals that match the elemental material in the ore body."

"Is that all?"

"No, it doesn't have to be nanotubes."

"That's not what I meant," Trakalo sighed.

Ignoring the rebuff, Robb continued, "It could be *graphene* sheets with functionalized edges, something that can be rolled, zipped or unzipped—in the right chemistry, of course. But I believe, whatever it is, it will be a lattice of thin carbon sheets decorated with Rare Earth compounds."

"For what?"

"There's a better question than that."

Trakalo sighed, "such as?"

"What would the right chemistry be?"

"Okay, what would the right chemistry be?"

"Try Ringer's solution. Your chemist will know what I mean."

"Yeah, but I won't."

"It's a mix of electrolytes that match the human bloodstream in ionic strength and *pH*. It's used for all sorts of things, such as rehydrating people or animals, or delivering drugs and blood serums, or simulating the human blood environment in a lab."

"Okay, damn it, do you ever speak normally?" Trakalo blustered.

"I've got all day to explain," Robb teased.

"I have a regular life to live," Trakalo retorted. And then, he surprised him. Picking up phone, the cop dialed the chemical forensic specialist. Creasing a finger across his lips, he indicated that Robb should remain quiet. Robb settled back in his chair, sensing the privilege to be privy to this conversation.

"Got a genetic soup for you to analyze," Trakalo smugly declared.

Robb's jaw dropped open. The cop knew a hell of lot more than he'd ever let on. The rest of the conversation blurred, the scientist barely able to contain his surprise. Impatiently, Robb waited until the phone call ended.

"How did you know?" Robb immediately asked, perplexed.

"It was obvious," Trakalo spoke abruptly, deflating the young scientist's ego yet further.

Bewildered, Robb slumped in his chair, dejection clouding his face. Trakalo smiled wryly.

"You're pulling my leg?" Robb began to catch on.

"Yeah, just a little. I've not had much fun lately, you know."

"You knew about the synthetic biology?"

"Not at all," he admitted, "but your reactions clued me in, along with a short conversation with Yakov this morning. He has a couple of puncture marks on his backside that look like injection bruises."

"Seriously?"

"Of course," Trakalo assured, "the technical stuff is not my field of expertise."

"I've not been on top of my game," Robb confessed.

"Don't apologize," Trakalo reassured, "at least you have game."

Two days later, sitting at his hotel room desk catching up on communications, Robb's phone rang, beckoning him to the RCMP barracks. His anticipation surged.

Entering the cop's office, he found Trakalo behind his desk, a cynical expression covered his tanned face.

"So what was Ottley doing here?" the cop opened.

"Trying to stay off the intelligence grid," Robb began.

"What do you mean?"

"His organization had several choices. For one, it could broker the minerals, forging alliances with the corporate world or military supply sectors, in exchange for political support and influence."

Trakalo raised his eyebrows.

"There is the complication that it's on foreign soil, but over time, that could have been worked out. Instead, I think they were pursuing an immediate alternative."

"Keeping an important find under wraps? Why?"

"The minerals are a springboard to a ledger of new technologies. With untraceable access and a head start, they could ready the next-generation applications. I doubt Ottley is really in charge. I imagine he is backed by those currently within the military-industrial complex. This is a methodical approach to fortify a position. It is about long term power."

"Explain further." Trakalo started taking notes.

"I believe Ottley is a field general, if you will, for this first phase. From his workplace, he can strategically access 'eyes on' intelligence as well as critical edge research. A dual skill set that keeps his activities compartmentalized. Less risk. He might need only a small and minimally-staffed lab to advance intriguing ideas."

"How could he have so much expertise at his disposal?" Trakalo countered.

"I'm overstating his technological capabilities," Robb backpedaled. "He or they have diversified several applications from a single biological concept. I don't think they're developing electronics, but they can tap into the core expertise as needed. Rather, I believe he excels in acquisition—that is, marshaling component contracts through private vendors. In the near term, his charter seems to be management and assembly to feed a greater political ambition."

"How have you learned this?" Trakalo voiced in reservation.

"It's taken time to filter through what I saw and heard in the office," Robb answered, somewhat sheepishly. "To find commonality, I followed the funding trail. Authors acknowledge their research sponsors."

Trakalo listened. Robb was introducing him to an overlooked investigative method.

"For starters, Ottley monitored a bevy of technical projects, most funded for nobler purposes. By trading grant money, they commission small, critical side projects and keep abreast of internally published classified papers."

"For their core competency, which is the replication technique, they followed blueprints, recipes used in making substances far less sinister in application. On the most dangerous applications, I believe they're acting alone. The related principle projects at university research labs are benign."

"Such as?" Trakalo queried brusquely, not meaning to scoff.

"Solving the world's energy demands, bettering global communications, understanding human genetics," Robb replied, unperturbed. In his short career, he'd already silenced many skeptics. Trakalo was an easy convert. "The genetic project in particular is well known and very well respected—trying to correct genetic disorders, not just isolating causal links to an appropriate DNA chain."

"That explains the high tech gadgetry," Trakalo agreed, "but not the dead man or what happened to Yakov."

"Actually, it does," Robb disagreed.

"How?"

"At first I thought that the Rare Earths were being used only in electronic devices, such as a flying *bug*. But the scale was all wrong, the limits of range and mass required that a payload had to be very small, effective, and difficult to analyze if it were intercepted or confiscated by the law. That's an extremely tall order, one that won't be met for some time."

"But it will be made some day?"

"Of course. Next, I considered the idea of synthesizing replacement proteins in the body, ones that could be used to create artificial diseases or control behavior, but that's a field fraught with road blocks, there's too little understood, and a successful result could be extraordinarily lethal, maybe even virulent. It made no sense. Instead, they are using a simpler and altogether more elegant approach."

"Which is?"

"They are *templating* DNA using the minerals."

"*Templating?*"

"Yes, creating a blue print, a stencil if you will, of its genetic program."

"Impossible."

"Why?"

"That would take forever. Even a supercomputer can't sequence an entire DNA strand for months—much less create one from scratch."

"That's the beauty of biology," Robb chuckled, "you can use living processes to circumvent electronic limitations."

"What does that mean?"

"Why re-invent what is already perfected? Why not find a way to duplicate the methodology?"

"Oh." Trakalo pondered. "So how are they copying DNA?"

"I believe they are encasing an unzipped DNA strand in a carbon nanotube and, for each component along the backbone, attaching selected Rare Earth ions to the inner tube wall."

Trakalo stared, fascinated.

"At the right conditions, each type of Rare Earth is attracted to a specific segment, one of the four groups in DNA, and locks its spatial location. Each chemical island now identifies an image of the adjacent strand."

Trakalo looked incredulous.

"After extracting the template, the backbone is inserted into a culture of human tissue, lab or live subject, and it goes to work, drawing building material from the host's cell to build a new DNA strand from the stencil. Within hours, the synthesized DNA migrates..."

"Migrates? How?"

"The cell divides. The new DNA is detected by the host cell, initiating reproductive cell division. The template remains in one new cell, doesn't matter which, and continues to replicate and divide. The other cell may not survive, having been robbed of considerable energy. Eventually, enough manufactured DNA is present to begin having effects."

"You don't even have to know what you are copying," Trakalo breathed.

"Not at all. Biological fabrication and replacement of DNA within a living body—not by lab synthesis, but by a person's own healing processes."

"How the hell would they know what to copy?" Trakalo wondered.

"I have some ideas, but more importantly, I'm pretty sure they aren't achieving their goal yet."

"Meaning?"

"Right now, I'm guessing they've mastered *templating* only fragment segments of DNA—instructions creating poisons and maybe longer, virus-like chains. The point is, I think the templates are not cellular, rather they're floating around in Yakov's bloodstream. His symptoms are similar, but slower acting than Shaparell's, who I think was poisoned by a self-made neurotoxin."

"How?"

"During his capture in Mexico, Shaparell was administered drugs, cocktails of chemicals, maybe as a smokescreen to hide something else. I asked Ottley if Shaparell had been x-rayed and he threw me under a bus for being naive. But he didn't answer the question, an omission I found disturbing. I continued to follow up on the idea of an embedded device until the logistics proved insurmountable."

"For example, each time Shaparell flew, an airport scanner would have imaged a metallic object. And, as his body healed from his assault, he should have been able to feel the presence of a foreign object underneath his skin."

"But, not so with carbon-based materials, which are flexible and transparent to full body x-rays. Implant a bunch of nanotubes, each a microscopic reservoir, each impregnated with a soup of poison-fabricating DNA, and you have injected a time-delayed killer."

"Not an IR-controlled electronic device?"

"Not yet, I don't think the technology is ready."

"Then why didn't Shaparell die right away."

"Action was purposefully delayed. In case Shaparell escaped or was rescued, the grunt work would still be done. The perpetrators would never have to make contact again. I think a flying device was used to activate the templates. TV footage shows he slapped at something on his neck, something I could never make out, even in high definition. That close to his brain, it wouldn't take much poison to be effective. And, once triggered, his own body killed him."

"Where did you learn this?"

"Yakov clued me in." He held up a dog-eared and stained leatherbound journal.

"Where did that come from?" Trakalo demanded.

"Evan."

"You held out on me?"

"I didn't want you guilty of treason."

"Bullshit."

"Remember when I forgot my bag in Evan's room? When I went back to get it, he gave this journal to me and told me to destroy it."

"How did Evan..."

"Evan didn't. Yakov found the journal after his captors were killed. He thought it might explain what is happening to him. I take it he understood that the Air Force would make it disappear. He didn't tell Evan much, but he managed to put it in a place the troopers didn't check."

"Which was?"

"Underneath the trapper's splint."

"No shit," Trakalo chuckled, evidently amused. "Now that I know about it, I suppose I'll have to turn it over soon." Pointing at the journal, he returned to business. "What else is in there? Does it say more?"

"Much, much more. Based on this diary, they were hoping to develop full blown field combat uses. The ultimate application of the replication technique is far scarier, although, at present, it still seems somewhat farcical."

Trakalo caught on fast. "Replicating another person's DNA?"

"Exactly."

"How will they know what to start with?"

"It would be semi-empirical, a guess: It's been long wondered if deviations in human behavior might have chemical or biological connections—tendencies that might be present at birth or develop over years of time. People who take antidepressants seem to develop a resistance to avoiding depression, even if the medication is changed. More debatable, if a killer is angry, does his anger further alter his chemistry, making him more likely to kill again? Some think so."

"More than a mental illness?"

"Sure, why not. Stress from worry and fear contribute to hypertension or diabetes, either condition is a physically degenerative sum of systemic chemical changes associated with environment, psychological or genetic stimuli. Sure, no one knows the pathway, but the cause and effect is statistically clear."

"It's a big leap to go from diabetes to something murderous."

"Yeah, it is. Even so, neurologists continue to find links between one's consciousness and one's brain chemistry. Some of the correlations known now were, only a generation past, laughed at as pure poppycock."

"So pathological killers are made, not born."

"Or they make themselves, through their life's experiences and the way they respond to them. The idea will stay pretty controversial, though, since nobody can isolate and study the pathological subject in the making. But, hindsight is 20-20, right?"

"I still don't believe it. Are you saying...?"

"By extracting DNA from mature people who possessed the attributes they wanted, they could harvest seed material and culture it in a foreign body."

"You're kidding."

"Not at all. Inject a living human with a well-fashioned template, and within minutes, the body begins replicating it. In short order, his own genetic make-up begins to tilt, presumably followed by changing attitudes and behavior. It might not take much to unbalance the scales."

"Nurturing nature?"

"Yeah."

"Can you prove it?"

"In what way?"

"Fix Yakov."

Chapter 24

Litmus Test

Poring through the smuggled journal, Robb struggled to unlock its secrets. It was a daunting effort, deciphering an unfamiliar coded science, while lacking the key. Achieving limited success, he pleaded with Trakalo to enlist an expert.

Since his meltdown Yakov had withered, devoid of his characteristic robustness. Constantly infecting, the neurotoxin degenerated his psyche, sentencing him to life in a maleficent wasteland.

Following up on Robb's needs, Trakalo requested conversations with leading in-house bio-chemical field agents. It was a hard sell, convincing bureaucrats that his international fugitives were anything but liabilities, but with the promise of the mineral lode, he prevailed. After a short delay, the phone began ringing with calls from federal scientists whose specialties were in the inorganic chemistry or bio-chemical arenas. Professionals of a similar ilk, Robb easily connected and downloaded His suspicions generated interest, and soon he was faxing journal sheets and participating in a conference call that spanned all three coasts.

Page-wise, the team unlocked the hieroglyphic text, at least in principle. Even with expert eyes, some of its acronyms would not yield to absolute identification. Even so, a general understanding emerged, complicit with Robb's suspicion that Yakov was infected with an *in situ*, self-manufacturing neurotoxin. This consensus simplified the approach at remediation.

By late afternoon, the lead scientist committed to delivering a best-guess antidote within twenty-four hours, the soonest he could arrange transportation. Based on the chemistry of the substances and Yakov's reactions to stress, he was recommending a three-step purging: unlock, bind and remove. He described a concoction of lab chemicals that would unzip the nanotubes, detach the rare earths, and secure them in a nonreactive molecular wrapping.

"*Chelation*," he asserted, "is nature's elegant solution to transporting heavy metals within the bloodstream."

The chemical treatment would be followed by a thorough blood transfusion to remove the admittedly caustic elixir.

It seemed risky, but Robb was unable to convincingly argue any alternatives, the basic science not his forte. Instead, tasked with the duties of informing Yakov and obtaining his consent, he arranged to meet the geologist the following day, only after sleeping on the idea. Before returning to his hotel room, he stopped by Trakalo's office.

"Sir, I'm leaving for the day, is there anything else I can do?"

"No, it's finally under control," Trakalo smiled, but worry lines creasing his brow indicated a different brew.

"Are there any further...developments?"

"Regarding your status as a *man on the run?*" Trakalo surmised.

"Yes."

"HQ is convinced it will wash out in the next twenty-four to forty-eight hours. A senior diplomat flew to Washington today to present your case. The possibility of a mineral source will go a long way to argue for a positive, judicious result."

"I'd hate not to have a bargaining chip," Robb remarked, with a tinge of sarcasm.

"Indeed."

"How about yourself? How are you holding out?"

"I'll be transferred soon, I imagine," Trakalo confessed. "Insubordination, no matter how righteous, does not endear allies."

"So true," Robb rued. "I'm sorry. I feel somewhat to blame."

"Not at all, we have had a northern frontier problem for some time, and it took my barnstorming to alert a few bureaucrats that it has moved south," Trakalo soothed. "Unfortunately, I embarrassed at least one cabinet member and he won't get over it soon." He sighed, "It's time to move closer to the urban part of this country again, but it'll never the replace the excitement of working out here. On the other hand, never will I regret escaping the remoteness of this outpost."

The next morning Robb returned to the RCMP barracks, eager to join forces with a new colleague, still uncertain how to broach the subject with Yakov. Granted a spare cubicle and an internet connection, he puzzled through the proposed remedy for Yakov, trying to sort out his misgivings. He couldn't sell a salvation he couldn't understand. His greatest concern was that they couldn't possibly know the dosage of trace materials that the Russian's bloodstream held. The possibility of unleashing a lethal dosage was an issue he could not assure against, with any conviction, if Yakov asked him.

A preoccupied Trakalo kept busy at his desk, occasionally relaying the progress of the traveling scientist. As the morning progressed, the federal employee departed from Ottawa, passed through Toronto, and headed toward Winnipeg, by way of Thunder Bay. From the Manitoba capital, he would take a charter.

At 11 AM, Trakalo announced a mid-day arrival, hours earlier than expected. A national security committee in Ottawa had delegated a military jet from Thunder Bay.

"Let's go grab lunch now," the cop suggested, "we have a lot of preparations to make."

Half an hour later they dined, ironically at the same restaurant they had patronized weeks earlier on Robb's first visit. It was surreal. Nothing had changed at the humble diner. Needing to stay alert, Robb ordered a tomato and cheese sandwich on toasted rye, no mayo, and a bowl of borscht with honey.

"Watching your waistline?" Trakalo teased while selecting similarly health conscious nutriment. Robb grimaced in acquiescence. After the food arrived, they ate slowly, mostly in silence, thoughtful of their impending duties and life-altering changes.

Swallowing a tall glass of sun-steeped ice tea, Robb rinsed the remnants of his light meal. The sandwich had been well chosen, but the borscht was not, a bitter concoction his palette could not embrace.

Trakalo's cell phone rang, and Robb chuckled as he promptly answered it The Mountie was tethered to technology after all. He barely noticed as the cop's face clouded, but caught the crisp dismissal as the call was disconnected.

"What's up?" Robb queried.

"The plane went down."

"The jet carrying the scientist?"

"Yes...missing, presumed dead," he answered to Robb's disbelieving eyes.

"How?"

There was no answer.

"How?" Robb asked again, his chest tightening.

Trakalo's eyes drilled across the table, "it wasn't an accident."

How much of my own plan do I really trust? Robb questioned. En route from the hospital, Yakov, Trakalo and he were returning to the RCMP barracks. With no time for further debate, he alone was on the hook.

Yakov's immediate health was in his hands.

The hospital's resident MD, a youngish man scarcely beyond residency, was overwhelmed by the audacity of his suggested treatment plan. Through a thick Indian accent, the doctor agreed to supply basic medical equipment, but prudently abstained from assisting. By virtue of the partial victory, they had acquired an IV drip, filtration equipment, liters of blood serum and a blood electrolyte solution of Ringers.

Yakov concurred with Robb's most basic apprehension: Unzipping the nanotubes *in situ*, and liberating an unknown quantity of poison metal in his body, might be lethal. Instead, they decided, Robb would remove small volumes of blood, perform some magic in a hastily assembled chemical reactor, then return the effluent. Robb was still troubled. He had ideas, not magic. Neither did he possess the equipment to test the results. He would be working blind.

Skirting the issue, Trakalo and Robb instead discussed moving Yakov to a major urban hospital, but it wasn't an option, both aware that transportation by plane, even military, was now suspiciously dangerous. Adding to their urgency was the correlation that the man from the train had expired within days of his apparent seizure.

How he met his death was uncertain, but they couldn't rule out a similar cause.

From there, the tale grew even more bizarre. Several days after Robb had observed the consumed carcass, it was reported that a male polar bear had gone berserk. At first, neurotically attacking phantoms in garbage dumpsters, it then moved aggressively through the shipyards, bullying dockside cranes and sending dockyard workers scrambling for protection. After slaying his imagination, the bear had calmed, meandering to an elementary school yard where he tore up the grass foraging for small rodents. By the time he began ripping through backpacks, the authorities were ready.

Concerned for the children's safety, the bear was tranquilized and crated. During relocation, it died, apparently from cardiac arrest. With Trakalo out of town, no autopsy was ordered and the carcass was burned in an open pit.

Anecdotally, some onlookers reported seeing unusual bursts of color, green, pink and purple, flashing in the flames.

Even if the bear story was embellished, it provided Robb ammunition for thought.

Although the town appeared unchanged, Trakalo assured him that the military was present, subtly fortifying positions within the village and along the coast. A small squadron and an aircraft carrier were ready offshore. All tourist traffic from any port of call was monitored and no one would be allowed in without close scrutiny.

On the water, however, their presence could not be missed. The propagated guise was that assistance was needed to aid a coast guard search and rescue effort for a billionaire activist, ostensibly mapping the early summer Arctic ice range, who'd ignorantly ventured into a drifting, late season ice floe. He'd transmitted a distress signal before losing radio contact. A piteous fool.

It was a trite ruse, well trodden and sufficiently effective. While the military attempted to appear in foxholes, Robb took up his own arms; chemical buffers, blood serum, charcoal and filters. Trakalo secured supplies from the high school, basic scientific instruments including a pH meter, conductivity meter, peristaltic pump and *Tygon* tubing.

There wasn't enough blood plasma to perform a complete transfusion, the quantity was sufficient only for Robb to test his best guess without bleeding Yakov to death. In that vein, periodic bloodletting, drawing and discarding a couple of liters at a time, might have worked. If the nanotubes weren't migrating out of his bloodstream, why not force his body to produce new serum, thereby diluting the remaining concentration and weakening its impact.

Arguing against the simple approach was Yakov's health. The math and Yakov's health predicted there wasn't enough time to make it work. The geologist would be fortunate to survive a few bloodletting cycles. The templates had to be tackled in a single operation.

"Do you wish some sedation, Yakov?" Trakalo asked.

Before the geologist could answer, Robb interjected, "it cannot be risked." They both looked at him with concern.

"Look," Robb explained, "I don't know all the triggers, but when I upset Yakov, the effects were immediate. It reminded me of the man on the train, and how in an instant, he nearly passed out. The reaction could be set off by stress, heat or hormones, I just don't know. Since DNA is organic, I'm guessing a hormonal influence is partly to blame. Since sedatives are organic, taking a tranquilizer might bring on an episode."

He turned to Yakov, "I'm sorry."

"I do not wish to be sedated," Yakov agreed. Trakalo nodded.

"Then let's get going," Robb gritted.

Setting the blood siphon, Trakalo drew the first liter while Robb tested his assembly. He was overcome with questions. How could he be sure this amateurish reactor was being effective? Could he trust his training and his instincts? How could he quantify improvement?

Without access to high tech equipment, a chromatography column or a mass spectrometer, he was just guessing.

And a man's life hung in the balance. Could he stomach a failure?

Chromatography! Impulsively, he breathed heavily.

"What is it?" Trakalo asked, worriedly, plugging the siphon's end.

"I need a pin and a lighter," Robb requested.

"In some parts of my district, that's the start of illegal activity," Trakalo chuckled. But Robb's face was blank, not understanding the reference.

Trakalo sighed, "it's not worth describing. I'll get you what you need."

"Thanks, and some hydrogen peroxide, too."

Minutes later Trakalo returned. The apparatus was working. Using the peristaltic pump, Robb was sending the drawn unit of blood through filter paper, separating the plasma from the cells into an Erlenmeyer flask. Taking a pin from Trakalo, he dipped it into the flask and inserted the wetted metal into a lighter's flame.

Instantly, the yellow eye flickered with bursts of firework color.

"Just as I hoped," Robb muttered.

Sterilizing the same pin with peroxide, he scooped a fraction of the filter's crimson jelly on its tip. Repeating the test, the flame smoldered, first drying the damp biomass before it burned, but it did not flash with a rainbow of luminescence. A peculiar odor of grilled steak wafted through the air.

"Yes!" Robb triumphed, "it's only in the plasma."

Trakalo's eyebrows raised.

"Heavy metals, like the Rare Earth's, give off characteristic flashes of color when stimulated," Robb explained. "It's a poor man's test at metal detection. The human eye is very sensitive."

Trakalo shrugged, but his confidence in the scientist was soaring.

"Now the tough part," Robb muttered, "coaxing the metals from the nanotubes."

While Robb separated the sieve's effluents into a row of small beakers, Trakalo drew a second liter. Purging the filter with Ringer's, Robb injected the backwashed slurry into Yakov's bloodstream. Repeating the process, he withdrew a third and fourth liter, filtering, recovering the cells and replenishing with Ringers. After several cycles, spent of manufactured fluid, Trakalo sat back, awaiting the scientist's efforts.

The onus was on Robb, but his test array was ready. He tried multiple approaches. Raising the pH of one, he reduced another. A third he passed over charcoal, and the last several he inoculated with medicine cabinet extracts, powdered DHEA, hydrogen peroxide, and a combination of pH buffers with a hormone. The remainder of the plasma was sieved continuously through a micron filter.

Subjecting each aliquot to his flame test, the results were refreshing. The weakest flame signals appeared in filtered samples. The more the liquid cycled through a filter, the fewer flashes appeared. Simple mechanical filtration alone was effective at ridding the nanotubes. Relieved, he discarded the chemical techniques, and his uncertainties of their risks.

For the next several hours, they repeatedly extracted and cleansed Yakov's blood until Robb declared that less than one part in 100,000 remained.

The Russian tolerated his phlebotomies, occasionally squirming in discomfort as the needle's bore seemed to enlarge with every operation. Yet, each transfusion was transforming, returning the physical vitality he'd been losing. Yakov's eyes blazed, thankful for his new life. His mental health was at the doorstep.

Chapter 25

Detainment

The four men sat around a small, collapsible card table that Trakalo had smuggled into the hospital. Evan occupied his bed while Robb perched cautiously on the steel barrels of an unused radiator and Yakov and Trakalo were in comfort on metal folding chairs.

Trakalo dealt the cards skillfully from beneath his massive hands, seamlessly varying the order of delivery with the practiced hand of a seasoned card dealer.

Evan and Robb smarted, having been skunked in the last match. They constructively dealt with the angst, drowning their bitterness with a full measure of rye. Even Evan did not deny the whiskey. For two days, he had refused the pain killers. This was a small step on the way to recovery.

"You're a helluva card player, Yakov," Trakalo bolstered his partner.

"I've had my share of practice," Yakov admitted, a viscosity in his voice conveying a reluctance to say more.

Trakalo changed the subject, turning to Robb and addressing his struggling opponent.

"Stop studying and play," he needled.

"You're just jealous that I'm a celebrity," Robb returned, leading with a queen to start the cribbage game.

The curing of Yakov had been sensational.

Following a few tentative hours as his body first metabolized the residual neurotoxin, he fairly flew through a rapid process of improvement. Overnight, his tremors had ceased. By the following afternoon, he was steady enough to venture outdoors for a long walk along the bay's shore.

But not everyone was impressed. There was an understandable skepticism expressed from the *round-table* experts. To expunge the doubt, Trakalo air-freighted a blood plasma sample to the RCMP forensics lab, where an electron microscopist quickly confirmed Robb's hypothesis.

Not surprisingly, the results were immediately filed under...*Classified*.

Robb cared little about the technology's dispositioning. Now both he and Yakov had high-value bargaining chips.

Trakalo relayed that Yakov's future was a topic of discussion at the senior cabinet level in Ottawa. It was rumored that he would quietly be offered a government post to continue mineral exploration. For the time being, he was too valuable to incarcerate or deport.

Trakalo was accepting a transfer. For the next year he would split his duties between Ottawa and Regina, first leading a task force to develop strategies for policing the mineral-rich north and then teaching new recruits at the RCMP Academy. It was a promotion of sorts, albeit fraught with the risk of having to tender and defend one's opinion amongst others accustomed to swimming with political sharks.

"I think HQ wants to keep me in sight," the cop worried, "they're afraid I've become too much of a cowboy out here." He thought further, "I suppose I have—by necessity, of course."

Earlier in the evening, Trakalo handed Evan a sealed envelope. In addition to a pardon signed by the Governor General was a scholarship to the RCMP academy.

"What is this?" Evan asked, a chagrin prompted by memory of the last packet of papers the Mountie had delivered.

"Your new career if you want it," Trakalo grinned.

Evan's eyes opened wide, and then clouded over.

Reading his mind, Trakalo pitched, "I should expect you will have your choice of posts. Who else wants to live up here all year?"

And Robb had the green light to cross the border. But his future seemed less certain. He still had to earn back Paulina's trust. As the drink calmed his anxieties and the unfamiliar protocol of a new card game consumed his intellect, he forgot his burgeoning worries.

Evan and Robb lost the second game, but the margin narrowed.

By game three, they were threatening and on the fourth game, Yakov was finding ways to communicate his cards to Trakalo, just to keep an edge. The geologist was smiling.

They played through midnight and adjourned only after the night nurse threatened to call the RCMP barracks.

The resident Sergeant was being promoted, too.

As Robb walked to the hotel, a nagging thought frayed the corners of his mind. In a few hours he would depart, taking the train to Winnipeg. Although he was free to travel across the border, it had taken a little longer to arrange than Trakalo had predicted.

Why?

*   *   *

"Step inside, please, sir," the customs officer commanded, his politeness a facade of pleasantness.

"May I ask why?" Robb asked, matching the agent's gambit by conjuring an innocuous demeanor himself.

"Park your car to the right. Don't lock it. Report to the officer inside the building behind the counter."

"Where?" he questioned, continuing the innocent and confused pretense.

"Sir, park your car in the first space on the right," the agent enunciated crisply. "Immediately in front of the stall, you'll see a pair of doors. Proceed through them to the counter inside."

Registering the official's agitation, Robb decided to surrender before he tripped the hair trigger agent.

He drove forward and parked in a wide, white-framed space, pointedly locking three of the doors and leaving the driver's side unsecured. In the adjacent stall, officials were methodically removing and searching luggage from an ancient Volkswagen bus.

Masking his unhappiness, he entered the depot, joining a queue of similarly unfortunate trans-nationals who shuffled between movable stanchions and cloth tape barriers with varying degrees of reluctance. Complicit with Robb, they exuded an aura of frustration and impatience. Nobody talked, except over wireless devices, and even then, conversations were muffled or subdued. Amongst them was an attitude of deference and suspicion.

Everybody else was a threat to a timely departure.

At the front of the line, separating the citizens from the government officials, was an austere counter coated in a bone white enamel. Behind it, smartly dressed, uniformed officials unhurriedly interviewed each detainee. The agents' mannerisms were brusque and unsympathetic. Above the counter top, a bulletproof polycarbonate window poised beneath an acoustic drop ceiling. Set on wide metal tracks, it was readied to plunge downward at a finger's touch.

Robb wondered if the transparent shield had ever been deployed or tested. Sophisticated barriers need to be serviced at regular intervals to operate reliably.

An hour later, an animated French man in a tight business suit standing immediately in front of him was unsuccessfully pleading a tragic case to a young square-jawed agent wearing a tight crewcut. The officer, probably on his first assignment out of language school, was struggling to fulfill a dual role of customs agent and translator. At the gracious best, his command of French was rudimentary. Unsurprisingly, his lack of linguistic acumen was a major hindrance, and he was unable to placate the anxious traveler, although the greenhorn was taking pains to make up for his shortcoming by being conscientious and attentive.

It wasn't working, the cultural barrier was insurmountable. After an intense, but polite argument, the Quebecois surrendered his cherished purchase, a bottle of Cask No. 16 rye whiskey, mistakenly tagged tax-free by a nearby duty-free shop, for a significantly inflated re-pricing.

As the irritated man settled his tax bill, Robb awaited his own tempest of turmoil. Before he left Churchill, Trakalo had confirmed that he was exonerated, and that the *Internationally Wanted* order was rescinded. This delay suggested otherwise, that he was ballistic toward a cross-woven tangle of legal proceedings.

Perhaps they didn't get the memo here, he seethed, worrying that denial of access was preceding indefinite incarceration.

"Next," he heard. And Robb stepped forward.

"Your passport, please."

Dutifully, he proffered the precious document to the customs agent.

"Bit of a mess," the officer chided, noting its haggard condition.

"I've sent it through a washer a couple of times by mistake," he apologized.

"I see."

Robb held his tongue. The less he said the better.

"Just a moment," the agent declared, smartly spinning on her heel.

My passport! Robb nearly exclaimed, as the agent briskly strode away. He was powerless to pursue.

Twenty tedious minutes elapsed before she returned. Behind him, the queue was bustling impatiently. Now, served by only one agent, its numbers were building and its tolerance decreasing.

"It will take a bit more time," the agent mouthed to Robb's sinking heart. Her voice was distant, spoken from a vacuum, devoid of apology or concern. Pointedly, she did not return his passport.

"What is the delay?" Robb asserted a feeble stab at control.

"You can wait more comfortably over there," the agent replied, pointing to a row of plastic chairs aligned against a wall, indicating where he was expected to wait.

"May I have my passport?" Robb requested politely.

"Please take a seat, sir," the agent leveled. Then she walked away from the counter toward a side office, keeping a watchful glance behind her until she disappeared through the open door.

Shit!

Robb slunk past the grumbling array to the *comfortable* seating and collected his thoughts.

He had not been refused entrance, nor was he been locked down. His immigration status was an enigma, both to himself, and perhaps to the border agent, who seemed to have carefully distanced herself from him. Surely she now knew who he was, having run his passport through the database, but she didn't seem certain about what to do with him, except not to let him pass through.

He was a dangerous curiosity, a man once accused can never be completely exonerated, even with truth.

Three hours later, Robb still waited, mired in the increasingly uncomfortable plastic seat. Irritated and restless, he was *free* to move, in a limited sense, about the public portion of the building. Most of the time, his movements were confined to an ill-at-ease shifting on the molded chair.

His passport had not materialized, although the agent had long ago returned to her counter station. She completely ignored him, refusing to make eye contact.

Oddly, she seemed out of place. When she had questions or requested assistance, she had a particularly difficult time getting anyone to help her. It wasn't a matter of administrative workload preventing her from being helped by her colleagues, she seemed to be genuinely disliked and disrespected. Caught in the crossfire of her office politics, Robb understood that he wasn't going anywhere soon.

He located a restroom and a courtesy room outfitted with a pot of ancient coffee, *sans* creamer. Frequent partaking of the horrid beverage kept him on a constant journey between all three rooms. It was better than sitting still.

Loitering in the courtesy room was no small frustration. For one, he barely tolerated the repetitive, annoying broadcast TV tuned to a channel that *objectively* covered only the most sensationalized news from the government, the markets and occasionally the globe.

The first viewing of a rapid-fire newscast was entertaining, the second, illuminating, but the third and fourth repetitions degenerated to a clamor less compelling.

The scales were falling from his eyes.

Tabloid TV for the politically addicted, he surmised. With each airing, and more so during periods of soundless watching, his comprehension of the spoon-fed tidbits increasingly refluxed to an inescapable conclusion.

It was not news, rather it was unconscionable theater, unadulterated propaganda for an economic entity with a political agenda.

Distilling themes he perceived a clear message, cleverly supported by pathos, images, hand-picked *expert* interviews, and, most unprofessionally, journalists' opinions that were little more than volatile diatribes.

The most amazing revelation was that during his first viewing, the message had emotionally resonated. Had he not been subjected to a half dozen replays, he might not have severed his affectations, and might have remained in tacit agreement.

Now, he found the message intellectually insulting.

Yet it was no wonder the broadcast was so popular, he realized. In a fast-paced, overpriced society, with most people struggling to make ends meet, few have the luxury of free time for critical thinking. It was sobering.

He felt ill, a synergism of brainwashing drivel and excessive coffee.

He could deal with his churning stomach by sipping several cupfuls of water, but no matter how well he tuned out the broadcast, his disgust would not neutralize.

"The solution to pollution is dilution...for both my gut and my mind," he chuckled, looking for reading material. Ever true in cliché, the *end results* kept him moving.

His frequent excursions to the amenities were noticed, monitored behind suspicious glances or blatant frowns each time he walked the corridors. The watching eyes seemed to convey more than mere disapproval. Were they setting him up by caging him, daring him to bolt, thus exposing a fettered conscience?

Robb knew better. Running to freedom was as much a myth as a growing obsession. It was the one impulse he was precisely focused on resisting. Instead, he stayed put and seethed, rooting his body onto the petrochemical seat top.

It wasn't easy.

Frustration has a way of riveting one's attention on details. Details such as his inability to go home or return to his car or even make a simple phone call without feeling like he was under observation. The harder he tried, the worse he felt.

As the hours consumed the afternoon, he grew hungry, needing food to quell his angry alimentary still smarting from the caffeine assault, but there was nothing of substance to eat in his shoebox of bureaucracy.

Neither could Robb sit still for long. For a scientist, a lack of knowledge is most unnerving.

Each attempt to elicit an explanation for his delay was met with a firm, well-practiced, rebuff. Whatever the border officials were waiting for or researching was remaining a mystery. He became convinced that nobody was extending any realistic effort into releasing him. In fact, it was transparent from their bland responses that he was not allowed to leave the building until something significant transpired. And, in spite of several polite inquiries, he still didn't possess his passport.

Robb found their callous demeanor infuriating, if not downright spiteful. Especially after being falsely accused of engaging in treasonous activity.

The only explanation he'd gleaned, which he did not believe, was that a nearby air force base had been overrun by hooligans. Their passports were, coincidentally, issued from the same agency as his. And with an investigation proceeding regarding the drunken invasion, the regular channels of communication were occupied, having been diverted to the more urgent need.

His short stint in government employ cast light on their behavior. Their reluctance to expedite his processing was borne of political fear, wary of ruffling the feathers of someone more important or better connected. In effect, their hands off attitudes were speaking volumes, answering his queries. Either their excuses were a smokescreen, or they had a need to be rigidly adhering to protocol.

He certainly wasn't the unlucky tourist, a randomly selected individual eliciting additional scrutiny. But, no matter the cause, he wasn't getting through easily, and he sure as hell didn't like serving as the poster child for a day's training activities. He stayed put.

The sun perched at early evening above the horizon.

"Robb?" a female voice called sharply.

Finally!

"Would you please step over here?" she demanded.

The waiting room was empty, as it had been for the better part of an hour. Those needing to cross the border early to reach a myriad of destinations had already blitzed through and were well on their way to homes or hotels or the next major town several hundred miles down road.

A dozen long haulers stretched into a train. It was the drivers' supper hour and few were inclined to leave their vehicles and loiter within a government facility, preferring instead to pass their mandatory break time within the comforts of growling cabs pragmatically equipped with the latest in mobile digital entertainment. Those that were working were efficient, presenting orderly carnets that elicited mere cursory glances verifying their cargo before being summarily waved through.

Robb envied their smooth passage and sighed. Having been delayed until shift change, she was probably handing him over to a different customs agent. As a teaser, she held a green manila file folder with his passport clipped on top.

Robb assented to her order, precariously lured by the siren of an escape ticket. Tremulously aware he was heading into danger, he crossed that invisible landing separating unstable sand from quagmire. In short order, it would entrap, engulf and entomb his future. Recklessly, he consoled himself, agreeing that his escape was forthcoming from spending hordes of money he might eventually earn.

She led him to a small, unoccupied room, sparsely furnished with a single, small metal desk and two folding chairs. The gray metal chairs were placed for an interview, set on opposite sides of a flat, barren desktop.

Pausing beside the desk, she methodically rifled through the clipboard layers, tarrying until he crossed the threshold. With a quick snapping motion of an open hand, she beckoned him to occupy the seat in front of the desk.

As he complied, she busied past.

"Just a minute," she sang, and pranced out the door, closing it firmly behind.

The passport left with her.

This is it, Robb ceded. He was caged, unable to wander without breaking the implied contract he'd involuntarily signed. Immediately, he began wondering how long it would be and how much effort it would take until he regained his liberty. And, once he did walk freely, with how much stain would he be permanently tainted?

How negatively would these accusations of treason tarnish his reputation, affect his graduation and future job prospects or hinder his ability to earn a living throughout his life?

The desire to flee grew exponentially, wickedly tempted by Trakalo's offer for a safe haven. Robb sat only for a moment. Fed up with the hours of immobility and uncomfortably hard seat tops, which had seemed more like cowering than waiting, he alighted and began pacing—treading a small circle in the tiny room. Pouring out his nervous energy, he debated his next moves.

Even out of sight, he was sure his every movement was being observed, analyzed and interpreted in the least favorable light.

The hell with them! He vowed, defiantly asserting himself, forging a small measure of peace with his fears.

The doorknob clicked, interrupting his silent disobedience. Hustling into the seat, he grimaced in disgust, less a defiant patriot than the fugitive cur he actually was.

A senior agent entered, tucking a clipboard in the crook of his elbow.

"Good evening, Mr. Davis."

He placed the clipboard on the desk and pushed it towards Robb. His passport was on top.

"I see you've been with us a few hours," he began.

"Yes, I have."

"Well then," the agent smiled ambiguously, "let's get to business. How long were you out of the country?"

"Nearly a month."

"Where did you visit?"

"I was in Churchill, Manitoba."

"The whole time?"

"Mostly."

"Where else did you go?"

"I drove a few hours east of town to see a mineral quarry."

"Where exactly?"

"I'm not sure. There weren't any towns."

The agent made a note. "Do you have friends or family there?"

"No." Robb was puzzled. The questions were routine.

"What were you doing there?"

Robb paused momentarily. There was no lie he could easily construe nor was there truth he wished to convey.

"What were you doing there?" The agent repeated with emphasis.

Robb felt his exasperation cresting. By this late hour, there wasn't anything about him that the customs agents didn't know. This was a ridiculous line of questioning.

"Where are you going with this?" he snapped.

"Just answer the question, Robb."

"I'm sure you know exactly why I was in Churchill," he pushed back.

"Yes, I do," the official said, a trifle menacingly.

"Then what else do you wish to know?" Robb glowered across the table.

"You have a questionable history," the agent threatened. "Your file is quite thick."

"Do I?" Robb argued.

"You've been in the wrong places at the opportune time. I don't believe in happenstance"

"Then why am I sitting here?"

"Yes," the agent smiled. Robb had called his bluff. He gestured at the passport.

"Take it."

"I'm being allowed through," Robb buffaloed.

"Of course."

The agent smiled mirthlessly and leaned back on his chair, one hand pushing the clipboard toward Robb, the other clasped behind his neck.

Robb's face flushed with a mixture of relief and anger. It was too surreal. Reaching forward, he lifted his passport from the clipboard and stopped in horror.

The blood drained from his face. On the paper beneath was a hand-written scrawl.

God does not roll dice.

"What the hell?" The agent swore. The annotation was a surprise to him, too.

Immediately, the border official sprung into action, lunging across the desk and grabbing Robb's elbow. From behind his neck, he raised a filled hypodermic.

A bead of liquid glistened at its tip.

Robb twisted in vain, unable to extricate his arm. The needle flashed downward through the air.

Impulsively, Robb jerked his arm backward, disrupting the heavier man's balance and pulling him over the table. The lethal projectile missed its mark, driving into the flat surface and bending. A clear fluid dribbled from the tip.

"You son-of-a-bitch!" Robb hissed, but the throttling pain in his still-gripped arm arrested a follow-up epithet.

The agent recovered quickly, twisting Robb's elbow hard and spinning him in place, efficiently lifting him out of his chair with one hand efficiently pressed against middle of his back. Shocks of pain seared through the scientist as sinews stretched tightly in his shoulder, debilitating his efforts to wrest free.

The agent pressed the plunger. Although the needle was bent askew, the syringe still worked. He shoved Robb toward the wall, trying to wedge him into place.

A commotion erupted outside the door.

"Get back!" He heard a man yelling.

"It's not him!" A woman shrieked, a familiar voice from his distant past.

"Get down!" the man commanded.

Robb dropped toward the floor, grunting out a guttural wail as his shoulder dislocated.

The door burst open. Through pain-streaked eyes, Robb saw a woman—the first agent who he'd spoken with earlier in the afternoon—burst through the portal.

"Drop it—and him!" she ordered.

"What are you gonna do about it?" He sneered.

"There is no escape. You're through. Ottley is finished."

"You've gone soft," he mocked.

"You'll hang for your treason."

"We'll see about that," the man replied calmly, releasing his grip on Robb and placing the syringe on the table. "You know I'll invoke the secrecy acts."

Robb passed out.

An hour later, Robb came to, lying shirtless on a gurney in a first-aid room. A medic hovered above his chest, searching every square inch of his skin. Axles squeaked as a portable x-ray cart was wheeled out of the cramped confines.

"There's no puncture," the medic announced, gently placing Robb's damaged arm over his breast and securing it in a sling.

Robb winced.

"Thank you," the female customs agent answered.

The medic hurriedly left the room. She glanced at Robb with a tight-lipped smile.

"Does it hurt much?"

"Like hell," he replied, gingerly donning his shirt.

"I'll get you some painkillers and an anti-inflammatory in a few minutes."

"Thank you."

"Sorry I took so long."

"No, thank you for the warning."

"We were both deployed here barely a month ago," she rambled nervously. "Ottley suspected you would come through this border post again."

"Did you send me the first message?"

Her eyes darkened.

"And the photograph?"

She said nothing, but her eyes blinked furiously.

Robb waited.

Finally, she spoke. "I started working here exactly four weeks ago."

Robb did the math. *The same day I was fired.*

"Good," he smiled, "there's more of you."

She busied herself to leave.

Robb had a sudden thought.

"What was in the syringe?"

"You were in no danger," she replied.

"How do I know?"

"It would be unethical."

"Of course it would be," Robb challenged.

From beneath the board's clip she withdrew a filled hypodermic barrel and detached a bent needle taped alongside. Producing a pocket lighter, she held it to the metal tip and rasped its flint. Reluctantly, a weak flame ignited, fizzling in a harmless amber glow.

"It's glycerin," she remarked, returning the parlor trick implements to their previous stowage.

Robb felt sick.

"There's a visitor here to see you," she said as she departed.

"Hello Robb," he recognized a familiar voice.

"Paulina?"

"Good to see you..." Paulina began, but the aggravation on Robb's face silenced the insincerity.

"I...I owe you an apology," his advisor stammered. "I had no idea where you went and I never would have approved. I didn't know." Looking Robb in the eye, she sought a fleeting measure of acceptance. There was none.

"What's worse, it would have escaped my attention except for the news...the accusations, the arrests. The lab was raided!" she rambled.

"How could you?" Robb responded fiercely, fully intending the double meaning, unable to interpret Paulina's ambiguous apology? Was it was well meant or simply another ill-formulated attempt to elicit his sympathies?

"I should have been suspicious when my grant proposals were unequivocally awarded."

Robb wanted to lash out, instead he griped along a parallel tangent. "Strange coincidences are rather normal for me, lately."

Looking at him oddly, Paulina struggled to find an appropriate response.

"Yeah, I'll bet," she muttered, failing to express any more.

"Paulina, it's good to see you," Robb asserted, "but why are you here?"

"I've come to vouch for you," Paulina responded, truthfully.

"For what?"

"For not being the agent of a foreign government."

"What makes you so sure?" Robb challenged.

"Huh," Paulina backpedaled, "I would never have considered it possible. Your work is detailed, imaginative, and profound. How could you show such promise and have time to spy?"

"I couldn't," Robb admitted. "I just wanted to make sure you trust me."

Paulina's surprise showed again. Her star student had developed a darker, sinister side.

"I'm sorry," she apologized once more.

"Thanks," Robb acquiesced. "I just want to get home. But I don't know when they'll let me go."

"They weren't detaining you just to flush out a rogue agent." It was Paulina's turn to surprise. "They were also waiting for me."

"Why?"

"Uh, there are still complications. You can't go home yet—for two reasons."

"Why not?" Robb sighed, regretting what came next.

"First, it's about my student, Wei-Ahn. He's been deported."

"We both know he wasn't a spy," Robb growled.

"No, he wasn't," Paulina soothed, "but neither was he clean."

"What are you talking about?" Robb glowered.

"It seems he was bending laws to save a buck or two," Paulina explained.

"Like what?" Robb remained suspicious.

"His cell phone account, for one," Paulina started, "was not in his name. It belonged to an acquaintance. And, it had been passed on to him from a previous student. No contract, no commitments."

"Big deal," Robb scoffed. "I hate the contracts, too."

"Then there were his textbooks," Paulina continued. "He used soft-bound 'International Version' copies. These aren't licensed for distribution in the US, they cost about a tenth of what the hardcover books sell for in the school bookstore, and there is no royalty paid to the authors from overseas printings. It's a bit like patent infringement." Paulina smiled wistfully, validating Robb's argument from months past. "Most are bootleg copies, too."

"Still not a compelling reason to deport someone," Robb pointed out.

"No, it isn't," Paulina sighed, "but the fouls were additive. A list of Social Security numbers was found in his possession. Numbers issued to foreign nationals, students that had lived in the US for a spell, but all had returned home. These SSNs were being used to establish lines of credit, some of which were being maxed out and defaulted. The cash was then used to purchase property, sports cars or electronics. He was using one to claim a dependent on his tax return so he could obtain Child Tax Credits."

"He was doing all that?" Robb was clearly surprised.

"No, as a point of fact, he wasn't that involved," Paulina acknowledged. "It was the owner of the phone contract. Your friend was slowly being drawn into a lucrative money laundering front operated by a local gang. They were building up a line of credit for his use and would eventually sell it to him in return for money laundering services. So, within a few months or a year, he might have been."

"I'm sure he didn't," Robb sounded confident.

"No, he didn't," Paulina agreed, "but unfortunately, neither could I convince him that his activities were illegal or unethical. He was convinced that the authorities were looking the other way, that the government needed scientists and engineers like him. Most of his colleagues are in some form of a similar scheme. It was part and parcel of being invited to this country. In the end, I had no choice but to let him go."

"Shit!" Robb swore, suddenly understanding Paulina's apprehension.

"Why else can't I go home?" He asked, a trace of humility in his voice.

"You need to talk to a few folks in Washington."

Chapter 26

Motivation

Days later, Robb was seated again in a classical power office, housed within a DC government building. This time, to his appeasement, he was not squirming among law enforcement personnel or intelligence agency drones. Rather, he was conversing comfortably with the Secretary of Energy, a kindred mind. The dialogue was easy, a chronological threading of his narrative, pinning the timeline of significant events and discoveries and his reactions.

It wasn't all business; they frequently digressed along tangents of salving scientific think tank hypotheses.

Off the record, he learned that Shaparell's body had been briefly exhumed and tested positive for a Rare Earth-nanotube complex remarkably similar to Yakov's infection.

Robb's relief was palpable, not needing to venture again into the bowels of the agency's edifice. Whoever had arranged the interview must have been clairvoyant. Had the meeting been with the FBI, the CIA, Homeland Security or a congressional committee, he might barely have restrained himself from bolting. He was a novice in their arena. Mostly, he feared that his inexperience under cross-examination would unwittingly lead to accidental self-incrimination.

Not that he held any illusions that the agencies weren't privy to the present discussion.

Before arriving in DC, the Secretary of Energy explained, the ring of treasonous perpetrators had been apprehended. Details from the ledger smuggled out by Evan held critical evidence, and was being shared between governments. The documents were immutable testaments, sufficiently strong to potentially prevent Robb from testifying.

For this Robb was hopeful. He did not want to be paraded in the public eye nor be forever associated with events surrounding acts of treason.

Ottley was a dead man, at least figuratively. The literal sentencing would be a much more delicate operation to enact. At the most fundamental level, exactly who or whom he represented just starting to become clear. It had yet to be decided how public Ottley's trial would be, or how much detail could be freely released, but there were tangential indications logistically connecting others in league with him, some who had been orchestrating and financing his rogue army. Ottley's abrasive mannerisms certainly annoyed enough during his departmental reign that he should have long ago been finished. On several occasions, key connections had interceded, thwarting his removal.

As the scapegoat for the most influential, he would bear the sins of many, unfortunately preventing the atonement of the much more pervasive political gracelessness.

It was hardly fair, Robb regretted, but his cowboy instincts were tempering, and as he'd reached a maturation point, he accepted the limits of his ability to seek a more satisfying judicial outcome.

"No, it isn't fair," he heard across the desk. "Perhaps I can help you make some peace."

"Why kill the ex-president?"

"Because we missed our chance when he was still in office," came Ottley's smart-ass reply.

"Don't be a dumbass, he was doing exactly what you wanted him to do."

"Of course he was, but the economy was so fucked up, we were bound to lose the election. People had tuned him out: his message was being lost in people's realities. By killing him, we could blame the terrorists, regenerate a frenzy and keep the country divided and distracted. In creating a state of fear, we would easily regain power for several terms. Then we could have really changed things, legally and politically."

"Why did you fail to kill him in Mexico?"

"We didn't fail at anything," he scoffed, "the kidnapping was a low-risk solution. We hoped a near miss would be sufficiently alarming to put a scare into our base supporters. You know, assassination attempt on foreign soil, miraculous escape..."

"Hand of God?"

Ottley stared at him, disgusted with the interruption.

"All that. Rile up the grass-root supporters, stir the pride, churn the fear, but it backfired. It didn't have the desired effect."

"Which was?"

"Disgrace the opposition, make them look inept. Degrade the public's confidence in their ability to defend our nation. Instead, polls indicated an unfortunate sense of pride had been stirred. It caught us off guard, but in hindsight, it wasn't so unremarkable. An over-the-hill moron outwitting young professionals trained to kill. We'd outsmarted ourselves."

"Then what happened?"

"We gave Shaparell's incident some time to shake through the public's mind. But we weren't idle. We spread a ton of misinformation. Over time, casual observers began associating the event with a terror plot. We fertilized the airwaves, motivated the talking heads, cultivated a slanted perception. We created a new opinion by fabricating an alternate reality."

"Even though the story kept changing?"

"That's just ignoring facts. We cemented belief subconsciously by increasing the anger. Most people have a hard time truly believing the press, and in their confusion, we have an opening to create an emotional connection."

"Why wait a year to try again?"

Eyes gleaming greedily, Ottley enthused, "The backup plan presented a better opportunity. Hand power over to the opposition, watch them navigate the inevitable economic avalanche, and let them take the blame for the prolonged economic downturn. In the meantime, it wasn't like we were going away. We were just waiting for our turn again."

Robb held his tongue. Ottley was sensational.

"We have money, we have power...we have time. The wars we engineered were channeling extremely lucrative fiscal revenue streams to us. The next administration could not undo them easily without admitting there had been serious wrongdoing."

Ottley chuckled, then continued, "That would have been a judicious catch-22, the world screaming for blood while the American public circled camp and resisted. We knew from our polls that our citizens would never allow a former presidential administration to face the ultimate humiliation of trial and conviction. Hah, if the opposition pursued them too vigorously, they'd have to defend two fronts, severe worldwide repercussions as well as a complete erosion of their national political influence. We had them between a rock and hard place."

"Weren't you managing a risk, too?"

"Yeah, we really didn't want to face the chance he would be indicted for war crimes. There's just enough groundswell every once in a while to have him investigated—we had concerns it could erupt uncontrollably, against our favor, killing our agenda."

"What more did you want to change?"

"We want to keep the American way—what we always have had. Cheap oil, cheap labor, unregulated markets, a fast-churning money supply. That's our economy. It sure as hell isn't manufacturing. It doesn't matter to us if we produce goods here or overseas, as long as we control the flow of commerce, and skim a little off each transaction, or manage the market's movements."

"And you didn't give a damn if ordinary Americans were impoverished in the process."

"The average American is subjugated, nullified. Angry, bereft of a coherent opinion, they side against each other and vote against their personal best interests." He chuckled. "Friendly fire cowboys. On the educated side is a bunch of smart people possessing an overpriced, worthless education, in debt to their eyeballs. Each has to work his ass off or lose his job and face bankruptcy. Just in case he develops a little political ambition, we derail him. We flood the media with nonsense, keeping the grass roots political will misinformed, stifled in indecision and fragmented with issues that roil the blood, but are of little consequence."

"The ironic thing is," Ottley continued, "the more needy an American is, the more likely he or she is to align with our agenda. Conservatism sells, salt with patriotism and scent with the essence of a self-made soul. It works every time..." he paused. "Well, most times."

"You're a real American hero, you know?" Robb laughed, unwilling to spare his disdain.

"You're a fool."

"Rot in hell."